Rattlesnake Wells, Wyoming
Right Between the Eyes

Rattlesnake Wells, Wyoming
RIGHT BETWEEN THE EYES

WILLIAM W. JOHNSTONE
with J. A. Johnstone

PINNACLE BOOKS
Kensington Publishing Corp.
www.kensingtonbooks.com

PINNACLE BOOKS are published by

Kensington Publishing Corp.
119 West 40th Street
New York, NY 10018

PUBLISHER'S NOTE
Following the death of William W. Johnstone, the Johnstone family is working with a carefully selected writer to organize and complete Mr. Johnstone's outlines and many unfinished manuscripts to create additional novels in all of his series like The Last Gunfighter, Mountain Man, and Eagles, among others. This novel was inspired by Mr. Johnstone's superb storytelling.

All Kensington titles, imprints, and distributed lines are available at special quantity discounts for bulk purchases for sales promotions, premiums, fund-raising, educational, or institutional use. Special book excerpts or customized printings can also be created to fit specific needs. For details, write or phone the office of the Kensington sales manager: Kensington Publishing Corp., 119 West 40th Street, New York, NY 10018, attn: Sales Department; phone 1-800-221-2647.

PINNACLE BOOKS, the Pinnacle logo, and the WWJ steer head logo, are Reg. U.S. Pat. & TM Off.

ISBN-13: 978-0-7860-4486-3
ISBN-10: 0-7860-4486-1

First printing: July 2017

10 9 8 7 6 5 4 3 2

Printed in the United States of America

Electronic edition: October 2018

ISBN-13: 978-0-7860-4017-9
ISBN-10: 0-7860-4017-3

CHAPTER 1

Buford Morrison pushed back from the table and proclaimed with a wide, satisfied smile, "Now *that* was a meal worth makin' a long, hard ride to enjoy!" He paused to sweep his one good eye over his tablemates and brought it to rest on Bob Hatfield at the head of the table. "And you, you lucky so-and-so, being married to the prettiest gal in Wyoming and having her be able to cook that good to boot . . . Doggone if that don't seem like more good fortune than any one man deserves."

Bob grinned amiably. "What can I say? I guess clean living and pure thoughts sometimes pay off in the end."

Seated next to Bob, his wife Consuela rolled her eyes. "I don't know about that," she said. Then, turning her dazzling smile on Buford, she added, "But I do know that flattery can be rewarded by another piece of blueberry pie—are you sure you don't have room for one more, Marshal?"

"Yes, sad to say that's the case," Buford answered. "Not that the desire ain't there, I promise you. But if I ate one more bite I'm afraid I might blow up and bust." He gestured toward Bucky, Bob's eleven-year-old son, seated next to him. "Save it for the boy here. Young lads always got room for more pie, ain't that right?"

"Most always," agreed Bucky. Then, holding his hands to his stomach, he added, "But right at the moment, I'm afraid I'm in the same fix as you. I don't think I can hardly hold another bite."

"The only solution, then," said Consuela, "is to arrange for each of you to have some later on. That's easy enough for you, Bucky; there'll be a piece waiting in the pantry. For you, Marshal Morrison, I will wrap a slice in waxed paper and you can take it with you. Since you are spending the night at the jail to keep an eye on your prisoners, you can either have it before you go to bed or perhaps when you wake up in the morning with some coffee."

"She's a beauty, she can cook, and she thinks good. The complete package," said Buford. "The only thing is—and I say this with all proper gratitude and meaning no offense—I will gladly take the pie to have later on. As far as having it with a cup of coffee from your jail, though, Bob . . . there's where I'd have to consider a serious change in plans."

"All right, all right. I get your point," said Bob.

Buford wagged his head. "I've made coffee out on the trail under the worst conditions you can name. Wind, dust, rain, snow . . . But even for all of that, I ain't *ever* made a pot as awful as what you and your deputies regularly brew down at that jail of yours."

"I said I got your point, didn't I? With nobody

arguing against you, where's the need to carry on about it?"

Buford was a deputy U.S. Marshal, operating out of Cheyenne headquarters. Pursuing owlhoots of every stripe throughout all of Wyoming, and sometimes farther, he intermittently passed through Rattlesnake Wells. In the course of these stopovers, he'd gotten to know and become friends with Bob, who was the town marshal here. This also meant exposure to the notoriously vile coffee that Bob and his deputies had a knack for making. No matter who took a turn at the brewing or how they altered their technique, the results were equally dismal. These doomed outcomes had created a reputation of sorts and had even given rise to speculation that the marshal's office/jail was perhaps built over some ancient Indian burial site that was retaliating with a bizarre curse.

Buford referenced this wild speculation now, continuing with a sly smile, "All I'm saying is that your luck with bad coffee is enough to make a body wonder some about that Injun curse business. I don't normally take stock in that kind of mumbo-jumbo, but whenever I hear an odd creak or a low moan of wind tonight, I expect it'll cross my mind a time or two."

On this occasion, Buford had shown up in Rattlesnake Wells riding escort to a tumbleweed wagon, a sort of mobile prison with barred sides and reinforcements all around. In such a conveyance, prisoners were collected from different points around the territory and hauled back to Cheyenne for further incarceration until a trial was held to decide their final fate.

Buford had arrived on this trip around the middle of the day, with three prisoners already in custody. He also had a wagon driver, a man named Crispin, a gout victim so hobbled by the disease that he hardly ventured more than a few feet away from the wagon. Waiting for the federal lawman at the town marshal's office was a telegram out of Cheyenne informing him of two wanted men—Abner and Ulmer Silas— reported to be in the area, working at one of the gold mines in the Prophecy Mountains north of town.

It was the Prophecy gold strike that had turned Rattlesnake Wells from a quiet farming and ranching community into a sprawling, often boisterous boom- town with no sign of the ore petering out any time soon. This made it an attraction that drew a steady stream of newcomers, every sort from hardworking, hard-luck dreamers looking to strike it rich and turn their lives around to opportunistic entrepreneurs planning to cash in by supplying goods at inflated prices to take advantage of those with sudden wealth lining their pockets; and in between, the hustlers, schemers, and double-dealers out to make a profit by playing every crooked angle there was. It was a steadily churning mix that also served as a good hiding place for men on the dodge from past mis- deeds . . . men like the Silas brothers, wanted for bank and train robberies and a handful of murders along the way.

The telegram awaiting Buford provided an al- legedly solid tip on where to find the Silases and instructed him to apprehend them while he was in the area and then bring them back to Cheyenne along with his other prisoners. In order to carry out this assignment, Buford had asked and been granted permission to house his current prisoners in Bob's jail while he went after the Silases.

Not only that, Bob had volunteered to side Buford in rounding up the outlaw brothers. The lawmen were set to head out for the high country in pursuit of their quarry first thing in the morning. The supper at Bob's house was a combination of professional courtesy and plain old hospitality.

"The offer to spend the night in our spare bedroom still stands," Consuela reminded Buford, following his remark about the night noises he might encounter at the jail. "You already have your assistant spending the night there because he doesn't get around well enough to go any farther than necessary."

"I appreciate the kind offer, ma'am, I really do," Buford assured her. "But I'm afraid I gotta turn it down. It's sort of a habit of mine to stick pretty close to the prisoners I take into custody until I've got 'em turned over to the federal lockup in Cheyenne."

"It's a habit you ought to be familiar with, 'Suela," Bob said. "It's the same one I follow whenever we throw troublemakers in the clink and keep 'em overnight. Either me or one of the deputies bunk on that cot in the storeroom overnight, too, to make sure there's no funny business."

"And I've never understood that, either," said Consuela stubbornly, giving a faint head shake that caused her long, glossy black hair to ripple down either side of her lovely face. "Once you have them secure behind bars, why the need to continue watching them so close? To me, it seems overly cautious."

Buford smiled wryly. "Been more than a few lawmen who figured that same way. Once they had some varmint in handcuffs or behind bars, they reckoned they could relax and let down their guard a mite. Not always—but too often to ignore—that turned out to be a mistake. The only good thing to be said afterward in most of those cases was that it was the last mistake they ever made."

"You teach a harsh lesson, Marshal," Consuela conceded when he had finished.

"It's a harsh life I lead, ma'am." Buford's wry smile turned into a lopsided grin. "But such as it is, it's one I'd just as soon keep living for a while. And hard as it might be to believe, there are a few others who I think sorta like having me around, too—Crispin, my wagon driver, for example. He's a good man, and under different circumstances I might very well take you up on your offer and leave him looking after those prisoners at the jail on his own tonight. But with his gout giving him the miseries as bad as it is, I don't want to stick him with being the only one to handle that pack of rascals. Knowing I wasn't around and also knowing Crispin's ailing the way he is, it'd be like 'em to raise a ruckus and keep him hopping the whole while, just for lowdown orneriness. With me on hand, that ain't apt to happen."

Standing six feet four inches tall and weighing in at well over two hundred pounds carried on a rugged, barrel-chested frame, Buford Morrison wasn't somebody too many men wanted to trifle with. In addition to his intimidating appearance, there was the near-mythical reputation that had taken root about his sheer toughness—starting with the shoot-out during which a ricocheting bullet fragment had taken out his left eye. Hardly slowed by the misfortune, Buford had kept on fighting, bloody mucus running down the side of his face, until he'd cut down the last of the desperadoes who'd been gunning for him and he alone was left standing.

After that he took to wearing an eye patch, but it did nothing to slow his effectiveness as a lawman willing to go after the worst owlhoots in the territory. He'd never back-shoot a man merely to gain advantage over him, nor did he treat his prisoners with undue harshness. But by the same token, neither did he hesitate to blast someone who made the mistake of trying to put up a fight, and his treatment of anyone he took into custody was humane only to the extent the individual's behavior warranted.

"I won't say you've completely convinced me, but it's hard to argue against the logic of your experience," Consuela told him. "What there can be no argument with, however, is that your remarks reminded me of something I would have felt very guilty over had I left it unaddressed. If I send a piece of pie with you for later, you see, then I surely should include one for your friend Señor Crispin. And, since Fred will be there with Señor Crispin until you return, I *really* can't send pie anywhere near his vicinity without making sure there's some available for him, too."

"I don't know that you have to go to all that trouble," said Bob. "Fred was going to see to it that Crispin, the prisoners, and himself got a good supper by having it fetched from the Shirley House kitchen. May not be as good as your cooking, but they put on a decent spread."

"I know they do," agreed Consuela. "But I'm not thinking about Fred going hungry as much as I am hurting his feelings."

"Not that I don't fight goin' to gut myself," Morrison admitted, "but having gotten a good look at your Deputy Fred, yeah, he's a good-sized boy. Don't appear he's missed too many bites of pie or anything else that's passed his way for a while. And as far as Crispin goes, he may be scrawny as a tumbleweed twig but he can pack away chow with the best of 'em. So I feel safe in speaking for him and assuring you he'd also be real grateful for a piece of that pie."

Consuela rose to her feet. "It's a good thing I made a second one. I'll go slice and prepare some pieces to take with you."

Buford watched her leave the table and then his gaze returned to Bob. "Like I said, there's a heap of good fortune for just one man."

"You say that like I haven't scraped against some rough edges in my time as well," Bob reminded him. "What's more, you half make it sound like I got such a dose of good fortune all in one swoop—and I ain't saying 'Suela's not a fine prize, mind you—that I should start figuring on nothing but torment and misery the rest of the way forward."

"Naw, I never said no such thing. Sure never meant it that way, anyhow," Buford protested. "I'll even go so far as to say that if anybody rates callin' the lovely Consuela his missus, and it can't be me . . . well, I reckon you ain't all *that* undeserving. How's that?"

Bob cocked a single eyebrow. "I think there *might* have been something close to a compliment in there."

"How about you, lad?" Buford asked, turning his attention to Bucky. "How do you like having Consuela for your new mom?"

The red-haired youngster appeared to consider the question very earnestly before answering. "Well, so far it's not really anything too different. I mean, Consuela's been cooking and cleaning for us and taking care of me for almost as long as I can remember. My true ma's been dead for nearly three years now, and even before she passed, she was sick and weak most all the time. Consuela was there, taking care of her, too."

"Doggone it, that was a blunt, stupid thing for me to bring up," said Buford, looking suddenly uncomfortable. "I'm sorry for that, lad. Truly I am."

"You don't need to be. It was a fair question," Bucky said. "I think about my ma a lot, and I loved her a whole bunch. I hope it didn't sound like anything less. I was just trying to say that Consuela has always been right there, too, almost like a *second* mom all along. So when her and Pa finally decided to get married—after folks around town kept wondering why it took so long on account of how it was so plain the way they felt about each other—well, it really didn't make that much of a change for me. *Calling* Consuela my ma is the only thing I'm having a little trouble getting used to."

"It'll come in time," Bob said. "And if it doesn't, Consuela has already told you that she understands if you don't feel comfortable calling her Mother."

"I *want* to," insisted Bucky. "Like I said, I feel about her almost the same way and everything. It's just that . . ."

"Let it go." Bob's tone was sterner this time. "That's for you and 'Suela to work out between the two of you, and you got plenty of time."

Nobody said anything for a minute. Until, with his mouth curving into an impish grin, Bucky added, "I'll tell you the hardest thing for me to get used to, Mr. Marshal Morrison. And that's seeing Pa and Consuela making cow eyes at each other and sneaking smooches once in a while when they think I'm not looking."

Buford emitted a hearty chuckle.

Bob felt his ears burn a little and knew they'd be turning as bright a red as his thick head of hair, its shade matched perfectly by Bucky's. Still, he couldn't quite hold back a grin of his own. "I'll tell you something that might be even harder for you to get used to, buster—and that's going without the piece of pie Consuela won't be saving for you if I tell her you were being a smarty-pants in front of our guest."

"Aw, I was only funnin' a little, Pa. You even grinned some yourself. And you and Consuela *do* smooch and cuddle an awful lot since the wedding."

Bob tried to glare at him, but he couldn't muster much heat. The boy was right. What was more, Bob decided, there wasn't a darned thing to be embarrassed about for cuddling and smooching his new wife.

CHAPTER 2

A short time later, Bob and Buford quit the Hatfield house and started down the slope toward town and the marshal's office. It was a clear night, early spring, still with a bite of leftover winter in the air.

As they walked, the two men made quite an imposing pair. Bob was a couple inches short of Buford's six-four and not as thick through the torso, but nevertheless plenty solid and every bit as wide across the shoulders. Both men wore Colts on their right hips, displayed prominently in holsters attached to fully loaded cartridge belts. In addition, Buford carried a Winchester '73 rifle chambered for .45-caliber rounds, same as his sidearm. He strode along carefully balancing a plate of neatly wrapped pie slices in his left hand and the Winchester gripped casually in his right.

"You're never very far from that Winchester, not even in town, are you?" Bob observed.

"Nope," Buford answered. "It gives me added range and added punch, and I decided those are benefits I kinda like, no matter where I'm at. Plus, having it openly displayed tends to discourage certain proddies who might otherwise be inclined to try and start some trouble with me." He paused a moment before adding, "And then, probably above all, there's the fact that I ain't exactly greased lightnin' when it comes to yankin' out my hogleg and puttin' it to use. The rifle solves that problem, too."

"From all reports, it seems to've solved it pretty good. You've cut a wide swath all through the territory with that rifle and that badge, and you're still going strong."

Buford grunted. "Trust me, I keep at this only because no better opportunity has come along. If I could ever quit law-doggin' altogether, or maybe at least settle down to a sweet setup like you've got here, I'd jump on it in a heartbeat."

"How come you never?"

"I just told you. Lack of the right opportunity. Leastways, none that seemed right at the time." Buford cut Bob a sidelong glance. "Did you ever know I considered takin' on the marshal's job here at one point?"

Bob shook his head. "No, I never heard that."

"Well, I did. But it was before the gold boom." Buford smiled wistfully. "Things were so quiet around here back then that I feared I might die of boredom and dry up like an old buffalo skull. So I passed, and then the gold strike came along only a few months later."

Bob eyed him. "I hope you ain't looking to edge

me out of a job and take over in my place now, are you?"

"Are you kidding? As rowdy and troublesome as this place is turning into? I'd want to ease back a notch and take it easy, not plunge into steadier action than I already got."

"I think I might be detecting a pattern. The right opportunity hasn't come along because of you being a mite too particular."

"A possibility, I reckon. But don't get too cocksure. If I could figure out a way to get rid of you and be left with the responsibility of consoling Consuela, now *there* would be an opportunity I'd be willing to put a powerful lot of effort into."

"Good thing we're having this conversation," Bob said dryly. "I'm gonna have to start paying closer attention to which way you swing that Winchester when we head up into the high country on the trail of those Silases tomorrow."

They'd reached the flat area at the bottom of the slope, a spot the locals had taken to calling the Point. Angling to the southwest from there, Front Street ran through the heart of the original community, nowadays called Old Town. This was where the town's longer-established businesses were clustered, along with residences lining a handful of side streets. Branching to the northwest from the Point was what had been dubbed Gold Avenue, the main artery of New Town. The newer businesses that had sprung up to serve the flood of gold seekers pouring in were strung out there—predominantly tents of all shapes and sizes, mixed with a few of hastily slapped-together wooden structures.

At this time of evening, the stores along Front Street were closed, with the exception of Bullock's Saloon and the Shirley House Hotel. Lanterns hanging on poles issued pools of light at regular intervals, and the windows of the houses on the side streets glowed with illumination. In the other direction, up Gold Avenue, it was a different story. For the tent saloons, gambling joints, eateries, and whore cribs, this was a peak time for doing a noisy level of business.

The jail building where Bob and Buford were headed was at the far end of quiet Front Street. For Bob, lingering for a while in this part of town was only a temporary reprieve. After he'd escorted Buford to the jail and got him settled there, the marshal would be relieving Deputy Fred of his duties for the night and would then be taking the standard evening turn around the rest of the town—boisterous Gold Avenue very much included. Bob's two other deputies, Peter and Vern Macy, were on leave for a few days, visiting and taking supplies to their younger brother Lee and Uncle Curtis up in the Prophecies, where Curtis had a long-standing, low-yielding dig (but with the promise of a big payout any time now, he kept insisting) that Lee was working with him.

As Bob and Buford passed in front of Bullock's Saloon, the strains of an accordion playing what sounded like a lilting Irish ballad drifted out to them. The Irish part certainly fit, given the proud heritage of saloon owner Mike Bullock, but accordion music was something new for the establishment. Bob took note of this, more a point of interest rather than concern, and reckoned he might poke his head in at the start of his rounds to get a closer look and listen.

Two blocks down from Bullock's, having also passed the Shirley House Hotel, the street took on deeper cuts of shadow between the pole lamps. The sturdy log jail building up ahead showed only a few thin slivers of light through its shuttered windows.

The accordion tune was still playing faintly inside Bob's head when it was suddenly interrupted by a harsh voice speaking from out of the shadows off to one side.

"That's far enough, law dogs. Hold up right there."

Bob and Buford stopped walking. Bob's right hand automatically drifted down to hover claw-like over the .44 on his hip. Buford's Winchester remained pointing down alongside his right leg, muzzle lifted slightly, the grip of his big paw tightening.

Half a block ahead, two men reverse-melted out of the shadows on either side and edged to the middle of the street in slow, cautious steps. Both wore long, rust-colored dusters, unbuttoned and flared wide open to reveal the guns buckled about their waists. The one on the left packed a converted Navy Colt in a cross-draw holster. His companion exhibited no holsters at all but had two pearl-handled revolvers thrust behind a fully loaded cartridge belt.

"Buford Morrison, you one-eyed human hound dog," spoke the same harsh voice, coming from the one flashing the Navy Colt. "Do you have any idea who it is you're standin' face-to-face with?"

"Well," Buford drawled in a flat, emotionless tone, "given the poor lighting and my afflicted eyesight, which you so disrespectfully just made reference to, the best I might could do was hazard a guess. But by the way you're paired up and the rotten stink floatin' off you, that helps me do some closer calculatin'—I make you for Ulmer and Abner Silas."

"Enjoy your successful calculatin'," said a new voice, just as guttural and unpleasant, coming from the one packing two pistols. "Because the clock on your time for enjoyin' anything has about run out."

"Here I was hopin' you fellas had clumb down outta the Prophecies to save me a trip up to fetch you," said Buford, faking genuine disappointment. "You sayin' that ain't why you're here?"

Now it went back to Ulmer, the one with the Navy Colt, for an answer. "Not hardly, you smart-mouthed old bastard. What we're here for is to end your days of fetchin' back hapless souls to face a hangman's noose for things that should've been long ago forgot. We heard you was in the area and was gonna be comin' after us next, so we decided to come after you instead. What's more, we freed those other three prisoners you been haulin' across the country like freaks in a cage—and they're of the same mind as us when it comes to puttin' a stop to your ways!"

"What of the men who were guarding those prisoners?" Bob demanded. "What did you do with them?"

"Ha! Wouldn't you like to know?" taunted Abner, cocking back his head and thrusting out the swell of his belly with its two pistols on proud display.

"If you harmed those men," Bob said through

clenched teeth, "you won't make it to a hangman's noose!"

"See," said Ulmer, "if we was the kind of low skunks ol' One-Eye and others have falsely painted us to be, bringin' bad harm to those deputies is exactly what we would've done. But we didn't. We saw 'em as a couple of poor slobs hired out for work that didn't have nothing personal against us. So all we did was chunk 'em in the head and lock 'em out of the way in your own jail cells."

"You *might* have got the same treatment, since our main purpose here was to square things with ol' One-Eye and get him off our backsides," said Abner. "But now your snotty attitude and threats has earned you the same treatment as him!"

"I wouldn't have it any other way," rasped Bob. "All I want to know is if you figure to talk us to death, or are you gonna pull those hoglegs and try to do something with 'em?"

The nearly empty street suddenly became crowded with tension.

"What about the other three?" Buford prodded. "They shy about joinin' the party—or are they just too chicken-shit to show themselves?"

"They'll join in when it's time," Ulmer assured him. "And when they do, you'll wish they *had* stayed too shy."

Out of the corner of his mouth, too low for the Silases to hear, Buford said to Bob, "You think they're bluffin' about the other three?"

"No. They're just stacking the deck in their favor," replied Bob. "I think I saw a flicker of movement on your side, to the right, in the mouth of that alley. I expect there's another one on my side. The third one I'd figure to be somewhere up high, a roof or second-floor window."

"Yeah. Reckon that's how I'd do it—if I was a pack of ambushin' polecats like them, that is."

"You take the alley on your side. Then swing that Winchester and find the one up high. I'll clear the middle and then go after the one on my side."

"Wait a minute. You sure you can—"

"I can do what I say. Trust me."

"Hey! Knock off the mumblin', you two," barked Ulmer. "You got any talkin' to do, you talk to us."

"The only thing we got left to say to you we'll be obliged to say with lead," Buford told him. "You ready to set it in motion, you gutless bag of wind?"

Everything froze for a long, tension-heavy moment. Bob could hear the accordion music from inside Bullock's playing ever so faintly . . . And then the evening seemed to explode all at once.

Ulmer and Abner grabbed for their guns. Quick as an eye blink, Bob had his .44 drawn and was fanning four shots so rapidly it sounded like one elongated roar. The brothers each took two rounds, dust and blood spurting from their shirtfronts as they were slammed backward, chins dropping, mouths falling agape. They tipped inward, against one another, then dropped to their knees for a second before toppling back and down. Ulmer had managed to clear leather with his Navy Colt, but got no further; it slipped unfired from his dead fingers as he hit the ground. Abner's guns stayed jammed behind their cartridge belt. He died with his hands closed on their grips, never having the chance to pull them free.

While the Silases were dropping to the dirt, Buford was levering and firing his Winchester with practiced precision, raking the alley mouth on the right side of the street. He inadvertently chewed some wood off the corner of a building, but the rounds immediately following that found what he was seeking. First came a yelp of pain and then Slick Stansberry, one of the three prisoners Buford had hauled into town behind the bars of the tumbleweed wagon, staggered into sight clutching his stomach and chest. A revolver he'd been grasping in one hand dropped to the ground as Slick tried to put that hand to better use squeezing shut the bullet holes in him. But it wasn't enough, not anywhere close. He pitched forward and was dead before he landed facedown in the dust.

Buford shifted his position slightly, dropping into a bit of a crouch as both his one good eye and his Winchester muzzle tilted upward, sweeping across surrounding rooftops and second-story windows.

To the left of Buford, Bob shifted, too. With the Silases down, he turned his attention to his side of the street, the shadowy doorways and the darkened alley. He only had two rounds left; he couldn't afford to pour random shots like Buford had done. He'd have to wait for a surer target.

And then he got one—almost too late.

The tip of a rifle barrel poked out of the alley, visible for barely a second before it was spitting red flame and lead. The wind-rip of a bullet passed close enough to scorch the fine hairs in Bob's right ear.

But then he was returning fire, emptying the last two cartridges in his cylinder, aiming tight into the blackness around the rifle tip as flame licked out once again.

The alley shooter's second round went way wide this time, whining off to slam harmlessly into a building across the street. But at least one of Bob's shots scored truer. First the rifle fell clattering to the ground. Then came the sound of a body dropping heavily. A second later, one foot and part of a man's leg became visible, thrusting out of the alley's darkness at ground level. Three or four violent tremors passed through the foot. These turned into a pair of weak kicks, barely enough to stir a tendril of dust. Then the leg and foot became very still.

Four down, one to go.

As he broke open his .44 and started to reload, Bob turned back to Buford. The federal man was still sweeping his eye and his Winchester muzzle high, looking for the fifth ambusher. Bob's gaze lifted as well.

It was only the warning cock of the fifth shooter's gun that saved one or both of the lawmen from taking a serious hit. The fifth man was not at a higher level at all. In fact, he was hunkered down about as low as he could get—down in behind a watering trough just short of the alley where Stansberry had bit the dust.

Thinking the errant gazes of both Bob and Buford gave him the opening he needed, this fifth gunman— one Marvin Porch, by name—popped up behind the far end of the watering trough and extended a Colt .45 at arm's length. He aimed at Buford first and even succeeded in planting a pill in the old bull with his shot. Trouble was, the hammer cock required to make that shot resulted in it being the only one he got off. A fraction of a second later, slugs from both Bob's .44 and Buford's Winchester were hammering mercilessly into Porch. He jerked upright, spun in a full circle under the pounding of the bullets, and then fell forward into the trough.

Everything went quiet almost as quick as it had erupted.

For several clock ticks, the only sound was the water slopping back and forth in the trough where Marvin Porch's body now floated facedown.

Slowly, the trample of feet and the excited murmur of voices began pouring out of Bullock's and the Shirley House.

CHAPTER 3

"They waylaid me as I was coming back with our meals—supper for the prisoners, and for me and Crispin," Deputy Fred was explaining. "When they shoved me through the jail door under gunpoint, I saw the three prisoners were already released from behind bars and had the drop on Crispin."

"Those blasted Silases tricked me by calling out like it was Fred returning," joined in Crispin. "When I opened the door to 'em, they swarmed in and knocked me to the floor. I was too hobbled up, too slow to stop 'em. Next thing I knew, they was turnin' loose those other prisoners, once they'd agreed to pitch in and help . . . Damn me and this gout that makes me so close to useless! You should've left me behind like everybody told you, Buford."

Crispin was a lean, balding man in his middle forties. Straightened up, he probably topped six feet by a half-inch or so. But trying to stand or move around with the gout currently coursing so painfully through his feet and legs caused him to hunch over and drag along in a way that made him seem considerably shorter and smaller.

"Knock that shit off," Buford admonished him. "You got fooled by a couple scalawags who've turned the tables on many a good man before you, gout havin' nothing to do with it. I brung you along with me on this outing because you were the man I wanted, the man I wanted sidin' me over any of the others who were available. I knew I could count on you, even getting around poorly, more than them. You bein' hobbled, I can tolerate. Whinin' and carryin' on about it, I won't."

"Any way you cut it, we both got snookered real good," added Fred, also hanging his head. "After they had us both under their guns, they roughed us up a little, then shoved us in a cell, cuffed and gagged so we couldn't call out no warning."

"The main thing to remember," responded Bob, "is that it turned out okay. You two don't have a patent on getting fooled by owlhoots. Hell, me and Buford did some wrong figuring of our own—if we hadn't, he wouldn't have ended up with that bullet hole in his side."

"That's for damned sure," muttered Buford. "Stinkin' little worm like Marvin Porch—I should've known better than to expect a worm like him would seek out a high position to do his shootin' from."

"Regardless of where he fired from," said tall, lanky Doc Tibbs as he was bending over to put the finishing touches on the wide bandage he was applying to Buford's side, just above his beltline, "you're lucky his bullet didn't hit an inch or so more toward your middle. Number one, it likely wouldn't have passed clean through the way it did and, number two, that means it probably would have done some tumbling and tearing up of a few important internal organs."

"You make that sound plumb distasteful, Doc," Buford allowed. "But on the other hand, the way you was pokin' and proddin' around in that bullet hole a few minutes ago wasn't doin' much to make me feel exactly lucky, either."

"Luck is a relative thing, Marshal," said the doctor, smiling as he tied off the last tail of his bandage. "A man who falls off the side of a mountain and breaks his leg is far luckier than a man who falls off the side of that same mountain and breaks his neck . . . Wouldn't you say?"

This combination discussion/medical treatment was taking place in the marshal's office of the jail building just down the street from where the recent shoot-out had occurred. Also present were Mike Bullock of Bullock's Saloon and Frank Draeger, who ran the Shirley House Hotel with his wife Freda. Several customers from each of those establishments were milling in the street directly out front of the jail, and others were strung out up as far as to where the bodies of the victims were being gathered and loaded onto a wagon by town undertaker Titus O'Malley and his assistant. The murmur of voices coming out of the gathering was like the amplified drone of mosquitoes on a hot summer night.

In no mood for a discussion on the philosophy of luck with the good doctor, Buford said, "All I want to know is, will this patch-up job of yours be good enough so's I can ride out of here tomorrow like I planned?"

"How far do you intend to go?" Tibbs asked.

"Cheyenne. I've got to report in, fill out the blasted paperwork on those fugitives." Buford paused, made a sour face. "Come to think on it, I guess I won't be ridin' out hardly like I planned at all. Our load will be considerably lighter than we figured on, eh Crispin?"

"For a fact. But we still need to take back the wagon and the team."

Buford sighed. "Yeah. And there'll still be the blasted paperwork." Buford's eye searched out Bob. "Be a big help if I can take along a sworn and signed account from you on how things went down here tonight."

"Be happy to. I'll have to write up one of my own anyway," Bob told him. "Might be in the morning before I can get it done, though. I've still got to take a turn around the town after we break up here."

"I can take care of that for you, boss," spoke up Fred.

"You already put in a full day. Plus you got knocked around pretty good by those varmints," Bob reminded him. "Best you call it a night and just go ahead and—"

"I'm fine, other than my bruised pride," Fred protested. "I'm all revved up and not fit for sleeping nohow. Might as well walk it off and do some good in the process." Fred was a large, heavyset man just short of thirty. The extra padding around his middle and his generally mild manner caused some folks to mistake him for being soft all over; they overlooked the spread of his shoulders, his thick wrists, and blunt-fingered, powerful hands. In his years as a deputy and now chief deputy under Bob, Fred had come a long way from the pudgy, insecure person he'd been when he first pinned on a badge. And a seldom seen—though fierce when it did rear its head—stubborn streak was part of the package.

"Okay. If you're sure you feel up to it," Bob conceded.

"I'll be fine," Fred assured him.

Partway out the door, the big deputy paused and looked back. "I see O'Malley, the undertaker, is about done loading up the bodies out here. You made up your mind yet what you're gonna want to do with 'em? He'll likely ask me. You figure to bury 'em here, or is Marshal Morrison gonna take 'em back with him?"

"Oh, no. We ain't gonna have to haul a bunch of stinkin' corpses all the way back to Cheyenne, are we?" groaned Crispin.

Buford made a face. "Sure as hell ain't a notion that sits any more favorably with me than you," he said. He looked thoughtful for a minute. Then: "Far as I can recollect, ain't none of 'em got kin anywhere around close who'd take any interest in claimin' the bodies. Bob, you willin' to plant 'em here on your Boot Hill? Sell their horses and gear, put whatever you get toward the burial expense, and then bill the balance to the U.S. Marshal's office in Cheyenne. I'll see to it you get squared up with pronto. And if any family members should happen to come 'round wanting any of the varmints, they can come here and dig 'em up. How about that?"

"Sounds okay to me." Bob cut his gaze to Mike Bullock. "Mike, you're on the town council. Any objection?"

Bullock spread his hands. "If we can't trust the U.S. Marshal's office, who can we? By all means, go ahead and do it that way."

Bob nodded. "You heard the man, Fred. Give the word to O'Malley, okay?"

Once Fred had gone on out the door, Doc Tibbs said to Buford, "As far as your question about riding to Cheyenne with this wound, that's mainly up to you. If you can stand the discomfort—"

"He can," Crispin vouched.

"Then by all means, go ahead," the doctor finished. "I'd ask that you stop and see me in the morning, before you head out, so I can change the dressing and make sure the bleeding is still clotted good. And then I'd recommend checking in with another doctor as soon as you get to Cheyenne."

"Reckon I can handle that," Buford said, knowing full well that he probably would check with a doctor in Cheyenne only if the bullet hole was bothering him more than he expected it would be. Since this was hardly the first time he'd been shot, he had a pretty good sense of how serious this latest encounter with a chunk of lead was, and he didn't rate it as all that bad.

A handful of minutes later, once the doctor had packed up his bag and taken his leave and Bob had gone out into the street to clear away the lingering gawkers, things turned quiet and peaceful in the jail office. Bullock and Draeger had also left, and Crispin, after gobbling a handful of pain pills the doctor gave him for his gout, had gone back to an empty cot in the lockup to sleep.

Bob sat behind his desk. Buford was in a chair hitched up before it. They were passing back and forth a bottle of good bourbon that Bob had produced from a desk drawer.

"Mighty smooth stuff you're serving up here, barkeep," Buford said as he handed the bottle back after taking a touch.

"Glad you find it to your taste," Bob responded. "Afraid I'm not a very discerning judge because, to tell you the truth, I don't do a lot of drinking. Still, there are times . . ."

"Like tonight."

"Uh-huh."

"Five men dead under our guns," Buford mused. "They weren't much but, still, they were men. Takin' a human life ought not ever come easy . . . But I gotta admit, the longer I'm in this business, the less I find it botherin' me. Especially when it comes to ambushin' skunks like the Silases. In fact—and I know this is gonna make me sound almighty cold—for the way things turned out tonight, I'm feelin' more sadness for those pieces of pie that got smashed in the street than I do for the men we cut down."

Bob cocked an eyebrow. "Yeah, I have to allow as to how that does sound a mite cold." His expression stayed blank for a minute, then it was split by a lopsided grin. "On the other hand, that *was* some tasty pie."

Buford held out his hand and Bob handed the bottle back.

After he'd taken a long pull and then unbent his elbow again, Buford said, "Comes to mind something else I want to comment on."

"Such as?"

Buford gestured. "You. Your speed with that .44 you pack."

"Make for a problem?"

"Not really. Although the Silases might have a different opinion, if they was around to spout it . . . The thing is, I've seen fast draws before. And God knows I've heard enough gut wind from those who've *claimed* to be fast. But I've never stood alongside anybody with lightning in their hand the way you've got." Buford wagged his head. "All the times I've passed through here since you took on the marshal's job, I guess I only vaguely picked up the notion you was pretty good with a shootin' iron. 'Sundown Bob' I've heard some call you. But I also heard how you don't like being referred to that way, so I didn't spend much time reflecting on it. Can't help wondering now, though, if that came from you setting the sun for a few *hombres* with that lightning draw of yours?"

Bob grinned tolerantly. "That'd make a better story I reckon. Leastways for some. Truth of it ain't nothing like that, though. It came from my flaming red hair. 'Red as a sundown' somebody once said, and damned if it didn't stick—not particularly to my liking, as you already know."

Morrison grunted. "You're right, my version makes a better story. Bottom line, as far as I'm concerned, remains that I somehow never got the full impression of how good and how fast you really are. Sorta caught me by surprise when I saw it on display out there a little while ago."

Bob shrugged. "It's a thing that comes in handy when called for. That's all. Don't mean it's something I advertise or make a big deal of. We both know what too often follows when word spreads about somebody being quick on the draw . . . That kind of attention I neither want nor need."

"Nobody does," Buford said. "Trouble is, not too many who've got the gift—if you want to call it that— are smart enough to play it that way. Makes you a rare bird, Bob. One I'm honored to know and call a friend."

"I appreciate that and feel likewise about you." Bob grinned. "Hell, I'd even drink to it if you ever hand that bottle back."

CHAPTER 4

**BLOODY AMBUSH IN THE STREETS
OF RATTLESNAKE WELLS ! ! !**

*Five Desperadoes Fatally Rebuked
by Brave Lawmen*

So read the front-page headline in the *Wells Gazette* when it hit the street two days following the shoot-out with the Silas brothers and their freed-prisoner accomplices.

A newspaper in Rattlesnake Wells was still a relatively new thing. It had started up right after the first of the year, the timing happening to coincide with the marriage of Bob and Consuela. In fact, the first issue of the *Gazette* had carried, also on its front page, a full article on the wedding. The coverage was more than warranted by the popularity of the couple, not to mention the fact that the event proved to be a town-wide shindig rivaling the recent New Year's Eve celebration. Bob himself could have done without all the fuss and attention, but seeing the happy glow that emanated from his bride and feeling the swell of affection and pride that filled him to near bursting, even he had to admit in the end that it was a grand time well worth recording for posterity.

In the weeks and months that followed, getting used to being married came a whole lot easier for Bob than getting used to the *Gazette*—or, more to the point, its publisher/editor/star reporter Owen Dutton. As Bucky had explained to Buford Morrison, having Consuela now transitioned into Mrs. Hatfield didn't really bring about that many changes to their household since she had, in essence, already been part of the family for so long anyway. It had taken her abduction by the vile Shaw clan the prior fall and the prospect of possibly losing her forever to jolt Bob into finally fully realizing and admitting to himself his deep feelings for her (something that had been apparent to others around town all along). Once he and a select posse of men had succeeded in rescuing Consuela and another hostage from the Shaws, it hadn't taken Bob long to confess his feelings and ask for her hand. Having never made a secret of the feelings she in turn had long harbored for Bob, the answer was an immediate yes. Initial plans to hold out for a spring wedding had quickly eroded, resulting in a ceremony just after the first of the year. No plans for a honeymoon were made, at least not any time in the foreseeable future. That part was taken care of in the privacy of Bob and Consuela's now shared bedroom, the biggest—not to mention easiest and most pleasant—change to their prior arrangement.

So while these adjustments were occurring on the home front, the adjustment to having a local newspaper was happening throughout the town. For the most part, it was a welcome thing. After all, a community claiming its own newspaper was a good sign—a sign of healthy growth and significance, like the spur rail line that had been put in and other positive changes that had come with the gold boom. (As opposed to the less positive things associated with Gold Avenue and the flow of lowlifes and schemers it unfortunately attracted along with those seeking only a chance to work hard in order to try and catch a lucky break.)

It was Owen Dutton's personality more than anything—his over-eager determination to find a story, no matter how obnoxious he had to be in order to dredge one up—that tended to rub some folks the wrong way, chief among them Marshal Hatfield. As far as the lead story in this latest edition of the *Gazette*, it was straightforward and accurate enough, albeit embellished with a good deal of sensationalized touches like the headline itself. That's mainly what it came down to with Dutton and his articles: He always got his facts right, he just couldn't keep from pushing too hard to find the most sensational angle, even in the simplest story. He did this both with his interviewing technique and then with the manner in which he wrote it down.

A classic example of this, Bob recalled with a wry grin as he scanned the current copy Deputy Fred had shoved under his nose, was the interview Dutton had tried to conduct with Buford Morrison on the morning the federal man was getting ready to leave. Dutton had been out of town chasing what turned out to be an empty lead on some alleged cattle rustling activity the evening of the Silas shoot-out so hadn't had the chance to start catching up with all the details until the following morning. His timing, as a result, caught Buford sore and cranky from his bullet wound, from also being a tad bit hungover, and anxious to be on his way for Cheyenne. It had taken only a few minutes of Dutton's persistent, rapid-fire inquiry before Buford lost his patience with questions like "how did you assess the danger factor in your opponents in order to select the best sequence for you to cut them down?" or "why did you shoot to kill in every instance, rather than merely disarm?"

"Tell you what," Buford had interrupted with a growl. "How about I throw your ass in the back of my tumbleweed wagon—it's all cleaned out, nice and fresh and empty—and you can ask questions all the way to Cheyenne? We'll keep a tally. If you ask some good ones, by the time we get there you'll have a helluva story. Not just about this here shoot-out but plenty of others that are sure to come up, too. Enough for a whole book. But if you keep askin' dumb-ass questions like the ones you've been spoutin' so far, then when we get to Cheyenne I'll turn you over to the judge and recommend charges against you for impersonatin' an actual journalist. You willin' to take the gamble?"

Not surprisingly, Dutton had turned down the offer.

So Buford went on his way and Dutton found other sources, primarily Bob, to put together his story. As he finished reading it now, the marshal saw that it was the usual factual account, dressed up with plenty of gory details and dramatic phrasing. Not for the first time, Bob mused that wherever Dutton had done his journalism training he'd clearly found time, in addition to his scholarly reading, to devour more than a few of the action-packed dime novels of the day that were so popular throughout the country. The influence was unmistakable in his writing.

"Well? What do you think?" Fred asked when Bob lowered the paper.

"Same thing I always think," Bob answered. "In among the overwrought passages and between all the exclamation points, Dutton gets his names and facts straight."

"Aw, I think you're sometimes too hard on the man, boss. I know he can be an annoying little pipsqueak from time to time, but he don't really mean no harm. Yeah, he comes on a little strong, always trying to pump more excitement into a thing than is truly there. But, overall, he ain't so bad. Plus he does a lot of, whatycall, human interest pieces that folks enjoy. Recipes and new babies and reports of family gatherings around town. Stuff like that."

Bob jabbed a thumb toward the battered old coffeepot over on the stove. "The day he prints a recipe we can follow to get a decent cup of coffee out of that thing, I will take back every uncharitable word or thought I ever had about ol' Owen. Is that fair enough?"

"No, it ain't fair at all. That would be bordering on the impossible, maybe even talking about tampering with the spirit world," Fred said stubbornly. He slapped the headlined article on the paper he was now holding. "There's nothing here that you got any business finding fault with. He made the bad *hombres* look bad and us fellas fighting on the right side look good. He even downplayed the way me and Crispin got hornswoggled and ended up locked out of the fight. And you and Buford? Look there, right smack in the headline—'*Rebuked by Brave Lawmen.*' That ain't nothing to grouse about, if you ask me."

"Okay, okay," Bob said with a weary sigh. "It's a splendid piece of journalism and deserves to be on display in a museum somewhere. Is that better? Now can we move on to other things? After all, that shooting was two days ago and it's been awful quiet around here ever since. Not that I'm complaining exactly, but I start to get a little itchy when things are too doggone calm."

"Be careful what you wish for, boss," Fred cautioned earnestly. "We're coming off a pretty hard winter, not too far into spring. But summer's just around the corner and you know how things tend to bust open more when the weather gets hot."

"Yeah, I guess I should appreciate the calm while it lasts." Then, stealing a line from Buford Morrison, Bob added, "I just don't want to die of boredom and dry up like an old buffalo skull."

"Huh?"

"Never mind. Just something I heard somewhere."

"Well, I wouldn't worry too much about the calm or the boredom. Take a closer look at a couple more things right here." Fred waved the newspaper again. "I can spot trouble brewing that I got a pretty good hunch we're bound to get involved in sooner or later."

"You mean that piece about the cattle rustling that's supposedly going on west of town? The rustling that Dutton got a big 'lead' on and went out to see for himself the other night? Trouble was, he came back without ever catching sight of anything, not even a scrawny coyote. Yet it still didn't stop him from running his article just to help keep things stirred up, did it? You see, *that's* the side of him I find so damned annoying."

"Maybe so. But you know who's behind those rustling claims, don't you?"

"I know who and I've got a pretty good idea why." Bob frowned. "The who is Ed Wardell. The why is because he's had a burr under his saddle ever since last summer when Carlos Vandez bought those sections of land off the Widow Terlain and expanded his V-Slash spread so it borders Wardell's Rocking W property for a good long stretch."

"Near to five miles," Fred said.

"Wardell hates Mexicans. Can't say I've ever heard exactly why, but it's a fact he's made plenty clear on more than one occasion. So now, all of a sudden, he not only has a Mexican for a neighbor but the Mexican's spread has expanded bigger and, by all accounts, is more successful than the Rocking W. This leaves Wardell in a seething rage pretty much around the clock. The only way his pride will let him face the fact that a greaser could pull off something like that is to start believing something underhanded must be going on."

"Underhanded like rustling?"

"That'd fit the bill."

Fred's face scrunched up. "You mean you think Wardell is making it all up?"

"I got no proof of that. I'm just sort of thinking out loud. But neither does Wardell have any hard proof to back up his rustling claims. That's part of the problem. Even if it was within our jurisdiction, he can't offer a trail or a sighting or an altered brand—nothing that makes a starting point to go after any culprits. All he does is keep claiming he's got missing cattle. Like you said a minute ago, we're coming off a hard winter. Maybe he lost an undue number of head to the weather or maybe some have wandered off and his brush poppers haven't rounded 'em up yet."

"So it could be that Wardell is jumping the gun with his rustling claims. And because he hates Mexicans so much, he thinks—and he's hinting hard for others to think—that Carlos Vandez might be behind it."

Bob shrugged. "Remember, I'm just thinking out loud. But nobody hates cattle thieves worse than I do. Even if it is outside our jurisdiction, if I truly thought a mangy pack of long-loopers was at work anywhere in our area, I'd probably still offer our services to try and run 'em down. But I ain't sold on the idea. Remember, too, neither has Wardell been able to convince the U.S. Marshals to send anybody to look into it."

"Yeah, he's made plenty of noise about that, too.

And when he heard Buford Morrison passed through the other day without even a glance in his direction, it set him off all over again." Fred paused, his expression darkening with a deepened concern. "In fact, that's actually what I meant when I said I could spot trouble brewing in this newspaper article about the rustling. It reminded me of what else Wardell said about the law refusing to get involved."

"And what was that?" Bob wanted to know.

"He said he was sending for some special men to hire on to his ranch crew—hardcase wranglers who knew how to work cattle and also how to deal with trouble in cases where men had to make their own justice."

Bob scowled. "You sure he said that?"

"I didn't hear it with my own ears but I sure heard about it secondhand from plenty of folks. There was still some talk about it in the Bluebird Café this morning when I stopped for breakfast."

"Well, that's just great. Why didn't I hear about it before this?"

"I figured you had. I guess that's why I didn't say anything. It was just a couple days ago. Like I said, after Marshal Morrison left without making a swing out to the Rocking W."

"Now I suppose I'm going to have to," Bob said with a sour look. "First, to see if Wardell went ahead and _did_ send for some hardcases. Second, to see if I can get him to ease up and call 'em off. That's all we need is for _hombres_ like that to show up and set a damn range war in motion over something that amounts to nothing."

Fred shifted his feet and looked anxious. "There's,

er, something else we haven't talked about yet that I think you're gonna want to pay closer attention to also."

"Something else covered in the *Gazette?*"

"Uh-huh."

Fred smoothed out the elongated, single sheet of paper on Bob's desk once more, then leaned over and pointed to another small article on the back side. The header for this one read: JOHN LARKIN RELEASED FROM PRISON—REPORTEDLY ON HIS WAY BACK TO RATTLESNAKE WELLS.

CHAPTER 5

"Close to five years ago, it would've been. A few months before you showed up and took on the marshal's job. The gold boom was under way, really starting to pick up steam. Gold Avenue was stretching out daily, though still a far cry from what it is today. You remember how it was back then."

Fred had settled onto a wooden chair that he'd hitched up in front of Bob's desk as he related this background information.

"Jackson Emory had the biggest mining operation going up in the Prophecies at that time. Angus McTeague was coming on strong, but he wasn't yet top dog like he's become these days. So, anyway, Emory had two foremen helping him run things. Saul Norton—you know him, he's still around—and John Larkin, the fella mentioned in that article. They were both a couple of aggressive go-getters, really worked their tails off for Emory."

Bob arched a brow. "Then that means Norton ain't changed much. He's still aggressive, though

ornery would be more like the word I'd choose. He
drives those Emory digging crews hard and with little
or no letup. I'm surprised he can keep finding men
to work for him."

"I know what you mean. He wasn't always quite
that bad, though. He pushed himself hard and expected everybody around him to keep up, but he
didn't used to seem so . . . well, okay, I guess 'ornery'
is as good a word as any. Since Larkin got sent away
to prison and old man Emory got stove up the way he
did, the responsibility for keeping up the output of
the Emory Mining Company has fallen mainly on the
shoulders of Norton. You got to give him credit for
sticking with it, I'd say, but the strain of it has taken
its toll. The two Emory daughters do their best to be
involved, but, from some reports, they may be almost
as much bother as actual help."

"I thought Norton and the oldest sister, Victoria,
were kinda sweet on each other."

Fred nodded. "That's the way Norton would like it
to be, that's for sure. And I guess there've been a few
signs of Victoria maybe showing some interest in
return, but not as strong as Norton would like for
her to show."

"Okay. I already know the situation with Norton
and the Emorys pretty good," Bob said. "But what
about this Larkin and the likelihood of his return?
Your tone and Dutton's implication in this article
seem to suggest that he might be a threat of some
kind."

"No doubt that's the concern of certain people. It

was another subject of conversation at the Bluebird this morning, I can tell you that."

"Sounds like I ought to start stopping by the Bluebird more often in order to stay on top of things." Bob scowled. "How does anybody even know Larkin got out anyway? How long was he sentenced for?"

"Five years in the Laramie pen," Fred answered. Then he went on. "But he got out early for good behavior. That means he's on parole for the balance of the five, and, if he does as directed, he's supposed to check in with the local law officials wherever he decides to settle on the outside.

"How does anybody know about this? Try chalking it up to the Emory money and influence. Somebody on the Laramie parole board saw fit to notify the lawyer who represented Emory Mining on the original case, and he in turn let the old man know. How, exactly, it traveled from there I don't know. But newspaperman Dutton caught wind of it somehow and made sure word got spread good and proper. So now it's wagging on tongues all over town."

"Yet, for all the wagging, I still haven't heard the full story on Larkin. What did he do to get himself sent to prison, and what makes folks think he might be coming back for some kind of revenge?"

"He got convicted of stealing from Emory. He swore his innocence throughout. The most damning testimony against him came from none other than Saul Norton, who spotted Larkin pocketing small amounts of gold dust from the mine. He went to Emory, who went to old Hector Goode, the town marshal at that time, who called in a U.S. Marshal.

With the name 'Emory' involved, there was no foot-dragging by anybody. Larkin was formally charged and there was an immediate investigation that turned up two small sacks of gold dust hidden among Larkin's personal effects. Once that was presented in court, along with Norton's testimony, the jury didn't have to waste a whole lot of time deliberating."

"Classic open-and-shut case," Bob said solemnly.

"Uh-huh. But a lot of folks—folks not on the jury or not in any other kind of position to have an official say in the matter—still had a hard time buying it."

"Why?"

Fred squirmed a little in his chair. "Mostly because Larkin was such a well-liked fella. Aggressive and nose-to-the-grindstone when it came to his job, like I said before, but somehow still likable and friendly. His men worked hard for him because they saw how much he cared and they wanted to please him, not because he pushed 'em and drove 'em."

"The way Norton did."

"Yeah. Did and still does." Fred paused, frowning, mentally sorting to choose the right words. "Why it was hard for so many folks to buy Larkin as a common thief had to do with more than just finding him likable, though. In about any way you could figure, it just didn't make sense for him to risk so much by pilfering that way. He had a good job, was earning—without having to steal—good money, and was clearly looked on with favor by Jackson Emory himself. Favorably enough to be seriously courting

Victoria and doing so with the full blessing of the old man and his wife."

"But there was no getting around the sworn testimony and the hard evidence found against him."

"That's the way the jury saw it."

"Any reason to think it was a frame-up? Somebody looking to gain by getting rid of Larkin?"

"Who? Norton hasn't gone anywhere, hasn't gained anything except a crushing added workload. Old Judge Bricker, the circuit judge who ruled over the trial, died of a stroke six months afterward. Hogan, the lawyer for Emory, is still practicing down in Cheyenne at about the same level he was then. And the U.S. Marshal who conducted the investigation, a fella named Mulhaussen, got shot to death three years ago up in Deadwood. You remember hearing about that, right? All that leaves is Jackson Emory himself, the victim of a wagon crash less than a year after the final trial that killed his wife and left him a cripple, only a shell of the man he was." Fred paused again and wagged his head slowly. "No, it'd be kinda hard to find anybody who you could say *gained* from Larkin going off to prison."

"So why do folks think he's coming back to make trouble? For who?" Bob said.

"Well, Norton would be the most obvious choice, wouldn't he? It was his accusations that started it all, and then his testimony and the rest that sealed it. And I know a few of the jury members who ruled on a guilty verdict are sweating a little, too. Larkin's last words, after the judge sentenced him and gave him the chance for a final statement, was to turn to the whole court and say this . . . I was there that day, I remember it word for word . . . 'You've just sentenced an innocent man to a prison hellhole. I mean to come back some day and show all of you the error of your ways.'"

"That was it?" said Bob, sounding almost disappointed.

"It was enough. If you were in court that day hearing him say it, it was plenty."

Bob pursed his lips thoughtfully. "I guess it could be taken as a threat. But it could also simply be the words of an innocent man stating his aim to try and one day set the record straight."

"One way or the other, I expect we're gonna be finding out one of these days before too long."

"You're convinced he'll be showing up?"

"For better or worse."

"Interesting choice of words. The oldest Emory daughter, Victoria, the one you said Larkin was sparking pretty seriously before his trouble . . . She figure into any part of why you're so sure he'll be back?"

"Not due to any encouragement from her, if that's what you mean. But for the first couple of years, Larkin sent her letters almost weekly. All they did was pile up at the post office, unopened, until they eventually quit coming . . . But just because he gave up on sending letters don't mean he's given up on his feelings for Victoria."

"Only now the feelings between her and his old friend Norton have been added to the picture."

"Yeah. There's that."

Bob leaned back in his chair. He puffed out his cheeks, then slowly expelled the air. "Fred," he said. "I want you to do me a favor."

"Sure, boss. What is it?"

Leaning forward again and planting his elbows on the desktop, Bob said, "The next time I open my yap about maybe feeling a little bored because things seem a mite too calm . . . Don't work so hard at cheering me up by painting all the trouble brewing on the horizon. Okay?"

CHAPTER 6

Bob didn't know exactly what to expect when he rode out to the Rocking W that afternoon . . . But what he for sure *wasn't* counting on was finding a necktie party under way once he got there.

After taking an early lunch at home with Consuela, the marshal had saddled up and headed out with the intent of discussing Ed Wardell's alleged rustling problem with him. As part of that, he figured to confront Wardell about the rumor of him bringing in hardcase wranglers.

The sky was clear, the air warm and sweet with the smells of spring's first greening. It was a good day for a ride, a chance to get away from the confines and increasing crowdedness of the town. Although he took a lot of satisfaction in being the marshal of Rattlesnake Wells, Bob had grown up on a sprawling Texas ranch so it never took very long out in the open spaces for him to be reminded it remained a setting that would always have an appeal and a strong hold on at least part of him. What was more, he knew Consuela felt the same. Their shared dream, once his days of wearing a badge were behind him, had now become to find a little outlying spread where they would run a few head of cattle, maybe some horses, too, and finish out their time together.

Such pleasant thoughts drifted in and out of Bob's mind as he rode over the rolling, grassy hills. But for the most part, he stayed focused on the upcoming meeting with Ed Wardell. He hadn't had a lot of contact with the rancher over the years, and what there'd been failed to leave a very favorable impression.

For one thing, there was Wardell's blatant dislike and distrust of Mexicans. During his formative years in Texas, Bob's closest friend had been Ramos Diaz, Consuela's brother. Their father, Alberto, was ranch foreman and trusted right hand to Bob's father. So all of his life—albeit never more so than now, subsequent to his marriage to Consuela—Bob had felt an affinity and appreciation for Mexicans. To hear others disparage them for no good reason other than ignorant bias (something all too common where he came from back in Texas) chafed him mightily.

Furthermore, in Wardell's case, he was a cold, sullen, generally unlikable individual to boot. It would be hard to find anybody around Rattlesnake Wells who regretted him not coming to town more often.

In fact, as he neared the Rocking W's main ranch house, Bob was starting to seriously question the wisdom of going through with this visit. Changing Wardell's mind about Mexicans wasn't going to happen, that much was a certainty. Nor was he apt to dissuade the man's belief that some of his cattle were being stolen. The best Bob could hope for was to find that Wardell hadn't yet sent for those Texas hardcases or that he'd be willing to call them off if Bob expressed some willingness to look into the suspected rustling. As far as the latter, though, Bob knew there was only so much he'd be able to offer.

And, looming over it all, would be the question of whether or not the two of them would be able to hold their tempers long enough to have any chance at ironing out anything at all. If Wardell got too mouthy, as he had a habit of doing, and Bob was entering into it already disliking him . . . well, how constructive was that likely to be?

From the crest of a long slope looking down on the ranch, Bob reined up and leaned across his saddle horn, pondering if it would be worth it to go the rest of the way or if it only stood the risk of making harder feelings.

That's when a pair of horsemen came in sight, each dragging on the ground behind him a hog-tied man lassoed at the ankles. As Bob watched, the two riders galloped hard toward a cluster of trees located off one end of a well-maintained corral. Four or five other horsemen were sitting their mounts there, waiting. A couple of them were waving their hats and cheering the approaching riders, reveling in the way the hog-tied men twisted and bounced cruelly on the rugged ground as they were dragged along.

Bob spat a curse and his right hand instinctively drifted down to touch the handle of the Colt riding on his hip. And then his gaze locked on something else. A rope had been tossed up and over a high,

horizontally extending limb on one of the trees . . .
and its free, dangling end was fashioned into a
hangman's noose!

An instant later, Bob was spurring his horse forward, down the long slope at a hard run. Instead of
drawing the Colt, he pulled his Winchester Yellowboy rifle from its saddle scabbard. Holding it out at
arm's length, he whirled it one-handed, working the
lever to chamber a round. Then he thumbed back
the hammer, aiming skyward, and triggered a jarring
shot.

A half dozen startled looks cut in Bob's direction
as he whirled the Winchester once again.

He came thundering up to the group of men less
than a minute behind the two riders dragging their
hapless victims. The two abused men were left lying
on the ground, all but smothered by swirls of yellow-
ish dust from the horses' hooves. Through the haze,
Bob could see feeble movement in the tattered, battered shapes, signaling they were at least still alive.

"What the hell's going on here!?" Bob demanded.
He raked a blistering gaze over the group of men,
looking for the face of somebody he possibly recognized, might at least know the name of. A couple of
the men dropped their eyes, unable to meet his. The
rest looked back at him with flat, impassive expressions. Three of them held their hands close to the
guns worn around their waists, marking themselves
as the ones Bob would go for first in the event this
showed signs of getting out of hand.

"What the hell business is it of yours?" came the
response to Bob's question.

Not surprisingly, this was voiced by none other

than Ed Wardell himself. He sat the saddle of a blaze-faced black gelding, a little deeper back in among the other men, only a few feet to one side of the dangling noose.

"You know the answer to that," Bob told him. "Crime and lawbreaking *are* my business."

"Not out here they ain't," Wardell was quick to remind him. "Your jurisdiction ends at the city limits marker of that shithole town of yours. Recall that little detail, Marshal? You ought to, you told it to me enough times when I came to you seeking help."

"You're right," Bob conceded. "When it comes to investigating an alleged crime or trying to put somebody under arrest, there are jurisdictional limits I'm bound by. But coming upon something like this—a crime clearly in progress—is something no self-respecting lawman or any decent citizen would turn his back on. I not only have a right but an obligation to intervene."

Wardell chuckled nastily. "Wow. You really take that law-dogging serious, don't you? You must be reading books and memorizing the fancy lingo and the whole shot." He nudged his knees against the sides of his horse and threaded his way forward, separating himself slightly from his men and emerging from the shade of the trees out to where he was able to put on a better show of brazenly facing up to the marshal. "You hear that, boys?" he said over his shoulder, even though his eyes were locked on Bob's. "We're being *intervened* on because the noble marshal here feels the obligation to stop our lowdown, lawbreaking ways."

Physically, there wasn't much of anything noteworthy or impressive about Wardell. Average in height and build, crowding fifty, with gray-flecked sideburns bracketing a somewhat pushed-in face. Watery blue eyes, a slightly pugged nose, strong lower jaw that thrust the chin forward, exposing his bottom row of teeth when he talked.

"What about the lawbreaking ways of these two skunks? Don't that count for anything?" said one of the horsemen whose lasso was still tied to a dragged man. He was a long, lanky number with a salt-and-pepper walrus mustache, hook nose, and mean eyes under bristly brows.

"Whatever they did, it don't count enough to warrant a lynching," Bob responded.

"And no lynching has taken place. That part ain't been decided yet," argued Wardell.

Bob's eyes cut meaningfully to the noose dangling down and then back to the rancher. "Oh? Sure could've fooled me. From the look of things, it appears somebody has already made up their mind."

"That's just a little window dressing. A persuader, if you will . . . to help loosen the tongues of those two varmints so's they'll tell me what I want to know."

"What about the dragging 'em behind horses part? What's that supposed to do besides loosen their hides on their bones?"

Wardell's chin thrust forward a bit farther. Challenging. Defiant. "How about we call that a message-sender? Any saddle tramps crossing my property are welcome to stop the night, camp, graze and water their horses . . . But *not* to make a meal out of one of my beeves."

"And lynching 'em would be the exclamation point on the message. Is that it?"

"I already told you—"

"I know what you told me. I'm calling you a liar." Bob's narrowed eyes raked once more over the others. "And the rest of you are a pack of gutless curs who couldn't stomp a stringy jackrabbit unless you ganged up to do it."

"That's mighty bold talk for somebody buckin' one-to-seven odds," sneered the hook-nosed horseman who'd spoken before.

Up to that point, Bob had been resting the butt of his Winchester on his hip, barrel angled skyward. Suddenly its muzzle was level and steady, aimed square at Wardell's chest. "You want to try laying down a bet on those odds, go right ahead," the marshal grated out the side of his mouth, addressing the sneering horseman but keeping his eyes locked on Wardell. "But as soon as you start turning cards, I guarantee your boss will be the first one to cash in his chips."

"Smoky, you damn fool! Knock it off!" barked Wardell, all color instantly drained from his face. "This badge-toting bastard will kill me sure as hell."

"And a good chunk of the rest of you, if it comes to throwing lead," Bob warned.

Wardell licked his lips. "All right. What do you want? How do we play it from here?"

Bob held everybody within the range of his direct and peripheral vision. The Yellowboy muzzle never wavered a whisker from Wardell. "For starters," Bob told him, "you light down out of that saddle. Shuck your guns and drop 'em to the ground. Real slow.

Then walk over here and stand close beside me, like we're best pals. Remember, the rifle will be on you all the way. And when you're sided up good and close, it'll be practically stuck in your ear. You might want to consider that a persuader, if you will . . . You know, helping persuade you and your boys not to even *think* about trying anything funny."

Wardell glared hatefully at the marshal. But he followed his instructions precisely. After he'd dropped his guns and started walking, he muttered a strained reminder to his men, saying, "Do whatever he says. No need to risk anybody getting killed . . . We'll have our turn another day."

Once he had Wardell positioned the way he wanted him, Bob said, "Okay, now the rest of you. Stay mounted but, one by one, real slow and careful, shuck your weapons. Sidearms and saddle guns alike." While this was taking place, he kept an especially close watch on the men who'd shifted their hands closer to their guns when he first rode up— making sure they didn't decide to try something brave and stupid in spite of what their boss said. When their guns obediently hit the dirt, Bob hissed out a sigh of relief.

Next his gaze sought out the two men who'd averted their eyes when he initially confronted the group, signaling they weren't entirely comfortable with the proceedings he'd ridden up on. "You and you," Bob said, indicating the pair with a jerk of his chin. "Climb down. Grab your canteens and go cut loose those men on the ground. Cut the lassoes and cut their other bonds, too. Then see if they're able to take some water. Not too much . . . The rest of you stay mounted and stay bunched together. Once the lassoes are freed, back away some."

In a matter of minutes, the abused men had been untied and were sitting up, though still on the ground. After they drank thirstily and poured some of the canteen water over their faces—erasing the layer of grime and dust and some patches of crusted blood—Bob was surprised to see they didn't appear to be quite as battered as he'd expected.

"You fellas in good enough shape to ride a horse instead of being dragged along behind one?" he asked.

The revived men looked up at him. "Our own horses are tied somewhere back in those trees," said one of them in a somewhat raspy voice. "Give us a chance to get back on 'em and, yeah, we're in good enough shape to ride."

"If it gets us away from these crazy bastards," amended his partner, "you damn betcha we are!"

CHAPTER 7

Their names were Al Hicks and Ron Streeter. Their story was a simple one: They were a couple of drifters from off Utah way on their way to the Prophecy Mountain gold fields hoping to sign on to a mining crew until they could make enough money for a grubstake to start their own dig in the hope of hitting it big one day. The same dream as countless other souls lured by the yellow ore—some coming to work hard for a shot at their share, some coming to find an easier angle.

In the case of Hicks and Streeter, they struck Bob as two hard-luck sorts who were willing to sweat for the chance to get ahead; they just never realized much good fortune from their efforts. Before making it to the Prophecies, as they were crossing the Rocking W range, they found themselves flat broke, hungry, and down to a half-empty jar of jam in their supply pack. That's when they came upon a sickly young calf, apparently abandoned by its mother, with no sign of the rest of the herd anywhere around.

"The poor, wobbly-legged little critter looked like

he'd never make it through until morning. So we decided we'd save him from his misery and save our empty, aching bellies from theirs, too," explained Hicks, what some might call a boyishly handsome individual despite being well into his thirties. His beard stubble had a blondish tint to it, matching the spare sideburns extending down from under his hat. He was average in build, not exactly soft looking but hardly exhibiting the kind of wiry toughness you saw in most drifters, either.

"And you can believe this or not," Streeter added, "but we had in mind the whole while that if we saw any wranglers or spotted any ranch buildings the next day, we'd 'fess up to what we'd done and offer to work it off as repayment." He was maybe a decade older than Hicks, taller and slower moving, with a long, sad face, dark whiskers, and, when he lifted his hat to sleeve away sweat, a shining bald dome except for a fringe around his ears.

The drifters were telling their tale on the ride back to Rattlesnake Wells. Their horses had been returned to them and they clambered aboard with a minimal show of difficulty for the battering they'd endured. Still, Bob was setting a steady but easy pace in recognition of what they'd been put through. Hicks appeared to be in the worst shape, sagging weakly in the saddle now and again, but then he would bolster himself and raise stubbornly upright once more. Mostly for his sake, Bob called a halt a couple different times, passing around a canteen and allowing a short breather.

Also accompanying them, for at least part of the way, were the two Rocking W wranglers Bob had singled out to cut Hicks and Streeter loose. Their names, he learned, were Temple and Reese. The marshal had further enlisted them to round up all the guns from Wardell and the others and bring them along until they were well removed from the ranch. Bob didn't really think the ranch owner or any of his men would be foolish enough to retrieve their shucked weapons and mount an actual assault on him—no matter how far out of his jurisdiction he was—yet he nevertheless figured it was better to be safe than sorry. After all, he'd done a pretty good job of humiliating Wardell in front of his riders and had backed the lot of them down without firing a shot. That kind of thing could rankle some men past the point of showing good sense.

When they had covered more than half the distance back to town, Bob called another halt, this time for the purpose of allowing Temple and Reese to return to the Rocking W.

"I want you to give Wardell a message for me," he told them. "Tell him I'm willing to consider this incident finished. Over and done with. If he insists on pushing it further, then what it leads to probably won't be pretty but it will be strictly on him . . . You got that?"

The two wranglers nodded solemnly.

"All right. Get on back to your ranch, then."

The two men hesitated. After exchanging looks with his partner, the one called Temple said, "Me and Reese here just want you to know, Marshal, that the whole business back there . . . well, it was settin' mighty uncomfortable with us the way it was headed before you showed up. And we was awful glad to see you when you did."

"When you say 'the way it was headed' . . . you figure a lynching was where it was gonna end up?" Bob asked.

Temple nodded. "That's sure how it looked and felt."

"When it comes to havin' his cattle rustled," said Reese, "Mr. Wardell is . . . well, he gets kinda crazy. He pure hates cattle thieves, especially when it's his cattle gettin' took."

"And even more especially when he thinks it's Carlos Vandez, a Mexican, who might be behind it. Right?"

"*That's* the name he kept throwin' at us," spoke up Streeter excitedly. "He kept insisting we worked for Carlos Vandez and wanted us to admit it."

"Yeah, he's got no love for Vandez, that's for sure," said Temple.

"How much rustling is actually going on? How bad is the Rocking W getting hit?" Bob wanted to know.

Again Temple and Reese exchanged glances.

"Well. That's kinda hard to say," said Temple. "I guess nobody knows for sure, not as good as Mr. Wardell and maybe Smoky Barnett, his ramrod. *They're* convinced the Rocking W has been losing a lot of head."

"But you're not?"

Reese said, "We're coming off an awful bad winter, Marshal. You know that. The weather took a toll on everybody's cattle. And for a spread the size of the Rocking W, what didn't freeze got scattered from hell to breakfast. Some of us fellas are thinkin' there's maybe still pockets of animals we just ain't caught up with yet."

"Only Wardell don't see it that way."

Temple scrunched his face into a perplexed expression. "It's almost like he *wants* it to be rustlin' . . . wants to be able to blame it on that."

"And blame Carlos Vandez specifically," said Bob, thinking out loud, stating his suspicions more to himself than anybody. Then: "Let me ask you this—either of you heard any talk of Wardell bringing in some new wranglers? Hardcases. Gunnies, in other words, to help fight this rustling problem he's so dead set exists?"

Yet again the Rocking W men exchanged glances before Temple answered, "Yeah, we've heard some talk like that. Smoky Barnett mentioned it a time or two."

"Names?"

Both men shook their heads. "None we ever heard."

"Either of you got any way of knowing if it went past more than just talk? Was anybody actually contacted or sent for?"

"We can't say on that, Marshal. Not one way or the other."

After Temple and Reese had ridden off, Hicks and Streeter, the unlucky drifters, finished rounding off their tale of the encounter with Wardell and his men up until Bob showed up.

At first light, some Rocking W riders had noticed their night camp and came riding down on it. Once there, it didn't take long for them to also notice the carcass of the dead calf and the uneaten slabs of meat still hanging on a spit over the cold campfire. Things turned worse for the strangers in a hurry. They were cursed and thoroughly roughed up. Every time they tried to explain their situation they got knocked down again. Until finally the leader of the Rocking W men, the one they called Smoky, decided the trespassers should be taken to ranch headquarters, to Ed Wardell himself. A rider was sent ahead to advise Wardell what the others would be bringing in.

When they got there, Wardell was waiting. So was the noose over the tree limb. Wardell wouldn't listen to a word they tried to tell him about who they were and why they'd butchered the calf. All he wanted to know was how long they'd been working for Vandez and where were they keeping the rest of the cattle they'd been stealing.

Not getting the answers he wanted, Wardell didn't waste much time giving the order to put them under the hanging noose. It was Smoky who halted that, at least temporarily, by suggesting that once the noose tightened around their necks they for sure wouldn't be able to provide any information. It was his idea to tie Hicks and Streeter behind horses and drag them around for a while in a last-ditch effort to get them to spill the truth about their connection to Vandez and the V-Slash.

"I guess you know the rest from there, Marshal," Hicks summed up the telling.

"And thank God you do," added Streeter. "Thank God you came along when you did."

"I don't know about reading God into it with me," Bob said. "But for the sake of you gents, I'm glad I arrived in time to break up Wardell's plans . . . You both convinced he would have gone ahead with the hanging?"

"Not a doubt in my mind," said Streeter.

"Same here," confirmed Hicks. "If Smoky hadn't come up with the idea to drag us around some—not that that was any picnic, I'll tell you—all you would have found when you got there was a couple of choked-out corpses swinging by our necks."

As soon as they hit town, Bob led the way to the doctor's office. He was pretty sure Hicks had some busted ribs at the very least. Plus he judged a handful of the gashes and lacerations visible on each man probably warranted stitches.

"In case you forgot, Marshal," Streeter said, his brow wrinkling with concern when he saw the doctor's shingle hanging over the door of the building where they swung in to tie their horses, "we ain't got a lick of money to pay no sawbones."

"Doc Tibbs is a reasonable man," Bob told him. "If I put in a good word for you, he'll agree to some payment arrangement. Then I'll see to it you follow through and square up with him."

Holding his middle and wincing in pain as soon as he'd climbed down off his horse, Hicks said, "Oh, we'll be sure and do that. First chance we get."

Bob pointed down the street to the log building that housed his office and the jail. "After I talk to the doc and drop you fellas off, you come on down there when he's finished with you. I'll have a report made up of today's incident that you can sign. Just for the record. Then we'll see what we can do about finding you someplace to stay and maybe some short-term work to help you get on your feet."

"I don't know why you're going out of your way to be so friendly, Marshal," said Streeter. "But we sure appreciate it. And you can count on us not playing you false for all you've done."

"I am counting on it," Bob replied bluntly. "Just keep in mind that it would cause me considerable annoyance if I found out I went to all the trouble of saving you from hanging only to have you turn out to be a couple of lowdown ingrates."

CHAPTER 8

"So, basically," Bob was saying, "all I accomplished out at the Rocking W was to make things worse. Usually, when Wardell or some of his boys come to town, they ain't too rowdy. Not near as bad as some of the other outfits around. After today, after I stuck a burr good and deep under the saddles of about half a dozen of 'em, I doubt that will remain the case. I expect they'll be showing up with fire in their eyes, primed for the least excuse to raise some hell."

"If that's what they're looking for, we can sure accommodate 'em," said Fred.

"Yeah, I suppose so. We've done it before." Bob sighed. "It's just that, doggone it, I went out there with the intent of calming things some. I sure missed that by a mile."

"I doubt those two fellas who dang near got hung saw it that way. You calmed things a whole lot where they were concerned," pointed out Fred.

"I guess there's that," Bob allowed. He got up from behind his desk, went over to the stove, and poured himself some coffee. This late in the day he

knew the brew would be stout enough to disintegrate
a stirring spoon, but that fit right in with his mood.
"I'm still finding it hard to believe Wardell has got
himself worked into a state where he'd try something
like that. One of his own men said he acts crazy over
the thought of somebody rustling his cattle. And that
same fella admitted it's kinda iffy whether or not
there's even that big a loss. Most of it could have
been just winterkill."

"So you continue to think that most of what's driving him is his hatred for Carlos Vandez and Mexicans
in general? That he just can't stand the thought of
sharing a property line with the V-Slash?"

"Hell, I don't know," said Bob, grimacing after
he'd taken a drink of his coffee. "Seems like a lot of
bother to go to out of just blind hate. But I've seen
that kind of thing before in old Indian fighters—
ones who harbored the 'only good Indian is a dead
Indian' mentality all the way to their own graves. So
I know that kind of attitude exists."

"Yeah, that's unfortunately true." Now it was
Fred's turn to heave a sigh. "And as further proof
that Wardell is ready to push to the limit his notion
about fighting rustlers—even if they don't really
exist—I found out some things about that while you
were away."

Bob sat down behind his desk. "Okay. Let's hear it."

Fred hitched up a seat for himself. "I got to thinking about the question of whether or not Wardell
went ahead and sent for some hardcases to add to his
crew. It dawned on me that the only way he could
have done it—since he only just started talking about

it a day or so ago, after Marshal Morrison failed to go out and see him about his rustling problem—was by mail or telegraph. Right?

"Now I know that neither Old Man Higby, the postmaster, nor Harold Feeney at the telegraph office are supposed to discuss what passes in or out under their noses. And I gotta say that they're both pretty tight-lipped about their business. But I also know that, with a little patience and the right approach, each of them *can* be nudged into revealing certain things."

"How about you?" Bob said, an edge of impatience cutting into his voice. "What's it gonna take to nudge you into revealing whatever it is you're working up to?"

"Okay, okay. Long story short: Neither Wardell nor any of his men has mailed anything at the post office for weeks. But . . . Smoky Barnett, Wardell's ramrod out at the ranch, did send a telegram on the afternoon Marshal Morrison rode out of town without stopping at the Rocking W. The telegram went to the Concordia Hotel in Denver. The words were something to the effect of: *Have your kind of work here after all. Come right away.* And even though Barnett was the one who sent it, he signed it as "E. Wardell" . . . I think that's why Feeney was willing to talk about it. He thought it was a strange message and, ever more, he thought it was suspicious that Barnett didn't sign with his own name."

"Yeah. That is a little odd," Bob said with a thoughtful expression. "Of course there could be all sorts of logical explanations."

"Yeah. But it could be summoning a hardcase like

Wardell talked about, too . . . *'Your kind of work after all'* . . . Makes it sound like there was some prior discussion but Wardell held off. Now he's no longer willing to."

"Well, we'll just have to keep a sharp eye out. Forewarned is forearmed, as they say. Good thinking and good work on getting the information, Fred. Feeney didn't happen to remember a name, did he?"

Fred nodded. "Matter of fact, he did. Like I said, the whole business had been eating away at him some. I think he was glad to get it off his chest. I checked the name he gave me against my memory and our Wanted files. Nothing came up, for whatever that's worth. In case it might mean anything to you, I wrote it down on that piece of paper I laid there on your desk."

Fred pointed.

Bob glanced down at his deputy's neat scrawl. *Rance Brannigan*, it read.

CHAPTER 9

Bob spent the next forty-five minutes feeling like he'd been gut-kicked by a mule. That's how hard the name Rance Brannigan hit him.

The worst part was trying not to show it, fighting not to reveal that the name had a connection to his past and what that dark, buried (he thought!) past was. Having Fred know him so well and being so perceptive only made it worse. Bob could tell right away that Fred sensed the change in him after hearing the name. At first, out of courtesy, the deputy held back from saying anything. But it was just a matter of time before his caring nature would cause him to start prying a bit.

Luckily, it wasn't long before Hicks and Streeter showed up following their sessions with the doctor. That shifted the direct focus away from Bob.

After necessary introductions were made, it was revealed that Hicks did indeed have three cracked ribs and both men received some stitching up. But other than a wealth of additional scrapes and bruises, there was nothing more—no broken bones or internal injuries or anything of that sort.

"For as bad as I ache all over," Streeter said wryly, "it seems like the damage oughtta be worse. But I reckon I'm willing to settle for some aches over what almost was. Had they gone ahead and stretched our necks, we wouldn't be hurting at all—but we'd also been slightly dead."

Following some additional small talk, Bob turned the two drifters over to Fred. Nobody knew more people or more about what was going on around town than Fred. This made him a natural for fixing Hicks and Streeter up with somewhere to stay and finding some short-term work to help them get back on their feet. He was already chattering with ideas and possibilities as he led them out the door.

Alone, Bob slumped in the chair behind his desk.

Rance Brannigan.

Jesus Christ!

Of all the names or situations to crop up out of his past, few could have been worse. Was there a chance it could merely be somebody with the same or similar name? No, that seemed highly unlikely. Rance was a pretty distinct handle. Attach the hardcase gunny description and it only served to solidify the identification all the more. And, yeah, Bob's past encounter with Brannigan had been down in Texas. But so what? A man could travel, couldn't he? After all, Bob had found his way from Texas to Rattlesnake Wells. No reason Brannigan couldn't find his way to Denver . . . and from there now summoned to be on his way here as well.

Bob sat staring at the handwritten name on the

piece of paper for several minutes, his mind and stomach churning. Then, abruptly, he grabbed the paper and balled it in his fist, squeezing as hard as he could, as if trying to squeeze away the existence of the person represented there.

Releasing the crumpled wad of paper, he got up and went out the door.

There was only one person he could talk to about it.

One person who knew the full story of his past.

One person who could calm him and help sort out some kind of rational plan for dealing with this unexpected twist that threatened their way of life here and everything they'd worked so hard to establish.

"Maybe he won't recognize you," Consuela said. "It's been nearly seven years. And for all that time everyone has believed the Devil's River Kid to be dead. Is it not possible that Brannigan will see in you merely the resemblance without believing you to actually be one and the same?"

"That's mighty thin, 'Suela," Bob replied. "It'd be real nice to think he could shrug it off that easy. But it's too risky to count on. He was there that day when I killed Sam Ramsey and those other three men. When Ramsey went down, Brannigan was the one who took charge of chasing me into the teeth of that blizzard . . . He was the last one to give up, almost at the cost of losing his own life to the storm."

Bob was sunk deep in the oversized easy chair in the living room of his home. Consuela was wedged in beside him, her legs across his lap, her head resting on his chest. Bucky was out playing with some of his school chums.

"And even after everybody else was willing to write me off as dead," Bob continued, "Brannigan was the last holdout. Since my body was never found to give absolute proof I was a goner, he continued to have doubt. I learned that pretty convincingly during those weeks I was holed up at my folks' place. He kept coming around, kept watching."

"Yes. He also came around there before Priscilla, Bucky, and I left for Chicago. After we believed you were dead," Consuela admitted. "He was a very determined man."

"The kind of man, you think, who would mellow so much with the passage of a few years? The kind of man who would take a good look at me and shrug it off as just a strong resemblance?"

"It's not totally impossible," Consuela insisted, though the conviction in her voice was weaker. "In such an unlikely place after so many years . . ."

"It wouldn't be so bad if he was just passing through, only gonna be in town for a day or two," Bob said. "But if he hires out to Wardell and hangs around for a while—especially after the way I tangled with that Rocking W bunch today—he's bound to be aimed at paying particular attention to me. How long, then, before he hears about you and Bucky and how hard will it be for him to get a good look at the both of you? Given all that, you really think there's any chance somebody like Brannigan won't be able to add up the pieces and get them to total Bob Hammond, the Devil's River Kid?"

"Okay. So what?" said Consuela, trying to sound defiant but not quite hiding a faint tone of anguish. "What can he prove? What harm can any accusations he makes truly do to us? Who's going to take the word of a stranger, a hired gun, against that of a trusted town marshal like you've proven yourself to be?"

Bob hugged her closer, appreciating her support and encouraging words. "That might work with the local folks. For a while, anyway. But the Devil's River Kid is wanted on some pretty serious charges back in Texas. Five or six counts of murder—no matter how justified—don't get easily set aside. Especially not with somebody like Cameron Bell hell-bent on seeing punishment dealt out. If he got word from Brannigan that I was still alive, he'd bring every ounce of his wealth and influence and thirst for personal vengeance to bear all over again, and it wouldn't be no time before proper Texas authorities—maybe even a Ranger or two—would come looking for me. If not them, Bell would reissue his Dead or Alive reward, and you'd see gunnies of every stripe flocking to try and claim it. It'd look like a second gold rush on our town."

Consuela lifted her face and looked up at him. "You make it sound so . . . hopeless. Is the answer, then, to pack up our things and leave here before Brannigan shows up? We could make up some kind of excuse—who could dispute it? Brannigan would never see you, so he could never recognize you. Your secret would stay safe. We could find somewhere new to settle and—"

"No!" Bob surprised even himself with the firmness

of his refusal. Then, softening his tone, he said, "I don't know yet what the right or best answer is . . . But running away ain't it. What about the lives we've built here? What about Bucky? What will he think? He was too young before to fully understand. If he must find out that I'm a wanted outlaw, then so be it. I'll explain the whole story and, if I've succeeded in being the father I tried to be, he'll understand. But to break all of that to him and then have him see me run away on top of it?" Bob gave a fierce shake of his head. "No. No, I'm not ready to do that."

A curious smile, proud and loving yet with a trace of uncertainty, maybe even fear, played across Consuela's lush mouth. "I'm glad you don't want to run. I don't want to, either. And nothing anybody could ever tell Bucky would stand a chance of diminishing his father in his eyes. You never have to worry about that."

Bob pressed his lips to her forehead, murmuring, "However this turns out, I'm just sorry I have to drag him and you through it with me."

"I took a vow only a few months ago, remember?" Consuela said. "I meant every word of it, including the 'better or worse' part. Bucky's vow is in the blood he shares with you. So going through this—or whatever else life might throw our way—together is all part of the deal."

"You're right," Bob said, feeling his own pride and affection well inside him. "I guess I'd be a lot sorrier if I *didn't* have you and Bucky in my corner, no matter what comes along."

CHAPTER 10

Texas, seven years earlier

The Devil's River Kid had become his identity in the minds of most people.

All but forgotten was Bob Hammond, son of Rafe and Martha Hammond, husband to Priscilla, and father to Bucky. Only that precious handful, along with Consuela, younger sister to Bob's best friend Ramos, remembered him for who he truly was, who he'd always been. After his retaliation for the murder of Ramos—and that's what it blatantly had been, no matter how the influence of Cameron Bell's money and power had corrupted the local law into seeing it differently—Bob Hammond was the one branded an outlaw, a killer.

Enraged, fueled by the thirst for payback and still more vengeance, Bob had declared war on cattle baron Cameron Bell and the insatiable empire he'd built up under his Liberty Bell brand. If they wanted to call him an outlaw, by God, he would live up to it in spades.

So for the better part of a year Bob had been raiding and raising hell with Bell interests all through Calderone County.

*Scattering cattle and horse herds, wrecking containment
pens and fences, blowing up irrigation canals, burning
down barns, destroying storages of grain and hay, and
threatening those who did business with Bell to break with
him and his corrupt ways else they suffer some of the same.
Through it all, he avoided capture by repeatedly fleeing into
the Devil's River wilderness area that he knew so well from
having explored and hunted in it since boyhood days with
Ramos—hence, the Devil's River Kid tag being slapped
on him.*

The Kid's ultimate goal was to cause so much trouble
throughout the region and break down the defensive layers
around Bell to a point where the local law could no longer
cover up for him and the Texas Rangers would be called in.
They, the Kid was confident, would dig until the evidence
of Bell's intimidation and extortion and overall bullying
tactics to build his empire at the expense of all the smaller
ranches around him was sufficient enough for them to bring
action against him. As part of all the havoc he was wreak-
ing and in spite of the small army of gunmen Bell hired to
ride against him, the Kid took great pains not to harm or
kill any individuals.

Although the county sheriff named him a murderer for
the shooting death of Willis Breen, Bell's first hired gun,
who had goaded Ramos into a fight he had no chance of
winning, the Kid knew there were those who'd seen the truth
of his encounter with Breen as a case of him simply being
faster on the draw than the vaunted gunman. Therefore, as
long as his subsequent actions refrained from more killing,
he calculated that the Ranger investigation he was hoping
to bring about would ferret out that truth and clear him of
the charge for Willis's murder.

As the months passed, however, the Kid was discouraged

to discover that others who'd been intimidated and cowed by Bell—men he'd counted on to be inspired by his acts and then make their own break with the corrupt, power-hungry cattle baron—showed no signs of doing so. The irony of it being that, as long as the Kid was unwilling to kill and go the full limit, the others remained too fearful of crossing Bell. And as long as they stayed cowed and the local law kept covering up and making excuses, the hope of drawing necessary attention from the Rangers was stillborn.

The grueling months of being on the run, living in the wilderness, and having to stay separated from his family eventually took its toll on the Kid. Especially as it grew increasingly clear that his hopes of bringing Bell to his knees were falling miserably short. The final straw was seeing—during the infrequent visits he managed to sneak in—that his always-frail wife appeared to be fading a little more each time and his toddler son was growing up with a stranger for a father. As a particularly bitter winter neared its end, the plan was made for Priscilla and Bucky, accompanied by Consuela to care for them, to return to Priscilla's hometown of Chicago as soon as the weather was finally clear. When sufficient time had passed and it could be determined that prying eyes were no longer watching them, Bob would slip away and join them. Reunited again, they would leave Chicago under altered identities and find somewhere to settle and begin new lives.

Had it not been for a freakishly fierce spring blizzard, it could have worked out that way.

Instead, that planned sequence of events was dramatically changed when the Kid, bent on harassing Bell interests for as long as he could, barely managed to escape a fiery trap set for him at a remote line shack. In order to make good his getaway, he'd been forced to kill again—a total of four

*men from among the dozen gunmen who'd been lying in
wait for him. His victims included Sam Ramsey, former
chief deputy for Calderone County's crooked sheriff, Tom
Garwood. Only a few weeks prior, Ramsey had given up
all pretense of not being in Cameron Bell's pocket and had
turned in his tainted star to assume leadership of Bell's
army of gun wolves. Seconding him in command was one
Rance Brannigan. Thus it was that, when Ramsey went
down, it was Brannigan who'd led the immediate pursuit
of the Kid as he fled the scene of the failed trap.*

*On foot (his horse having been shot out from under him),
with limited weaponry and supplies, far from the Devil's
River wilderness that had provided haven so many times
before, the Kid found himself in a desperate situation. Only
the intervention of a sudden, powerful, late-season blizzard
saved him. At first, the storm in and of itself had presented
a significant threat against his survival. Determination,
a touch of luck, and wilderness lore he had honed since boyhood helped him win that contest, however, while at the same
time the blizzard turned back his pursuers. The ferocity and
duration of the storm, combined with the conditions under
which the Kid had been driven into it and the fact no sign
of him could be found after the weather broke, gave many
cause to believe he must have gotten disoriented and perished somewhere in the blinding snow and knifing, freezing
wind.*

*Although unaware of this belief, the Kid inadvertently
gave it impetus by going to ground and remaining silent
and inactive for nearly three weeks. Having made it through
the blizzard and finally reaching the security of his familiar
Devil's River terrain, he had holed up in a small cave that
he'd previously stocked with supplies for just such an emergency. Aware that the additional killing he had finally*

resorted to was sure to intensify efforts to apprehend him, he figured it best to lay very low for a while and let things cool down, even after spring-like weather had firmly set in.

Finally, on a heavily overcast night, he'd cautiously paid a visit to his father's ranch. There, he learned of the widespread belief that he was dead. Further, he found out that his wife and son were among those who accepted this and had therefore gone ahead, accompanied by Consuela, with their planned departure to Chicago. After the initial disappointment over not finding them awaiting him, the Kid quickly saw the benefit in such a turn of events. If the belief in his death took root deep enough, then any monitoring of his wife and son to watch for possible contact by him would be minimal and short-lived. Meaning that when he was ready to rejoin them, the way ought to be that much clearer and easier for them to go on with relocating and starting their new lives under new identities.

To play it as safe as possible, Bob remained at his parents' home for an additional three weeks. Never venturing out, careful to stay away from windows and open doors, once again laying very low. Inasmuch as they all understood that when Bob did take his leave it would be for good, meaning they'd likely never see one another again, it was a time of deep, special bonding with his parents that made his departure, when it came, somewhat easier to bear.

Twice during those three weeks, Rance Brannigan came around. He looked, asked questions, made a few thinly veiled threats, and let it be generally known that he wasn't among those who bought that the Devil's River Kid—well known to be the Hammonds' son—was dead. But, at the same time, he also revealed that he stood virtually alone in his refusal to accept that fact. Even Cameron Bell had come around to believing it.

When the time finally felt right, Bob Hammond put the ghost of the Devil's River Kid behind him, said his farewells to his parents, and struck out for Chicago. He made it without incident and there reunited with Priscilla, Bucky, and Consuela. Things went smoothly yet Bob nevertheless kept looking over his shoulder, expecting/half-fearing someone to show up and try to nab him. But no one did. Even through the ongoing struggle with Priscilla's poor health that eventually claimed her, they forged on with the implementation of the rest of their plans—assuming the new family identity of Hatfield as opposed to Hammond, and relocating eventually to Wyoming Territory in a place called Rattlesnake Wells . . .

All those early times when Bob would look fretfully over his shoulder, fearing to see someone closing in on him, the face of the "someone" invariably envisioned by his anxieties had been that of Rance Brannigan. And now, after all the intervening months and years, irony of bitter ironies—it looked like he would be coming face-to-face with Brannigan once again after all.

CHAPTER 11

Knowing he was in for a restless night anyway, Bob had once again taken the late turn around town. Even apart from his worries about Rance Brannigan, he also had concerns about the hornet's nest he had stirred up with Ed Wardell and the rest of the Rocking W men. In case any of them decided to make a special trip to town that night with a chip on their shoulders, Bob wanted to be sure he was the one on hand to deal with it.

No such trouble occurred, however. In fact, the night was basically without incident. Never one to foolishly look for trouble, at least not at this stage of his life, Bob was left feeling somewhat empty, almost disappointed. In the edgy state he was in, he realized, a part of him had actually been *hoping* for a little excitement.

He didn't like admitting that about himself and vowed not to let it become a habit. Still, he couldn't deny it might have helped take the edge off the way he was feeling . . .

In the morning, despite the near-sleepless night

he'd fully expected, Bob maintained his habit of rising with the sun. Consuela, who no doubt had gotten little sleep, either, lying next to his restless tossing and turning, rose to prepare his customary breakfast of two boiled eggs, a tortilla-wrapped scoop of spicy sausage, and coffee. Consuela did not eat with him; she would have her breakfast a little later with Bucky, after she got him up for school. She and Bob spoke little while he ate, and not at all about Rance Brannigan.

When the meal was finished, Consuela prepared him a second mug of coffee, this time doctored with two heaping spoonfuls of sugar and a splash of milk. His morning treat, they called it. The only time in the many cups of coffee he consumed during the course of most days when he did not take it black. Maintaining another habit that he followed on most days when the weather was nice, Bob took this second cup of coffee out onto the front porch and leisurely sipped it out there. Sometimes, since they'd been wed, Consuela came out and sat with him. This morning, sensing that he would rather be alone with his brooding, she did not.

During this time, Bob generally looked down on the town, perhaps planning his day if there was some particular event scheduled or expectation in the air, but almost always with a sense of satisfaction for the way things had turned out here. This morning he again felt that sense of satisfaction but he was also keenly aware of the threat now looming over it. By the time he'd finished his coffee, he had resolved that—whatever it took—he was damned if he would let that threat ruin everything he and those he cared most about had worked so hard to establish in this place.

As usual, Bob got to the office first that morning.

Fred was only a few minutes behind him, however, and came bearing good news. Bob's other two deputies, Peter and Vern Macy, had returned from the visit to their uncle and younger brother up in the Prophecies. Fred had come by their place on the way in and they'd called out that they would be showing up not very far behind him. Bob digested the news with a nod of approval; it would be good to have Peter and Vern back, especially if the expected trouble with the Rocking W flared up.

"Also, I thought you'd like to know," Fred reported, "I was able to get those two fellas you saved from hanging some short-term work at Peterson's Livery. Joe Peterson is holding a couple dozen horses for some Army buyers who ain't due for another week, maybe ten days, so he's in need of some extra help. He offered the two of 'em a place to sleep, a noon meal, and a few dollars a day to care for those horses and whatever other odd jobs come along. How they divvy up the work—Streeter figured he'd handle the heavier stuff, on account of Hicks's busted ribs, while Hicks did the grooming and lighter duties—is up to them, as long as it gets done. It ain't much and it won't last forever, but it's a stopgap to tide 'em over for a little while and at least give 'em some time to heal up a bit."

"I figured you could scare up something to help them out," Bob said. "And if I know you, there's a good chance you'll have something more lined up by the time they need it."

Fred shrugged. "If I can help out, I will. They got one big break from you, and they seemed genuinely grateful. Fellas like that I don't mind lending a hand—Lord knows that in our line of work we run into enough ungrateful lowlifes, it's good to be reminded there are other kinds out there, too."

"As long as you don't let your guard down too low and always keep in mind there still *are* plenty of skunks in the mix as well," said Bob, his mood not up for an excessive amount of optimism and good fellowship. "I worry sometimes that your amiability might do you in one of these days, Fred. Be careful it don't."

"That's a heck of a sour outlook," said Fred, frowning. Then, remembering how his boss's mood had shifted the previous afternoon, his frown deepened. "What's gotten into you lately, anyway?"

Before Bob had any chance to answer, they received a visitor. The front door opened and a small, bespectacled, middle-aged man came in. Bob recognized him as Myron Poppe, a somewhat timid and always exceedingly polite teller at the Starbuck Territorial Bank. He was dressed for work, white shirt and bow tie, but the bank wasn't scheduled to open for another forty-five minutes or so.

"I hope this isn't too early or that I'm not interfering with more important business," Myron said. "But, if not, I was hoping I could have a few minutes of your time, Marshal."

"Of course, Myron," Bob told him. "Have a seat, why don't you? Would you like a cup of coffee?"

"Oh, no, thank you." The answer came so swift and firm that at first Bob suspected the man had heard the horror stories about the coffee served here. But then Myron clarified his response a bit further. "I've quite had my morning quota of coffee— or tea, I should say, in my case. Once we tellers take our positions at our windows, you see, Mr. Starbuck is very strict about us not leaving our stations for any reason. Even to, er, evacuate any excess morning beverage. I therefore have learned how much intake I can tolerate in order to make it to my scheduled lunch break, and I am very careful not to exceed that."

"Okay," Bob said measuredly, thinking he'd rather have been left with his assumption about Myron's fear of the jail coffee instead of getting quite so much personal information. It gave him pause to ask the next question, but he went ahead with it anyway. "So what is it that brings you here, Myron?"

Myron hitched forward on the wooden chair where he'd seated himself. "Are you familiar with the name John Larkin?"

"Yes, I am."

"He was in the paper yesterday."

"Yes, I know."

"He was part of our community up until a few years ago. That was before your time."

Bob nodded. "I know. But Deputy Fred here has brought me up to date on Larkin and the circumstances surrounding his, er, leaving."

"Good. That's good." Myron bobbed his head in Fred's direction, acknowledging him. Then, turning back to the marshal, he said, "Did he tell you that I was on the jury that sent Larkin away?"

"No, I don't believe we touched on that particular detail."

"Well, I was."

Bob waited for him to expound on that. When it appeared he was going to need some prodding, the marshal cleared his throat and said, "I trust, then, that the community was sufficiently grateful for your time and the performance of your civic duty."

"I suppose so," Myron allowed. "But I'm not looking for gratitude. What I want to know is what do you intend to do about John Larkin returning?"

"I guess I don't quite understand your question," Bob said. "My understanding is that Larkin has been paroled following good behavior for time served. If that's the case and he reports same on his arrival here, then there's not a lot I can do. Providing he keeps his nose clean and doesn't get in any new trouble, that is."

Myron looked anxious. "Then you don't know about his threat?"

"Threat to who?"

"Why, to me . . . Well, to be exact, to each and every one of us who were on the jury that sent him away. After he was sentenced, he swore he'd come back and get even with us."

"Now wait a minute, Myron," Fred spoke up. "I wasn't on the jury that day, but I was in the courtroom and heard what Larkin said. It wasn't quite like that."

The little man in the bow tie suddenly looked very

defiant. "He said he'd come back and show us the error of our ways. If that's not a threat, what is?"

Bob cleared his throat again. "With all due respect, Myron—er, Mr. Poppe—I think I have to agree with my deputy. Larkin saying he was going to come back and show everybody they'd made a mistake about him doesn't really amount to a threat. I suppose it *could* be taken like that, if you look at it in a certain way. But it could also simply be the statement of a man bent on proving he's innocent of the charges made against him."

"You think Larkin was an innocent man?"

"I'm in no position to comment on that. I believe that judges and juries usually reach the right conclusions, even though there sometimes are mistakes made. All I'm really saying is that, to my ear, Larkin's words don't sound exactly like a hard threat."

"It was the *way* he said it."

Bob wanted to hear the man out and have sympathy for his concerns, but he was growing weary of this. He said, "Look, no matter how he said it or what he truly meant, my position is this: Larkin served his time and was properly released. If he comes here and follows the procedure he's supposed to, like I told you before, there's nothing I can do to stop him. It's not like I can turn him away at the city limits just because he makes certain people nervous."

"That's too bad," Myron said somberly.

"My deputies and I will naturally keep a close eye on Larkin for however long he sticks around. Sorry I can't promise you any more than that."

"Very well. I guess that will have to suffice." Myron stood up. "You and your men do a very good job of protecting our town, Marshal. I appreciate that and I hope I haven't taken up too much of your time. Before leaving, let me say one more thing, though . . . I don't profess to put words in other people's mouths. But since the news started to spread about Larkin's return, I can assure you that I am not the only one with the concerns I have just expressed to you."

Behind his desk, Bob stood up, too. "I'll be sure to keep that in mind, Mr. Poppe. And like I already told you, me and my deputies will also be sure to keep a close eye on Larkin if and when he shows up."

Myron gave a faint nod, turned, and walked out as quietly as he'd entered.

CHAPTER 12

The door had scarcely closed behind Myron Poppe before it opened again to the entrance of Peter and Vern Macy. Greetings and a round of updates, sprinkled with a bit of good-natured ribbing, quickly followed. The easy camaraderie among the four lawmen was enough to lift Bob's mood, at least for a time, and even made cups of the notorious jail coffee tolerable.

For their part, Peter and Vern didn't have a lot new to report. Their uncle and younger brother were doing well and remained optimistic, even though they hadn't struck the big vein yet. They were nevertheless finding enough color to have built up a nice nest egg and had plenty to offer payment (even though the gesture was declined) for the supplies brought in as part of the visit. Tales of his older brothers' badge-wearing adventures (no doubt embellished a bit during the telling) were exciting for young Lee to hear, though he remained committed to the prospecting life and it was clear Uncle Curtis was grateful to have him.

On the receiving end, the brothers had already caught wind of the shoot-out involving Bob and Buford Morrison against the Silases and the prisoners they'd freed to aid them. Regardless, they were still hungry for some firsthand details. After that, they were also filled in on the situation with the Rocking W brand—the alleged rustling, the attempted hanging, the anticipated trouble next time any of Wardell's riders came to town, and the rumors of a hired gun (or guns) being brought aboard. No mention was made of the specific name Rance Brannigan. Finally, Bob left it to Fred to tell them about the returning ex-con, John Larkin, as far as his history and the concerns of certain citizens based on his statement after being sentenced.

When all of that had been laid out, Peter emitted a low whistle and said with mock exaggeration, "Whew! Good thing we got back when we did. Sounds like the town's about ready to blow wide open." He was a compact, muscular young man, not yet twenty-two, with thinning blond hair, a ready smile, and a devilish glint in his eyes that signaled an equally devilish sense of humor.

"Let's hope it don't quite come to that," said Bob. Then he grinned. "But it is good to have you back."

"I'll second that," agreed Fred.

"I won't say we missed the times we've had lead flying in our direction, but otherwise I reckon we're glad to be back, too," said Vern, a close image of his brother, though a year younger, a couple inches taller, and generally more serious in nature. "I think it's safe to say, for both of us," he went on, "that the rock-choppin' life up on that cold mountain ain't something that holds a lot of appeal."

Bob nodded. "Okay then. Since everybody's so danged happy you're back, how about going to work? You can start by giving your legs a stretch and taking a turn around the town."

"You got it, boss."

Once the brothers had taken leave, Bob turned to Fred and said, "How good is your memory when it comes to who was on that jury for Larkin's trial? Can you put together a list for me?"

Fred looked thoughtful for a minute and then said, "Yeah. Sure. Any blanks I got, I can ask around and get 'em filled in quick enough."

"Start putting it together, then. If Myron Poppe's right about some others besides him being nervous over Larkin coming back—and you suggested the same thing, come to think of it—then I'd like a chance to see who else we might be hearing from . . . For that matter, who else we might need to keep an eye on if and when Larkin does show up."

"Okay. That's a good idea. A couple are dead, a couple have left town. I can tell you that much right off. Oh, and one of the jury members was your pal Mike Bullock. You might want to check with him. If folks are buzzing about Larkin's return, Mike likely has heard talk of it in his place."

"He probably has," Bob allowed. "I've got an errand to run, then I'll swing by and have a talk with him. In the meantime, you get started on that list."

"I'll have it waiting when you get back."

* * *

Before going home for his talk with Consuela the day before, Bob had stopped by the telegraph office for the purpose of sending a wire to Buford Morrison, whom he hoped would still be reachable at the U.S. Marshal's headquarters in Cheyenne. His message read as follows:

URGENT FOR INFO ON RANCE
BRANNIGAN STOP MAY BE WANTED STOP
LAST KNOWN AT CONCORDIA HOTEL
IN DENVER STOP ANY NEW INFO
GREATLY APPRECIATED

He'd told Harold Feeney, the telegraph operator, not to deliver any reply that came in and not to hand it over to anybody else, to just hang on to it until he came by to check. That's what he did now. The response waiting for him was this:

NO WANTEDS ON BRANNIGAN STOP
DEPARTED DENVER ONE DAY AGO STOP
DESTINATION UNKNOWN STOP
SORRY NOT MORE

Bob wadded the response into a ball and shoved it in his pocket. He thanked Feeney for his time, cautioned him not to speak to anyone about the exchange, and left.

An inquiry from one U.S. Marshal to another—Morrison in Cheyenne to a counterpart in Denver, for example—was bound to have gotten a quicker reply than if Bob had sent his inquiry directly to the Denver authorities. Trouble was, for all its promptness the answer was neither what Bob wanted to hear nor was it something that did him any good. "Departed one day ago" pretty much confirmed that Brannigan was on his way here. And the fact he had no Wanted papers on him meant that Bob couldn't do anything when he showed up except wait for him to make a wrong move.

Just like John Larkin.

While the return of the ex-con posed less of a threat, in Bob's opinion—and certainly less of a personal one—he was potential trouble all the same.

Forewarned is forearmed, that's what he'd told Fred. But knowing a double dose of trouble was likely on the way yet not being able to do anything about either one except *wait* . . . old adages aside, that was worse than having all hell just go ahead and bust loose.

CHAPTER 13

Even though he was a man seldom given to drink, Bullock's Saloon was one of Bob's favorite places. The prime reason for this was the friendship that had developed between him and owner/proprietor Mike Bullock over the years. Bullock was a bullet-headed, barrel-chested, gregarious Irishman, and his saloon was one of the oldest businesses in town. A boisterous good time could be had there, but the limits on behavior were firm and anybody who got out of line had to answer to Mike and his rock-hard, lightning-fast fists.

An additional attraction when it came to Bullock's, and not just for Bob, was Mike's right-hand gal, Maudie Sartain. She was a curvaceous eyeful who didn't mind showing off her physical charms, usually in low-cut dresses that displayed enough cleavage to guarantee increased sales of cold beer in order to offset the dry throats she caused. At one time, Bob and Maudie had had a flirtation going on between them that hinted at perhaps turning into something more—until Bob came to his senses and realized his true love was Consuela and he'd better follow through on that rather than continue to hold off and risk losing her. Their marriage left his relationship with Maudie somewhat strained for a time, but that had gotten ironed out and now they were back to being good friends once again. (Although Bob had to be careful not to let it appear *too* good, inasmuch as Consuela had a jealous streak and a corresponding temper to match.)

When he entered the saloon that morning, there wasn't much of a crowd yet. It was more than an hour until noon, when things would really pick up. In preparation for that, a couple members of the kitchen staff were already putting out trays of cold cuts, sliced cheese, slabs of bread, and a big bowl of boiled eggs.

Otherwise, there were only three elderly gents, all dressed in collarless white shirts and dark vests, puffing long cigars, earnestly playing dominoes at a round-topped table near the front door. Toward the back, Merlin Sweeney—the tall, wiry black accordion player Bob had first heard the night of the Silas shoot-out but who'd now become a regular, performing for tips—was quietly practicing some new songs on his instrument. In between, at the far end of the bar, awaiting the lunch rush, were Mike and Maudie. He was leaning on the bar from the back side, she was perched prettily on a stool in the front.

First making a slight detour to spear a couple sweet pickles out of a jar just being added to the lunch spread by one of the kitchen helpers, Bob headed down the length of the bar toward the pair.

"Here comes the party pooper now," Bullock greeted.

It took Bob a minute to catch his drift. "How's that?"

"Well, from what I hear, you broke up a perfectly good necktie party just yesterday, didn't you?"

Bob rolled his eyes and said to Maudie, "Anybody ever tell him his sense of humor is a mite twisted?"

"Try being around him as much as I am each day," she replied dryly.

"I am but an observer of the human condition as seen through the filter of a wry Irish wit," said Bullock.

"You're something, that's for sure," muttered Bob as he settled onto a stool next to Maudie.

Bullock sighed. "Did you come here just to free-load pickles and run down my sense of humor, or are you going to buy something for a change?"

"To prove once and for all that I'm not a freeloader, I'll buy *you* a drink. And you, too, Maudie, if you're in the market for one," said Bob. "As for me, I'm hoping you've got some tea brewing in the back."

Maudie was a tea lover who was always experimenting with different blends and, whenever Bob stopped by, he liked to sample whatever her current one was. He liked some better than others, but it was a safe bet that the worst she served would be better than the jail coffee.

"It's a bit early for me to be in the mood, but it would be rude to turn down such a rare and generous offer," said Bullock, reaching to pour a shot of redeye.

"I'll pass on that," Maudie said. "But yes, I do

have some tea brewing in the back. I'll go get us each a cup."

As Maudie departed to fetch some tea, Bullock threw down his shot and then smacked his lips approvingly. When Bob reached to pull some coins out of his vest pocket, the saloonkeeper quickly waved him off. "Don't you dare. If you start paying for anything when you come in here, it will take away all the fun of me giving you a hard time about *not* paying."

Bob grinned, leaving his money where it was. "I guess there's some logic in there somewhere. But I'm not going to strain my brain trying to figure it out."

"Good enough then. Now, tell me about your run-in with Ed Wardell and his Rocking W boys."

"First you tell me how you even know anything about it."

It wasn't like Bob meant for the incident to be a big secret. But nevertheless, he was genuinely curious how news of it had spread so quickly. If he hoped to keep any trouble tamped down when Rocking W riders came to town, it wouldn't help if they immediately ran into grumblings and accusations about the attempted lynching.

"Well, the two fellas you saved are put up over at Joe Peterson's livery, ain't they?"

"That's right. They needed a place to sleep and some short-term work while they healed up some. Deputy Fred took 'em over to Joe and they made the necessary arrangements."

"Uh-huh. And don't Joe stop over here each evening for a couple beers before he goes home to turn in for the night?"

"If you say so."

"I say so." Bullock shrugged. "So, when he stopped in last evening, Joe told us about the whole thing."

Maudie had returned with two cups of tea by that point. Placing one on the bar top in front of Bob, she said, "Were those Rocking W rowdies really going to hang those two men?"

"That's sure the way I saw it," said Bob. "Ed Wardell tried to argue it was all just for show, to scare 'em. But it looked mighty intense and for real to me. And those fellas with the shadow of the noose dangling over 'em thought it was for real, too."

Maudie shook her head. "The audacity to try and pull off a lynching in this day and age. That's almost too shocking to believe."

"Not so much when it's Ed Wardell you're talking about," said Bullock. "He's got a cold, mean streak in him that runs deep and is as solid as an iron bar. Especially when it comes to rustling beef that rightly belongs to him."

"He come in here much?" Bob asked.

"Now and then. Fact is, he don't come to town all that much. But when he does, he usually makes a stop here."

"And you've heard him complain about rustling?"

"Not always. But that's sure been his favorite theme the last few times."

"Ever since Carlos Vandez bought that land bordering Wardell's," Maudie said. "He hates Mexicans with what you can only call an obsession. The thought of the V-Slash range just *touching* up against his is too much. It's like it's making him insane."

"That might be closer than you think," Bob allowed. He tried a sip of his tea. It was a blend he couldn't remember having before, but a good one all the same. "I'm beginning to question if the rustling is even real—or if Wardell is mostly imagining it because he's bound and determined that's how a lousy greaser neighbor would act."

"You've looked into it?" Bullock said.

"Very little. It's out of my jurisdiction. That's something else Wardell can't seem to accept."

"And when Buford Morrison passed through the other day and failed to show any interest, either, that was *really* hard for him to accept," said Bullock.

"You heard about that?"

"Hard not to. Wardell wailed it loud and clear, all over town."

Bob took another sip of his tea. He hadn't come in here intending to talk about the situation with Wardell. But input from Mike and Maudie was always worthwhile.

"During the course of his wailing, you happen to hear anything about him planning to bring in a hired gun?"

Bullock scowled. "Yeah, he spouted some about that. I figured it just for hot air. You thinking it's for real?"

"Yeah. There's pretty good indication that's the case."

Maudie regarded him closely. "It's understandable that's not welcome news," she said. "But we've all seen you handle gunnies plenty of times before. You look like you find the prospect of this one particularly troubling, though. Why is that?"

"Somebody you know?" Bullock asked.

"No," Bob lied, the response coming a little too

quick. Then he tried to smooth it over by adding, "Nobody anyone around here has ever heard of. But whether I know whoever it is or not, that don't mean I've got to like it. What I especially don't like is that damned Wardell and his Mexican-hating ways bringing in a gunny over something that may only exist in his twisted outlook on things. If him and his riders were already geared up enough to attempt a lynching, think what adding a fast gun to their mix might do. And especially when you stop and think that Vandez ain't exactly the kind of man who'll stand for much pushing or harassment. Just like a spark to a grass fire, the whole situation would become primed to flare into a range war."

"There's nothing you can do to prevent it from getting to that stage?" said Maudie.

"I don't know what," Bob said, grimacing. "I rode out to the Rocking W yesterday with a notion to try and calm things down. You heard how far I got with that. And if Vandez finds out Wardell is throwing around all kinds of accusations against him and is bringing in a hired gun, how willing do you figure he'll be to stay peaceful and reasonable about the whole thing?"

"Not very, I don't suppose."

"Uh-huh. I suppose the same. Plus—and Wardell was mighty quick to remind me of this—there's the problem of my actual jurisdiction only reaching as far as the city limits. By rights, even if it *did* break into a range war, I wouldn't have any legal say in it."

Bullock said, "But if feelings get too raw between the two brands, you know damn well it'd be just a matter of time before some of the trouble spills into town."

"You think I don't know that?" said Bob. "It still don't give me a way to step in before it comes to that."

"What about your pal Morrison, the U.S. Marshal? If he didn't feel he had cause to go out and see Wardell when he was here last, how about now? The attempted lynching, a hired gun coming in . . . I'd say that changes the situation quite a bit, wouldn't you?"

"I reckon," Bob allowed. He'd already thought about notifying Morrison. But, number one, he was reluctant to ask for help with a situation that basically was right in his backyard. More than that, he was worried about having the federal man on hand if Rance Brannigan showed up and started laying down accusations about Bob's past as the Devil's River Kid. Bob had already made up his mind that, if given no choice, he'd fight his way clear of any attempt to take him back to Texas as the result of anything Brannigan had to say, but Buford Morrison was about the last person he could think of that he'd want to make that fight against.

"I've already been in contact with Buford," Bob added, not exactly telling another lie. "I'll have to see what else he's got going on when he gets back to me."

CHAPTER 14

When Maudie left to get more tea, Bob said to Bullock, "Look, before you start getting busy with your lunch crowd, there's something else I want to talk to you about. Actually, it's what I came in here for."

"Let 'er rip. What's on your mind?"

"Fella by the name of John Larkin. I got reason to believe you're familiar with him, right?"

Bullock pursed his lips. "Yep. Know—or knew, I guess I should say—him real well."

"So you know he's supposed to be on his way back to town after his prison hitch."

"Saw it in the paper. Heard talk of it . . . been hearing a fair amount of talk about it, as a matter of fact."

"So have I. You were there at the trial, I understand. On the jury. You got any feel for whether or not Larkin might be coming back with some revenge in mind for the town that sent him away?"

Bullock poured himself another shot of redeye

before answering. While he was doing that, Maudie returned with freshly filled cups of tea for her and Bob.

"Whoa. What's going on?" she asked. "You two look even grimmer than when I left."

"I was asking Mike about John Larkin," Bob explained.

Maudie's own expression tensed. "Oh. Him."

"What to expect out of Larkin if and when he returns." said Bullock, staring down into his drink without lifting it to his lips. He lifted his gaze, still without taking a drink. "The truth is, Bob, I'm damned if I know. The John Larkin I knew—or thought I knew before he got convicted—didn't seem like the type who'd come around seeking vengeance. But then, neither did he seem like a thief. And we all know how prison can change a man."

"A good man is a good man," Maudie said with somewhat surprising firmness. "Everybody all over town knows John Larkin was a decent man until he got caught up in that mess. Earl says he's coming back that same person. Looking to restart his life, not make trouble."

Bob didn't know for sure, but he had to guess that the "Earl" she was referring to was Earl Hines, the town blacksmith. Hines had long harbored feelings for Maudie that everybody else could see but he'd been too shy to make known to her; in recent months she'd finally become aware of the fact and they'd begun spending a good deal of time together.

In response to the puzzled look on Bob's face, Maudie said, "Earl and Larkin were good friends before the trouble happened. Earl believed at the time, and still does, that Larkin was innocent of the things he was charged with. They've corresponded while Larkin was in prison, and I think Earl even went to visit him a time or two."

"A lot of folks around town wanted to believe Larkin was innocent," Bullock said. He finally threw back his drink, then added, "But doggone it, the evidence presented at the trial didn't leave any choice but to find him guilty."

"When you say Larkin is coming back to restart his life," Bob said to Maudie, "what does that mean exactly? Does he have family here?"

She shook her head. "No. None."

"I understand there was a sweetheart involved—Jackson Emory's oldest daughter. Do you think part of his intended restart is with her?"

"All I know is what I told you, based on what Earl has said to me," Maudie answered rather stiffly. "Maybe you should talk to him, maybe he can give you a clearer understanding."

Bob took a drink of his tea. Lowering the cup, he said, "Sounds like a good idea."

Earl Hines's blacksmith shop was located on the southeast side of Front Street. It sat a ways back off the street, a moderate-sized barnlike structure containing, apart from the forge and working area, a handful of horse stalls and a small corral out back. Hines's living quarters were above the shop, attainable by an outside stairway.

It was a warm, sunny spring day, and activity up and down the street had increased significantly during the time Bob had been inside Bullock's. He donned a vague smile and an expression aimed at being more pleasant than he actually felt as he passed among the citizenry, nodding politely in response to the greetings that came his way.

Approaching Hines's shop, he saw the wide front doors standing open. At first, given that no one was in sight, Bob thought maybe the smithy had taken his lunch break a little early. Curious, though, that he hadn't run into him since he knew that Hines usually took lunch at Bullock's where he could have a few words with Maudie while partaking of the luncheon spread there. Also, he was pretty sure that Hines generally closed the front doors when he left for any length of time.

As Bob stepped through those open doors, his attention was drawn by odd sounds coming from back in the horse stalls. Walking on back, he quickly saw the source of the sounds.

There was a total of five men engaged in activity back there. In one of the stalls, a man with a drawn handgun was holding it aimed at Earl Hines, forcing him to stand very still with his hands balled into fists hanging at his sides. In another stall directly opposite that one, two other men were using their own fists to beat the hell out of a third man they had pinned in a corner.

Before any of them realized he was there, Bob drew his .44 and fired once, shooting the gun out of the hand of the man who'd been holding it aimed at Hines. The gun flew away and thumped against the side of the stall. The man let out a shriek and reached with his opposite hand to grasp the one that had been gripping the pistol.

Bob swung his Colt and brought it to bear on the two men who were administering the beating. "That's enough!" he said sharply. "Back away from that man. Turn to face me and don't even think about reaching for your guns."

The two men twisted at the waist, their hands automatically dropping closer to the six-guns holstered on their hips. When they saw Bob standing there with his .44 leveled on them, their hands froze. The man they'd been beating sagged against the back wall of the stall. The pair who'd been pounding on him slowly did as Bob had ordered, backing a couple steps away from their victim and turning to face the marshal.

The loud smack of a fist colliding with meat and bone caused Bob to give a quick glance over his shoulder. He saw Hines, the burly blacksmith, just completing the delivery of a hard right cross to the jaw of the man who'd been holding a gun on him. The latter collapsed to the floor, dropping like a sack of oats.

"That's enough," Bob said out of the corner of his mouth. Then: "Somebody tell me what the hell's going on around here."

"These three rannies from the Rocking W showed up a few minutes ago with a couple horses they wanted reshod," Hines said. "This other fella had just showed up to pick up some bridles I'd repaired for Joe Peterson down at the livery. Soon as they laid eyes on him, they lit in. One of 'em held me at bay, like you saw, while the other two yellow skunks commenced to ganging up on the poor devil."

The lighting was rather dim this far back in the barn, so it had taken a few minutes for Bob's eyes to fully adjust. Now that it had, he was able to recognize some faces. One of the two men who'd been dishing out the beating was Smoky Barnett, Ed Wardell's ramrod out at the Rocking W. The man on the receiving end of the punishment was none other than Ron Streeter, one of the men the marshal had saved from a lynching yesterday.

Bob's eyes locked on Barnett. "You're pretty thick-headed at learning a lesson, ain't you?"

"Ain't nothing you got to teach that I *want* to learn," Barnett snarled.

"So you're thickheaded *and* mouthy. That's a combination that can get an *hombre* in a lot of trouble."

"I been in and out of trouble all my life. None of it stuck yet. And I sure as hell ain't worried about the amount of trouble no hick sheriff in a shithole town like this is gonna make for me."

Bob cut his eyes momentarily to Hines. "Help this other fella to his feet, will you? His name is Streeter."

"I'd rather help that mouthy one *off* his feet," said Hines. He was a big man, thick through the shoulders and gut, too, but none of it was what you would call soft. His arms, bared by a sleeveless shirt under a leather apron, were corded with muscle. He had a broad, blunt-nosed face with deep-set dark eyes and coal black hair combed straight back from a slight widow's peak. "Strip 'em of their guns, Marshal," he pleaded, "and give me five minutes alone in a stall—

both of 'em at once—and I'll teach the cowards a lesson they won't soon forget."

"That's a tempting proposition," Bob said. "But I'm afraid it don't work that way. Just do like I asked, okay?"

Hines went over to Streeter and leaned down to assist him.

While he was doing that, Barnett glared at Bob. "So what *have* you got in mind for us? You try to get too cocky, it won't set good with Wardell, you know."

Bob showed his teeth in a humorless smile. "Mister, you could fill a real big bucket with how much I don't give a damn about what don't set good with Wardell."

Streeter was standing up now, brushing loose straw and dust off his clothes, backhanding a trickle of blood that ran from the corner of his mouth.

"You hurt bad?" Bob asked him.

"Nothing serious. I got a sister hits harder than those nancies."

"All the same, you want to press assault charges against 'em?"

Streeter took a step forward and did some glaring of his own. He held his mouth clamped tightly shut, chin thrust forward, and air whistled audibly in and out of his nose. After a minute, he said, "Naw. That'd just be a lot of bother for you and your deputy. They ain't worth it. All I want—and I know I speak for Hicks, too—is to get on without no more trouble."

"How about you, Earl?" Bob asked the blacksmith.

"I already told you what I want," Hines answered. "Barring that, no, I don't want to fool around with no legal charges against these varmints." Then he directed his attention to Barnett, saying, "But as long as he's got yellow skunks like you working for him, you go back and tell Wardell that no more Rocking W business is welcome here at my shop."

"You might want to be careful about cuttin' off your nose to spite your face, bub," Barnett said.

"You let me worry about that," Hines was quick to respond. "What you'd better be careful about is not letting me run into you again—or either of these other two, especially that one who stuck a gun in my belly if he ever wakes up—under different circumstances. I do, we'll finish this little get-together and I'll show you my personal version of settling assault charges."

"That was a downright threat against me and my pards," Barnett wailed. "You heard him, Marshal. You gonna let him get away with that?"

"I don't know what you're talking about," said Bob in a flat, emotionless tone. "I didn't hear a thing except these two men giving you a break by refusing to file formal charges against you. Was I you, I'd consider myself lucky and let it go at that."

Barnett's eyes narrowed. "So that's how it is, eh? All hands turned against the Rocking W, just like Wardell has suspected all along—even the so-called law."

"You're the ones who put yourselves crossways of the law, buster. And if you ever *really* get on the wrong side of me, you'll know it, and it will be too late for standing around whining about it. Now roust your friend off the ground and haul your sorry asses out of here . . . except for one final little detail."

"What's that?" Barnett wanted to know.

Bob gestured with his Colt. "Shuck your guns. Pull 'em slow and easy, toss 'em to the ground, and kick 'em over here toward me . . . Earl, I'd be obliged if you'd gather 'em up. Don't forget the one over in the other stall that was aimed at you a couple minutes ago and also any rifles they might have on their saddles. After these gents have taken their leave, you have my permission to break down those weapons and feed the metal into your forge. Take whatever you pour out and feel free to form it for repairs and such. Courtesy of my office."

"Wait a minute. You can't do that!" protested Barnett. "Guns don't come free, you know."

"Yeah, I know," allowed Bob. "There's dealers who sell 'em—unfortunately sometimes to idiots. I made the mistake of sending you back your guns yesterday. And here you are, just a day later, bringing 'em into my town and causing more trouble with 'em." Bob wagged his head. "I ain't gonna make that mistake again."

By now Hines had gathered up the hardware, the shucked handguns along with two Winchesters from the saddle scabbards of the horses the three had ridden in on.

Bob again gestured with his Colt and said to Barnett, "Now scat. I'm sick of looking at you. Gather up your fallen friend and make dust out of town."

The Rocking W men did as ordered. After swinging up into his saddle but before riding away, Barnett said, "You think you're hot stuff with that Colt in your hand, don't you?"

"Hot enough for the likes of you, sonny," Bob told him.

"Everybody's heard how fast you're supposed to be with that thing. But that don't mean there ain't those around who are faster."

"Always some who think so. But it ain't you, Smoky. Not today, not on the best day you ever had, not if you had guns stickin' out your ass. Now beat it!"

As he wheeled his horse about and put the spurs to it, Barnett called over his shoulder, "Your day's comin', Hatfield. And a faster gun is comin' with it!"

CHAPTER 15

Because the blacksmith barn sat a ways off the street and because the confrontation with the Rocking W men took place deep inside the interior of the building, the single shot Bob had fired went without drawing undue attention. One shot—or maybe only what sounded like one to folks out on Front Street, then not followed by any sights or sounds of a bigger ruckus—wasn't enough for anybody to get too alarmed over.

So once Barnett and his buddies rode away, the scene of the altercation was left suddenly quiet and calm.

"Seems like you got a way of showing up whenever I'm in a fix, Marshal," said Streeter.

"Seems like you got a way of getting yourself in fixes," replied Bob. "Just so you know, I had a full-time job before you came along. I don't need your help finding ways to keep busy."

Streeter grinned ruefully. "I'll try to keep that in mind and not put myself in a position to need saving by you again. But in the meantime, I purely thank you for stepping in on my behalf once more."

"Seems like I'm caught in the middle of something besides what just happened here," said Hines. "Somebody mind filling me in?"

Bob gave him a quick rundown on what had happened out at the Rocking W yesterday. He didn't really like playing it up any more than necessary, but word of the near lynching was already starting to spread just as was bound to happen with what had occurred here. So Hines might as well hear a factual account from those directly involved rather than some secondhand exaggerated version. Especially since Bob still intended to pump the blacksmith about John Larkin and expected straight information in return.

When the marshal had finished his telling, Hines furrowed his brow and said, "Damn. Sounds like Wardell is getting crazier and more dangerous by the day. He always was a moody sort, but these suspicions about rustling are making him worse than ever."

"Yeah. I know," said Streeter, absently touching a hand to the base of his throat. "Me and my buddy got a pretty good taste of his bad mood—almost a permanent one."

Hines cut his gaze to Bob. "What Barnett said when he rode away. About a faster gun coming? You caught that, didn't you?"

"Hard not to."

"Ain't the first time I heard words like that. From Barnett and a couple other Rocking W hands. Up until now I took it for hot air passed along secondhand from Wardell. And even if there was anything to it, it sounded like it was meant to be aimed at their rustlin' problem." Hines's expression grew very earnest. "But given what you just told me on top of this other dustup that took place here only a bit ago, I think I'd be reckoning that any hired gun brought in by Wardell would likely have your name whispered in his ear, too, Marshal."

A corner of Bob's mouth lifted in a wry smile. "I reckon your thinking probably ain't far off the mark."

"You believe Wardell really has sent for a hired gun?"

"Seems to me he's done too much talking about it not to."

"Yeah, that's pretty much the way I see it."

Streeter emitted a nervous laugh. "Although we'd likely be pretty far down on the list, if Wardell starts siccing a gunslinger on everybody he's got a reason to be sore at, then that means he might even get around to me and Hicks sooner or later."

"You can go ahead and fret over it if you want," Bob told him. "But before that, my guess is that you'd better get those repaired bridles back to Joe Peterson, if they're ready, or he'll be giving you something to fret about right in the here and now."

"They're ready," confirmed Hines. He pointed. "They're hanging on that sawhorse right over there. Go ahead and take 'em, and tell Joe I'll bring a bill around later this afternoon or tomorrow."

Streeter gathered up the armload of bridles,

thanked Bob again for showing up when he did, then headed off for the livery.

As soon as he was out of sight, Hines said with a lopsided grin, "That was pretty smooth, Marshal, helping him remember there was someplace else he needed to be. Seems clear you came here to talk to me about something besides the fracas you walked in on, and I take it it's something you'd as soon keep between just us. That being the case, I got a sort of office in the corner over yonder. You want to go sit down and get to it in there?"

"Up to you. This won't take long; we can do it right here as far as I'm concerned."

"Hitch up a bale of straw and take a seat then. What is it brings you around?"

"Wanted to talk to you about John Larkin," Bob said, getting right to it.

Hines went a little tight around the mouth. "I see. Word's getting around. Big, bad ex-con on his way back, looking for revenge against those who wrongly convicted him—is that it?"

"You tell me. I understand you were pretty good friends with him."

"Was. Still am. And not one lick ashamed to admit it."

"Nobody said you should be. All I'm trying to find out is what me and my deputies—seeing how we're in charge of keeping the peace around here—ought to expect when he shows up. Like you just said, word's getting around about Larkin's return, and there are those who are worried that he'll come seeking revenge. Since you're friends with him and I believe you've even had some correspondence with him while he was in prison, I thought maybe you could tell me what his mind-set is."

Hines shook his head. "Nothing like that. He's not coming back to make trouble. All he's looking to do is come home and restart his life."

"That's a pretty broad statement," Bob said. "Restart his life how? I'd say it's a pretty safe bet that resuming his employment with Emory Mining ain't in the cards."

"There are plenty of other job opportunities in and around Rattlesnake Wells. More all the time." Hines scowled. "And John still has plenty of friends around town besides just me. Friends who believe he got a raw deal at that trial and are more than willing to give him a second chance. For starters, I've already told him he can stay here with me when he gets to town. It ain't nothing fancy, but it's better than where he's been for the last four-plus years. It'll give him a place to stay until he gets squared away and back on his feet."

"That's mighty decent of you."

"Like I told you, I consider John Larkin a friend. I don't turn my back on friends."

Bob thumbed the brim of his hat up a bit and then said, "Speaking of 'friends,' like the other ones you say Larkin has all around town . . . You count one of 'em as being Victoria Emory? I understand her and Larkin were sweethearts before he got sent away."

Hines gave a disdainful grunt. "Hell no. That lousy little . . . No, *Miss* Emory has made it plenty clear she's no longer a friend to John."

"And he's willing to accept that?"

"If he ain't got the message, then some of those rocks he's been breakin' in the Laramie prison yard must have somehow dribbled in through his ears and replaced his brains."

"Comes to Miss Emory, the way I hear it is that her current, er, romantic interest is none other than Saul Norton—Larkin's former co-worker who first turned him in for stealing and then was the prosecution's star witness at the trial."

"A pair of two-faced snakes tangled together. They deserve each other," muttered Hines.

"And not even that—finding his former sweetheart now in the arms of the man who ratted him out and got him sent off to prison—would be enough, you don't believe, to strike a revenge spark in Larkin?" asked Bob.

Hines's expression clouded and he raised his voice, saying, "Is that what you're hoping I'll say? You're starting to come across like somebody who *wants* to hear that John is coming back for revenge. Christ, don't you have enough on your plate already with the Wardell trouble and a hired gun on his way for you to deal with?"

"That's exactly my point. I'm damn well aware of the trouble I already have. What I'm trying to find out is how strong's the likelihood of me and my men needing to be prepared for even more coming from Larkin."

Hines held Bob's eyes for several beats and then abruptly looked away, his shoulders sagging. "To the best of my knowledge, John ain't coming back looking for trouble," he said. "But you've got a point—it'll be just a matter of time before he runs into Saul Norton, whether he goes looking for him or not. And I don't doubt for a minute that the blamed fool is gonna make a run at trying to patch things up with Victoria. What'll happen when he actually gets here and is faced head-on with those situations . . . I can't say."

"But as far as the men on the jury who found Larkin guilty—you don't see him looking to try and get even with any of them for their verdict?"

Hines shook his head firmly. "No. That's ridiculous. I don't believe for a second John has anything like that in mind."

"I hope you're right." Bob stood up from his bale of straw. "Appreciate your time, Earl. When Larkin shows up, make sure he comes around to see me. Tell him I harbor no kind of ill will toward him and I'll do everything I can to treat him square . . . I hope you believe that, too."

Hines nodded. "I do. You're a fair and decent man, Marshal. Whatever else happens, I know John has no worries about you playing him false."

CHAPTER 16

Before going home for lunch, Bob stopped by the jail long enough to pick up the list of jurors Fred had ready for him. He also took time to tell his chief deputy about his encounter with Smoky Barnett and the other two Rocking W men.

"When Peter and Vern get back, make sure to tell them about that as well," Bob added. "For the foreseeable future, I suggest we all keep a sharp eye on any Rocking W men who come to town. I've done a pretty good job of riling the whole nest, so I expect they'll all be on the proddy side."

"Not much doubt about that, the way they ganged up on poor Mr. Streeter all over again. Good thing you showed up when you did," said Fred.

Bob frowned. "For Streeter's sake, I guess it was. But, like I said, it sure added to riling up the whole works. Barnett made a point of saying how Wardell was bringing in a hired gun, so that sure as hell ain't gonna settle things down."

"No, that's for sure. But hey, did Earl Hines have anything worthwhile to say about Larkin coming back? It was a smart idea to go talk to him, I'd forgot how good a buddies him and Larkin were."

"Nothing I'd want to take to the bank," Bob said with a shrug. "He freely admitted to being good friends with Larkin, so naturally he tried to put him in the best light. The two of 'em have been corresponding while Larkin was away, and I guess it's set up for Larkin to be staying at Hines's place for a while when he gets back to town." Bob held up the list of jurors and waved it. "Hines made a pretty convincing case for none of these men having to be worried about Larkin. But he couldn't say the same for Saul Norton. And he—Hines, that is—seemed to think there wasn't much doubt that Larkin would be trying to make contact with Victoria Emory as soon as he could."

Fred winced. "Ugh. That'll stir the pot in a hurry. Every indication is that Miss Victoria won't like it. And you can bet Norton won't. And old Jackson Emory—no matter he's wheelchair-bound and keeps mostly to himself these days in that big old house— has still got the teeth to do some chomping if his daughter starts squealing that Larkin is bothering her."

"Boy, I'm sure glad I stopped by long enough for you to cheer me up with your sunny outlook on things," said Bob as he started for the door. "There I was, on the verge of thinking things appeared a little gloomy."

At home, Consuela had lunch waiting. Although she could never be exactly sure when Bob could get away—and sometimes it wasn't at all—she always managed to have something ready. Today it was a beef sandwich on sourdough bread and a cup of corn chowder.

As they ate, Bob filled her in on the morning's events. Consuela was a good listener, attentive and seldom interrupting until the telling was done.

"It sounds to me," she said now, when that stage was reached, "like you are making sure that if and when Rance Brannigan gets here, he will have no shortage of reasons to pay attention to you."

"I doubt he needs much more reason than our unfinished business from the past," Bob replied with a faint smile. "But you're right, I seem to keep finding new ways to tangle with Wardell and his current crew. So, from Wardell's perspective, if he adds Brannigan to his payroll, then part of the way he'll expect him to earn his keep will be dealing with me."

"But you do not fear him, do you?" Consuela said, regarding him closely.

Bob took a drink of his after-meal coffee. Then: "I don't fear him in a face-to-face confrontation, if that's what you mean," he said. "But that doesn't mean I don't have a cautious . . . respect, I guess is the right word . . . for his toughness, his skill with a gun, his craftiness. But those are things I think I can overcome. What I fear is that, even if I beat him, the secret of my past as the Devil's River Kid will be revealed. *That*, I don't know how to overcome."

Consuela gazed even deeper into his eyes, as if she were seeing all the way to his soul. "But you'll find a way. I know you will."

She reached across the table and put her hand on

his. Bob looked down as her smooth, silky palm slid across his knuckles and her fingertips slipped under this thumb. She held her hand there and squeezed. Not hard, just gentle, steady pressure. Yet there was a strength there far beyond the mere physical kind. Consuela was silently conveying the existence of the unbreakable bond between them.

CHAPTER 17

On his way back to the jail, Bob encountered just about the last person in town that he wanted to run into.

As he was passing in front of the Shirley House Hotel, a voice hailed him from the middle of the street. "Marshal! Marshal Hatfield!"

Bob turned his head and saw newspaperman Owen Dutton hurrying in his direction. Sighing resignedly, he paused in a slice of shade thrown by the strip of shake-shingled awning that extended out above the boardwalk in front of the hotel.

Dutton stepped up on the boardwalk next to him. Pulling a wrinkled handkerchief from his hip pocket, he lifted his bowler hat and used the hanky to pat the beads of sweat standing out across his forehead.

"My goodness," the newspaperman said. "These spring days are getting warmer and warmer. If they're any indication of what's to come, I fear this summer is going to be a scorcher."

"We'll have some days like that, for sure," Bob said amiably.

Dutton replaced the hanky, resettled the bowler, and adjusted the spectacles riding near the tip of his nose. He was a smallish man in his middle twenties, four inches shorter than Bob, with rounded shoulders, hands that had never seen a callus, and the beginnings of a paunch pushing out above the waistband of his trousers. His most distinguishing feature was a pair of thick, curiously dark—almost black—eyebrows that stood out in sharp contrast with the reddish hair in evidence on his head and in the bushy muttonchop sideburns obscuring the hinges of his jaw.

"Speaking of things heating up around here," Dutton said, cocking his head back to peer up at Bob through the thick-lensed spectacles perched on the end of his nose, "makes a very good segue to the matters I have sought you out to discuss."

Bob frowned. "I've got a lot going on, Dutton. If you want a piece of my time you're gonna have to come up with something a little more serious to talk about than the warming weather."

"Very well," said Dutton, poking out his lower lip in a smug manner. "How about non-weather-related subject matter like the rustling that Ed Wardell insists is taking place out on his spread and the hired gun or guns that he therefore feels forced to bring in because the law isn't doing anything to help him? How about the near-lynching that took place yesterday out at the Rocking W? How about the vengeance-seeking ex-con due back in our town any minute now . . . ? Don't you think these matters are significant enough for the public, via me and my newspaper, to know your thoughts and intentions regarding them?"

"You're blowing each and every one of these things out of proportion, Dutton, and you damn well know it," Bob said through clenched teeth.

"Am I?" the newspaperman challenged. "Then, as I just said, tell me your thoughts and intentions regarding them and help me gain a different perspective."

Bob looked around at the street busy with activity and people starting to gawk. "Okay," he muttered grudgingly. "But standing here ain't the place to discuss it. Come on with me to my office."

"Delighted to," said Dutton, falling in step behind as the marshal resumed heading for his original destination.

When they got to the jail, they found Peter and Vern leafing through a stack of wanted posters, refreshing their memories of fugitives suspected to be in or near the area and familiarizing themselves with anything new that might have come in while they were away.

"You boys take your lunch yet?" Bob wanted to know.

"Not yet," said Peter. "We came in from rounds not too long ago. Told Fred to go ahead and take his, we'd wait until either him or you got back."

"Well, as you can see, I'm back," said Bob. "So go ahead and strap on the feed bag somewhere. Then, since I'm gonna want you to cover late hours tonight, take the rest of the afternoon off. Come back around five or so."

The two brothers nodded and then, in almost perfect unison, which was an eerie habit they had, said, "You got it, Marshal."

As soon as the Macys went out the door, Dutton said, "They make a couple of fine-looking peace officers."

"More important to me than how they look doing it is that they're mighty good at their jobs," said Bob.

"Yes. Of course that is the most important thing," said Dutton. "I haven't seen them around for a few days . . . I was beginning to wonder if they'd quit or something. All things considered, it would be most unfortunate timing for you to lose two-thirds of your deputy force right about now."

Bob sighed. "Number one, that ain't gonna happen. They were off on leave for a few days visiting their uncle and younger brother, that's all. Number two, the cloud of doom you seem so hell-bent on picturing as hanging over our town I don't believe is nearly as ominous as you're making it out to be." The marshal waved an arm at the chair positioned in front of his desk as he settled into his own seat behind it. "Sit down. Take a load off and let's try to hash out the horse apples from the buffalo chips about these matters that have got you so worked up."

"Very well," said Dutton, dropping onto the chair. "But before we get into those other things, I'd like to ask you a simple question."

"I thought that was the whole idea. As a reporter, asking questions is what you do, isn't it?"

"To be sure. But this is more of a personal nature. What I'd like to know is, why do you dislike me?"

This bluntness of the inquiry took Bob by surprise. He didn't answer right away. Then: "I guess I've got to come back with a question of my own. What makes you think that?"

"The way you act toward me makes it plain enough. Can you deny that I annoy the hell out of you?"

Bob emitted an abrupt chuckle. "There you go. Yes, you *do* annoy the hell out of me. But that doesn't mean I dislike you as a person."

"Isn't it the same thing?"

"Not the way I see it. Angus McTeague, one of the wealthiest, most respected men in town, annoys me with those cheap-ass, stinking cigars he smokes. Abe Starbuck of the Starbuck Territorial Bank annoys me with his arrogance and the way he treats his employees. But I can't say I actively dislike either one of them."

"So what is it about me that annoys you, then?"

Bob pointed. "That right there. The way you keep digging. You get an answer to something but you're not satisfied, you insist on digging deeper."

"That's what a good reporter does."

"Then it's lucky I haven't ever been around many reporters. Sounds like I'd find them annoying, too."

"The first answer someone gives is what they *want* you to accept. A good reporter has to consider there may be more behind it. Almost all of us have secrets we are reluctant to open up about. Don't you also find that as a law officer?"

"This is the West, Dutton. On top of that, Rattlesnake Wells is a boomtown. A big share of the folks around here left some kind of past behind to make it this far. And you're right, a lot of them want what's behind them to stay there and don't want to 'open up' about it. I see my job as dealing with the fresh wounds in front of me, not picking the scabs of old ones."

"But I see a story as more than just what's on the surface, I see it going all the way to its roots. I guess that's where we differ."

One corner of Bob's mouth lifted in a wry grin. "And that's what makes you so annoying."

Dutton blinked a couple of times and then emitted a somewhat uncertain chuckle. "Okay. I guess we've covered that, then." He shifted around some in his chair, produced a notepad and a pencil. "Now, as I know you are busy and I'm taking up your valuable time, let's get to those other matters I wanted to talk to you about."

"Okay. But you're probably gonna come away disappointed. Based on what you rattled off out on the street, I don't know that I've got a lot to add to what you already seem to know."

"But you're not denying any of it, are you?"

"None except for the rustling that Wardell keeps squalling about. I haven't seen anything to convince me it's taking place, at least not on the scale he claims. Even if it was, it's technically out of my jurisdiction so there are legal limits to what I could do. But if he came forward with some kind of proof, I might feel different."

"What would you do in that case?"

"I'm not sure exactly. But nobody hates cattle thieves more than me. For starters, if I really believed there was a big rustling problem, I'd probably lean on the federal marshal's office down in Cheyenne to send a man up. In that case, if he chose to, the U.S.

committed. So until or unless he does something that puts him back on the wrong side of the law, he deserves the same privacy and respect as anybody else. For you to deprive him of that by calling undue attention to him in your newspaper would be mighty ill-advised."

Dutton's face reddened. "Of course. Goes without saying. My remark to you certainly was not . . . No. You're right. What I said was unfair and uncalled for. It was inexcusable and certainly not the kind of attitude I would ever allow to seep into my writing."

Bob eased up a bit, somewhat surprised by the newspaperman backing down and admitting he'd been out of line. He said, "What I've told my deputies, and this applies to both Larkin and the situation with Wardell, is that we need to keep a sharp eye peeled and be ready to react to whatever happens. Don't seem like a bad tactic for you to try and follow, either—react with what you report, but don't jump ahead and give things a nudge that might help 'em swerve one way or the other."

Dutton gave his pencil a rest. "Doesn't sound like bad advice, Marshal. I just might give it a try. But in the meantime, you'd be well advised to know that there's a good deal of talk going around town on both matters. Word of mouth, or plain old gossip if you want to call it that, was spreading news and stirring up people's feelings about things long before typeset ever came along.

"I can't say about Wardell and his gunny, but there are two distinct camps when it comes to Larkin. A lot of folks see him as a nice fellow who somehow got a raw deal. But plenty of others don't trust him and

think he's on his way back looking to get even. He
runs into enough of the latter, things aren't going to
go easy for him."

"Yeah," Bob said in a flat tone. "This is not for
quoting in your paper but, much as I wish otherwise,
I've got a feeling there are quite a few things that
ain't gonna go easy in the days ahead."

CHAPTER 18

The previous year, a man named August Gafford had built in the New Town section of Rattlesnake Wells an impressive two-story structure that he called the Crystal Diamond Saloon. The main room was furnished with a specially imported bar and an array of dazzling chandeliers, and had a spacious performing stage where an exclusive dance hall revue was scheduled to put on nightly shows. Trouble was, a serious of violent events brought on by outside forces as well as Gafford getting caught in his own double-dealing caused the whole thing to fail spectacularly before it ever got off the ground. A great deal of blood was shed and lives were lost—including Gafford's, at his own hand—before it was all over.

Ultimately, after the bodies were buried and the wounds of the living patched up, the Crystal Diamond was stripped of all its glitzy furnishings and by the start of winter was nothing but an empty shell of a building. Enter a man named Roy Cormier out of Denver who paid the city for the land and the abandoned building, furnished it with the simple basics even though renaming it the Grand, and re-opened it as a workingman's saloon and gaming house.

The almost immediate onset of a hard winter, something many thought might be a factor working against the success of this new establishment, actually proved to be quite the opposite. While Bullock's Saloon and the restaurant bar at the Shirley House Hotel in Old Town were exceptions, most of the Grand's New Town competition was cramped, drafty, dirt-floored tent saloons and gambling joints. So when the snow and bitter winds started whistling under tent flaps and through frosted-over canvas walls, those inclined toward cheap drinking and gambling quickly found they could do so at only slightly higher prices but in the comfort of the warm, dry wooden structure that was the Grand. It wasn't long before Cormier's place was the most popular spot in New Town, drawing a near-capacity crowd almost any night of the week.

Helping matters along was the way the upper story of the Grand was put to use. Accompanying Cormier when he came to town was a sultry blonde with a thick German accent whom he introduced only as Duchess. As the ground-floor saloon was taking shape, Duchess was busy transforming the second floor into a six-bed bawdy house that operated pretty much independently from the saloon. It had its own discreet entrance by means of an outside stairway at the rear and a parlor complete with a limited bar where callers could socialize briefly before choosing one of the working girls to spend some private time with. All under the watchful eye of "Madam" Duchess, seconded by a gigantic black bouncer named Arthur. The girls, who were selectively brought in by Duchess, did not mingle with the drinkers and gamblers down in the saloon, such as was done in other places, but rather stayed exclusive to the second floor.

Unlike the pricing in the Grand's saloon, Duchess's second-floor entertainment came at a premium that was considerably higher than the crib whores available in tents and shacks at the far end of Gold Avenue. It took a while for this to catch on, but once talk started spreading through the mining camps and surrounding ranch bunkhouses and the town in general, the difference in quality and service soon was drawing a steady stream of customers willing to shell out a little extra.

While the Grand flourished, both downstairs and up, the tent saloons, gambling joints, and whore cribs farther down the length of Gold Avenue felt the pinch. Most of them managed to still survive, however, because there always remained a certain level of thirsty, horny men too broke or just plain too cheap to pay more than bottom dollar.

On this particular spring evening, Roy Cormier was in a reflective mood. He sat alone at the far end of the bar, a glass of good bourbon and a top-quality cigar burning in an ashtray on the bar top in front of him. Tonight's crowd was rather slim for some reason, but decent enough all the same. Two tables of gamblers giving the pasteboards a workout, a mix of miners and cowboys holding up the bar, and a handful of *hombres* shooting pool. The day's take would still be okay. And with the approach of summer and more and more suckers braving the elements to arrive in the area, drawn by the lure of hoping to hit gold up in the Prophecy Mountains, there was every reason to believe business would remain good.

Life, in general, was working out pretty good for him these days, Cormier decided. At forty-five, he would be considered handsome by any standards; tall, trim, an evenly featured face complete with strong jaw, faintly dimpled chin, and a classic widow's peak sweeping back to a headful of wavy dark hair. He carried himself with the measured bearing of a military man or aristocrat, though he was neither, and even his most casual apparel was crisp and clean.

Rattlesnake Wells was still rather primitive compared to the larger cities where Cormier had developed a taste for the finer things in life. But he'd found out the hard way that the competition in those places had ways of grinding a man down and spitting out the broken pieces over even the slightest miscalculation. Far better to be a big fish in a small, relatively calm pond, he'd discovered, than a minnow always struggling against the strong currents to be found in places like Chicago and Denver. And as long as he had Duchess at his side, he would never lack completely for a taste of life's finer pleasures.

As he sipped his bourbon and enjoyed his cigar this evening, Cormier's reflections drifted and he became idly focused on the games of pool taking place not far from where he sat. At first a young drifter Cormier hadn't seen around before had purchased a rack of balls and was playing by himself. Before long, though, three workers from the McT #3 mine showed up. They were regulars who always gravitated to the pool table whenever they stopped in. So it was only a matter of a few minutes before one of them put money down for the next rack of balls and, as was customary, challenged the young stranger to a game, winner take control of the table. The stranger agreed.

Now all of the miners were pretty good pool players, but the best of the trio by a considerable amount was tall, lantern-jawed, braggadocious Ray Monte. He was the one who stepped up to play the young stranger who introduced himself simply as John.

The game was straight pool, call every shot. It went quickly and stayed fairly close, but in the end it was John who sank the winning ball. Next to challenge him was Sam Ruckner, an older, quieter gent who got beat rather handily. The remaining member of the McT #3 trio was big, brutish Jimmy Russert, the poorest pool player of the three, yet he insisted on making a run at the stranger, too. The results were predictable and over with in no time at all.

Watching, Cormier saw that John, the stranger, was not a showboat and not much of a talker at all, really. A tall, pale individual sporting a ragged, untrimmed beard, he just took his time, concentrated hard, and stroked the cue smoothly and accurately.

By the time John had put Russert away, Ray Monte was ready to take another turn. Also by this time, the contest was starting to draw the attention of several of the men who'd been lining the bar. So when Monte suggested playing the next game for money and John sheepishly admitted not having enough to

cover the bet, one of the onlookers—Tub Simonson—
quickly offered to fade him.

With that, the game progressed and, once again,
John won. By this time, even more spectators had
gathered around and several of them were eager to
wager on the outcome of another game, some backing Monte, some going with John. The two men
agreed and so the balls were racked once more.

Looking on, Cormier had no trouble with the activity or the wagering as long as the shooters and onlookers were continuing to spend money on drink.
Something that did cause him a touch of concern,
however, was the look of growing frustration, hinging
on anger, that he could see forming in Ray Monte.
Monte had always been proud and loud when it came
to his pool-shooting skill and now to find himself getting repeatedly bested by this quiet stranger, especially
with his pards and other customers looking on, was
getting to him. This particular bunch of McT #3 boys
had never been particularly troublesome in the past,
but there was always a first time. And Cormier had a
hunch this had the makings of possibly turning into
that. Just in case, he caught the eye of each of his
bouncers—Jake Jocoby on a stool over by the front
door, and Miles Cray perched at the back of the room
beside a door that opened to the enclosed stairs leading up to the second floor—and gave them the "be
alert" signal. They nodded in response.

The next game started. It progressed notably slower
than any of the previous ones, each man being perhaps overly cautious with his shots due to the money
riding on the outcome. The click of the balls colliding

was the only sound as everyone, players and onlookers alike, focused with quiet intensity.

Finally, it came down to sinking the final ball, the game winner, and Monte had control of the table. He called his pocket and got lined up for the shot, a relatively easy one. When he made his stroke, however, the tip made the dreaded sound of striking off center and the cue ball reacted accordingly, striking off its intended mark so that the shot was missed. A collective groan escaped from all looking on.

Before the dismayed sound had died out, John stepped up, called his pocket, and made the shot. The game was over and he'd won again.

Now the sound that came out of the crowd was mixed, another groan from those who'd wagered wrong, elation from those who'd be collecting winnings.

But then all sound was cut short by Ray Monte's voice calling out loud and harsh. "I claim foul. That bastard cheated!"

CHAPTER 19

All eyes cut to Monte.

"What's that supposed to mean?" somebody wanted to know.

Monte and John were standing on opposite sides of the table. "I spoke in plain English, didn't I?" Monte said. He pointed at John, adding, "This cheatin' skunk purposely bumped the table when I made my shot. No way in hell I would have miscued like that otherwise."

"That's a lie," John said, flat and cold.

Somebody else spoke up. "Come on, Monte, how can that be? We were all standin' right here watchin'."

Monte thumped the butt of his cue stick on the floor. "That's exactly the idea. While everybody was concentratin' on me takin' my shot, this polecat gave a hip bump—just a sly one, so's nobody'd notice— and threw off my stroke."

"That's right," chimed in big Russert. "I seen the weasel do it. I think he's been doin' stuff like that right along. How else could he keep winnin' time after time?"

"How about he's just plain better?" came another voice out of the crowd.

"To hell with that, says I!" spat Monte. "He's a cheatin' skunk and that's all there is to it. The outcome of that game ought not count and no money should be paid. And this sonofabitch deserves nothing else but to be run out of the joint, and that's too good for him."

"I'll say it again. You're a liar. You and your pet bear, too," stated John. "And I ain't going no damn where, not on your say-so."

Roy Cormier slipped from his stool and took a step toward the crowd. "I'll second that last part," he said in a firm, sharp voice. "Nobody orders anybody out of my place unless the order comes from me or one of my assistants." He paused, cutting his eyes meaningfully to either side as the two bouncers also slid from their stools and stood ready, feet planted wide.

"As far as the outcome of the game," Cormier continued, "I saw no evidence of any cheating. You're good, Monte, everybody knows that. But tonight you simply ran into somebody better. It happens sometimes."

"You couldn't see good enough, sittin' clear over there where you were," Monte protested. "Especially not with everybody crowded around."

Cormier moved closer. "I could see good enough to stand by my statement. The game was fair. It's over, you lost."

"You ought not be buttin' into this," Monte said through clenched teeth.

"But I am. And what I say goes around here," Cormier responded icily.

"Don't let this fancy-shirted bastard back you down, Ray," urged Russert. "That dirty cheater called both of us liars, too. We ain't gonna let that stand, are we?"

"Don't forget this fancy boy has got those bouncers of his," muttered Kingston, the older, quieter McT man.

"To hell with him and his bouncers," declared Monte. "I'll stand for no man cheatin' me, and I'll damn sure not let some sneaky weasel call me a liar!"

Kingston heaved a sigh and then muttered again, almost softly. "All right. Go ahead and do what you're gonna do, then. I'll cover you." With that, he made a move that was totally unexpected and executed with surprising speed—yanking a six-gun from the waistband of his trousers and thrusting its muzzle up under Cormier's chin. Addressing Cormier but now in a raised voice, he said, "Tell your thumpers and your barman to just relax, mister, and you can keep that fancy shirt of yours from getting messed up with a lot of nasty blood."

The two bouncers at either end of the room and the stocky drink slinger behind the bar all three froze helplessly.

Whatever action Monte and Russert might have taken from there became a moot point because John didn't wait for it. Inasmuch as he wore no gunbelt or visible weapon of any kind, he instead reached for other tools at hand to fight the two-to-one odds that suddenly loomed before him.

First, he snatched the cue ball from the table and

flung it into the face of Monte. It struck only a glancing blow off the side of his head, but it was enough to make the wrangler jerk away and stagger backward, kept from losing his balance completely by a knot of men who were crowded close. With that much accomplished, John took the cue stick he still held in one hand and whirled it around until the fat, lead-weighted end was extending away from him.

Gripping the slender part of the shaft now with both hands, he spun to face the bull-rush of Russert coming around one end of the pool table. John met the rush by momentarily cocking the cue stick back over one shoulder and then swinging it like a base-ball bat, slamming the fat end hard across Russert's middle. The stick snapped in two but the big man stopped short and started to fold up. John tossed away the broken twig he now held in his hands and quickly closed on Russert, driving his knee viciously upward to pulverize the nose of the lowering face. Russert emitted a honking sound as he partially straightened up, twin jets of blood spraying out of his flattened nostrils, then tipped to one side and fell heavily to the floor.

John immediately turned back to Monte, who, on the other side of the table, had regained his balance and was shoving away those around him who'd helped keep him upright. Not wanting to allow the miner a chance to get any more set than that, John used his height and long legs to vault up onto the pool table and then leaped from it straight onto Monte. His crashing weight drove his adversary back and down, and both men tumbled to the floor in a tangle. Onlookers scattered frantically to get out of the way, tables and chairs were sent skidding and clattering every which way.

The two men rolled across the floor, kicking, gouging, throwing in-close punches and elbows. After a minute, they separated and clambered to their feet, fists raised, teeth bared, ready to slam into one another all over again.

That's when deputies Peter and Vern Macy came barging through the front door. Peter swept the room with a drawn Colt as Vern wielded a double-barreled shotgun. When the latter discharged one of its barrels toward the ceiling—an "attention-getter" load of bird shot that could be quickly followed with a twelve-gauge blast from the other barrel if the message needed to be made stronger—the room fell instantly silent and still.

"Everybody freeze!" Peter shouted, somewhat unnecessarily. "Stay right where you are, keep your hands empty and in plain sight!"

Sam Kingston withdrew the gun from under Cormier's chin and let it drop to the floor. Raising his hands to shoulder height, he turned slowly to face the deputies and said calmly over his shoulder to Cormier, "Nothing personal, mister. A fella's got to back the play of his pards, that's all there is to it. Even when they're mule-ass dumb, it's what you got to do."

CHAPTER 20

"When one of 'em gave his name as John Larkin," Peter said, "I figured you'd want to know right away. Otherwise I wouldn't have bothered you."

He was providing this explanation to Bob, who'd just entered the front office area of the jail building. When Bob arrived, Peter was behind the marshal's desk, filling out paperwork, and Vern was standing over by the stove with a cup of coffee in hand.

Trailing Bob as he came in was Ollie Sterbenz, an elderly gent who did handyman work around town including maintaining the street lanterns and lighting them each evening. Ollie had been one of the men drinking at the bar in the Grand earlier when the pool competition started getting out of hand. Having been around long enough to sense trouble in its early stages, before it flared into something bigger, Ollie had slipped out and gone in search of Peter and Vern on patrol. Thanks to Ollie's alertness, the deputies arrived in time to halt the fight before it went any further than it did. Subsequently, it had been Ollie whom Peter sent to notify Bob at home that John Larkin not only had arrived in town but also had already managed to get in trouble.

"You did the proper thing, letting me know right away," Bob said now, in response to Peter's remarks.

"Dang me for failin' to recognize Larkin as soon as I walked in that saloon," Ollie lamented. "We've all heard the talk about how he was comin' back. That raggedy beard of his and the fact he's gotten a lot skinnier than he used to be threw me off, I guess. If I'd've recognized him right off, I could've let you boys know even sooner and maybe stopped the trouble a-fore it ever started at all."

"You did fine as it was, Ollie," Bob told him.

"That's right," Vern added. "If you hadn't come and found me and Peter when you did, that situation likely would have turned a lot uglier. From what I saw when we got there, another minute and it would have busted out into a full-scale brawl."

"I agree," Peter spoke up. "You saved a lot of damage, Ollie."

"As a matter of fact," said Bob, "to show our appreciation for the help you've been, how about you go up the street to Bullock's and have a couple drinks on me for the ones that got interrupted at the Grand. Tell Mike I'll be around tomorrow to square the tab."

"Aw, you don't need to do that, Marshal."

"I know I don't *need* to. But I want to. So why don't you run along and take advantage of my generosity before I change my mind?"

"Okay. If you insist." Ollie grinned. "Hate to put you to the trouble of switching your mind back and forth."

As soon as the door closed behind Ollie, Bob

turned to his deputies and said, "Okay. Give some details."

Peter shrugged. "If not for Larkin being involved, it was just another saloon fight. An argument over a pool game."

"From most reports," Vern added, "Ray Monte, one of the workers from Angus McTeague's McT #3 mine, was the main instigator. Him and Jimmy Russert."

"Those McT boys generally aren't troublemakers," Bob mused.

"True," Vern agreed. "But tonight seems like it was an exception. Sam Kingston was also with 'em. He didn't engage in the fight with Larkin but he held a gun on Roy Cormier to make sure him or none of his staff interfered."

Bob frowned. "Hell. Sam oughtta know better than that. What's Cormier saying about it all? What kind of charges does he want to make?"

"Surprisingly," said Peter, "he was pretty calm about everything. I guess because there wasn't that much damage done. A broken cue stick, some tipped-over chairs, and spilled drinks . . . oh, yeah, and a very eye-catching shotgun blast pattern in the ceiling where Mr. Law-and-Order got in a hurry to bring things to a screeching halt."

Vern scowled, his face reddening some. "Hey. Like I said before, it looked to me like everybody in the joint was about half a second away from throwing fists. I didn't want that to get started."

Peter smiled. "And you made sure it didn't. That's all I'm saying."

"Getting back to Cormier," Bob said. "He going to press charges or not?"

"He said he'd stop by first thing in the morning and talk to you about that," Peter said. "He wanted more time tonight to finish checking for damages and whatnot."

Bob jabbed a thumb toward the heavy door at the rear of the room that led back to the cellblock. "I trust you've got all the ones involved back there?"

Vern nodded. "We figured you'd at least want to hold 'em overnight for drunk and disorderly . . . Although, truth to tell, none of 'em are all that drunk."

Bob skirted the end of the desk and headed for the heavy door. "Let's go find out what they've got to say for themselves."

There was a surprise waiting for the three lawmen when they walked into the cellblock area. It came from Ray Monte, who'd sprung to his feet as soon as he heard the door bolt sliding back. From the cot he'd been sitting on, he moved to the wall of bars that ran floor to ceiling across the front of the cell into which he'd been locked along with Russert and Kingston. John Larkin occupied the adjoining cell by himself. He also sat on the edge of a cot, but he neither looked up nor stood when the visitors came in.

"Marshal, I'm glad you're here," Monte said, a tone of urgency in his voice. He wrapped his big hands around the bars before him and squeezed them tight. "There's been a big mistake."

Bob smiled somewhat wearily. Like he hadn't heard this spiel before.

"Yeah, and you made it," he told Monte. "Saloon fighting pretty clearly qualifies as disorderly conduct, and that automatically earns you the right to spend a night in these cozy accommodations of ours. In the morning, if Roy Cormier decides he wants to press charges for whatever damage you caused, you might be staying a little longer."

Monte shook his head. "That's not the mistake I'm talkin' about. I know me and my buddies here— mostly me—deserve this. The mistake is with this other fella over here." Monte tipped his head to indicate Larkin in the other cell. "He *don't* belong behind bars. He didn't do nothing but defend himself against us . . . well, again, mostly me."

Bob cocked an eyebrow. "Oh?"

"That's not the song you were singing a little while ago," Peter was quick to say. "You were mighty loud about accusing him of cheating at pool and being the one who started the fight."

Monte loosened his grip on the bars and looked away. "I was wrong. I wasn't telling it straight."

"Why the sudden change of heart?" Bob wanted to know.

By now, Larkin had risen to his feet and moved closer within the confines of his own cell, paying tighter attention to what was being said.

Monte looked one way, tossing a glance at Larkin through the bars that separated the two cells, then turned his head briefly to look back over his shoulder at his pals Kingston and Russert. Kingston was on his feet, listening with interest, while Russert remained sitting on the edge of a cot, holding a bloody rag to his smashed nose.

Monte's eyes returned to Bob. "Since I found out this other fella is John Larkin, it's forced me to do some thinkin'. Reflectin', you might say, on how all this came about. Reckon I don't have to tell you that Larkin only recently got released from the pen down in Laramie. Been quite a bit of talk lately about him bein' on his way back." Monte paused, cleared his throat. "The thing is, it sets awful hard with me to think that some poor devil who just spent all that time in a prison comes home only to end up right off the bat smack in jail. And me bein' the cause of it . . . well, I just can't go with that."

"That ain't exactly your call to make," Bob pointed out. "He joined in the fight, just like you."

"But that's what I'm tryin' to explain, what I already told you about him just defendin' himself—against me and my accusations and the way me and Russert back here was proddin' him to where he had no choice. You can't fault a man for standin' his ground in a situation like that."

"What about your claim that he was cheating?" Vern asked. "Wasn't that the start of the whole thing?"

Monte hung his head. "That's why I keep sayin' it's all mostly on me . . . Larkin was never cheatin'. Not that I saw, not that anybody else did, either. I was just bein' a sore loser. I take a lot of pride—stupid pride— in bein' a good pool player. It humiliated me to have this stranger whip me so sound in front of my friends and everybody. Blamin' that some cheatin' went on seemed like a way out. That's all I was lookin' for, really. But once the words came out of my mouth . . . well, here we are."

"And we're supposed to believe that, all of a sudden, a guilty conscience is causing you to change your tune?" said Bob.

"It's the truth, dammit," Monte insisted, growing agitated. "Why else would I be sayin' it? I don't owe Larkin nothing, never saw him before in my life. And I ain't paintin' myself as no saint. Far from it . . . But neither am I so lowdown that I'd cause an innocent man to stand a jail hitch for me makin' a false claim on account of my feelin's got hurt. Way I hear tell, there's plenty to be found who think Larkin got a raw deal the first time around. I can't do nothing about that, but I *can* do something to try and see he don't do jail time this time around—leastways not on my say-so."

Bob exchanged uncertain glances with his deputies. Then he looked over at Larkin in the next cell. "You got anything you want to add to this?"

Larkin cut his eyes momentarily to Monte, then regarded the marshal. He came forward a bit more in his cell. "What do you expect me to say? Even if this man wasn't telling the truth—which he is, by the way—it would still be in my best interest to agree with him, right?"

Bob didn't respond right away. When he did, he came from a different angle. "How long have you been in town?"

Larkin took the change-up in stride. "Counting my time in here, only a couple hours or so."

"Since you got out of prison on early release and therefore are on parole," Bob said, "weren't you advised you're supposed to check in with the local authorities when you arrive in a town?"

Larkin nodded. "Yes, I was advised of that. But I understood I had twenty-four hours to do so. I intended to stop by your office first thing in the morning."

"But first you made time to stop by a saloon. Seems like your priorities might be a little out of kilter, mister," said Peter.

"Maybe so," Larkin allowed. "But I just got in from riding all day. And, for a lot longer before that, I was in a place where cold beers were few and far between. So having one or two to cut the trail dust and celebrate making it back home didn't seem like such a bad idea."

"And after you had those beers—providing this other hadn't happened—what were your plans for the balance of the night?" Bob asked.

"An old pal of mine offered to put me up for a few days once I got back to town. I was figuring to drop in on him and take him up on the offer."

"That old pal be Earl Hines, the blacksmith?"

"It would."

Bob considered for a minute. Then he said to Vern, "Go find Hines and let him know he's got a visitor in town, will you? Bring him back here with you."

Turning to Peter, the marshal then said, "Go ahead and unlock Mr. Larkin's cell. We'll discuss this further out in the office."

When his cell door groaned open, Larkin didn't exit right away. He paused to speak to Monte. "What happened earlier wasn't exactly a pleasant experience. Not for either of us, I guess. But it was mighty decent of you to speak up for me the way you just did. For whatever it's worth, I appreciate it."

Monte gave a one-shoulder shrug. "Least I could do. Maybe we'll run into each other again someday and shoot some more pool under friendlier circumstances. I'll be ready for you next time."

Partway out his cell door, Larkin paused again. "That big fella sitting back there on the couch," he said to Bob and Peter. "I damaged his nose pretty bad. He could use some attention."

"I tried sending for the doc but he's out of town on a house call. Not much more we can do for him right now," Peter explained.

"Maybe a pan of fresh water and a clean towel at least?"

"We can do that much," said Bob. "We'll bring something back."

CHAPTER 21

As usual, Bob was the first to arrive at the jail the next morning. In this instance, however, due to the policy of someone remaining at the jail when there was a prisoner in the lockup overnight, Vern Macy was there to greet him. The young deputy looked like he'd been up for a while. The cot he'd slept on over against the sidewall of the office area was made up and a pot of fresh-brewed coffee was on the stove. Still, once he'd informed Bob how things stood, he was more than ready to take his leave and head on home.

The only change since Bob had left there himself last night was that Doc Tibbs had shown up around midnight, having gotten back into town and found the note that was left on his door informing him there was an injured man at the jail. He'd treated Russert's nose, packing it with cotton to prevent any more bleeding and bandaging it to try and hold it in place so it could mend as straight as possible. He'd also left a small bottle of pain pills for the patient.

After that, the rest of the night went without incident and even Russert had rested fairly peacefully.

Vern hadn't been gone long before Fred reported in. Inasmuch as he'd made his usual stop at the Bluebird Café for breakfast, he'd already heard the gossip version of last night's fight at the Grand, most notably including how John Larkin was back in town and had been involved in it, and how he now was behind bars again for his trouble. It never ceased to amaze Bob how fast the local tongue-waggers could learn about and then spread the word on anything and everything that happened around town.

This time around, though, what the wagging tongues didn't know was that, after Ray Monte had admitted to instigating the whole incident and Earl Hines had shown up to take responsibility for Larkin, Bob had made the decision not to hold him.

"You mean you let him go?" Fred echoed upon being so informed.

"That's right," Bob said with a nod. "After Monte confessed to lying and causing the whole trouble, what grounds did I have to hold Larkin on? Like Monte himself kept pointing out, all Larkin did was defend himself."

Fred emitted a low whistle. "That'll set the town to buzzing even more than they already are."

"I can't help that. It was the right thing to do."

Fred nodded toward the cellblock door. "But the other three—the McT miners—they're still back there?"

"For now," Bob said. "I expect to let 'em out before too long. Call it disorderly conduct and time served. It's gonna depend on whether or not Roy

Cormier decides he wants to press any charges, though. According to Peter and Vern, it didn't look to them like there was much damage. The most serious thing, the way I see it, is Kingston pulling a gun on Cormier."

"That old fool ought to know better than that."

Bob grinned wryly. "Kinda what I thought. But he did it, nevertheless."

"Decent of Monte, though, to set the record straight like he did."

"Yeah. You got to give him that."

Fred scrunched up his face. "Saloonkeepers ain't exactly known for being early risers. When do you figure Cormier will be coming around?"

"He told Peter and Vern it wouldn't be very late. But in the meantime," Bob said, "I reckon we owe our prisoners some breakfast. How about you make a return trip to the Bluebird and have Mike and Teresa fix up some meals you can bring back with you?"

"Sure, I can do that."

As Fred started for the door, Bob added, "And Fred? Don't give the gossipmongers any new news to blab about while you're there. I don't know how the hell they find out half the stuff they do, but make sure it ain't from you. Make 'em work for it."

Roy Cormier came by a little before ten. He continued to have a very tolerant attitude about what had occurred in his establishment, stating that the damage done was too minimal to go to any added bother over. When he heard that Monte had changed his story, admitting to starting the trouble on a false-hood and thereby clearing Larkin of any wrongdoing except defending himself, Cormier seemed gen-uinely pleased.

"Good for Monte," he said. "He never seemed like a bad sort any of the previous times he's been in my place. And good for the Larkin fellow, too. I was never convinced he'd done any cheating. Especially after I heard about his past troubles, I was sorry to see him caught up in a sham."

"Well, he ended up getting out of it okay," Bob said, marveling once again at how everybody seemed to find Larkin so innately likable and wanted to give him the benefit of the doubt. "The only thing that leaves," he added, "is the matter of the gun that was pulled on you. That's too serious a thing to just ignore, wouldn't you say?"

Cormier frowned. "What do you suggest?"

"Well, I know the old-timer who did it. He's not really a bad sort, either, like you said about Monte. I'm surprised he was even carrying a gun. Still, he was and he used it pretty unwisely." Bob paused, then made a catchall gesture with one hand. "I can per-manently confiscate the weapon and fine him, say, twenty-five dollars. I figure that would make him think twice before he did anything so stupid again. Would that satisfy you?"

"It would, yes. But that's a pretty stiff cost to a working miner, isn't it?"

"I know his employer. Kingston's a good worker, been with the McT mines for quite a spell. I think

Angus McTeague will cover the fine and then let old Sam work it off once he gets back on the job."

Cormier nodded. "That sounds reasonable. I'm fine with that."

An hour later, Bob sent Fred back to the lockup to release the prisoners.

After all three had shuffled out into the front office area, Bob sat on the corner of his desk and addressed them. For starters, he advised Kingston that he wouldn't be getting his gun back and then informed him of the fine levied against him.

"I figure McTeague will be good for it and then let you work it out with withdrawals from your pay," Bob said. "If for some reason he won't, you'll have to serve some more time. You understand that?"

The old miner hung his head and nodded.

"It was a pretty dumb thing to do, Sam. I can't just leave it go."

"I understand, Marshal. You're bein' fair as you can," Kingston said. "Far as bein' a dumb thing, I can't argue that, neither. There was a lot of that goin' on right at the time and I guess I got caught up in it."

"Once again, mostly on account of me," Monte spoke up. "Sam's fine will get paid, Marshal, and he won't be servin' no more time over it. I'll chip in, too, to make sure."

Bob regarded him soberly. "You're proving yourself to be a pretty decent fella, Monte . . . But it's all coming after the fact. Next time, make sure your decent side shows a little sooner—before you run your mouth or lose your temper and drag yourself and your pals into trouble again."

"I get the message loud and clear, Marshal," Monte assured him. "You can count on that."

"I hope so." Bob jerked a thumb toward the front door. "Now beat it. Report back to your mine and stay out of trouble."

CHAPTER 22

Bob went home for lunch and enjoyed a light meal and some quiet, leisurely time with Consuela. It added to his improved mood, the best one he'd been able to manage for a couple days now.

Having Larkin back in town also helped with that. It was a relief of sorts, certainly better than waiting and wondering about his return. His intentions now that he was here still weren't entirely clear, but from the time Bob had spent with him he hardly seemed like the embittered, revenge-seeking threat that some feared he would be. Not to say he couldn't still display such inclinations, especially toward certain people, but Bob got no sense of that being the main motive driving him.

Nor did the appearance of Larkin do anything to erase the situation with the Rocking W and Ed Wardell's apparent hiring of Rance Brannigan. But at least the anticipation of one man showing up was out of the way, and the associated trouble at the Grand last night had occupied Bob's time and attention sufficiently enough to relegate thoughts of

Brannigan to the back of his mind, at least for the time being.

And now, as he came down the slope from his house, on his way back to the jail, he spotted someone waiting for him whom he was pretty sure represented something more that would be occupying his time and attention to kick off the afternoon.

The buggy parked at the base of the slope was not a showy affair, but the mere fact it *was* a buggy, as opposed to the buckboards and freight wagons more common to the streets of Rattlesnake Wells, made it stand out. Its two occupants—the tall, militarily erect man on the driver's seat and the small, hunched-over man riding as passenger—gave it added distinction. Both wore dark business suits, crisp white shirts, neckties the color of ink. The driver wore a bowler hat perched on a cleanly shaven head. The passenger wore a wide-brimmed slouch hat pulled low over his eyes and had a plaid shawl draped over his narrow shoulders despite the warmth of the day.

Bob strode up and stopped beside the buggy. "Afternoon, Mr. Emory," he greeted.

"And to you, Marshal," Jackson Emory responded with a bob of his head. Lifting a pale, heavily veined hand, he made a slight gesture toward his driver. "You know my man Graedon, I trust?"

"I've seen him around. Don't know that we've ever been proper introduced," said Bob.

"Well then, consider that remedied. Marshal, Graedon . . . Graedon, Marshal Bob Hatfield."

The two men exchanged nods.

Emory went on, "I presume you have gathered

that we were here waiting for you, Marshal. Can you spare me a few minutes of your time?"

"Sure. What's on your mind?"

"To talk," Emory said bluntly. Then he slowly looked around, examining their surroundings, and brought his eyes back to Bob. "As you undoubtedly know, I seldom venture out of my house these days. Especially during the cold months only recently behind us. But inasmuch as I am out today and it is such a fine spring afternoon, I would very much like to drink it in with a turn through town and out a ways into the countryside. Would you mind riding with me while we have our discussion?"

Bob shrugged. "Don't see why not."

He went around the rear of the buggy and climbed in from the opposite side. Both the backrest and seat of the passenger compartment were so plushly cushioned that Bob felt half-swallowed when he leaned back. "Wow," he said. "This is so comfortable you may have trouble getting me out of here, even when the ride is over."

Emory gave no response to that. To Graedon he said, "Head on south through Old Town and then out into the country. Hold an easy pace."

Up close, Bob was somewhat startled by how old and frail Jackson Emory looked. His skin was almost as pale as the tufts of white hair poking out from under his hat, and his hunched posture gave the impression that the weight of the shawl over his shoulders was pressing him down in the seat. It had been months, maybe close to a year since Bob had seen him last. When Bob had first come to town, Emory had been hale and hearty; never a particularly large man, just average sized, he was solid and square shouldered and made to seem larger by his self-assurance and the success of his two mines up in the Prophecies. But that was before the accident just short of three years ago, the wagon crash coming down off the mountain that had taken the life of his wife and left him without the use of his legs. Emory had been slowly withering away ever since then. But Bob had never seen him look this bad. Before long, if he didn't get turned around somehow, there wasn't going to be anything left to wither further.

They rolled down Front Street, past the jail and Peterson's Livery, veering wide around the depot and the roundhouse of the spur railroad line. Ahead stretched the rolling hills of the prairie, its grasses starting to take on a bright spring green.

"In case you're wondering, we can speak freely in front of Graedon," Emory said. "I trust him implicitly."

"Okay by me."

"I expect you can guess that what I want to discuss is the return of John Larkin."

Bob nodded. "Had a hunch that would be it."

"I understand he's arrived in town, just as we've all been anticipating, and he immediately got into a saloon brawl."

"It wasn't really what you could call a brawl. More of a scuffle between Larkin and a couple other men. McT miners, if it matters."

"What matters, to me, is that you put the ruffian behind bars as a result. But then you released him again after only a short time."

"That's right. Larkin wasn't the one who started

that fight; all he did was defend himself. There were no grounds for keeping him in jail."

"No grounds?" Spots of color appeared in Emory's cheeks and his muddy brown eyes sparked with a hint of his old fire. "The man is a thief and a betrayer of great trust! He's an ex-con come back seeking revenge and to make trouble—as he immediately proved only minutes after crossing the city limits line. What more in the way of 'grounds' do you need, for God's sake?"

"More than that, I'm afraid," Bob said, straining to keep his voice calm. "I can't arrest a man for what he *might* do. And as far as him being an ex-con, that's exactly right. The important part is the 'ex'—he served his time for what he did and was officially released for good behavior."

"That's absurd!" Emory huffed. "His sentence was never adequate to begin with."

"It was the ruling of a judge and jury. That's all I know."

Emory's mouth formed a thin, straight line and he didn't say anything for a long minute.

They were quite a ways out of town by now. The prairie spread on all sides, the green of new grass and even the faded, gold-brown remains from last year awash in bright sunlight. Up ahead, a tall, wide, flat-topped rock formation—a butte—thrust up like a lonely sentinel.

"Would you like to circle the butte as usual, sir?" Graedon asked over his shoulder.

"Yes. Yes, that would be fine," Emory said rather absently.

"Very good, sir."

Emory looked like he was ready to return to his silent stewing but then, abruptly, he motioned ahead and said to Bob, "Do you know the story of that butte up there?"

"No, I don't guess I do."

"The Indians had a legend about it. It doesn't get told much today. Maybe that's a good thing, but I think it's sad. We drove all the Indians out, seems we at least ought to hang on to some of their lore."

Emory's voice took on a wistfulness as he continued. "Long ago, according to the legend, there were two Indian tribes fighting over this land and the vast herds of buffalo that roamed here. They warred back and forth for years. During a particular battle, the braves of one of the tribes were decimated to a very small number and cut off from any escape except to clamber to the high ground on top of that butte. From there, they were able to hold off the superior number of the other tribe.

"But as you can imagine, that was only a very limited victory. It quickly became clear that they were trapped there. The braves on top of the butte could hold off the other tribe as long as they had the strength to fight, but without food or water they would eventually grow too weak to hold their ground or perhaps even perish of starvation. Their choices were to surrender, or possibly fling themselves from the high rocks rather than that, or try to fight their way back off the butte knowing they would certainly be slaughtered by the larger opposing force waiting at the bottom . . . They chose the latter," Emory concluded, "and were indeed slaughtered to the last man. But the fight they made of it so inspired the rest of their tribe that they rose up with great determination and ferocity and at last drove their enemies away forever. Afterwards, the butte came to be known as Massacre Butte and the legend of the great battle there was passed down through generations."

"Quite a story," Bob said.

"Not a pleasant one, I fear. I suppose that's why, when the settlers came to the area, they quit retelling it and also stopped referring to the spot as Massacre Butte. Now it has no name at all, as far as I know. And that, as I said, seems sadder to me than maintaining the rather bloody legend."

"But there's something more," said Bob, regarding Emory closely, "that gives it a special meaning to you."

The old man met his eyes. "You are a very discerning man, Marshal," he said.

"I try to be."

They had begun skirting around the butte. The sun, only an hour past its noon peak, poured straight down, creating minimal shadows in the seams that ran up and down the sides or among the rubble of boulders around its base. This served to enhance the streaks of color—reddish-brown, hints of pink, gold, yellow—that ran all throughout the high-reaching rock slabs.

"Right there. The coloring," Emory said. "That's what gives this place a special meaning to me. More to the point, it's what was so appealing to my late wife. She loved riding out here on sunny days or sometimes at sunset to watch the way the colors came out of the rocks. She was another one who hated hearing that old Indian legend, wouldn't let me speak of it, but she savored seeing the way the sun paints the rocks and never tired of coming out here to see it. Since she's been gone . . . well, on the infrequent occasions I leave the house, I still like to return."

"It's understandable—both why your wife liked coming here and why you like coming back," Bob said. "I must have ridden in sight of here a dozen times and never paid much attention. Saw it as just a pile of rocks. Now I know better. I'm pretty sure it's something my wife would appreciate seeing sometime, too."

"Yes, you should bring her out. That's what life is all about, Marshal. Family. Lasting memories from the special moments you spend with those you cherish the most." As he spoke, Emory was gazing up at the butte, but somehow Bob knew he was seeing something more, something beyond.

Abruptly, the old man turned his head and looked very directly at Bob. "That's my real concern where John Larkin is concerned. I don't dispute that the man has served his time and deserves another chance to get his life straight. But what I fear—what I cannot accept—is for his actions to bring any more pain to me and my family. I was once ready to accept that ungrateful pup as a son, a husband to my daughter. But he chose instead to betray me and break her heart. He'll not affect me any further, you can be certain of that. But my daughter, Victoria, I'm not so sure about. I've little doubt he still has intentions toward her. I won't stand for him intruding into her life and her happiness any more than he already has!"

"That's understandable," Bob allowed.

"Then what do you intend to do to stop him?"

Bob hesitated, looking to formulate the right answer—one that would address Emory's concerns while at the same time stating the legal limitations when it came to preventing Larkin from at least making an attempt to see Victoria. To do this without setting off the old man's anger all over again was the tricky part.

But, all of a sudden, none of that mattered so much.

What mattered was the bullet that came sizzling in and cut a slash across the top of the backrest smack between the heads of Bob and Emory! The boom of a rifle report came an instant later, sounding from among the boulders clustered around the base of Massacre Butte.

Bob's Colt was immediately gripped in one fist while, with his other hand, he was grabbing Jackson Emory and yanking him down lower in the cushiony seat. Another bullet cut the air just above their heads, followed by another jarring boom.

"We're being shot at, Graedon," Bob hollered. "Put the whip to that horse and get us the hell out of here!"

The buggy jolted into motion at an increased speed. Graedon's whip cracked above the tail of the sleek black gelding in the harness and the animal responded by breaking into long, smooth strides.

Bob twisted around in his seat and peered cautiously over the backrest, looking for some sign of the shooter. He caught a momentary glimpse of a telltale wisp of gunsmoke hanging above the low boulders, though the range was questionable for return fire from his pistol. But in a matter of seconds, the horse's pounding hooves and the churning wheels of the buggy kicked up a dust cloud from the dry ground under the prairie grass that boiled around the rear of the rig and obscured his vision of the spot.

But no more shots came their way. And, as Graedon veered them away from the butte and made a wide loop back toward town, no riders appeared in pursuit. Just to make sure, however, Bob remained vigilant, peering over the backrest with his Colt held at the ready while keeping Emory down low in his seat until they were well clear.

CHAPTER 23

On the outskirts of town, Graedon reined the buggy to a halt. He quickly hopped down and came around to the side. Bob was more than a little surprised to see a short-barreled, nickel-plated revolver gripped in Graedon's hand when he first hit the ground. The manservant quickly returned the weapon to a shoulder holster under his coat, however, and then both he and Bob got Emory situated upright in his seat again and checked to make sure the frail old man hadn't been too badly shaken up by being shoved low or by the rough ride that followed. Judging by the string of epithets Emory began spewing toward whoever had shot at them, he was feeling more pissed off than hurt.

"Who was that bushwhacking bastard who opened up on us back there?" he demanded.

"That's what I'd like to know," Bob answered. "All I saw was a telltale sign of gunsmoke from over in the rocks around the bottom of the butte. Being exposed out in the open like we were, we couldn't afford to stick around to try and get a better look. Graedon did a good job of getting us out of there and luckily there was no pursuit."

"He was a yellowbellied damn coward whoever it was." Emory scowled fiercely. "You figure it was somebody out to get even with you, Marshal?"

"I've made some enemies over the years, no denying that," Bob allowed. "But most of them are either in the ground or behind bars. The ones still running loose are nowhere in this area, not as far as I know. And even if they are, they'd have no way of expecting I'd be taking a buggy ride out close to that butte in order to be laying in wait for me there."

"So what are you saying?" Graedon asked.

Bob thumbed back the brim of his hat. "Well, I guess I'm thinking maybe the question needs to be turned back on Mr. Emory . . . Do you have any enemies, sir, or anybody wanting to get even with you badly enough to take a potshot at you?"

Emory's scowl tightened even more. "You don't reach my level of success and wealth without throwing some sharp elbows and making some enemies along the way. Especially not in a tough business like mining. But those days are mostly behind me. Ever since the accident, I haven't been . . . well, either as ambitious or aggressive. It's been years since I've clashed with anyone who'd be likely to harbor enough ill will toward me to try and kill me." He paused. The scowl left his face but his expression remained no less intense as he fixed Bob with a very direct gaze before adding, "With perhaps one exception."

Bob knew who he was talking about, of course. He

hated to put it into words but it loomed too large to try and step around. "John Larkin, you mean."

"Who else? So you admit to seeing it the same way?"

"I admit nothing. I was simply stating my recognition of what you were implying."

"It was more than an implication. It was a conclusion, and not a very hard one to reach."

"That might be one way of looking at it," Bob said. "But here's another: First of all, it's almost *too* obvious. A day after he hits town he goes after you? And for what purpose? You weren't on the jury that sentenced him, you brought no evidence against him. You were caught in the middle as much as anybody. And if Larkin continues to have designs on your daughter, as you believe he does, how would killing you—knowing he'd surely be a suspect—stand the chance of gaining him anything in that regard? What's more, how would he know to be laying an ambush out there at the butte any more than one of my past enemies would?"

"You sound like a defense lawyer for Larkin."

"I'm just pointing out some facts as I see them. The key, it seems to me, is that butte and how somebody—anybody—would know to be there waiting for either one of us."

"When we take our buggy rides, sir, a trip out to the butte *is* a rather common thing," remarked Graedon.

Emory shot him a *who's side are you on?* glare. "When we left the house today," he argued, "I had no intention of visiting that damned butte. My sole purpose was finding the marshal and having a discussion with him. It was a last-minute decision to ride out there—made only after I saw what a fine afternoon, weather-wise, it was shaping up to be."

"Nevertheless," Bob said, "your trips out there are enough of a pattern for somebody looking to gun you to consider as a possible opportunity for catching you under pretty vulnerable conditions."

"It still could be Larkin," Emory insisted. "He could remember how my wife and I used to enjoy riding out that way and have taken a chance on me still doing so."

Starting to get impatient, Bob said, "With all due respect, sir, you're being so mule-headed about *wanting* it to be Larkin that you've got blinders on to any other possibility. How would he even know you were taking a buggy ride of any kind today, let alone guess where you might be headed? If I were you, I'd start giving some consideration to those who are part of a tighter circle around you."

"And if I were you," Emory snapped back, "I'd give some serious consideration to being less rude to well-established citizens of your community and concentrate instead on the known criminal element."

"That's exactly what I intend to do," Bob told him. "As soon as we're back in town, I'll be sending out my two young deputies—who are as good trackers as any around—to examine that butte and see if they can pick up the trail of whoever the shooter was. While they're doing that, I'll be pinning down Larkin to see if he can prove his whereabouts over the past hour or so."

Bob paused for a moment, took a breath to try and calm himself some. But his teeth were still clenched when he continued. "That's more of an explanation than I owe you or am in the habit of giving. But since you *were* involved in the shooting and you *are* a highly regarded citizen of our town, I'm making an exception. I'll keep you posted if me or my men turn up anything pertinent. I expect you to do the same in return, in case you find out or think of anything useful. Now, all we're accomplishing here is wasting time. Get us back into town, Graedon, and drop me off at the jail."

CHAPTER 24

"So that's the way it's gonna be, eh? Every time somebody farts crossways in this town and the stink drifts in the direction of Emory, I'm gonna get hauled in for questioning. Is that it?"

"Nobody's hauling you anywhere," Bob pointed out to an indignant and overly defensive John Larkin. "I came here without making a big fuss and put it to you straight, simply asking if you could account for your whereabouts the past couple of hours. I can't help it if it ruffles your feathers—all things considered, it's a logical inquiry for me to make."

"Well, you got your answer. I been right here all morning."

"And I can vouch for that, Marshal," interjected Earl Hines. "John's been working at my side the whole time. We haven't even taken a break for lunch yet."

The three men were standing in Hines's blacksmith shop. Both Hines and Larkin were clad in leather aprons and each bore streaks of sweat and soot on their faces. Larkin had shaved off his beard since Bob saw him last, and the flush in his cheeks stood out in sharp contrast to the paleness of his skin.

When Bob had first entered the shop, Hines had been fashioning a piece of red-hot metal clamped in a pair of tongs while Larking was working a bellows to keep the forge superheated. Upon seeing this and comparing it to a mental calculation of how long it would take for someone to make it back from Massacre Butte, even riding full out, it seemed pretty clear that Larkin couldn't have been the shooter out there. Nevertheless, Bob had felt it best to go ahead and make his inquiry in order to remove any doubt.

"Reckon that gives me what I came to find out," he said now, accepting Hines's word as all the verification he needed. "I'll go ahead and leave you fellas to your work."

"Wait a minute," said Larkin. "What about the old man? Does *he* think I'm the one who did that shooting?"

"Your name came up," Bob confirmed. "With you fresh back in town, that shouldn't really come as a surprise."

"That's not fair, damn it! He can't go around making accusations like that."

"It wasn't exactly an accusation. Like I said, your name came up. Emory raised the question of the shooter possibly being you, that's all."

"No offense, Marshal, but what about you?" Hines asked. "You've surely made some enemies in your time. Isn't it possible—maybe even *more* likely—that shot could have been meant for you?"

"Possible, yes," Bob admitted. "That's why I mean to ask all the questions I can think of. Nobody's singling out just you, Larkin. All I know for sure is that somebody took a shot at the buggy Emory and I were riding in, and I mean to get to the bottom of it. Hell, maybe they were aiming at Graedon, the driver. Before I'm through, I may be chasing that line of inquiry."

Larkin scowled. "When you talk to Emory again, tell him this: I got no grudge or any kind of hard feelings against him. He got flimflammed by that whole business four years ago same as me. With all the lies and the false evidence planted against me, I don't blame him for believing I betrayed him . . . But I didn't. You tell him that."

Bob started to turn away but then halted. "What about his daughter?" he asked.

Larkin's scowl deepened. "Victoria, you mean? What about her?"

"Don't you want to convince her of those same things as far as your innocence?"

Larkin's gaze dropped. "I'd like nothing better," he muttered. "But I doubt I've got a chance of getting anywhere near her to tell her anything."

"No. Not if her father has his way, you don't," Bob said. "But that's for you to work out. Nobody can stop you from trying to see her. While we're on the subject, though, I may as well warn you that if she *doesn't* want to see you and you push it too hard . . . well, me and you will probably need to have another chat."

"Okay. You've made yourself clear." Larkin's face lifted and his scowl was back. "Weren't you on your way someplace else?"

* * *

Before returning to the jail, Bob swung by Peterson's Livery to see if anyone with a horse boarded there had ridden out in the past two or three hours and, if so, had they returned yet? Or, he also asked, had anybody come in on a hard-ridden animal within the past half hour?

"Been pretty dead around here all mornin'," Joe Peterson told him, "except for your two deputies ridin' out a little while ago. And they ain't come back yet."

"No, I don't expect 'em to return for a while."

"Some kind of trouble goin' on, Marshal?" Joe asked. "I saw you rollin' past at a pretty good clip with Jackson Emory in his buggy not too long ago. You usually see his driver movin' the old fella around mighty slow and careful."

"I guess they were in a hurry to get me back to the jail," said Bob, not exactly lying. "Listen, Joe, just keep your eyes peeled for anybody on a hard-ridden horse like I described, okay? Anybody like that comes around in the next half hour or so—or even if you just see 'em ridin' by in the street, comin' from the south—you let me know, okay?"

"Any luck?" Fred asked when Bob got back to the jail.

Bob shook his head. "Not so's you could notice it."

The marshal sank down in the chair behind his desk. Fred poured him a cup of coffee and brought it over.

"There's still hope that Peter and Vern might turn up something. They're awful good trackers," Fred said.

"Yeah, they are. That's why I sent 'em out."

Fred went back over to the stove and poured himself a half-cup of coffee. Turning back, he said, "So Larkin had a good alibi, eh?"

"Pretty solid by my standards," said Bob. "Earl Hines vouched that Larkin was with him in his shop all morning. Plus, time-wise, there just plain wasn't enough time for Larkin to have gotten back from the butte and be there in Earl's shop when I walked in."

Fred took a drink of his coffee, then said, "I know this probably ain't the right thing for me to say, being a law officer and all. But I'm kinda glad Larkin checked out okay."

Bob grinned wryly. "Yeah, I know. Because he's so doggone likable. Right?"

"You feel that way, too?" Fred asked, a little eagerly.

"No, I can't say as I do," Bob answered. "To tell the truth, the times I've talked with him have been a little contentious. But I keep hearing this 'likable' business from so many other folks—with the exception of Jackson Emory, that is—it's bound to rub off sooner or later."

"Well. One step at a time, I guess," allowed Fred. "For now, like I said, I'm just glad it didn't pan out there was any question Larkin might've been the one who took that shot."

"Maybe so. Trouble is, it still leaves the question of who *did* take it . . . and who it was meant for."

Fred frowned. "I got the impression you were

kinda locked on the notion that it most likely was aimed at Emory."

"Most likely, yeah. But only because I can't see how anybody gunning for me would know to be waiting for me out at that damned butte."

"Any chance they might've followed you out?"

Bob shook his head. "Mighty slim. It's wide open out that way. You can see for a mile in any direction. Even though I wasn't necessarily looking for any sign of trouble, I'm pretty sure I would have noticed somebody fogging us."

"Hey," said Fred, his eyebrows lifting. "It looks like we've got what's shaping up to be a genuine mystery on our hands."

"For crying out loud," Bob groaned. "Only you would find a cheerful side to something like this. Did it occur to you that the other end of your 'mystery'— unless or until we get to the bottom of it—is the shooter making another try, only this time maybe not missing?"

Fred spread his hands. "All the more reason for us to be clever enough to expose the mystery shooter before he strikes again."

Bob groaned some more.

And then the front door opened and he had even added reason to groan when he saw who was entering.

CHAPTER 25

"Ah, Marshal. I'm glad I caught you in," declared Owen Dutton, sweeping the door closed behind him. "And, of course, you too, Deputy Ordway."

"This ain't a particularly good time," Bob was quick to say. "We're pretty busy with some things right now."

"I should expect so," Dutton responded. "An ex-con returning to town with revenge on his mind, a fierce saloon brawl, the attempted murder of one of the town's most prominent citizens—all within the space of less than twenty-four hours. Yes, I can well imagine how that qualifies for giving you a very busy agenda."

"Now wait a minute. You can't—" Fred started to say before Bob cut him off.

"We've already been through that vengeance-seeking ex-con crap," Bob said through clenched teeth. "I thought we had it put behind us."

Dutton shook his head. "We may have placed it on hold. But it was never pushed out of the picture completely, not the way I saw it. And certainly not now that a veritable crime wave has erupted within minutes of Larkin's arrival."

Bob couldn't believe his ears. "Oh, for Christ's sake, Dutton. A 'crime wave'? A saloon scuffle and a potshot taken miles outside the city limits you call a crime wave?"

"I ran into Jackson Emory and his driver a little while ago out on the street. No matter where that 'potshot,' as you call it, took place, it nevertheless had them rattled. And rightfully so, I would say."

"I'm not arguing the things you spouted off didn't happen. I'm just saying it's a pretty big stretch to call them a crime wave."

"Very well. For the time being, I'll just call them facts," Dutton replied rather haughtily. "But they are facts my readers deserve to hear—and will. And, after I've printed them, I'll let said readers and the citizens of this town decide for themselves what to call them."

"Yeah. And you'll be sure to help them make up their minds by cramming your reports with every sensational detail and insinuation you can come up with, won't you?"

"That may be the way you choose to see it, but I still call them facts," Dutton insisted. "Now, if you're still too busy to spare me any of your time, I'll have no choice but to begin preparing my articles with the information I have. If you have anything to add that you think might alter my perceptions, then I'd suggest you make time to talk with me."

"Remember the other day when we were arguing about this little pipsqueak and I was defending him?"

Fred said to Bob. "Okay, now I think I'm coming around to seeing things your way."

"About time," Bob muttered.

"So," Fred continued, "you want me to hold the door open while you escort him out by the scruff of his neck? Or would you like me to just go ahead and take care of it for you?"

"You wouldn't dare!" huffed Dutton.

"Hold it," said Bob as Fred started for the newspaperman. Then, pinning the latter with a distasteful look, he added, "I'm gonna go ahead and spare you some of our time. But for one reason only. I mean to set you straight on your so-called facts and see to it you don't unjustly smear Larkin the way you're setting out to do."

"I have no problem with that," Dutton replied as he settled onto the chair in front of Bob's desk and took out his pencil and pad of paper. "If you can make a convincing case, then that's the way I'll write it. No matter what you think, I'm not predisposed to smearing Larkin. But surely you can see where the man's arrival followed almost immediately by these other incidents makes for an awfully strong dose of coincidence to try and swallow."

Bob nodded. "I'll grant you that. Nobody distrusts coincidences more than lawmen. But suspicion about them can't be taken for fact, either." From the middle drawer of his desk, the marshal pulled a rectangular log bound in cheap imitation leather. This pushed across the desktop toward Dutton, saying, "There's the log my deputies and I keep on the various things that happen around town—the ones that amount to anything, I should say—where we get involved. If you open it to the ribbon marker, you'll see the most recent entries.

"The near-lynching I broke up out at the Rocking W is there. Also the run-in I had the following day, here in town, with Smoky Barnett and a couple other Rocking W men. And then there are the details on the fight—and I say 'fight,' not a 'fierce brawl'—that took place at the Grand last night involving Larkin and three McT miners. But you'll note that Larkin is only mentioned in passing and was *not* held overnight on disorderly conduct charges like the others. That's because, based on the testimony of Grand owner Roy Cormier as well as the miners themselves, it was determined that Larkin was only defending himself and had nothing to do with starting the trouble."

As he scanned the log entries open before him, Dutton's heavy brows furrowed above the spectacles that had slid down to teeter precariously on the tip of his nose.

"You won't find any entry for the shooting that occurred just a little while ago," Bob went on, "because I haven't had the chance to make one yet. The way things stand right now, the only thing I *could* write down is that persons unknown took two shots at Jackson Emory and me while we were riding in his buggy out south of town, near a spot known as Massacre Butte . . . Oh, yeah, the one thing more I could add is that I've determined the shooter wasn't John Larkin. I found him working with Earl Hines in the blacksmith shop right after I returned to town—too soon for him to have made it back from the butte if he'd been the one who took those shots. Plus Hines vouched for Larkin having been with him in the shop all morning."

"If not Larkin, then who would have had reason to try and shoot Emory?" Dutton asked.

"That's a good question," Bob replied. "Unfortunately, at this point I have no good answer—not even a decent guess."

"And," Fred interjected, "we can't even say for certain that Emory's who the shot was meant for."

Dutton's eyebrows lifted. "I never thought of that. No doubt someone in your position has made enemies, Marshal. But none in particular come to mind?"

"None that seem likely."

"What about the gunman Ed Wardell supposedly has hired?"

Bob shook his head. "I can't see that as a fit. Number one, it's awful soon for anybody he sent for to even have arrived in the area yet. Number two, even though Wardell has some differences with me and might get around to siccing his gunny on me eventually, the main reason he's bringing a man is for his alleged rustling problem. Seems like that'd be his first priority."

"So what does that leave?" Dutton wanted to know. "With no idea who the shooter was and not even knowing for sure who he was aiming at, do you just wait for him to try again?"

"It might come to that," Bob admitted. "I've got two deputies out now trying to pick up any sign the ambusher might have left when he came or went from the butte. Barring any luck with that, we don't really have much else to go on."

Dutton closed the report log and leaned back in

his chair. He reached up and readjusted his glasses. In a more subdued tone than before, he said, "It appears you once again have saved me from my hastiness to jump to some wrong—or at least premature—conclusions, Marshal."

"That's good to hear."

Dutton tapped the log. "Seems like this would be a worthwhile thing for me to check from time to time, to make sure I've got my facts straight. Going forward, can I presume it will be made available to me again?"

"It's a matter of public record," Fred answered. "We got nothing to hide."

Dutton put away his notepad and pencil, then placed the report log back on the desk. Standing, he said, "Speaking of hiding," he said to Bob, "with the shooter unidentified and neither you nor Mr. Emory certain which of you was the target, I trust you will be taking some very strict precautions in the days ahead?"

"If my deputies don't succeed in picking up the shooter's trail, yeah, I'll call on Emory and not only recommend he takes precautions but try to work out some protective arrangement to help make sure he does so. As for me, there's not a hell of a lot I can do different. I'll keep alert, keep extra sharp. I can't very well stay home and hide. When a fella puts on one of these"—Bob tapped a thumb against the badge pinned to his shirt—"you go out every day facing the possibility of it making a nice shiny target for some skunk who might not see eye to eye with the law—just naturally comes with the territory."

CHAPTER 26

The spacious parlor of the Emory home was well appointed without being overly extravagant. The furnishings had an equal mix of masculine and feminine touches, ranging from dark wood trim and an elk's head with a truly magnificent rack mounted over the fireplace to colorful bits of bric-a-brac placed here and there, overstuffed silken pillows on a long chesterfield, and an elaborately carved china hutch against one wall.

Already present when Bob was ushered in by Graedon were Emory, his two daughters, and Saul Norton. Emory was seated in a high-backed leather chair near the fireplace, the ladies occupied the chesterfield, and Norton stood at the end nearest Victoria, his hand resting on the backrest just above her shoulder. The pose, Bob thought, seemed to convey—either intentionally or perhaps just by chance—a message of possession. *This girl is spoken for, and she is mine.*

"I am pleased, albeit a bit surprised, to have you stopping by so soon after our little adventure earlier this afternoon," greeted Emory. He still wore the tie, white shirt, and trousers from before, but gone were the slouch hat and suit coat. In place of the latter he had on an unbuttoned knit sweater. "Could it be you are here to report some positive news on the identity and/or purpose of the cowardly dog who attempted the ambush on us?"

Bob shook his head. "Sorry. I wish that was the case. But I'm afraid it's just the opposite—every early lead we've attempted to follow has come up empty."

"That's rather surprising," said Norton. "The only lead you need to bother following at all is the one that leads directly to John Larkin. How difficult can that be?"

He was a tall, even-featured man—classically hand-some, many would be inclined to call him—of about forty. Solidly built, with a good set of shoulders and big hands that looked to have done some hard work in their time though not any time recently, and dark, wide-set eyes bracketed by neatly trimmed sideburns showing faint streaks of gray. He wore tan work trousers, a brown corduroy jacket, and a pale blue shirt with a black string tie. In the hand that wasn't resting on the back of the chesterfield, he was hold-ing a chunky glass of amber liquid.

"Following the lead to Larkin wasn't difficult at all," Bob replied evenly. "But getting it to yield any-thing that provided any kind of answer to the shoot-ing turned out to be another matter. Larkin had a rock-solid alibi for the time of the attempted ambush—for all day up to the time I spoke with him, as far as that goes."

"Isn't that just the way for a lowdown crook?"

Norton sneered. "Always make sure they have their ass covered with a good alibi." Right after the words were out, he clapped his mouth shut tight and a flush of color spread up over his face. Cutting his eyes to the sisters, he quickly said, "I beg your pardon for my coarse language, ladies. It's just that the thought of your father coming so close to harm and the certainty down deep in my gut of who's responsible has got me boiling almost uncontrollably inside. I want to go after the dirty coward with my bare hands!"

Victoria reached over her shoulder and placed her hand on Norton's, the one on the backrest behind her. "Calm yourself, Saul. Take some deep breaths, take another drink if you need to. We all know Marshal Hatfield to be very competent at his job; we must trust his handling of this."

She spoke with a soothing, well-modulated voice that seemed perfectly fitted to her graceful beauty. In her late twenties, slim and very poised in her bearing and movements, Victoria Emory was quite a stunning creature. She had glossy hair the color of rich cherrywood, porcelain skin, ripe red lips, and blue-green eyes. The dress she wore was a simple, full-skirted affair with three-quarter-length sleeves and a snug bodice that revealed her figure to be trim yet possessing no shortage of womanly curves.

"Thanks for the vote of confidence," Bob replied to her remarks. Then, shifting his gaze to Norton, he said, "And the last thing anybody needs is for you to lose your temper and try to confront Larkin. Trust me, it won't help. There's a good chance it'll only make matters worse and you may run the risk of getting yourself in trouble."

"You defend Larkin but warn *me* about getting in trouble?" said Norton, stiffening to his full height, pulling his hand out from under Victoria's. "That takes a lot of gall, don't you think?"

Before Bob could respond, Emory said softly but forcefully, "That's enough, Saul."

Once again Norton clamped his mouth tightly shut. It was obvious he was still simmering and had more he wanted to say, but he held his tongue.

Now it was the younger sister, Brenda, who spoke up, saying, "Enough indeed. Enough of treating Marshal Hatfield like he's some sort of intruder, an unwelcome guest in our house. We haven't even offered him a seat . . . or perhaps something to drink?"

Three or four years younger than Victoria, Brenda was also very attractive but in a different, more subdued kind of way. No doubt to her frustration, she was likely still referred to on occasion as being "cute" rather than lovely or beautiful. She had the same delicate facial features and full lips, but her nose was slightly pugged, with a dusting of stubborn freckles across the bridge. Her hair was also red, though more of a rust shade, and she had her father's brown eyes. She gave the impression of having been a bit of a tomboy in her younger years, but there was nothing boyish about the way she filled out the otherwise demure dress she wore.

Replying to her, Bob said, "No thanks to a drink, miss, and I'm fine with standing. Also I understand that I am an intruder of sorts, coming here when all of you are still trying to digest something as troubling as your father being shot at. I wish I had better news to offer as far as being able to identify who was behind it and what their motive might have been."

"What about the deputies you were going to send out to try and pick up the trail of the ambusher?" Emory wanted to know.

Bob shook his head. "No luck. They found the spot the shooter fired from, and they found a couple of spent .44-40 cartridges, a caliber common to fifty or sixty percent of the weapons to be found in these parts. But when it came to spotting a trail left by whoever fired those shots, the spring grass out that way is too thick for them to have been able to pick up anything."

Brenda's pretty face pulled into a thoughtful expression. "Why is everyone so certain those shots were meant for my father?" she asked. "Isn't it equally possible—maybe even probable—that they could have been aimed at you, Marshal? In your line of work you deal with miscreants and outlaws all the time, don't you? Haven't you left behind some of that sort who harbor ill feelings toward you?"

"More than I care to think about," Bob admitted. "Trouble is, there are none who seem logical for this particular time and place. But that don't mean I'm not still giving that possibility some consideration. In the meantime, though, there's something else that also deserves consideration. In fact, it's the main reason I came here."

"What are you getting at?" Norton said.

"What I'm getting at is the fact that whoever took those shots today missed," said Bob.

"Thank God!" exclaimed Victoria.

Bob nodded curtly. "Yes. But if whoever it was had

reason enough to try once, then we have to figure he still has reason to try again. And since God might be busy with something else next time, I'm suggesting you take it on yourself to exercise some precautions, Mr. Emory."

"What kind of precautions?" Emory said, scowling.

"Nothing overly elaborate. Since you don't venture out of the house very much anyway, that would be the main thing right there. Make sure you keep inside, stay away from the windows, simple measures like that."

The old man's scowl deepened. "Make myself a prisoner in my own home, you mean? Incarcerated by a yellow scoundrel, by something that only *might* happen?"

"Father, you seldom go out as it is," Victoria pointed out gently.

"And nobody's talking forever," Bob was quick to add. "Just short term, just until me and my deputies have a chance to get to the bottom of this."

"But what about your own safety—in case it's you the shooter was aiming at?" Brenda said.

"I can take care of myself. It comes with the job," Bob told her.

"Protecting the citizens of this town also comes with your job," said Norton, doing a pretty good job of scowling himself. "If you think Mr. Emory is in danger, isn't it up to you and your deputies to keep him safe?"

"It is," Bob allowed. "And we'll do everything we can to keep a close eye on things around here. But there's a limit to how much attention we can focus on one person. All I'm suggesting is that Mr. Emory—and all of you here—work with us."

Emory bobbed his head in a single nod. "That's not unreasonable."

"Father employs armed guards out at the mine," Brenda said. "Might it be a good idea to station one of them around here for the time being?"

"I don't know that it's necessary to turn your home into an armed camp," said Bob. "But that's up to you. If they're competent men—"

"They are or they wouldn't be in our employ," Norton interjected.

"If they're competent," Bob continued without acknowledging him, "and you *do* make that decision, all I ask is that you be sure and let me know. Since my men will also be patrolling by here regularly, I'll want them aware so they can act accordingly."

"I don't think we need to go to quite that extreme," said Emory. "We naturally have some weapons of our own in the house. And there's also Graedon. With his background, he's more than a common manservant."

"Yes, I noticed the gun he was ready to use out on the prairie this afternoon," remarked Bob.

"He has a background both in the military and as a big-city police officer," Emory explained. "If the need arises, he can function very effectively as a bodyguard."

Norton looked surprised. "I wasn't aware of that."

"Well, now you are," Emory replied rather stiffly.

"Something else occurs to me, Marshal," spoke up Victoria. "Not to sound overly melodramatic, but if someone is out to harm Father, there could be other, more indirect ways to do that. Do you think my sister or I may be in any danger?"

Bob's expression sobered nearly to the point of turning grim. "I'm not ready to discount anything. If the target is me instead of your father, then the same could be true for my family. But whichever of us he was after, my gut says whoever took those shots earlier was out to kill, not looking to harm indirectly."

"It's unthinkable to believe otherwise!" hissed Emory.

Bob shook his head. "Like I said, we still shouldn't discount anything. Yet, at the same time, there's realistically only so much we can do. It all comes down to keeping on guard and staying sharp at all times."

"That I can manage," stated Brenda. "But, speaking for myself, what I won't agree to is putting my life on hold and being cooped up—hiding out from the mere possibility of danger."

"There's such a thing as being *too* headstrong," her father warned her.

"I can't help it, Father. That's the way I feel."

"You're a woman grown. It's your call," Bob said. "Just try to have the sense to take some precautions like I suggested."

CHAPTER 27

That night, the quiet evening Bob had planned to spend at home with his family once again got interrupted by violence in town. Supper was over, the dishes were done and put away, and Bob, Consuela, and Bucky were seated around the kitchen table playing cribbage when a heavy knock rattled the front door.

It was Stan Brewster, a clerk at Krepdorf's General Store, bringing word that Bob was wanted as soon as possible at Doc Tibbs's office. That's where they were taking Saul Norton, Brewster explained, after he'd been found beaten to a bloody pulp in an alley beside Bullock's Saloon. Because he happened to be present when the discovery was made, playing cards and having a few drinks inside, Brewster had been sent to fetch the marshal.

Taking time only to strap on his gunbelt and express his regrets to Consuela and Bucky, Bob was out the door in a matter of minutes.

When he got to the doctor's office, he found a small knot of men gathered there. A few were standing outside, a few more were inside, in the waiting area that adjoined the examining room. The inside group consisted of deputies Peter and Vern Macy, Mike Bullock, and Earl Hines.

"What happened?" Bob asked.

"The doc's got Saul Norton in there," Peter said, tipping his head toward the closed door that led to the examining room. "Somebody jumped him outside of Bullock's, dragged him into the alley, and pure stomped the living hell out of him. He's busted up real bad."

"Any idea who or why?"

Peter tipped his head again, this time toward Earl Hines. "Hines there is the one who found him. I'll let him tell it."

When Bob's eyes cut to him, Hines straightened a little in his stance and cleared his throat. "I was inside the saloon, having a few drinks and chatting with Maudie. When she was ready to take a break, we stepped outside to catch some fresh air. We'd no sooner sat down on one of the boardwalk benches there in front than I heard a sound coming from the alley along the south side. It was a long groan, or moan maybe you'd call it. Anyway, I listened and when I heard it again I got up and went to check it out. I found a man, just barely conscious, laying about half a dozen yards in from the mouth of the alley. I lit a match to see better. It was Saul Norton and, like the deputy said, it was pretty clear he'd had the holy hell beat out of him."

"Was he able to say anything? Give any clue why he was attacked—or by who?"

Hines glanced uneasily at the others in the room,

then his eyes came back to Bob. "He claimed it was John."

"Larkin?"

Hines nodded.

"Have you followed up on that?" Bob asked his deputies.

"Just like last time," Vern answered, "once Larkin's name came into it, we figured you'd want to hear about this right away. We helped carry Norton over here and put him in the doc's hands. Nobody outside this room heard Larkin mentioned as being any part of it. Knowing you were on the way, we decided to wait and see how you wanted to play it. You want us to haul him to the jail for questioning, or do you want to be part of going after him?"

"That I do," said Bob. He turned once more to Hines. "Any idea where we'll find Larkin?"

"Far as I know, he's back at my place. My apartment over the shop," Hines said. "That's where I left him about an hour and a half ago. When I told him I meant to go over to Bullock's for a few drinks and some socializing, he said he wasn't interested. Said he'd just stay in tonight."

"Apparently he changed his mind," muttered Peter. "Apparently he decided to go out and do a little socializing of his own."

Mike Bullock spoke up. "Did Norton say he got a good enough look to be sure it was Larkin? As dark as it is in that narrow alley, tight between the buildings, how could he be positive?"

Hines frowned. "He was barely conscious and hurtin' bad. He only muttered a couple words . . . 'Larkin,' he said. Then: 'Getting even' . . . That's all."

"He mumbled a couple more things when we were picking him up to bring him here," said Peter. "But nothing anybody could understand."

"So it stays with Larkin as being the best we got to go on," Bob said. "We've got to go talk to him."

"Can I go along?" asked Hines. "Maybe I can . . . Look, I don't want John to react badly to still another accusation by the law, okay? If I'm there to help explain maybe it will also help . . . I just don't want tempers to flare and things get out of hand, all right?"

"We're not going there to accuse, we're just going with some questions," Peter said.

"And if Larkin's done nothing wrong, then why the worry about his temper flaring?" added Vern.

"It's probably none of my business," said Bullock. "But I think it would be a good idea if Earl *did* go along."

"You're right, it's none of your business," Bob told him. "But I'll agree to letting Hines come—as long as he keeps his place and follows my lead."

"You got my word on that," Hines responded.

Hines's apartment over the blacksmith shop was accessible by means of an inside stairwell and also by an outside set of steps angling up the side of the building. Inasmuch as the shop was buttoned up for the night, Hines led them up the outer stairs. There was enough moon- and starlight pouring down from a clear sky to provide adequate illumination.

Bob and Peter followed Hines up the steps; Vern stayed below.

The apartment had two rooms: a large main space with a doorway on the back wall that led to a small bedroom. The bedroom door was closed. The main room was divided into a kitchen area at one end, complete with stove, table, chairs, and food cabinets; the other end was a parlor of sorts with a long, low couch and a couple easy chairs. The couch was made up as a bed with no sign of having been slept in recently. An open book lay facedown on the covers. On the kitchen table a coal oil lantern was burning low, but still providing a soft glow that filled the room.

There was no sign of John Larkin.

"Damn stupid of him to go out and leave the lantern burning," Hines grumbled.

Bob caught Peter's eye and jerked his chin toward the bedroom door.

Peter strode to the door and rapped his knuckles against it, calling, "Larkin?"

When there was no answer, he turned the knob and shoved the door open. Enough light poured into the darkness to show there was no one in there. Peter closed the door again.

Earl Hines went over to the lantern and twisted the wick up brighter. When he turned back to face the two lawmen, he wore a troubled, somewhat confused frown. "I hope you don't think I was giving you some kind of bum steer," he said. "John was here when I left and said he had no interest in going out. I guess he must've changed his mind. But where he took a notion to go I don't—"

The rest of the sentence was cut off by a voice floating up from outside, through the stairway door they'd left open upon entering.

"Hey, Marshal," Vern called. "We got something down here. You better come have a look."

"Bring that lantern," Bob said, starting for the door.

A minute later they were all back at the bottom of the outside steps. Vern was some distance away, standing at the back corner of the building, motioning them toward him.

When they reached Vern and followed him around the corner of the building, they found themselves facing a small corral where Hines sometimes kept a horse or two that he was getting ready to fit for new shoes. The corral was empty. Against the rear outer wall of the building some bales of straw had been placed. Sitting together on one of them, with a candle resting on the ground at their feet, were John Larkin . . . and Brenda Emory!

"What in tarnation is all the commotion about, Earl?" Larkin said, looking up at the sudden cluster of men, squinting slightly against the brightness of the lantern.

CHAPTER 28

In the darkness, lying in bed beside Bob, Consuela said, "So it was *Brenda* Emory who was able to provide him an alibi?" Her voice carried a note of incredulity.

"None other," Bob confirmed. "She claimed she was with him the whole while, from within just a few minutes of when Earl Hines left and went over to Bullock's. She saw Hines going out as she was coming down the street. When she got up to the apartment, Larkin didn't think it would be proper for the two of them to be alone there. So, it being a clear, warm night, he suggested they go down and have their visit in the corral area out back of the shop . . . That's where they still were when we found them."

"But I thought it was the older Emory sister, Victoria, who was Larkin's romantic interest before he got sent away to prison."

"It was," said Bob. "But while Victoria was quick to decide she no longer wanted anything to do with a convicted thief, apparently Brenda was like a lot of others and refused to believe Larkin was truly guilty of the charges brought against him. In fact, from talking with her tonight and even a little earlier, when I was at the Emory house, I got a hunch she had a sort of baby-sister crush on Larkin."

"*Had* . . . and perhaps still does?"

"Could be."

It was late when Bob got back home. Bucky was in bed asleep. Consuela had gone to bed, too, but was still awake when Bob came in and slipped under the covers beside her. As soon as she draped a slender arm over his chest, she could feel the tension in him. At times like this they often lay and talked. Consuela had proven to be an invaluable sounding board. Bob often told her this, and then would invariably add, "As if anybody as soft and curvy as you could ever be called any kind of board."

Continuing their discussion now, Consuela said, "Whatever her reasons, the fact Brenda was together with Larkin tonight is bound to raise a few eyebrows—and none higher than in the Emory household. Wouldn't you say?"

"Oh, yeah. I think it would be a real safe bet to lay money on that," Bob agreed.

"It also puts Saul Norton in a rather questionable light, doesn't it? I mean, if Brenda's telling the truth, then where does that leave Norton's claim that it was Larkin who attacked him?"

"That's a good question. By the time we got back to Doc Tibbs's place, after talking to Brenda and Larkin, Norton was heavily medicated and in no condition to get any more out of him. *Somebody* attacked him and did a helluva good job of it, that much is for certain. Broken ribs, fractured cheekbone, one tooth knocked out and several others loosened. The doc is pretty sure he has a concussion, but how severe he can't say yet . . . We *may* be able to talk to him in the morning, but it will likely be limited at best."

"So that leaves hanging the matter of why he identified Larkin as his attacker."

"It was plenty dark in that alley he was dragged into," said Bob. "I suspect what it'll come down to is that Norton didn't really get a good look at whoever was beating on him and only *figured* it had to be Larkin because he'd been more or less expecting something like that."

"Yes. If Larkin truly did come back with revenge in mind, then—even more than all those now worried jurors who found him guilty—the single person *most* responsible for his conviction was Norton."

"If I was in his shoes, that's the way I'd look at it."

"But if Brenda is telling the truth, then the assault on Norton *couldn't* have been by Larkin . . . Do you believe her?"

"Yes, I do," Bob was quick to reply. "I don't see where she has anything to gain by lying for him. In fact, like you already pointed out, taking his side, being there with him at all, gives her plenty more to lose—with her family and, when word gets around, no doubt in the eyes of the more prudish-minded around town. Her behavior will be considered scandalous."

"That's not fair!" Consuela said indignantly. "She went there to show support to somebody she felt had been wronged in the past. And then she had guts enough to stand up for him against a new accusation that, this time around, she could prove was false."

Bob felt her small, delicate hand ball into a

sharp-knuckled fist resting atop his bare chest, and it made him smile. "Take it easy, tiger," he told her. "Brenda Emory will come out of this okay. A person can seldom go too far wrong by sticking to the truth."

"What if the truth is that John Larkin really didn't commit those crimes four years ago? If so, things still went pretty far wrong for him, didn't they?"

"Whoa. Let's not get too carried away." Bob put his hand over hers and held it there until she slowly unclenched her fist. "I've got enough to handle with stuff that's going on in the here and now. I don't need to look four years in the past and try to untangle something from back then. Okay?"

"Of course. You're right," Consuela said, softer now. Her flattened palm grew very warm against his skin. "I almost forgot that, in addition to the trouble surrounding Larkin and the Emorys, there's still the matter of Ed Wardell and his alleged rustling problem . . . and whether or not he's actually sent for Rance Brannigan. You've hardly spoken about that in the past day or so."

"Been a little busy. Too busy to fret over what ain't here yet."

"But you still believe he's on his way?"

"Been too much talk to rule it out. Expect we'll be finding out soon enough."

"More trouble from years past. Trouble that unjustly branded *you* an outlaw." A trace of bitterness crept into Consuela's voice. "Maybe that's why I have a certain empathy for John Larkin and the thought he may have been wronged in a similar way."

Bob gave a small grunt. "You and half the rest of the town. Half think he got a raw deal; the other half thinks a fair trial took place and that should be the end of it. Trouble is, all or most of 'em seem to be in agreement on one thing: thinking Larkin might have come back aiming to get even, whichever way it was. And now—after the shooting earlier this afternoon and the beating of Norton tonight, even though he's been cleared of both—it's almost like somebody is trying awful hard to make that look like a legitimate worry."

"But who? Who would benefit from that?"

Bob responded negatively, rolling his head back and forth on his pillow. "Damned if I know."

Neither of them said anything more for a couple of minutes.

Until Consuela lifted her hand slightly and began moving her index finger in small circles through Bob's chest hairs. At the same time, she shifted her supple body tighter against his. Neither her curves nor the heat of her were contained in the slightest by the thin material of her sleeping gown.

"I suggest," she said in a husky whisper, "we have covered enough nasty business and nagging questions for the time being. Don't you think we could come up with a more pleasant and relaxing way to finish off the night?"

"I don't know about relaxing, leastways not right at first," Bob said, grinning as he rolled to face her. "But the pleasant part, with you in my arms, is pretty much a guarantee."

CHAPTER 29

"How the hell do I know what I said last night? I just got done getting my brains bashed in. It's a miracle I was able to say anything at all. If I did, I must have been talking out of my head."

Sitting propped upright on a narrow bed in a spare room at Doctor Tibbs's place—the room serving as a hospital of sorts for patients who needed care and observation overnight—Saul Norton was a much sorrier sight than the tall, handsome, self-assured presence he'd been when Bob last saw him at the Emory house the previous afternoon. This morning, the wraps of bandages around his head, the twin black eyes and bruised, swollen cheek-bone, the split lower lip, and the thick wrapping of bandages around his middle combined to not only paint him in a different light but also attested to the severity of the beating he'd endured. The dull tone of his voice and still semi-dazed look in his eyes were added indicators that his spirit, too, had suffered a beating.

"So you didn't get a good look at your attacker

and can't really say who it was. Is that what you're telling us now—in spite of saying the name 'Larkin' and the words 'getting even' last night?" asked Bob.

In addition to Bob and the patient, the room was also occupied by Deputy Fred, Victoria Emory, Graedon, and of course Doc Tibbs.

"Like I just got done explaining," Norton half-groaned, "you can't take to heart anything I said last night after I was assaulted. In those first few seconds after I got slugged and dragged into that alley, while I was still conscious, I'll admit my first thought was that it must be Larkin. I mean, everybody in town figures he came back to make trouble and who does he have a bigger reason to hold a grudge against than me . . . Right . . . ? But as far as getting a look at whoever it was who jumped me—no, I didn't. It all happened so fast, I . . . I . . . ."

"Doctor, please!" Victoria implored. "Is this necessary? Let alone advisable? He's already told the marshal everything he can. When is enough, enough?"

The doctor looked over at Bob. "She makes a valid point as far as pressing him too hard in his condition. I'm surprised he woke as lucid as he did this morning. He truly needs a lot more rest and quiet. Actually, I've recommended he stay here for another day or so but—"

"No, I won't hear of it," Victoria said. "He's coming home with us. Graedon has the buggy waiting outside and has it prepared to transport him comfortably. We've also made necessary arrangements at the house. Saul will get all the rest and care he needs there—with, of course, regular visits by you, Doctor."

Tibbs's mouth pulled tight, just short of a frown, but he said nothing.

"I really hate for you to go to all that trouble, dearest," Norton said halfheartedly. "Your father already requires a great deal of your attention, you don't need me to—"

"Nonsense. It's all decided," Victoria cut him off, just as she had the doctor. Then she turned to Bob. "Are you quite finished, Marshal?"

Having seen this demanding, rather shrill side of the eldest Emory daughter, Bob decided that she wasn't quite so fetching after all. The exterior of some things definitely didn't tell the whole story. He smiled mildly and said, "I've got just one more question for Mr. Norton, then I'll let him rest."

Victoria sighed impatiently. "Very well. But make it short. You heard what the doctor said."

Addressing Norton, Bob said, "Since we've established that it couldn't have been Larkin who assaulted you, I'm wondering if you can think of anybody else who has hard feelings toward you that might have led them to take it out on you in that way?"

Norton shook his head, quickly wincing in an indication that it hurt to do so. "No. No, I can't think of anybody like that . . . Sure, I'm the boss over a couple crews of hard-nosed miners who don't always like the rules I lay down . . . But there's none of them I can picture resorting to something like that."

"Nobody you've fired or had to recently discipline in some way they thought unfair?"

Norton started to shake his head again but then held it in check. It still made him wince, though. "No. Nothing like that I can think of."

"You said one more question, Marshal," Victoria reminded him.

Bob nodded. "Okay. I'm done." He cut his gaze back to Norton. "You get some rest. But I'd appreciate it if you do some more thinking on who might have been behind that attack. I'll check in on you later today or tomorrow in case you come up with anything."

"While you're checking up on things," Victoria said rather haughtily, "I strongly suggest you do some further checking on John Larkin and his so-called alibi . . . I don't care *who* provided it for him!"

"Whew!" Fred exclaimed after he and Bob had left the doctor's office and were walking toward the jail. "That Victoria gal seems like one bossy handful, don't you think?"

"Yeah, I sorta noticed," Bob agreed.

"She sure is pretty, though."

"Too bad she brings with it a reminder of the old saying about beauty only being skin deep."

"I guess. What she said there at the end, which amounted to calling both Larkin and her own sister a pair of liars, was kinda ugly."

It was the middle of the morning. Front Street was moderately busy with folks going about their business, a few probably out and about on some menial excuse just to enjoy another fine spring day.

"What do you think about that?" Fred said, continuing to talk as he and Bob strolled along. "About the kid sister, Brenda, I mean. You think there's any chance she *could* be lying to cover for Larkin?"

Bob shook his head firmly. "Nope. I'm convinced she's on the level."

Fred frowned. "What the heck's going on then? It almost seems like somebody is trying to put Larkin in a bad light with these things that keep happening—the saloon fight, the shooting out by the butte, now the beating of Norton—but so far he comes out in the clear."

"Either that," Bob said, "or somebody has it in for the Emorys and they're using the return of Larkin as cover for themselves. Way I see it, you can't really count the fight in the Grand—that was an outlier, strictly Ray Monte bringing it on by acting like a jackass. But the other two incidents . . . yeah, there's something calculated—something more than just the incidents themselves—going on there."

Fred's eyes widened. "Wow. Our mystery deepens!"

They'd reached the jail by that point. With his key inserted to unlock the door, Bob shot a look over his shoulder and growled, "Don't start that again or I swear I'll throw you in a cell and not let you out until you promise to never carry on about 'mysteries' anymore."

CHAPTER 30

Merlin Sweeney, the accordion player who'd recently settled in town and worked most nights in Bullock's Saloon, playing for tips, sat on a bench toward one end of the wide porch that ran across the front of the Shirley House Hotel. He was leaning back against the side of the building, his long legs stuck out before him, accordion resting on his lap. From time to time he played a portion of a tune, maybe even sang along a little bit, but his mind wasn't really about music this morning.

One of the few benefits of being a wandering musician was that a body could usually laze around in a public place, playing and singing a little bit, and not get hassled. Not even if you was a black man, not as long as you smiled wide at folks passing by and looked harmless and didn't linger in one place for too long. Most people liked music.

But the smiles Merlin flashed this morning were infrequent and more than a little strained. He was worried. Deeply worried. And the activity taking place at the doctor's office located catty-corner across the street was the focal point of his concern. He didn't know what all was going on inside. He could only imagine, and that was worse than knowing.

The one thing Merlin knew for sure was that the injured Saul Norton was in there—*still* in there, after being kept under the doctor's care all night. That was bad, not a good sign at all.

Oh, Lord, why had he hit the man so hard? So hard and so often?

"Come on, you black bastard, is that the best you got? Hit like you mean it . . . Make it look like something . . . ! You were paid good money, now earn it, you damned ungrateful nigger!"

From his vantage point, Merlin had seen people come and go from the doctor's office. A high-toned lady had rolled up in a buggy driven by a tall, stiff-backed driver—a servant of some kind, it was clear—who'd assisted her down and then the two of them had gone inside. They hadn't come out yet. A little while later the marshal and one of his deputies had gone in. A short time ago, they'd come back out and gone on down the street.

But no sign of Saul Norton coming out. A horrible thought bolted through Merlin—maybe Norton *couldn't* come out. Maybe he'd never come out, not under his own power. Maybe he'd died from the injuries he suffered.

A spasm gripped Merlin that caused him to squeeze a sour squawk of sound out of his accordion. Unpleasant as the sound was, it somehow seemed to fit the wretched knot of anxiety jerking steadily tighter in his gut.

"You were paid good money . . ." Those words kept

RIGHT BETWEEN THE EYES   there was a

...ating through Merlin's thoughts. ...he when he thought any money gained sho...t of theft was "good" money. All he'd wanted when he came to Rattlesnake Wells was to put together enough money for a grubstake—some simple food ...s, a few tools, and a decent pack animal—so he mor... ca... up into the Prophecies and try his slowly. The ...ing out little extra he earned, in beating was four ti... accum... of the store- so far. Damn near enoug... for admi...bar each his grubstake. That's what ma...imped toget... made it seem like such "good money." ...d there for

Even at that, it might not have been so bad i... hadn't lost his temper and gotten so carried away with the task. But all the taunts and humiliations he'd swallowed down over the years weren't lying as dormant inside him as he'd thought. With "black bastard" and "ungrateful nigger" ringing in his ears after he'd already started the beating, something snapped inside him and a wave of savagery was unleashed that propelled his fists and feet to a heightened level of fury . . .

And now he was sick over it. Sick over having committed the act at all, and sicker still with the worry of how badly he might have damaged his victim.

The refrain of *Please God, don't let him die* kept pulsing inside Merlin's head. As if God would heed any pleas coming from the likes of him now.

Merlin was ready to r... would be tight, but he ... with the money h... deal on a pack ... hand to ... to, a... ...animal of some kind, buy some secon... ...Scrape together sufficient food ... ...last resort, he'd hock his acc... But before he lit out, he had ...

He badly wanted to... ...ured he could make it work ...ad now. He could haggle out a

He had to stick around ... ...e getting ready was a murderer ...d out for lunch when ...ore noon. For several horses galloping ...lock up the...and then reining up in front of the they hea...g. This was unusual enough—both the do... ...ber of horsemen involved and the big hurry they seemed to be in—to draw the prompt attention of the two lawmen

Stepping outside, they found a half dozen riders milling before the hitch rail. A seventh had climbed down from his saddle and had been preparing to come in.

"Ah, *buenos dias*, Marshal," greeted Carlos Vandez, pausing with one foot planted on the short section of boardwalk that ran in front of the jail. "And also to you, Deputy Fred."

"Good morning to you, too, Señor Vandez," Bob replied.

"I am glad I found you present, I feared maybe you would already be gone for lunch," said Vandez. "In that case, of course, I would have waited to discuss my business rather than interrupt."

Bob nodded. "I appreciate your thoughtfulness. But you've ridden a long way, and I would have spared you some of my time in any event. Would you like to step inside and talk?"

"If it's all the same to you, I don't mind having our discussion right here. It is a fine morning and I am used to being in the outdoors. Plus, there is nothing I have to say that I can't say in front of my men."

Well into his fifties, Vandez was a ramrod-straight individual with a deeply tanned complexion that, somewhat surprisingly, was not as weather-lined as one would expect for a rancher and outdoorsman of his age. He stood only slightly over average height but carried himself with a bearing that made him seem taller. He had bright, alert brown eyes, a black pencil mustache in contrast to his thick snow-white hair, and a wide mouth that was quick to flash a smile but looked as though it could be just as quick to bark stern orders.

"Okay by me," Bob responded with a wave of his hand. "It *is* a fine morning, especially after the nasty winter only recently behind us."

Vandez nodded. "I will keep this short as I know the demands of your job make you a very busy man."

"Whatever it takes. What's on your mind?"

"I am not one to listen to rumors and certainly do not base my actions upon them," Vandez began. "But there has been talk. Too much talk to ignore."

"Talk about what?" Bob said.

"Talk coming from my neighbor, Ed Wardell. His claims and accusations about me, his alleged plans to bring in a hired gun. I'm sure you must have heard some of these things, too—is it not so?"

"Yes, I've heard the noise coming from Wardell and the Rocking W. I've even had a couple run-ins with him and some of his boys." Bob regarded Vandez flatly. "I expect that you, in turn, have heard some things about that."

Before Vandez could reply, one of the V-Slash riders still on his horse, a runt with butter yellow hair spilling out from under the brim of his hat and down across his forehead, spoke up. "Yeah, we heard all about 'em. We heard how you had run-ins but we also heard how not much came out of 'em. Even though most would say their behavior—an attempted lynchin' and all—surely deserved it, you dang sure ain't got no Rockin' W rannies in that jail behind you, do you?"

Fred immediately bristled. "You'd best put a muzzle on that snotty attitude, bub, or you might get a real up-close look at what's inside our jail."

The yellow-haired runt smirked. "Oh, that's rich. You threaten to toss me in the clink for makin' a remark, but a gaggle of Rockin' W boys who tried to hang a couple fellas are still runnin' loose?"

"That's enough, Billy!" snapped Vandez. "I said I could speak freely in front of my men, but that was not an invitation for any of you to speak freely during my discussion with the marshal."

"Everybody needs to take it easy," Bob added, sweeping his gaze over all of the V-Slash riders and finishing up with a cut to Fred at his side.

Fred and Billy continued to exchange blistering glares but neither said anything further.

"Yes, it's true I broke up what appeared to have the makings of a possible hanging out on Rocking W property a couple of days ago," Bob went on. "And no, I didn't attempt to arrest anybody and put them in jail. There were what you could call mitigating circumstances—one of them being that I was well out of my jurisdiction. I was satisfied that I was able to break up the play and ride away with the two men who'd been in danger."

"Considering how, from all reports, you were up against a superior number of men," Vandez said, "I would say that was a brave and significant accomplishment."

Billy made a soft sound that came close to being a disdainful sniff, but nobody called him on it.

"But I did not come here to challenge you on the performance of your duties to date," Vandez continued. "What I would like to know are your thoughts and intentions regarding this—this *gunslinger* Wardell is reportedly bringing in. What are your thoughts on that? Do you believe it to be true and, if so, what are your plans for dealing with him?"

"As far as the truth of whether or not Wardell has sent for a hardcase, a hired gunman . . . yeah, I have pretty good reason to believe he's done so." Bob fought hard to keep his expression from revealing that the man Wardell was bringing in was much more, on a personal level, than just another hired gun. "If that's the case, then how and if I end up dealing with him will mostly depend on what he does after he gets here. I can't stop Wardell from hiring somebody nor can I stop that somebody from coming here. And again due to jurisdictional boundaries, there's even a limit to what I can do as far as the actions this so-called gunman might take out on the open range. I can handle any trouble he causes in town. But outside of that, a U.S. Marshal would have to be called in."

Now Billy openly sneered. "That's real convenient for you, ain't it?"

For the first time, Bob fixed his full attention on the mouthy little runt. He looked to be no more than twenty and was lucky if he topped five-four standing on the ground. But the twin-holstered gun-belt strapped around his waist and the ivory-handled Colts riding prominently in those holsters made up the difference—in the kid's mind, at least. It was one of the oldest stories in the West. Another young punk who finds out somewhere along the way he's fast with a gun and then allows that to make him believe he's something special. Another fool thinking the gun makes the man, instead of the other way around.

"Just who are you, bub?" asked the marshal.

"Billy Clairmont," came the answer.

"Billy, I told you—" Vandez started to say.

But Bob cut him off. "No. Let me and Mr. Clairmont chat for a minute, if you don't mind. He's got something stuck in his craw, so let's give him the chance to spit it out."

All of a sudden, under the steady gaze of the marshal and the scowl from Vandez, Billy looked a little uncomfortable and not quite so cocky.

"Sounds like you don't think I'm very good at my job and that you know a better way of handling the Rocking W bunch," said Bob. "That about sum it up for your way of looking at things?"

"I never said that," Billy protested. "I don't know nothin' about how you do your job."

"You as much as did," Bob pressed. "You said my jurisdictional limits were real convenient, sounding to me like you meant I was hiding behind 'em."

"No. No, I never meant it that way." Billy's face started to turn red. "I-I don't even rightly know what those jurisfractional things are."

Some of the other riders to either side and slightly in back of Billy grinned a little at his flusterment.

"Well, let me tell you," Bob went on, "they're not a convenience at all. As a matter of fact, they're a pain in the ass. But for the sake of holding on to my job and to keep the town out of legal entanglements, I have to pay attention to them. Some sly skunk like Wardell would love to see me overstep my bounds so he could sic a hotshot shyster on my ass and bottle me up so I was next to worthless. Or, like I said, out of a job altogether."

"I didn't know it worked like that," Billy muttered.

"Well, it does. Now let's move on to the part about dealing directly with this hardcase Wardell is reportedly bringing in. You don't figure it really matters whether I get involved or not, do you? Not as long as Señor Vandez here has got you and those fancy tie-down guns of yours on his side. Ain't that the size of it?"

Billy's chin lifted and suddenly some of the fire was back in his eyes. "Yeah. Yeah, that *is* the size of it. You're damned right I figure me and my guns are up to facin' any gunslick Wardell brings in."

A corner of Bob's mouth quirked up in half a wry grin. "Pretty good with those hoglegs, eh?"

"Not just pretty good—*damn* good." Billy waved

his arm in a catchall gesture. "Ask any of these other fellas, they'll tell you the same."

The other riders, the men Billy had indicated, put away their grins and looked sober. A couple of them nodded faintly.

"If you're so good, why haven't I ever heard of you before?" Bob asked. Over his shoulder, he said to Fred, "How about you, Fred? You ever heard of a fast gun named Billy Clairmont?"

"Can't say as I have. Quite a few fast-gun Billys around, but none named Clairmont that I ever heard tell of," Fred answered.

A flush of color poured over Billy's face again. This time from being taunted, not from being flustered. "You ain't heard of me because I'm young and never been nowhere yet. 'Cept around here," he said through clenched teeth. "But that don't slow the greased lightnin' in these hands none. When it's my time to move on away from here, then you can bet your ass you'll hear about me. You'll hear plenty, you wait and see."

"Billy is the only son of my late ranch foreman," Vandez explained tolerantly. "William Clairmont passed on just short of two years ago, joining his beloved wife Helen, who had left us some years earlier. Billy has basically grown up on the V-Slash. He's a fine wrangler and he *has* gotten to be very good with those guns of his."

Billy said, "I'm beholden to Mr. Vandez, to the memory of my pa, and to the V-Slash in general. That's why I've stuck around this long. And I sure ain't goin' nowhere now, not with all this trouble brewin' and with some gunslick supposedly on his way in to make things even hotter for our brand."

Bob nodded. "I can't fault your loyalty, son. But I sure got reservations about what you're so eager to set yourself in the path of."

"What choice do we have?" said Vandez. "You answered what I came here to find out. You said yourself there are limitations to what you can do if and when Wardell brings in a gunman. If his purpose to push the falsehood of rustling and try to lay it at the feet of me and my men to use as an excuse to make trouble for us, then we will have to fight. Not just Billy, but every man who rides for me is prepared to protect our property and the integrity of the V-Slash brand."

"All that gunslick has to do is have the guts to plant himself in front of me," said Billy, his cockiness fully returned, "and I'll settle his hash in a quick hurry. Then it'll be just a matter of moppin' up."

"That's what it always comes down to in the end," Bob said with a weary sigh. "I just wish there was a way to stop it before it reaches that far."

CHAPTER 31

"Maybe I should just shoot the sonofabitch at the first sight of him," Bob said, stabbing his fork hard into the slice of ham on the plate before him. "Look at the problems that would solve. All in one swoop, it would chill the range war that's heating up and it would eliminate the risk of Brannigan ruining our lives by revealing my past."

Seated across the table from him, Consuela said, "Sure, that sounds like a good idea. While you're at it, after you shoot Brannigan, why not go ahead and shoot Wardell and Smoky Barnett, his ramrod, too? If you don't, they'll only bring in another gunman, maybe more than one. And if you really want to make sure everything stays peaceful, go ahead and shoot John Larkin as well, just in case he has come back to make trouble like so many people believe."

Bob paused with the piece of ham raised partway to his mouth. Frowning, he said, "Do you really think sarcasm from you is what I need at a time like this?"

"If you keep making ridiculous statements, it's what you're going to get," Consuela answered. "I surely cannot support that kind of foolish talk coming from you."

Bob shoved the ham into his mouth and chewed aggressively.

Following the meeting with Vandez and his men, Bob had come home for lunch and had related to Consuela how the discussion had gone. In doing so, he'd allowed his frustrations to boil to the surface.

"We both know you're not going to do any of those things," Consuela said now, her voice softened. "You're too good a man for that. That badge you're wearing has come to mean too much to you. You're going to confront Brannigan and deal with him the best way you can—the best *legal* way you can. And you're going to do the same thing when it comes to a conflict between the Rocking W and the V-Slash."

"The trouble is, I can't deal with Brannigan in a legal way because, when it comes to him, he knows better. He knows I'm an outlaw."

"That was a different time and place," Consuela insisted. "He can prove nothing. He has no kind of authority here or anywhere else."

Bob made a sour face. "We've been through all this before. He doesn't have to have any authority to run his mouth. He carries on long enough and loud enough, it's bound to set some folks to wondering. All it would take from there is for somebody like that nosy newspaperman Dutton to do some checking and raise a fresh wave of interest down in Texas."

"But everybody down that way thinks you're dead," Consuela reminded him.

"If I know Cameron Bell and if he caught even a

whiff that I might still be alive, he wouldn't leave it to chance. He's bound to have a long memory and a big hate where I'm concerned. And it's doubly certain that his money has a long reach. If he can't stir the Texas authorities to try and take action this far north, then you can bet the reward he'll once again offer will bring the bounty hunters swarming like bees to honey. Hell, if he can get big money riding on it, Brannigan will likely make a direct move on me himself."

"In that case," Consuela said sternly, "you'd have every right to kill him in self-defense."

"Uh-huh. But by that point, if he had sufficient doubt whipped up about me and enough bees were swarming my way, our identities and our standing in this community might already be ruined."

"But you'd still be alive."

"By the time this is over," Bob said in a somber tone, "that might be the best we can hope for."

"See. Right there." Fred bent over and extended his arm downward, pointing at the ground. "That's what I wanted to show you."

Bob moved up beside him and leaned over, too, taking a closer look at where Fred was pointing. It was an oval of wet ground near the back end of the alley that ran beside Bullock's Saloon. A shallow puddle stood in the middle of the oval and, since there'd been no rain for days, Bob reckoned the spot to be where somebody regularly dumped a pan of dishwater or maybe a mop bucket out the back door of the saloon.

When Bob was returning to town from having taken his lunch at home, Fred was waiting for him at the mouth of the alley and eagerly motioning him over, saying he had something he wanted the marshal to see. What that something was, what Fred was now pointing out, was a single distinct footprint in the damp earth on the outer edge of the wet oval. It was the mark of a man's shoe, the left foot, a good-sized one.

"Okay," Bob said, frowning. "Why are you bothering me with this? Is there supposed to be something special about it?"

"Yes. Two things," Fred told him. "First, that's the print of a flat-heeled shoe, not a cowboy boot like is more common around here. True, a lot of the miners wear shoes rather than boots, but most of that type hang out up in New Town. The drinkers who come around Bullock's are more apt to be ranchers, wranglers—boot wearers, in other words, who spend their time in the saddle with their feet hooked in stirrups. That makes it a little unusual in and of itself. The second thing is the marking inside the heel area. See it there? It's clear as can be in the soft ground."

Bob studied a little closer and then he could make it out. A series of small dots inside the outline of the heel formed a cross with the long end pointing in toward the rest of the foot.

Bob straightened up. "Okay, so the whole thing is a bit unusual. But I still don't see your point."

Fred straightened up, too, and suddenly his expression looked a little uneasy. He held up one hand, palm out in a *take it easy* gesture. "Okay, now don't bite my head off when I say this, but I'm gonna use a mystery-solving term. I'm suggesting this might be a clue to the identity of whoever beat up Saul Norton last night."

The word "clue" made Bob scowl a little, as Fred had feared, but he held off saying anything until his deputy could explain further.

"I got to thinking, while I was at lunch," Fred said, "that in the dark and all the excitement last night after Norton was found so badly beaten, nobody probably had the chance to explore the alley where the beating took place. In the dark, like I said, it would have been hard to see anything anyway. So I thought it might be worth taking a look now, in the daylight.

"Back there, closer to the front end of the alley"— Fred pointed again—"you can make out where the struggle took place, the ground is all chewed up. Otherwise the ground all through here is pretty sandy so it doesn't leave much in the way of clear markings or footprints. Except here, where it's damp."

"But if this ground stays damp from dumping water out of the saloon," Bob pointed out, "that footprint could have been put there anytime. It might be fresh from this morning or maybe a couple days old."

"True," Fred admitted, "but it *might* be from last night, too. This alley doesn't see a lot of foot traffic, there's no need for it. And Bullock doesn't like for customers to enter in from the back; yet if you look at that footprint, the way it's turned, it appears to have been made by somebody rounding the corner like they were intending to go in the back door."

Over the years, Fred's knack for noticing things that most others either missed or paid no attention to had proven too valuable to ignore. So, while Bob didn't exactly see the point in what Fred was showing him now, neither was he willing to dismiss it out of hand.

As if reading the marshal's mind, Fred was quick to add, "Look, all I'm saying is that it might be something worth keeping in mind. I know we can't hardly go around town asking everybody wearing flat-heeled shoes to hold up their feet so we can check the bottoms. But if we happen to run across that mark on the ground again or if we get lucky and run across somebody who *does* have a cross on his heel . . . Well, I think that would be somebody we'd want to have a long, serious chat with."

Bob grinned tolerantly. "That's fair enough. It was good thinking on your part to come back here and check it out at all, Fred. But now that you've had your look-see and you've shown it to me, what say we get out of this alley—it stinks back here."

CHAPTER 32

When Bob and Fred got back to the jail, the Macy brothers were there, having reported in for late duty. The next several minutes were spent updating them on the morning's events—the status of Saul Norton, including his back-peddling on the identification of John Larkin as his attacker; the visit from Carlos Vandez and some of his men, signaling the rising tension between the V-Slash and the Rocking W; and Fred's discovery of the curious footprint in the alley beside Bullock's.

"Sounds like what it boils down to," Peter Macy summed up, "is that we need to be keeping a double-sharp lookout for a particular passel of things outside the normal trouble signs we stay on alert for. Starting with the appearance of any new *hombre* in town who might be the hired gun Wardell has called in. Even without him, with feelings starting to simmer now among the regular riders for both Wardell and Vandez, there's the makings right there for a pot of trouble to boil over if crews from each outfit happen to end up in town at the same time.

"On top of that we got some skunk lurking around who was behind the ambush attempt on either the marshal or Jackson Emory. And, latest, there's another ambusher who dragged Saul Norton into that alley and beat the crap out of him."

"Do you think there's a chance that whoever beat up Norton might be the same varmint who did the shooting out by the butte?" said Vern.

"I thought about that," admitted Bob. "While it's true there's a connection between the two, the difference in the methods of attack hardly seems to jibe. A bullet is a lot more permanent than a beating. If the overall target is old man Emory, then beating a business associate of his is an awfully indirect way to get at him."

"Unless the two acts were only meant as warnings," Fred said. "The bullet wasn't really permanent because it didn't hit anything, remember."

"But warnings about what? And why?" Vern asked.

"It'd have to be something about the Emory Mining Company," said Peter. "That's the connection between the old man and Norton."

Fred said, "There's another . . . Victoria. Emory's daughter, Norton's sweetheart."

"But still, toward what end?" said Vern, frowning. "If the varmint is after money, which is the next thing you'd think of if he ain't simply out for blood, then the threat of continuing to make trouble for the company—by hurting its two key men with the threat of something worse to come next—sort of fits. Pay me or I keep doing bad things. The daughter . . . I don't know."

"What about kidnapping?" said Peter. "Emory would certainly pay ransom to get her back safely."

"But if that was this skunk's game, why wouldn't he just go straight to it?" pointed out Fred. "Why fool around with this other stuff at all?"

"I think we might be getting carried away with what amounts to mostly just speculation," said Bob. "In the first place, if somebody was trying to strong-arm money out of Emory, I don't know why he wouldn't say so. Especially when I was there for the attempted ambush and even more so now that Norton has been attacked and there are the two young women to think of." Bob paused, scowling thoughtfully. "I don't like coincidences any better than anybody else. But they *do* occur sometimes. So with nothing more solid to go on than what we've got, I say we can't automatically jump to any conclusions. The two attacks might be linked, they might be just coincidence. We flat don't know yet."

"Just like the coincidence of this John Larkin character returning home when all of it starts happening. There's that, too, ain't there?" said Peter.

"Larkin's got rock-solid alibis for both incidents," Fred was quick to say.

Peter spread his hands. "I'm just saying."

"Maybe he hired somebody else to do it for him," suggested Vern. "That way he could rig his alibis to make sure he was in the clear while still managing to get some pieces of his revenge."

"That's pretty far-fetched," said Fred. "He just got out of prison, in case you forgot. He doesn't have two nickels to rub together. How is he gonna hire anybody for anything?"

"I said that's enough," Bob growled, putting some heat in it. "It's good to air out ideas and observations, but too much gum-flapping becomes just a waste of time. Our best bet going forward is to go right back to what Peter said in the first place—keeping a double-sharp lookout for things outside the normal trouble signs we watch for. We do that, I'm confident something will turn up. Something solid we'll be able to take some action on."

Peter and Vern nodded agreeably. Fred, his face pulled by a thoughtful frown, nodded with notably less enthusiasm.

"What is it?" Bob wanted to know.

Fred met his gaze evenly. "One thing comes to mind out of all this 'gum-flapping.' It might prove a waste of time, but it also *might* narrow down an important question."

"Go ahead."

Fred turned to the Macy brothers. "When you fellas went out to the butte yesterday, you found the spot where the ambusher fired from, right? Did you notice any footprints on the ground or was it too rocky?"

Vern and Peter exchanged looks. Then Vern said, "Well, the ground was naturally pretty rocky in there among those boulders. But there were patches of sand and grass, too. There might have been some footprints . . . but to tell the truth, we weren't looking for anything like that. Once we found where the shooter fired from, we went on the lookout for his horse's tracks to try and pick up a trail for where he came from or where he went."

"I understand. That was your purpose for going

out there," Fred said, nodding. He then looked over at Bob. "You see what I'm thinking, don't you? It won't bring us any closer to an identity, but if the ambusher left any discernible footprints out there and they happened to show the same cross pattern in the heel . . . it would definitely narrow it down as far as whether we're looking for one man or two."

"Hey, that ain't bad thinking," said Peter.

"No it's not," allowed Bob. "It's sure worth taking the time to try and find out. Peter, you go with Fred. Ride out there to where you found those spent shells and this time look for footprints, too. See what you can find."

"No promises, boss. But I think it's worth checking out," said Fred.

"Didn't I just agree with you? Get going."

CHAPTER 33

A handful of minutes later, Bob was seated alone at this desk sorting through some mail that had piled up and updating his report log. Fred and Peter had ridden off for Massacre Butte and Vern had gone on patrol.

As he worked, the marshal's mind drifted in and out of things other than what was before him. He felt a little guilty that his thoughts most often came around to Rance Brannigan. He shouldn't allow his personal stake where that polecat was concerned to outweigh the risks posed to Emory or Norton or the innocent wranglers who stood to get caught up in the range war that was coming closer to busting loose. But Bob was only human. Brannigan represented more than just a personal threat. The well-being of Bucky and Consuela also were riding on the trouble he could bring.

Maybe I should just shoot the sonofabitch on sight.

If he had any idea how and when the specter from his days as the Devil's River Kid would be arriving, Bob wasn't altogether sure he couldn't bring himself to do just that. Ride out to face Brannigan before he ever had the chance to make it to town and send him to hell where he belonged . . . "*You're too good a man for that,*" Consuela had said . . . Bob was glad she thought so, and he wanted to measure up to everything she saw in him. But at the same time, he knew that even a good man would do a desperate thing to protect those he loved . . .

"Can you spare a minute, Marshal?"

Bob looked up with a start, only belatedly realizing someone had come in the front door. John Larkin stood there, a somewhat anxious expression on his face.

Bob cleared his throat. "Sure. Sure, come on in, Mr. Larkin . . . What can I do for you?"

"I'd like to talk to you about a couple of things."

"All right." Bob gestured to the chair situated in front of his desk. "Why don't you go ahead and have a seat."

"That's okay. I'll just stand, if you don't mind."

The man was dressed considerably better than the last couple times Bob had seen him. New duds from the skin out. Nothing fancy, just basic workman's attire bought off the store shelf. Trousers, shirt, shiny new shoes. No hat, hair slick with pomade and carefully combed into place. Bob had a pretty good hunch he was looking at the handiwork of Earl Hines, who likely had gone good for the cost of the new outfit.

"I want to say, first of all," Larkin started in, "that I appreciate how you've treated me square ever since I hit town. You've had to question me about some things, but I understand. You were just doing your job. You nor none of your boys have leaned on me unduly hard the way a lot of lawmen might have, especially with so many folks in town figuring I only came back to make trouble."

"I don't operate that way. I wouldn't allow any man working for me to, either," Bob told him.

Larkin nodded. "I know. I'm acknowledging that. I figured you for different at first, that's why I was kinda mouthy with you a time or two. I'll apologize for that now, while I'm at it. Like I said, you been square with me, I want to do likewise."

"Sounds fair enough."

"So part of being square is leveling with you about a couple recent things that happened. You may get a different slant from other sources; that's why I want to make sure you hear it from my side."

Bob hitched forward behind his desk. "These recent things . . . some kind of trouble?"

"Nothing serious, not to my way of thinking. But seeing as how it involved me, some might slant it as being more."

"How about you just tell me?" Bob suggested. "I hear a lot of different slants on how things happen. I'm pretty good at sorting out the horse chestnuts from the buffalo chips."

"At Krepdorf's General Store a little while ago," Larkin related, "I had some heated words with another one of his customers. You can see I've got on some new clothes, courtesy of my friend Earl—who I'll be repaying just as soon as I can. Anyway, that's how I came to be in Krepdorf's. He helped me pick this shirt and these pants off the shelf based on judging my size by eyeing me up. But just to make sure, he told me I should go in the back and try them on.

"This lady came in while I was picking out the clothes, see. And then, after I went back to try the fit, she couldn't see me and started yapping her mouth, thinking I couldn't hear. She scolded old man Krepdorf for doing business with the likes of me— '*the likes of that kind of person*' is how she put it. Like I was some piece of crud off the floor of a horse stall or something. Then she started in on how, if she was going to risk running into my kind when she came in his store, she would just have to take her business elsewhere. That's what made me lose my temper, threatening Krepdorf like that on my account. I'd been biting my tongue and just staying back out of the way, figuring I'd keep clear until after she was gone. Until I heard her say that. That's when I came barreling out and gave the old bat a piece of my mind and . . . well, I fear we got into a pretty good shouting match over it."

Bob almost wanted to grin. "And that's the spot of trouble you think might get blown out of proportion and make its way back to me?"

"Don't you? Standing nose to nose with an old gal and cussing her out—although I don't think I actually used too many bad words—don't paint a very good picture of a fella, does it? Especially not a fella with my background. What's more, the old bat turned out to be the wife of one of the jurors who sent me to the pen four years ago—you know, one of those dutiful citizens I'm supposed to have come back seeking revenge on. Now there's bound to be some who'll claim I was getting warmed up by picking on the poor helpless wife of one of my intended."

Bob said, "What's the old ba . . . er, what's the lady's name?"

"Poppe. Mrs. Myron Poppe. I think her name is Elvira. Her old man is a clerk at the Starbuck Territorial Bank."

"Uh-huh. Him I know. Can't say I ever had the pleasure of meeting his wife."

Abruptly, Larkin came forward and dropped down on the chair in front of Bob's desk. "So what do you think? How much trouble can she make for me over something like that? It's not enough to put a bad mark on my parole, is it?"

"It hardly sounds that serious." Now Bob did grin. "Didn't come to blows, did it?"

"No. Although there was a couple times when I thought she might haul off and slap me. And if she'd been a man, I'm pretty sure I wouldn't have been able to hold back from . . . well, let's just leave it at that. No blows were exchanged."

"Okay. Good. And Rudy Krepdorf was there the whole time, wasn't he? He's a fair man; he won't let the telling of the story become too one-sided."

"I hope not." Larkin took a breath, expelled an audible gust of air. "One of the reasons I wanted to get decked out in some better clothes in the first place was that I meant to go calling. And I did. That's the other thing I came here to tell you about."

Bob had a pretty good hunch what was coming next. "Let me guess. You paid a visit to Victoria Emory. Is that it?"

Larkin nodded. "You said there was no law against

me trying to see her. Right? I didn't hold out much hope for how it would go, but I still had to make the attempt. I had to get it off my chest, hear from her own lips she didn't want anything to do with me, that we were all through."

"And?"

"I got my answer." Larkin hung his head, gazed down at the floor. "She didn't even want to see me at first. The old man's big manservant, Graedon, answered the door and tried to run interference for her. But without pushing it too far, I was stubborn about being turned away. Finally, Brenda came to the door. She told Graedon to let her handle it and then, somehow, she went and convinced Victoria to come speak with me." Larkin paused for a minute, his head hanging still lower. But then he lifted his face and finished the telling. "It didn't take long. She pleasantly but firmly told me she no longer had any feelings for me. She said further that she was betrothed to another and asked that I respect her wishes and not make any more attempts to see her . . . And that was it. I could see in her eyes that she meant it, that there was nothing there for me anymore, so I turned and walked away.

"There was no big scene, no drama or anything. And there won't be, as far as I'm concerned. Like I said, I got my answer. But once again, I just wanted you to make sure you heard my side of how it went."

"I appreciate that, Larkin. I really do," said Bob. "I hope that, going forward, if you still intend to stick around you don't feel like you have to walk on eggshells and report every little thing to me. Whether you know it or not, you've got a lot of friends in this town. A lot of folks think you got a bad shake four years ago and want to see you make out better this time around. I wasn't here to know all the particulars from back then, but I find myself sort of leaning that same way. I believe you when you say you didn't come back to make trouble. I hope you don't prove me or the others who believe in you wrong."

"I don't intend to, Marshal." Larkin stood up again. "Oh, just so you know, there's been a couple other changes with me, too. I'm no longer staying with Earl Hines. I got me a job swamping out the bar at the Shirley House Hotel. It don't pay much, but it comes with a sleeping cot in the back of the storeroom. There might be some other odd jobs I can do for extra money as well."

"I thought that other fella, that Sweeney who also plays accordion at Bullock's, was doing that job," said Bob.

"He was. But he lit out on short notice, decided to head up into the Prophecies in search of gold instead. I heard about the opening and spoke up for it right away." Larkin made a catchall gesture. "Like I said, it ain't much but it's something. Earl's been great to me, but I feel like too much of a mooch the way things are. I don't want to take advantage of him. This way, I can earn a little money at the hotel and also do some part-time work for him if and when he needs a hand. I'll make out okay and I can start paying him back for everything he's already done to help me. Eventually, if I decide to stick around for good, something better will come along."

"Good luck with that," Bob told him. "Thanks for stopping by and keeping me up to date on things."

CHAPTER 34

After Larkin left his office, Bob leaned back in his chair and thought about the visit. He wasn't, by nature, a cynical person. Yet his dealings with corrupt power back in Texas and his run-ins with crooks and slicksters of various types since donning a badge had nevertheless implanted in him a layer of skepticism through which he tended to filter most situations he encountered. This left him questioning the exact purpose behind Larkin stopping in the way he had.

Had his visitor truly been interested in just staying "square" with the marshal and showing concern for his parole status? Or had it all been a play to influence Bob's perception of the encounters that had already taken place and maybe cast Larkin in an improved light for the sake of others he might be planning in the future? Bob didn't want it to be the latter—he was finding the former convict likable, too, just like so many others. But neither did he want to end up getting the wool pulled over his eyes. Since he wasn't doing a very good job of concentrating on the paperwork before him anyway, he decided a way to help quell the questions nagging him would be to go over to Krepdorf's General Store and talk with Rudy while the confrontation between Larkin and Mrs. Poppe was still fresh in his mind.

The activity up and down Front Street had tapered off considerably from earlier. There was hardly any foot traffic on the boardwalks though the street itself still had a number of wagons and horsemen moving to and fro.

Krepdorf's was two and a half blocks up from the jail, on the opposite side. Bob had drawn nearly level with the store and was waiting for a wagon to roll by, headed down toward the rail depot, so he could cross over.

That's when a commotion in front of Bullock's Saloon, another block beyond the general store and on the same side, suddenly reached a level of volume and intensity that drew Bob's attention.

The figure of a man strode somewhat unsteadily out into the middle of the street, waving his arms and shouting loudly. As Bob watched, the man wheeled about and faced back toward the saloon he had just exited.

The man hollered something, but the clatter of the just-passed wagon made it indistinguishable to Bob. The marshal stepped out into the street, too, angling now more toward the shouting man rather than the store directly across the way. Bob continued to advance, reaching down to slip the keeper thong off the hammer of his Colt.

The man up ahead shouted again, and this time his words were very clear. "Get out here, you yellow-livered, scum-sucking puke! You called down the thunder, now come and face what you asked for!"

Mike Bullock pushed through the batwings of his saloon and stood on the boardwalk, feet planted wide. He addressed the man in the street, saying, "You're the one who needs to get out of here, you damn drunken troublemaker. Go somewhere and cool off before somebody gets hurt!"

"That's the general idea, you thickheaded Irish fool," responded the man in the street. "I aim to hurt Curly Joe real bad and real permanent. He belittled me and dressed me down in front of all the boys. I take that from no man! He said my gun work was a joke, so I'm gonna give him a chance to have hisself a big laugh by tryin' to prove it!"

"He didn't mean nothing by it," Bullock said, trying to reason. "He's drunk, just like you, Billy, and he was only hoorahing you some. But he knows he ain't good enough to go gun to gun against you. He's ready to apologize if you'll just—"

"To hell with that!" the man in the street barked. "The time for him to be sorry was before he ran his jackass mouth! It's too late to apologize now. That only proves what a yellow, belly-draggin' dog he is!"

Bob was close enough to recognize the belligerent now. It was Billy Clairmont, the cocky young would-be gunny from Carlos Vandez's V-Slash crew. As Bob continued to move closer, walking slow and easy, he saw by a flick of Bullock's eyes that the saloonkeeper had taken note of his approach. Billy hadn't yet, though.

So as not to alarm the already agitated kid and possibly cause him to overreact by grabbing for one of his guns, Bob drawled nice and low, "Afternoon, Billy . . . What seems to be the trouble?"

Billy twisted in a half turn, both hands dropping to the guns riding low in tied-down holsters on each hip. But he had enough presence of mind to hold off from drawing either of them. Bob's own hand was poised above his Colt, but he'd purposely kept from closing on the grips so as not to stoke Billy's reaction any hotter.

"You!" Billy exclaimed, his eyes locking on Bob and then quickly narrowing.

Bob nodded. "That's right. Me, the marshal."

"So what? That badge don't give you no right to horn in on this," Billy sneered. "I'm callin' out a dirty bastard who insulted me. All I'm lookin' for is a fair fight to stand up for my honor."

"There won't be nothing fair about it, Marshal," said Bullock. "Curly Joe Hatch ain't no gunman, not by any stretch. This pup is just looking to make a rep for himself by throwing down a challenge he knows is bound to give him a quick, easy kill."

Billy's nostrils flared. "You'd best watch your own mouth, Mr. Saloon Man, or I might have to save a bullet for you . . . even though you're obviously too chickenshit to go around heeled."

"No, I don't think you're gonna do anything like that," Bob said, coming to a halt about ten yards short of where Billy stood.

"Who's gonna stop me?" Billy demanded to know. "I told you this ain't no concern of yours, law dog."

"You're wrong about that, too," said Bob. "In

my town, anybody threatening to shoot another person—especially a friend of mine—is damn sure my concern."

"Aw, I'd never shoot an unheeled fella," Billy scoffed. "I just said that to keep ol' Bullock from stickin' his nose in my business."

"You started this ruckus in my saloon with one of my customers, so I say that makes it my business, too," Bullock huffed. "What's more, take off those guns of yours and I'll do more than stick my nose in what you think is your business—I'll stick my fist elbow-deep down your gob!"

"If you think you're helping any, Mike, you're not," Bob told him. "I'd appreciate it if you just stood clear and let me handle this."

"Oh, that's rich!" Billy proclaimed. "*He* threatens *me* and you ask him to pretty-please back off. But what you call a threat when *I* want to give what's comin' to a lowdown insultin' skunk, *that* you try and stop me from doing!"

Bob gave an almost imperceptible wag of his head. "Not just *try* to stop you, Billy. I'm telling you flat that you won't be using those guns on anybody here in town today. Show some sense. Shuck that gunbelt and come with me to the jail where you can cool off. After you've done that, I'll give you your guns back and you can return home to the V-Slash. *There* is where you need to be ready to use your guns. Remember? To help protect the Vandez brand in case of trouble from the Rocking W."

Billy stood very still, eyeing Bob as he digested the words. For several clock ticks Bob thought he'd succeeded, thought Billy looked like he was ready to waver.

But then, abruptly, a shudder seemed to run through the kid, as if he was physically shaking off the urge to give in. His eyes went wide for a moment and then narrowed again.

"No. No, I ain't shuckin' my guns. And I sure as hell ain't lettin' you haul me to no jail."

Bob felt the muscles tighten across his shoulders, and his mouth pulled into a thin, straight line. "That wasn't an invitation that included you having a choice in the matter. Now you've run your mouth, put on a show out here in the middle of the street, and maybe even impressed one or two people with how tough you can talk. That's enough. The show's over, and it's time for you to stand down."

"To hell with that. You want me stood down, you're gonna have to make me." Billy cocked his head slightly to one side and eyed the marshal with added intensity. "I remember now how you and your fat deputy gave me a little ribbin' earlier, sayin's how if I was so good with my guns, then why did nobody ever hear of me. Yeah, the two of you thought you was mighty smug, didn't you?"

Bob said nothing, let his flinty gaze do the talking for him.

"Maybe this is even better. Maybe this is like fate," Billy went on. "Instead of settlin' the score with Curly Joe and his insults, it looks like it's in the cards for me to settle with you. Yeah, that's better yet. I hear tell you're supposed to be pretty hot stuff with that ol' .44, Sundown Bob. I drop *you* in the dirt, folks will damn sure start talkin' up my name."

"Don't be insane," Bullock said from the saloon doorway. "You go up against Bob Hatfield, the only place your name will end up is on a tombstone."

Bob started walking slowly forward. "I don't want it to come to that, Billy. I really don't. But if you leave me no choice, that's the way it will have to go. Unbuckle that gunbelt and hand it over. Slow. Your hands reach for those guns instead of the buckle, you'll be forcing me to kill you."

But Billy was beyond being reasoned with. He was too drunk, too stubborn, and he'd put on too much of a show not to try.

His hands streaked downward for the guns in their tied-down holsters. He truly was fast, faster than Bob would have guessed. But even at that, his guns were only starting to clear leather when the marshal's Colt spoke and a bullet smashed into Billy's right shoulder. That's where Bob had been aiming, never intending to actually go for a kill shot in spite of his warnings.

If Billy had been packing only one gun, that would have been the end of it. His shoulder was ruined, so he'd ceased being a threat with the gun hand on that side. But he was a tough, determined little bastard and as he twisted away to his right, his left hand came up with the gun that had been holstered on that side and he squeezed off a round. The shot came close to its target, sizzling only a finger's width from the side of Bob's face. The marshal jerked his head away reflexively and, because Billy's gun was still raised and aiming in his direction, he had no choice but to return fire with another shot—this one more hastily triggered and therefore not as carefully aimed. The bullet drilled into the side of Billy's neck, just below the hinge of his jaw. The impact caused the young man's head to flop over onto his right shoulder, and then his whole body pitched in that direction and collapsed onto the ground. His guns clattered to the dusty street on either side of where he fell.

CHAPTER 35

"It was the last thing I wanted. I tried my best to back him down, but he wasn't having any. Wasn't nothing else for it but to slap leather against him. I pulled my first shot, aimed for his shoulder . . . But he had two guns and there was no quit in him . . . When he damn near blew my head off, even after he was wounded, I had no choice but to return fire . . ."

Marshal Bob Hatfield spoke these words somberly from the back of his horse, reined up close before the front door of Carlos Vandez's sprawling ranch house. Fidgeting beside him, its own reins gripped in Bob's left fist as they had been all during the ride out from town, was Billy Clairmont's pinto gelding. The pinto's saddle was empty except for Billy's gunbelt lashed to the pommel.

In the doorway of his house, backlit by the soft glow of lanterns from within, Vandez's shadowy face hung heavy in response to the words he was hearing. When Bob paused in the telling, Vandez said quietly, "So the boy is . . . dead?"

Inside the house, somewhere close behind Vandez, a woman choked out a ragged sob.

In response to the question put to him, Bob set his mouth grimly and gave a single nod. Dusk was settling over the V-Slash ranch headquarters and the surrounding prairie. It was as if the long, grotesque shadows cast out from various objects had been summoned to fit the gloomy news the marshal carried with him.

Vandez spoke again, his voice a sandpapery whisper. "The body?"

"It's back in town, at the undertaker's," Bob said. "I didn't know if you'd want it buried in the cemetery there, or if you had a place out here."

Vandez's eyes cut involuntarily toward a hill in the near distance, rising up just beyond a low shed and some cattle pens. Following his gaze, Bob saw a half dozen or so crosses on the crest, silhouetted against the graying sky.

Vandez said, "Yes, we have our own plot. Billy's parents are there. He should rest with them."

"I can have O'Malley, our undertaker, prepare the body and bring it out to you," Bob offered. "Or you can go ahead and make your own arrangements."

"I'll take care of it." Vandez continued to gaze up at the hill dotted with crosses. "I guess what I didn't take care of very well was keeping my word to Billy's father. When he knew he was dying, he asked me to look after the boy, finish getting him matured and settled. There were already signs, once Billy discovered he had a knack for handling a gun, that he might take a wild turn one day if not held in check."

"Certain young men are like certain wild stallions.

Sometimes there's a streak in 'em you just can't break."

"Perhaps it is so." Vandez sighed. He pulled his gaze away from the hill and brought it to rest on Billy's horse and the gunbelt draped over its saddle. "My greatest fear was that one day he would ride off and end up facedown in the dusty street of a faraway town where he would be dumped in an empty hole by strangers and none of us would never know his fate . . . This, I guess, is somewhat better than that. At least he will rest for eternity beside his family."

Bob had nothing to say to that.

Now Vandez's gaze swung to him. "But for you, it is not better. I see guilt written on your face."

"No you don't," Bob replied in a low, flat tone. "I regret what happened. Regret it deeply. But I feel no guilt, because he gave me no choice but to do what I did."

Vandez continued to regard him. "You are a hard man . . . yet still a decent one. The mark of that is you bringing word of what happened yourself, rather than sending another. For that I am obliged."

"It was the least I could do," Bob said, holding out the reins of the pinto for Vandez to take.

Then he wheeled his own horse and rode away, back toward town.

Bob, Consuela, and Bucky sat talking at the kitchen table.

It was late, full dark outside. A softly burning lantern sat in the middle of the table, and another wall-mounted one cast an added warm glow from the adjoining room.

During the time it took Bob to make his visit to the Vandez ranch, Consuela and Buck had gone ahead and had their supper. The plate Consuela prepared and put aside for Bob now sat only half eaten on the table before him.

"You've had to shoot men before, Pa—as recent as only a few nights ago with Mr. Morrison, the federal marshal. I don't understand why this one is bothering you so much." Bucky's earnest expression as he said this was almost a match for Bob's somber one.

"It never *hasn't* bothered me when I've taken a life, son. Don't ever think that," Bob told him. "But there are degrees to how you feel about certain things. You understand what I mean by that?"

"Sorta . . . I think."

"Those men the other night were hardened, mean-spirited criminals with little or nothing to redeem them," Bob tried to explain better. "They were out to kill Marshal Morrison—and me—with no more thought or regret to it than you or I might swat a mosquito . . . Men like that, it's hard to have any charitable feelings toward. Therefore, having to kill their kind—especially in self-defense—don't leave you with a lot of remorse.

"But this fella today, he was so doggone young for starters. Not too many years older than you. He was cocky and wrongheaded and fueled by damn whiskey he couldn't handle . . . But he wasn't lowdown and mean spirited like those other men. Not yet, anyway. He still had some youth and innocence to him. Maybe he was on his way to become just like those

252 *William W. Johnstone*

other skunks one day, or maybe he would've got his head on straight and turned out okay . . . Only now nobody will ever know. Because I had to kill him."

Bob pressed his palms flat down on the table and peered intently at his son. "Do you see the difference? Do you see why having to shoot one kind bothers me more than the other? That's what I meant by different degrees. But either way, it's never something to take lightly."

"Okay, Pa. I think I see now."

"You'd better. I've begun to teach you about guns, how to handle one properly and use it to defend yourself. But always remember it's just a tool. How well it gets used—both from a skill standpoint and whether for good or evil—is strictly up to the person behind the trigger. It won't be too many more years before you'll be packing a gun of your own. You'd best have fixed in your mind before then how you mean to use it."

"Good heavens, Bob," said Consuela in a slightly chiding tone. "The boy's not even twelve yet. You sound like you're getting ready to pin a badge on him and send him out to help defend the streets of town."

Initially, Bob scowled at her words. But then, realizing she was right, he willed himself to relax some. Leaned back in his chair, expelled half a breath, even managed a ghost of a sheepish grin. "Guess I was laying it on a mite thick, wasn't I?" he said. Directly to Bucky, he added, "Sorry about that, pal. Didn't mean to unload on you quite so heavy."

"That's okay, Pa. I understand."

"Something else I'm sure you can understand,"

said Consuela, "is that it's time to be headed to bed. You've got school tomorrow, you know."

"But only for a couple more weeks, until summer break," Bucky was quick to point out. "And, boy, am I looking forward to that!"

"Well, it ain't here yet. So get washed up and hit the sack," Bob said. "We'll be up to say prayers with you in a few minutes."

"Okay, Pa."

As the boy rose from the table and started to turn away, Bob stopped him, saying, "Speaking of school tomorrow, pal, I want you to do something for me."

"Sure, Pa. What is it?"

"When you and your buddies start talking about this afternoon's big shoot-out right here in the streets of Rattlesnake Wells, like I know you're bound to . . . Let 'em go ahead and yammer about the excitement and the glory and all that. But somewhere in there, do me a favor and remind 'em, like I just did you, that a young man's life ended real sudden-like when all was said and done. He was looking for glory and excitement, too. What he found out was that there's always another side to it."

"O-Okay, Pa . . . I'll, er, try to work that in." But then Bucky continued to stand there, appearing uncertain or puzzled about something.

"What is it, Bucky?" Consuela asked.

"It's just that . . . well, no matter what I say, the fellas are really going to be carrying on about this. And me, I'm the one whose pa was right there in the thick of it—out-drawing and out-blasting a two-gun shootist right here in our very own town. Practically right outta one of those rip-roaring dime novels. I mean, that's how everybody else will be looking at it . . .

"I understand about the sad side to it. How the young fella's life got cut short, how nobody will ever know if he might've amounted to something better and all . . . But, holy cow, I don't want to come across like some stern and serious dope while all the other fellas are carrying on and play-acting the exciting parts and everything. You're my pa, Pa. They'll be bragging you up like the next Wild Bill Hickok or something. Can't I get in on at least *some* of the bragging along with 'em?"

Bob and Consuela exchanged looks. She smiled. Bob felt the corners of his mouth also lift a bit as a swell of pride filled his chest. "I reckon," he said around the lump in his throat, "if you feel the need to do some bragging on your old man, that'd be okay . . . Still try to fit in some of the other, too, if you can."

CHAPTER 36

After the talks with Carlos Vandez and then Consuela and Bucky, Bob found that he'd resolved the shooting of Billy Clairmont fairly well in his mind. Like he'd told Vandez, he had a deep regret over the incident but he felt no guilt.

In the arms of Consuela, he even got a solid night's sleep. It helped that, unlike the run of previous evenings, there'd been no interruptions due to trouble in the town.

Or so he thought.

When he got to the jail the next morning, he soon enough found out that, while it was true no one had felt it necessary to notify him at home, there *had* been a disturbance in New Town. The first indication of this had come when he arrived to find Vern Macy asleep on a cot over against the side wall of the office area. It was standard procedure for Bob or one of his deputies to stay on premises overnight when there was a prisoner in the lockup.

Vern woke when Bob came in, quickly shoving away the blanket that had been covering him and swinging his feet over the side of the cot as he sat up. He was fully dressed except for his boots and gunbelt, which hung from the back of a chair right beside the cot.

"Hey, Marshal . . . G'morning."

"And to you, Vern. What's the occasion?"

Stifling a yawn, Vern said, "We've got some overnight guests. I drew the short straw for sticking around to hold their hands in case they got scared of the dark."

Bob fed some kindling into the top of the stove and went to work setting a pot of coffee to brew while Vern stomped into his boots, then stood up and buckled on his gunbelt.

"How many and what did they do?"

"Three rowdies from down Texas way," Vern answered. "They were paying their respects to some of the gals in Duchess's bawdy house. One of 'em felt the need to get a mite too rough, and when the gal he was slapping around hollered for the bouncers, the other two Texans joined in to fight them off. It took me and Peter showing up to lay our gun barrels across a couple skulls before things got settled down."

Bob grunted. "Arthur must be slipping," he said, referring to the imposing black bouncer Duchess employed to keep things tamed down in her bawdy house. "Time was he would have handled only three troublemakers without hardly breaking a sweat."

"Yeah, that surprised me a little, too," Vern allowed. "I think one of 'em must have clubbed him from behind, right at the start, and knocked most of the starch out of him before he ever had the chance to get set. And I gotta say, these three *hombres do* have some pretty rough bark on 'em."

"Well, it sounds like you and your brother were still able to handle them okay. Glad to say it don't look like you're too much the worse for wear, except maybe for the damage sleeping on that old cot might've done to you."

Vern shrugged. "The cot ain't that bad. And by the time we showed up, those Texans were thankfully starting to get a little winded. At any rate, neither me nor Peter figured their hell-raising was worth notifying you. Not last night. Especially after the day you had and all the times recently we already had to bother you."

"I appreciate that," Bob told him. "But any time you figure the best call is to send word or fetch me at home, don't hesitate to do it."

"I'll remember that," said Vern. "As far as damage done, there was a pretty fair amount suffered at the bawdy house. Furniture and the like. And Duchess was real prompt about calculating it up and bringing over the amount practically before we had those jaspers locked up."

Bob grinned. "From all reports, Duchess is mighty quick about money when it comes to all of her business transactions."

"Those Texans claim they got money to pay whatever the charges are," Vern said. "But we explained to 'em that the amount of their fines would have to be set by you this morning. They deserved to cool their heels behind bars for at least one night anyway. Way I see it, you'll probably want to charge 'em with disorderly conduct, assault, and disturbing the peace at the very least. I entered all the details in the report log before I turned in last night."

"Okay. Sounds good. I'll take it from here. What you need to do is go on home and grab a few more hours of rest so you can report back at noon."

"Like you said, that sounds good."

"Before you go, though—anything else happen last night I oughtta know about?"

Vern cocked an eyebrow. "Oh, yeah. A few things that might come back around again today. For starters, you know that Fred and Peter had no luck finding any matching footprints out at the butte, right? Fred said he was gonna let you know."

"Yeah, he stopped by the house before I headed out to the V-Slash."

"How did that go, by the way?"

Bob twisted his mouth sourly. "About like you'd expect. Hard news for 'em to get hit with. Despite his young age, the Clairmont kid had rode for the brand for quite a while. Sorta grew up there. But Carlos Vandez had recognized a wild streak in him when it came to an itch for using his guns, so it didn't come as a complete surprise. He'll be coming in after the body sometime today I expect, to take it out for burial on a plot they've got out at the ranch."

"That shooting naturally got the attention of a lot of folks. One of 'em, one I'm sure you will be hearing from yourself, and pretty quick, is that newspaper-man Dutton. He came around yesterday with about a million questions. But since none of us were there to see it go down—except for Bullock, and I don't know how much Dutton bugged him—there wasn't a whole lot in the way of details we could tell him."

"He's the kind who'll make up what he needs to sensationalize his story anyway," Bob muttered. "With any luck, Mike may have stuffed him in an empty beer keg and shipped him off to the brewery for a refill."

"A couple more visitors you can probably look forward to," Vern went on, "are Saul Norton and Myron Poppe, the bank clerk. Seems they both have some complaints to register about our pal Larkin. Sounded awful petty to me, in both cases."

Bob frowned. "After the beating he took, I'm surprised to hear Norton was up and about at all. Especially for some petty matter."

"He didn't look so hot, you're right about that. He was walking with a cane and his movements were mighty stiff. Almost hurt just looking at him. But I reckon feeling the need to speak up for his lady love's honor was pushing him past his pain."

"So that was his complaint? Larkin going to see Victoria Emory?"

"You know about that?"

"Some."

"Okay. Yeah, Norton's worked up because Larkin stopped by the Emory house to try and call on Miss Victoria. She met with him at the door for a few minutes, I guess—long enough to tell him she never wanted to see him again—and then he left peaceful-like. Don't really know what else Norton wants. Sorta the same thing for Mr. Poppe. His wife ran into Larkin in Krepdorf's store and they exchanged some unpleasant words with one another. That was what he wanted to report.

"They came in at the same time. Apparently they'd

got to talking about it inside the bank, comparing notes I guess you could say, and decided they could make a stronger complaint if they pitched it together. So me and Peter listened to their tales of woe, then had to tell them that, since Larkin hadn't broken any kind of law or anything, there wasn't a whole lot we could do. But I got a hunch neither of 'em will be satisfied until they bend your ear about it, too."

"Thanks. You've given me enough to look forward to for one morning," Bob said wryly. "So beat it. Get out of here and go get some rest before you think of something else."

Once Vern had left, Bob poured himself a cup of mud and sat down behind his desk to read the report log from last night. Most of it, not surprisingly, had to do with the incident at Duchess's bawdy house. A piece of stationery folded into the log next to Vern's entry contained, in a flowery woman's hand, a listing of damages amounting to seventy-five dollars. It was signed simply "D." Bob grinned again at the madam's efficiently subtle demand.

A moment later, however, his grin fell away hard. He got to the listing of the three Texans who'd caused said damage. Their names were Charley Drake, Wilbur Nixon . . . and *Rance Brannigan!*

For several clock ticks Bob sat perfectly still, staring down at the name as if stunned.

The day had finally come. Brannigan was in town.

When Bob's brain started to work again, started to propel his thoughts past the impact of Brannigan's name, it replayed Vern's words from a few minutes earlier: "*Neither me nor Peter figured their hell-raising was worth notifying you.*" Not worth notifying him!? After all the talk of Ed Wardell bringing in hardcases to fan the flames of a possible range war, how the hell could his two deputies think the arrival of Brannigan wasn't worth . . . Then the rest of it hit Bob. There was the trouble, the shortfall. After Fred had gotten Brannigan's name from the wire Smoky Barnett sent to Denver and then wrote it down on a scrap of paper for Bob to see, the marshal had shoved that paper in a desk drawer and the name was never specifically mentioned to either Vern or Peter. Any subsequent talk they heard about the outside gun Wardell might be bringing in was merely indirect references like "hardcase" or "hired gun."

Bob expelled a long, ragged breath and leaned back in his chair, as if trying to distance himself from the name now appearing once again in the report log. No amount of fretting over the lack of communication or the failure of an earlier notification really mattered, not when it came right down to it.

Brannigan was here. That was the long and the short of it. And now Bob was going to have to deal with him . . . however it played out.

CHAPTER 37

Myron Poppe was very distressed that morning. It wasn't unusual for him to feel apprehensive as he left the house for work. After all, it was pretty much a given that in the hours ahead he could look forward to another dose of demands and cutting remarks from his boss, Abraham Starbuck. As the head teller for the Starbuck Territorial Bank, Myron was responsible for not only his own actions but those of all the other tellers as well. And hardly a day went by that Mr. Starbuck, a stern taskmaster by anyone's standards, didn't find fault with something he felt necessary to bring to Myron's attention.

All of that was bad enough. But while Myron certainly didn't look forward to more of the same, it was common, to be expected, and so he therefore was somewhat inured to it. What he didn't need on top of it, however—what was pushing his normal anxieties to a higher level—was having his wife on his back about her confrontation with John Larkin and demanding Myron do something to rectify it. What exactly it was he was supposed to do he didn't know, and neither did she. But she still expected him to do *something* and, until he did, there would be no living with her. Or, to be more exact, living with her would be unbearable. She'd make sure of that.

Myron was not one given to curses or epithets, yet he muttered more than a few of them under his breath as he walked from his house and proceeded down residential First Street toward its intersection with the main drag of Front. Myron prided himself on his punctuality when it came to reporting for work, but he had a full hour before the bank would open for business. Mr. Starbuck was almost as irritable about employees reporting too early for work as he was about anyone showing up late. The bank's owner and president was probably already there himself, but that didn't mean he wanted anyone else around yet. Some speculated he had a bizarre obsession about being alone with "his money" for a portion of each day. Whether or not there was anything to that, Myron didn't know and didn't join in on the speculation. Frankly, he didn't give a damn. Especially not this morning.

Myron had left the house so early partly to get away from his wife and partly with the notion to have time for stopping in and seeing the marshal. He'd already spoken with two of the town's deputies about the situation regarding Larkin and his wife. He'd done so, in fact, accompanied by Saul Norton who turned out to have a similar issue regarding Larkin's approach to Norton's betrothed, Victoria Emory. As Myron had expected, since there were no illegalities involved, there really wasn't much the deputies could offer in the way of help or advice. It would likely be the same result with Marshal Hatfield, Myron figured, but it was still worth a try. At least it was something more he could report to his wife . . . for all the good it would do.

Of course, Myron told himself, if he were a different sort—more of a manly man, a type possessing the potential for physical action—he could confront Larkin face-to-face. Demand an apology for his wife and threaten to thrash the scoundrel within an inch of his life if ever anything similar occurred again . . . At some base level, whether she even realized it herself, that might have been the very thing his wife wanted him to do. But the plain reality of it was the fact that Myron was *not* the confrontational type, and any pretense of such by him, given his small stature and timid nature, would fall short to the point of almost being ridiculous.

With these thoughts swirling in his mind, Myron reached the intersection with Front Street. At this early hour, there was hardly any activity in either direction. He paused, gazing down the street toward the jail building, his stomach now churning with indecision on top of everything else.

"I'm having the same problem," said a voice from the opposite way Myron was looking.

Myron jerked around, startled. On the other side of First Street, on the corner of the block that housed the Starbuck bank building, Saul Norton was sitting on a wooden bench at the end of the boardwalk. He was impeccably dressed, with a shiny black cane resting across his lap. But apart from his attire, he didn't look very good. He was very pale, showing in particularly sharp contrast to the purplish-black circles around his eyes and the large bruise on high cheekbone. His eyes looked somewhat pain-dulled though struggling to stay alert.

"Sorry if I gave you a start," the battered apparition said. "I've been waiting here a while, hoping you'd be along. I had a hunch you probably would be since I knew that, like me, you weren't satisfied with the answers we got out of those two deputies yesterday . . . I wanted to get an early start this morning in order to this time catch the marshal before he got involved with other things. I expected you'd be thinking along those same lines."

"Yes. Yes, that's exactly what I was thinking," Myron said. "Although, to tell the truth, I don't have my hopes up for results that are any more satisfying."

Norton issued a dry chuckle. "Once again we're thinking along the same lines. I've been sitting here with the same thought running through my head."

He stood up, the motion slow and rather jerky. He used the cane to push up and steady himself. Then he stepped off the boardwalk and started walking over to Myron, wincing with every other step.

"No offense, but you look dreadful. You're obviously in a great deal of pain," Myron said, his brows knitting with concern. "You belong home in bed, healing, not straining yourself so."

"I'll start healing only after that damned brassy John Larkin is put in his place," Norton declared. "A no-account lowlife like him ought not be loose in public, let alone free to accost fine, decent women. If it's not a crime, then it's still a dirty shame. And that's for certain."

"Yes. Yes, it is," Myron agreed.

"I can appreciate the limitations the marshal and his men have to operate under," Norton went on. "I don't like it in this particular instance, but at the same time I understand there have to be rules against lawmen running roughshod like some are known to do."

Myron frowned, not sure how to respond.

"So," Norton continued, now having reached him and coming to a halt at his side, "when the rules have the hands of lawmen tied, it sometimes falls to an individual to take care of his own problems. I think you and I may have reached that point with our respective situations."

"What do you mean? What are you driving at?"

Norton lifted his cane and pointed in the direction of the Shirley House Hotel across the street. "John Larkin is over there right now, swamping out the Shirley House bar. He's living and sleeping in the corner of a storeroom like a human rat. He took over the job that a lowly damn nigger didn't want to do—that's the kind of scum we're talking about. Scum that the law and its rules allow to roam the street and upset our womenfolk."

"I-I still don't see your point. I'm not saying I disagree with anything you just said," Myron replied, although in truth he hated anyone using the term "nigger," "but I'm not sure I understand what you're suggesting we do about it."

Norton lowered his cane and stabbed its point down into the ground. "I'm saying we forget the law, since we're convinced it can't or won't do anything to do us any good, and go over there and confront Larkin ourselves."

"Confront?" Myron echoed, his voice cracking slightly. "Again, I'm not arguing that doesn't sound like a wonderful notion . . . But not, I fear, for me. Take a look, Mr. Norton, and be honest. Do I strike you as the confrontational sort? Do I look like I could intimidate anyone more substantial than perhaps a grade school–aged child?"

Something akin to an impatient growl escaped Norton before he said, "For the love of Christ, man, I'm not suggesting we go over there and physically attack Larkin, try to *bully* him into seeing things our way. Do *I* look like I'm in condition for anything like that? Under different circumstances, yeah, I might try exactly that . . . But I'm not that stupid, not the way things stand now. Still, that don't mean we can't stand nose to nose with that sonofabitch—like *men*—and tell him to lay off our women."

"Or what?" Myron wanted to know. "Doesn't a demand like that—a threat, if you will—require something to back it up? We've each of us just got done admitting we're in no position to deliver that kind of follow-through."

"You'd be surprised," Norton countered, "how effective an angry cussing-out can be just in itself. Larkin's not going to lay a hand on us, either, not with both of us there to serve as witnesses we did nothing to provoke it turning physical. And if we've got the balls to look him square in the eye and demand he back the hell down and leave our women alone, how is he going to know we *don't* have a way to back it up? We're both men of means, right? The way his mind works, don't you think he might logically figure that—without us ever saying anything to suggest it, but given the self-righteous anger we'll be displaying—we might possibly be willing to *hire* some backup if we have to?"

All of a sudden, this was starting to sound like not such a crazy idea to Myron. His heart quickened and his mind raced. Him, getting in the face of somebody, demanding they "back the hell off," and enforcing it with the unspoken threat that he'd do whatever it took if they didn't pay attention . . . What would be the look on his wife's face when he told her he'd taken such action?

"Do you really think it could work?" Myron asked.

"I damn well do," Norton assured him. "What have we got to lose if it doesn't? At worst, it's a sight better than slinking around, frustrated and defeated because the law can't or won't do anything to help us, isn't it?"

Myron turned his head and looked across the street, setting his gaze on the Shirley House Hotel. Slowly his expression hardened and his gaze became a glare.

"All right, let's do it," he said, his tone uncharacteristically flat and steady. "Let's go confront that sonofabitch."

CHAPTER 38

"So are we gonna crowd 'em on it—on knowing that they're here as hired guns for Ed Wardell?" said Deputy Fred, who'd arrived at the jail and been promptly filled in by Bob about their guests back in the lockup.

Bob shook his head. "No. I don't want to give 'em the satisfaction of thinking they're important enough for us to have any advance concern over 'em. If they're what we think they are—*know* they are—they'll show their hands soon enough. When they do, that's when we'll show ours."

"Okay. However you want to play it," said Fred.

Bob leaned back, half-sitting on the corner of his desk, arms folded across his chest. "Go ahead and bring 'em out, then. Let's see if they've got the money they're supposed to have to pay their fines. If they do, we'll turn 'em loose and find out how fast they head for the Rocking W."

Fred took a ring of keys from a peg and disappeared through the heavy door that led back to the cellblock. Bob sat and waited, listening to the murmur of voices and the echoing clank of steel coming from back there. A curious kind of calm had settled over him. His jaw was set, his eyes were focused on the cellblock doorway . . . waiting for the first sight of Rance Brannigan. Now, after all the thoughts and emotions that had been roiling inside him these past few days, he actually wanted it to happen, wanted to make this initial eye contact in order to see Brannigan's reaction and find out where it was going to take them.

Three men emerged from the cellblock ahead of Fred. All were of a similar stamp—lean, unshaven, with hard, alert eyes and a way of carrying themselves that conveyed a sense of being poised for trouble. Fred directed them out into the office and then told them to halt in a line before Bob.

Brannigan had been the last of the three to come out. He was a couple inches taller than his two companions, topping out around six feet even. His hat rested back on his shoulders from a chin loop, exposing a headful of thick, dark hair and the narrow blade of a face that Bob remembered well. There was a thin scar above his left eye that hadn't been there before, the split it made in his eyebrow causing it to be more noticeable than it otherwise might have been. His eyes were restless, dark, and sunken deep in their sockets. When they settled on the marshal there was, at most, a split second where they widened ever so slightly with what Bob took as recognition. But then, immediately, any further sign of a reaction was gone and they merely were regarding him with a flat stare.

"This is Marshal Bob Hatfield, gents," Fred told them. "He'll be telling you the charges against you and discussing any fines due in accordance . . . Marshal, who we've got here is Charley Drake, Wilbur Nixon, and Rance Brannigan." Fred gestured to each as he named them.

Bob flicked his eyes only briefly to the other two, otherwise he kept his own flat stare locked with that of Brannigan. Waiting to see if the Texan would keep his cool or break down and declare recognition.

Charley Drake was a blocky, square-faced individual with a cruel twist to his mouth. Wilbur Nixon had a slight slump to his shoulders and an oversized nose protruding out from below beady, too-close eyes. The fact they made no attempt to say anything but cast their eyes expectantly over at Brannigan made it clear enough who was the headman of the trio.

"Well, Marshal Hatfield," Brannigan said, pronouncing "Hat-field" in two distinct syllables and dragging it out just a bit, tossing what Bob took as another sign of his recognition yet not stating anything openly. "I guess sayin' something like 'good morning' or 'pleased to meet ya' would be kinda dumb, wouldn't it? So, speaking for myself as well as my two pards here, what I *can* say is that a night in your jail has driven home to us the point that we got off on the wrong foot in your town with our bad behavior. We're rightfully sorry, are prepared to pay the fines you're about to levy, and give you our word that our future behavior will be restrained so as not to bring us before you again."

Bob cocked a single eyebrow. "Well now, you rattled

off that little spiel pretty slick. Almost sounded like you might have had some practice saying it before."

"I'm forced to admit that, in the past, we used to run with an ill-behaved crowd who *did* put us in similar fixes," replied Brannigan. "But although I guess some of their bad habits sorta rubbed off on us, we're tryin' our best to ride a smarter, better trail, Marshal."

Bob continued to eye him. "Uh-huh. It also sounds like you've come here with the intention of sticking around for a while. Is that so?"

"Indeed it is. We've been in contact with a local rancher by the name of Wardell. He's agreed to hire us on . . . I trust you're familiar with the Rockin' W operation?"

Bob had no way of knowing just how well informed Brannigan was of the whole Wardell situation. A man who hires out his gun does it for the money and more often than not doesn't care about the particulars other than who's paying him and what (or who) they want him to take care of. As far as Bob knew, Brannigan was merely responding to a summons to come do his kind of work, without knowing very many details. Yet there was a taunting edge to the Texan's question about Bob's own familiarity with the Rocking W that made the marshal suspect Brannigan might already damn well know that dealing with him would be part of the job.

For whatever reason, his old nemesis was in no hurry to reveal Bob's past and his true identity as Bob Holland, aka the Devil's River Kid. So okay, Bob would play along. For now. The lid would blow off soon enough; there was no need in rushing it.

"Yeah, I know the Rocking W," Bob said without elaboration.

"Well then, you must know Mr. Wardell better than we do." Brannigan paused and showed a sheepish grin. "But whatever kind of fella he is, I reckon he wouldn't appreciate us lingerin' here in town after he sent us travelin' money and all. So, if you'd be so kind, Marshal Hatfield, I'd be obliged if we could get to settlin' up our fines and whatnot so's we can be on our way out to the Rockin' W."

Once again Brannigan put that odd, broken emphasis on "Hat-field."

Their stares locked and, for several clock ticks, it was like everything and everybody else went away. It was just the two of them, glaring into each other's minds and souls . . . *Okay, you bastard. I know you, you know me. How long are we going to carry on this charade before we get to finishing the unsettled business between us . . .* Until, abruptly, Brannigan broke eye contact and glanced somewhat uneasily over at his companions.

"Okay," said Bob, reaching around for the papers he'd prepared detailing the charges and fines facing the trio, along with the damage compensation owed Duchess. "I hope you've got a good chunk of that traveling money left, because you're gonna need it . . ."

A short time later, the fines were paid and Brannigan and his cohorts had departed. Fred was standing by the office's front window, gazing in the direction the three had gone, toward the livery stable.

"You really think it was a good idea to give them their guns back?" Fred asked over his shoulder.

"It wouldn't have done us much good to keep 'em. Not like they can't easily buy more or get all they want out at the Rocking W," Bob replied.

"I suppose," said Fred, turning away from the window. "It's just that handing a fella a gun that you figure there's a good chance will be aimed back at you someday . . . doggone it, that's a little unsettling."

"There are guns already here and others coming in all the time that might be aimed at us someday, Fred. You ought to be used to that by now."

Fred sighed. "Yeah, I know. I guess there was something about those three *hombres* that unnerved me a little. Especially that Brannigan, who did all the talking . . . He was a cool customer, though, you got to give him that."

"You don't know the half of it," Bob muttered.

"How's that?"

"Nothing. Never mind." Bob held out an envelope. "Here's the money due Duchess over at the Grand bawdy house for the damage those three did there. Think you can take this over to her, get a receipt, and make it back without falling in love with one of her doves?"

Fred blushed furiously. "Aw, come on, boss. You know I never—"

"I know, I know. I'm just teasing you a little. But take care of it for me, will you? If I go over there myself and Consuela catches wind of it, I'll get cornered into giving explanations for the next three days."

Fred's blush turned into a grin. "The marshal getting the law laid down to him, eh? I'd like to see that."

"No you wouldn't," said Bob, shaking his head. "Sometimes, when she gets really mad, she starts jabbering in Spanish. Later, after she finally cools down, I ask her what it was she was saying and she translates it into words that make my ears burn."

CHAPTER 39

Fred was still grinning as he took the envelope and started out. When he pulled open the front door, however, Saul Norton immediately stumbled through and nearly fell into his arms.

"Marshal . . . Deputy," Norton gasped, partly out of breath, partly in pain. "You'd better come quick, I think there's going to be bad trouble."

Fred grabbed the man, steadying him as Bob hurried across the room to assist. Norton's cane slipped from his fingers and clattered to the floor.

"Here, get him into a chair. Be careful, he's battered from head to toe." As Bob said this, he ducked his head under one of Norton's arms. Cautious though the two lawmen were, their handling of him caused Norton to throw back his head, wincing, sucking a sharp intake of breath.

"You darn fool, you shouldn't be up and about," Bob said as he and Fred lowered the pain-racked man onto a chair. "But where's this bad trouble you're talking about—at Jackson Emory's place?"

"N-No, not there . . . Just up the street . . . at the Shirley House Hotel."

"The Shirley House? What's going on there?"

"It's Myron Poppe . . . He's going after Larkin . . . He's making threats and acting crazy."

"Myron Poppe!?" Bob and Fred echoed together. Then, needing to confirm even more the words he'd just heard, Bob said, "Myron Poppe is making threats against Larkin?"

Norton bobbed his head frantically. "Like I said, it's as if he's gone crazy . . . We'd arranged to meet early this morning . . . to come here and talk with you about the concerns we had with the way Larkin treated our women . . . But when Myron showed up, he was in a rage like I wouldn't have thought possible for him . . . I think his shrew of a wife must have been nagging him something awful . . . Anyway, he wasn't interested in coming here anymore. He wanted to go straight to find Larkin, have it out directly with him, he said . . . Somehow he'd found out Larkin was swamping at the Shirley House . . . I tried to stop him. When he found out I wouldn't go with him, he shoved me away. Actually knocked me down . . ."

"Does he have a weapon?" Bob wanted to know.

"I didn't see one . . . But he kept reaching into his pocket with one hand. I-I think he might have had something in there . . . I don't know exactly what he has in mind, and there's no way of telling what Larkin will do if Myron comes at him the way he's acting . . . But I don't think it'll be good . . . You need to get over there, Marshal!"

Bob swore under his breath. "You'd better stay here with him," he said to Fred. "I'll go see what's up."

* * *

John Larkin heard the faint scratching noise at the back door right after he'd finished emptying the last of the spittoons into the large wooden slop bucket. He paused, listening for the noise to repeat. When it didn't, one corner of his mouth lifted in a wry smile. He had a pretty good idea what it was anyway. Freda Draeger, who ran the Shirley House with her husband Frank, had a habit of tossing out bones and food scraps each morning from the rear door of the hotel kitchen, said door being only about twenty feet down from the back door of the bar area. Mornings when she was running a little late with this disposal, the stray dogs and cats who roamed the surrounding alleys and had become accustomed to the buffet Freda provided sometimes got impatient and demonstrated so by scratching at one or both of the doors that opened onto their alley.

Since John was ready to carry his bucket out and empty it in the big, four-holer outhouse that served the hotel bar, he figured he would soon encounter whatever hungry critter was out there. His smile stretching a bit wider, he muttered as he started for the door, "Scratch all you want, Mr. Mongrel or Miss Pussycat, I don't think you're going to be very interested in what it is I'm hauling out."

A moment later, as Larkin elbowed open the door and stepped outside, what he found waiting for him wasn't any kind of four-legged critter at all. There was a critter there all right, but it was the two-legged variety—a well-dressed man lying facedown on the alley floor with one arm stretched out, fingertips reaching to where they would have been scraping on the base of the door before it opened inward. This much registered only vaguely with Larkin. What really drew his attention was the handle of the knife poking up from middle of the man's back . . . its blade driven to the hilt through the victim's spine.

Larkin just stood there for a long minute. Frozen. Not moving, not able to take his eyes off the sprawled figure.

And then the man groaned and his reaching fingers twitched.

Larkin came out of his spell. He sat the bucket down heavily and dropped to his knees beside the man. He reached with one hand and very gently placed it on the man's back, very near where the knife was embedded. He fought the urge to pull it out. Something told him that wasn't the right thing to do. He might only make the injury worse.

"Jesus God, mister. H-Hold still . . . I'll go get help."

At that instant, the other door, the door to the kitchen area that also accessed the alley at the rear of the hotel building, opened and Freda Draeger stepped out with her pan of bones and food scraps. Freda's gaze fell first on Larkin and a pleasant smile started to form on her lips. Then her eyes dropped to the man with the knife in his back. Her expression instantly turned horrified, her pan of food scraps dropped from her hands, and her mouth opened incredibly wide to emit the most piercing, blood-curdling scream imaginable.

Larkin shot to his feet and extended his arms,

palms out. "No! No, it wasn't me . . . It isn't how it looks . . . Send somebody for the marshal!"

Those words were barely out of his mouth before a voice behind him said, "That won't be necessary. I'm already here."

Freda bolted back inside, still screaming her head off.

Knowing better than to make any sudden moves, Larkin turned slowly around. He found himself facing Bob Hatfield. What was more, he found himself looking down the muzzle of the marshal's drawn Colt.

"This ain't how it looks, Marshal. I swear . . . I just stepped out here to empty my bucket and found him laying there."

"You'll get the chance to tell your story. But for right now I'm going by the story my eyes are telling me."

"This man ain't dead yet," Larkin said frantically. "You need to get a doctor here and try to save him. He'll tell you it wasn't me who—"

Bob cut him off, saying, "I expect Freda's wailing will fetch the doctor and plenty of other folks pretty quick. In the meantime, you take these and clamp them on." With his left hand, at all times keeping the Colt leveled with his right, Bob pulled a pair of handcuffs from his belt and shook them open. As he tossed them to Larkin, he added, "I'm pretty sure you're familiar with how they work."

Larkin caught the cuffs, grimacing as he did so. "This is ridiculous! I don't even know this man!"

"Lying won't make it any better, son. If I'm not

mistaken, that's Myron Poppe lying there at your feet and you mentioned his name to me just yesterday— Now get those cuffs on!"

Larkin fumbled with the cuffs, attempting to get them untangled. "I don't give a damn who he is. I tell you I—" Abruptly, the cuffs slipped from his fumbling fingers and dropped straight down into the slop bucket, landing with a thick *plop!*

"That was an accident. I swear!" Larkin was quick to claim.

"That's too bad," Bob said through clenched teeth. "Reach in and get 'em out. Then get 'em on!"

Larkin's nostrils flared. "To hell with that! No way I'm gonna—"

Bob's Colt roared and spat a tongue of red flame. It also spat a bullet that tore into the ground a fraction of an inch ahead of Larkin's right foot.

"I'll take off a toe with the next one. Do like I told you and get those goddamn cuffs on!" the marshal ordered.

Slowly, Larkin sank back onto one knee. With his right hand, he reached into the bucket and thrust it into the sloppy accumulation of cigarette butts, tobacco juice, and spit. All the while he glared hatefully up at Bob.

Bob edged a little closer as Larkin continued to grope for the cuffs. "Come on, they can't be that hard to find in there," he said.

Larkin placed his left hand near the bottom of the bucket on the outside, holding it steady as he plunged deeper with his right. Then, in a sudden burst of desperation and rage, Larkin lunged to his feet as he simultaneously lifted the bucket and hurled it up into Bob's face. In its upward swing, the lip of the bucket caught the marshal's wrist, knocking his gun hand high as another shot exploded harmlessly from the Colt.

Blinded by the faceful of slop and bulled backward by the weight and force of Larkin barreling into him, Bob was driven to the ground, landing on his back with his attacker on top of him. Larkin hammered a furious rain of blows—right, left, right—down on the marshal. Unable to see, Bob had no chance to block or strike back effectively. When he was near the point of unconsciousness from the pounding, there was a momentary reprieve. But it lasted only for as long as it took Larkin to grab the fallen bucket and slam it down for a finisher that knocked Bob the rest of the way out cold.

CHAPTER 40

"No! I'm the one who let the sneaky bastard get away, that makes me the one to go after him. It's not a job that requires a full posse."

Bob Hatfield made this statement from the seat of a wooden chair in the barroom of the Shirley House Hotel. He was stripped to the waist, and on the table beside where he sat there rested a washbasin full of sudsy water with a washcloth floating in it. As he spoke, Bob was drying his freshly scrubbed face and torso with a large towel that bore lettering identifying it as belonging to the hotel.

A small group was gathered around the table where Bob sat—Doc Tibbs, Fred Ordway, Frank Draeger, Saul Norton, Peter Macy, and Earl Hines. A short distance from the table, the back door of the barroom remained open and the body of Myron Poppe was partly visible where it still lay on the ground. Less than an hour had passed since the discovery of the body and John Larkin's breakaway from the scene. In that time, even with the good doctor's arrival and his best efforts to prevent it,

Poppe had died. Someone had removed their coat and spread it over the shoulders and head of the little man, signaling the fact that the knife had taken its ultimate toll.

In response to Bob's statement, Doc Tibbs said, "Although past experience has taught me I'm probably wasting my breath, I'll go ahead and point out anyway that, due to the beating you suffered and especially the wallop to the head that knocked you out, you ought not be charging off anywhere. The smart thing would be for you to take it easy for at least twenty-four hours."

"You're right, Doc, you just wasted your breath," Bob told him. "But you said your piece, so now you can have a clear conscience."

"If anyone deserves to be questioning his conscience, what about the blacksmith here?" spoke up Norton, who also occupied a chair at the same table where Bob sat. His movements upon entering the barroom had been jerkier and his color even worse than when he showed up at the jail earlier. But none of that lessened the venom he now directed at Hines. "If you hadn't so obligingly provided Larkin a horse and gun when he came scurrying to you for help, nobody would have to worry about chasing after him at all."

"How was I supposed to know he was on the run from the marshal?" Hines said defensively.

"If Larkin hadn't got what he wanted from Hines," Fred interjected, "he would have gotten it somewhere else. And being a man on the run, he might have resorted to hurting somebody more in the process. We can at least be thankful for that much."

"And if you want to talk about a clean conscience," Hines said, directing some heat of his own back at Norton, "who's the one who helped egg Poppe on and got him agitated enough to go after John in the first place? We don't even know for sure if the knife that ended up in him didn't start out in his own hand."

"How vicious!" Norton snarled. "To talk so disparagingly of the innocent dead and, what's worse, to do it on behalf of a proven criminal who isn't fit to—"

"Knock it off!" Bob said through gritted teeth. "This is no time for bitching and blaming. Both of you could have done things different—maybe it would've helped, maybe it wouldn't have mattered at all. I could have been sharper when I had the drop on Larkin, too. But all of that is behind us now. What matters most, right at the moment, is running down the fugitive and bringing him back here so we can get to the bottom of it all."

"We're already *at* the bottom of it, aren't we?" said Norton. "A man is dead, murdered . . . one of the most gentle souls in town . . . and everybody here knows who did it. It's plain enough what has to be done with the killer once he's apprehended and returned."

"You sound like you'd be ready to hang him on the spot," said Peter, who'd been called back on duty early, along with his brother, due to what had transpired. "Aren't you forgetting a little something called a trial?"

"A trial!" spat Norton. "That conniving ingrate got a trial last time and all it did was send him to prison just long enough for him to grow more hardened and bitter. All it did was delay the inevitable, I say!"

"And that kind of attitude," Hines said, "may be exactly what caused him to run, even if he's innocent."

Norton pointed toward the open doorway. "Are you forgetting the dead man lying right there? How could the villain caught kneeling over him be innocent?"

"Maybe it was an accident," suggested Fred Draeger.

"Then why didn't Larkin stay and defend himself, try to explain? Innocent men don't run away!"

"You might be surprised," Bob said, not quite under his breath.

"What was that?" asked the doctor.

"Nothing. Must've been thinking out loud," muttered Bob.

Before he was called on to elaborate further, there was a stirring of voices and movement from up toward the front of the barroom. Looking around, Bob saw that Consuela and Vern Macy had entered and were moving toward him. Vern had a fringed buckskin war bag slung over one shoulder, and Consuela was carrying a folded article of clothing. The corners of Bob's mouth lifted and his heart swelled at the sight of his beautiful wife, the way it always did when he gazed upon her, no matter the circumstances. In return, however, Consuela's expression was etched with concern.

Bob had sent Vern to fetch his war bag from the house. He well knew that Consuela would realize what that meant—that he was heading out on a manhunt. The bag, which rested on the floor of their bedroom closet when not needed, was at all times packed and ready with certain items: a backup Schofield revolver; extra ammo, both for the Schofield and his .44; a compass; and a pair of high-quality binoculars. Consuela was the only person other than himself who knew the full story of how the bag and its essentials dated back to his days as the Devil's River Kid.

Bob was confident that, upon hearing his request for the war bag, Consuela would include some additional staples like a change of clothes and probably a pack of beef jerky. What he hadn't quite expected, because it had never happened before, was that she would accompany its delivery.

"You didn't have to come all the way down here," he said as she marched up and handed him the clean shirt he'd asked Vern to also bring him.

Very earnestly, Consuela said, "What kind of wife would I be if I did not come to see my husband off with no certainty for how long he'll be gone yet with a strong certainty he may be facing danger while he is away?"

Bob realized belatedly that, in spite of all the years Consuela had been part of his life and all the other occasions when he'd gone out leading a posse or on an individual chase, this was the first time he was leaving her behind as a wife. He realized further that he should have gone to her and told her himself what he was planning, not sent an intermediary.

He took the clean shirt she held out, set it aside, then wrapped his hands around hers. "There's only one kind of wife you ever could be . . . the best kind," he told her. "Surely one who deserves better than somebody as thoughtless and rude as me. I'm sorry

I didn't think to come and explain things to you myself. Try to forgive me."

"I will, but only on one condition," Consuela said sternly. Then her expression melted into a smile as she added, "And that is, that you make it back to me in one piece!"

"Sounds like a condition I can agree to," Bob said.

"Good. Now don't you think you'd better put a shirt on? You might have a hard time convincing folks you're a marshal if you go running around with nowhere to pin your badge."

A short time later, Bob was ready to ride out in pursuit of Larkin. He'd kissed Consuela good-bye and left it to her to give Bucky his love and explain why he had to leave with all haste. He knew that she also would take it upon herself to help calm the distraught Freda Draeger and then join other towns-women in doing their best to console the newly widowed Mrs. Poppe. Myron's mortal remains, in the meantime, were gathered up by undertaker O'Malley and his men and removed from the blood-ied alley where he fell.

Bob's three deputies walked with him down to Peterson's livery where a horse was saddled and wait-ing. At the last minute, before they left the Shirley House barroom, Owen Dutton the newspaperman had shown up clamoring for details on what had hap-pened. Inasmuch as Bob needed to be on his way and wanted some time to confer alone with his men, the sputtering, demanding Dutton was held at bay and told he'd have to wait until some appropriate time could be afforded him.

"I'm leaving you fellas with plenty in your laps," Bob said when it was just the four of them in the stable, "but dealing with that pain-in-the-ass pip-squeak might be the worst of it. I feel kinda bad, but I'd be lying if I said I was sorry I'm getting away from him."

"Don't worry, boss, we'll handle Dutton," Fred told him. "If he gets to be too big a pain we'll soak his head in a tub of his own ink until the bubbles quit coming."

"That'd give him a headline to write about," said Vern.

"And he won't have to bother other folks with questions because he'll know all the details first-hand," added Peter.

"Seriously," said Bob, "give him the least you can to satisfy him and try to keep him from stirring everybody up any more than necessary about this killing— or whatever else he might decide to go after. I don't want to bring John Larkin back to a whole town that's in a lynch mob mood like Saul Norton."

Fred made a sour face. "Yeah. Boy, he's really got it in for Larkin, don't he?"

"Nothing new about that," pointed out Bob.

"No, but the way he was acting back there a little while ago it was like he was practically foaming at the mouth over the thought of seeing Larkin with a noose around his neck."

"Maybe," said Vern, "he's overreacting out of guilt for leaving Myron Poppe and letting him go to see Larkin on his own."

"Could be that, could be more," said Bob.

"What are you thinking? You got a hunch about something?" Peter asked.

Now it was Bob's turn to make a sour face. "Not really. Something about Norton just chaps me, that's all . . . No more than that, I guess."

"But you *do* think Larkin killed Mr. Poppe, right?" said Vern, frowning. "I mean, you found him right there beside the body while it was still warm."

"That I did." Bob sighed. "Look, we're not gonna come up with any answers right here on the spot. The main thing right now is to catch Larkin and haul him back. The rest of it will shake out from there. That's what trials are for."

The marshal swung up into his saddle and swept his gaze over his deputies. "The main thing to keep an eye on while I'm gone—and a big reason why I'm leaving all three of you behind—is the situation between the Rocking W and the V-Slash." When Vern and Peter were called in early, Fred had given them a quick rundown on how the three Texans they'd jailed the night before were the expected hired guns Ed Wardell had called in. "With those gunnies on the scene now," Bob went on, "I expect that situation to build up pressure fast. As long as they keep it out on the range, there's only so much we can do. But if it spills into town, then it's a different story. That's the part I'm afraid of. Especially if Brannigan and those other two come back into town and run into any V-Slash riders who also happen to be here. The gunnies will try to crowd 'em, you can bet on that. And if the V-Slash boys do any pushing back, there will be bloody hell to pay."

"We'll keep a close eye on it, Marshal," Peter said in a somber tone.

"We'll stay frosty and have each other's backs," added Vern.

"You can count on us, boss."

Bob nodded. "I know I can. Look out for each other and look out for the town. I'll be back as quick as I can."

CHAPTER 41

Rance Brannigan sat on the open front porch of Ed Wardell's sprawling ranch house and listened to his new employer ramble on about "dirty, cattle-stealing Mexicans" and "the worthless local law" and how there came a time when a man had no choice but to "take the bull by the horns and by-God do what he has to do for the sake of protecting his own." Brannigan smiled slyly behind the rim of the glass of bourbon he lifted to his lips and sipped from. How many times had he heard a variation of those words from other men like Wardell? Men who weren't about to soil their own hands from "taking the bull by the horns" but rather relegated that kind of dirty work to the likes of Brannigan. What was more, they all felt they had to explain themselves in some way, justify their actions, when everybody knew all that really mattered to the Brannigans of the world was the money being offered to do what they were being asked to do.

What made this particular spiel especially tedious for Brannigan was the fact that, as he sat and listened to it, his mind was being tugged in a whole different direction. *Dirty Mexicans,* blah, blah, blah . . . *missing cattle,* blah, blah, blah . . . *worthless local law,* blah, blah, blah . . . Yeah, Brannigan absorbed enough to get the general drift. It wasn't very hard. But all the while, a larger portion of his thoughts were swirling around quite another subject: Bob Hatfield, the marshal of Rattlesnake Wells . . . aka Bob Hammond, formerly of Calderone County, Texas . . . aka the Devil's River Kid . . .

Here.

Alive.

Holy shit!

It was almost too incredible to believe. And yet, in what might be called a cockeyed twist of fate, it was really quite fitting and proper. After all, seven years ago, when everybody else was so damned willing to accept that the Devil's River Kid must surely have perished in that freak blizzard, it was Brannigan who'd held fast to the belief that the sneaky bastard had somehow gotten away. And now, after all the years and all the hard miles trampled in between, Brannigan had walked out of that cellblock this morning and looked the truth square in the face!

There was no doubt in Brannigan's mind that Hatfield and Hammond/Devil's River Kid were one and the same. He'd never stood face-to-face with the man before, but he'd sure as hell chased him for a long enough period and had gotten enough fleeting, though clear, glimpses of him through binocular lenses. Now, albeit joltingly unexpected, here he was again.

The only question nagging Brannigan, however,

was whether or not *he* had been recognized in return. His name had most likely been known to the fugitive, so there was one point right there that should have registered. And, if Hammond/Hatfield had a telescope or binoculars of his own, then it seemed reasonable to figure that he had gotten some good looks at Brannigan as well. Yet, if there *had* been recognition, the man behind the marshal's badge this morning sure as hell played it cool. Why? He could have easily sent the fat deputy on some bogus errand and then drilled all three prisoners—calling it an attempted escape—thereby immediately and effectively eliminating Brannigan as the threat he posed to revealing the marshal's outlaw past.

What had prevented him from doing that? Did he truly *not* recognize Brannigan—or was he calculating a more devious way to react? Or was he merely planning a simple ambush for some remote spot later on?

Brannigan's thoughts were jerked back to the matter at hand by Wardell saying in a rather sharp tone, "Mr. Brannigan! You'll forgive me if I say that it seems like your mind is on something else."

Brannigan sat up a little straighter in his chair. "No, not at all, Mr. Wardell. Just a little wore out from the trail, that's all . . . Ain't that right, boys?"

Drake and Nixon, who'd silently been nursing their own glasses of bourbon from where they sat at the same table with Brannigan and Wardell, bobbed their heads agreeably. Smoky Barnett, Wardell's ramrod, also present on the porch but only just leaning against one of the support posts, looked on with an expression that suggested he was neither convinced nor particularly impressed by the trio.

"From the things you've told us," Brannigan continued in response to Wardell, "you want the rustling of your cattle stopped and you want this unwelcome beaner neighbor of yours, this Valdez, gotten rid of. Ain't that what it boils down to?"

Wardell scowled. "His name is *Van*-dez, not Valdez. And when you say 'gotten rid of' . . . I never meant to imply I was advocating murder or anything like that."

After taking another long pull of his bourbon, Brannigan said, "The way I see it, you've got three problems. Number one, you're losing cattle. Number two, you figure this Vandez *hombre* and his outfit are the ones skimming them off. Number three, my read is that you neither like nor trust any damn Mexes and you definitely don't want one as your neighbor. Am I wrong on any of those?"

"Well . . . no, not exactly," Wardell said, fidgeting slightly under Brannigan's close scrutiny.

"Okay, then. If all we do is stop the rustling that's presently taking place but we leave Vandez alone, what does that get you? You still won't like having him for a neighbor and you still won't be able to trust that he won't start up pilfering your herd again at some future point. Right?"

When Wardell didn't answer right away, Brannigan continued regardless. "So here's the thing. Me and my pards didn't ride here to hire on for the long haul. We don't figure on popping no brush nor branding no cows' asses. We do what we do— what we know *how* to do, in order to make the fix permanent-like—then we ride on. Now if that ain't what you had in mind, if you ain't ready to hire us and let us operate the way we do, then there's no hard feelings except you're out the expense money you sent to bring us here, and we'll just drift on . . . What do you say?"

Again Wardell took his time responding. When he did, he said, "How about letting Smoky show you to the bunkhouse where you can pick a spot for your gear, wash up, and get ready for lunch at the grub shack? Afterward, he can show you around some. Then, this evening, you're invited back here for supper and we'll finalize our arrangement."

"Sounds good to me," Brannigan said with a nod. "Done and done."

In spite of the aches and pains from the beating he'd endured, Saul Norton felt pretty good. Finally, one of the plans he'd set in motion had panned out like he hoped—hell, had worked out *better* than he dared hope. He'd not only placed that troublesome damn Larkin in a knot but, with none other than the marshal himself finding the ex-con kneeled over the murder victim, it was so secure there was no imaginable way for him to wiggle out.

Once Hatfield caught up with the unfortunate wretch—which he would, he always did—one of two things was bound to subsequently happen. If Norton's streak of good luck held, the marshal would be forced to shoot and kill the fleeing man. That would end it once and for all. But even if he only captured Larkin and returned with him as a prisoner, a trial leading to a hanging was sure to follow. With two highly credible witnesses like Freda Draeger and Hatfield serving as witnesses to Larkin's heinous act just short of actually seeing him plunge the knife into poor, undeserving Myron Poppe, how could any other verdict be reached?

To help whip up the mood of the town in order to not only stifle John Larkin's "likable" image once and for all but to also help instill the mood for hanging justice, Norton had given a lengthy and impassioned interview to Owen Dutton, the newspaperman. He had painted Larkin in the darkest hues, going all the way back five years, and had praised Myron Poppe as the gentlest of souls driven to anger by Larkin's coarse treatment of Myron's equally sweet and gentle wife. "*Must a man pay with his life for merely defending the honor of the woman he loves?*" Norton had wailed. From Dutton's track record for heavily embellished style when it came to the articles he wrote, and by the way he was furiously scribbling down this quote and others, Norton knew that his article(s) on this particular matter would set exactly the right tone of sensationalism and outrage that Norton wanted to see grip the town.

All things considered, Norton was practically skipping (aches and all) as he proceeded up the graveled walk leading to the front door of the Emory home where he was still staying to convalesce. He would, of course, be in for a scolding from Victoria for venturing out again—just like when he'd gone out yesterday and fortuitously ended up running into little Poppe for the first time—rather than staying in and resting to aid his healing. But he would counter once again by arguing it was better to stretch his bruised, aching joints instead of letting them stiffen up from too much inactivity. And then, when he broke the horrid news of what had happened to Poppe, all else would be forgotten.

Upon being ushered into the Emory manse by the ever-present Graedon, Norton's expectations for what came next proved totally accurate. In a matter of minutes, after withstanding Victoria's scolding and then her gentle murmurings of concern for his battered condition, he'd asked for the rest of the family to join them in the parlor. With the patriarch and the two daughters seated expectantly and Graedon stationed on the perimeter, Norton related (with no small amount of dramatic relish) the shocking news from town—how Myron Poppe was found murdered and how John Larkin was witnessed kneeling over his body, the bloody knife practically still in his hand. Further, how Larkin then attacked the marshal to make good his escape and was even now in desperate flight with Marshal Hatfield hot on his trail.

"How dreadful! How terribly, terribly dreadful," gasped Victoria.

Jackson Emory pounded a frail fist down on the padded arm of his easy chair and swore with very unfrail gusto. "That double-dealing, betraying bastard! He should have never got out of prison. He should have rotted there!"

Brenda, however, showed quite a different slant on the news, saying, "It shouldn't surprise me to hear that kind of attitude from all of you—and yet, sadly, it does. When it comes to guilt and punishment, don't any of you recall a little thing called due process?"

"Due process for that incorrigible dog," her father hissed, "is a noose around his neck."

"How can you possibly defend someone who would murder such a kind, sweet soul as Mr. Poppe?" demanded Victoria.

"I'm not defending him," Brenda argued. "But neither am I willing to leap to the immediate conclusion of condemning him. I *know* John Larkin. Good God, we *all* know him! Have you forgotten that? Do you really think he's capable of cold-bloodedly killing an innocent like Mr. Poppe? There must be some other explanation."

"If he's not the killer, then why did he run?" said Norton.

"Precisely because of *this* kind of reaction!" Brenda shot back. "The rush to condemn and convict him without even hearing his side of what happened."

"It's hard to hear someone's side of an incident when they are running away from it," Emory pointed out.

"And how can you say you *know* John?" Victoria challenged. "You were a mere child when he was here before, before he was sent away to prison. If anyone knows him, it's me. And considering how nearly five years behind bars can change a man, on top of the way he betrayed and hurt me and our family the way he did to get sent away in the first place, I'm sorry but I have no trouble believing he could by now be capable of anything."

"I spent enough time with him the other night— at a time when, once again, everybody was ready to rush and condemn him for something he didn't do—to believe he doesn't have that kind of dark, dangerous side to him," insisted Brenda.

"And it's scandalous that you ever consorted in such a manner with that scoundrel," fumed Emory. "I don't want to hear no more talk of it!"

Brenda rose to her feet. "I'm sorry that I'm such a scandal and embarrassment to the family. Maybe I, too, should flee and then you can all condemn me and talk about me more freely behind my back!"

"I never said that. I never meant it that way," her father protested.

"I know what you said, Father. As part of it, you also made clear the kind of talk you refuse to hear. Well, I claim the same right. I shall no longer remain here and listen to this kind of abusive rubbish!" With that, Brenda stormed from the room.

CHAPTER 42

Knowing that Larkin had fled with no advance planning and nothing in the way of supplies except for the horse and rifle he'd gotten from Earl Hines, Bob had ridden out after him with hopes of achieving a relatively quick rundown. As the day wore into afternoon and then edged toward evening, however, the marshal began to sense it wasn't going to be quite so easy.

It was clear that Larkin was pushing his horse hard and fast, eating up as much ground as he could while he had the lead and for as long as there was daylight. It came as no surprise that he was headed for the mountains. Not the Prophecies, where the gold boom activities meant he might risk running into any number of miners, prospectors, freighters, and the like. He'd have to expect that word was bound to spread pretty fast about the killing, and along with it a description of him. Therefore, his trail veered north and east toward the Shirley Mountains. Inasmuch as no valuable ore had ever been found in the Shirleys, they remained wild and rugged and mostly uninhabited except for a handful of diehard trappers and hunters.

It wouldn't be hard for a man to obscure his trail and hide himself deep in the Shirleys. If he was savvy enough to build a proper shelter and hunt for meat and other sustenance, he could hole up and survive in there for quite a spell.

Bob had no way of knowing for sure what Larkin had in mind, but the marshal's guess was that he wasn't heading into the mountains with the intent of holing up there. He'd either forge on through, using the streams and rocky ground to try and erase his trail, and then likely cut more to the east and head for Deadwood. Or he'd use the same trail-erasing tricks but then double back and strike out south, toward Cheyenne or Laramie, maybe as far as Denver.

No matter what he tried, though, Bob was counting on his tracking skills being up to sticking with him. It was just a matter of time before he closed the gap. And when he did, Larkin's plans would undergo a sudden change and the only place he'd be headed would be back to Rattlesnake Wells.

"Any chance you recognize this?"

Maudie Sartain frowned down at the garment Deputy Fred held out before her, wadded in one of his big paws.

The early evening crowd in Bullock's was moderate in size, and the buzz of conversations being carried on across the room droned at a low pitch. Mike Bullock himself was tending bar, at the moment hunched forward on his elbows about midway down its length, swapping off-color jokes with a pair of derby-hatted drummers. Maudie had been sitting alone at the far end, sipping from a cup of tea and looking somewhat bored when Fred and Earl Hines walked in. She'd perked up at the sight of them, especially Earl, until the question Fred rather bluntly put to her produced instead the thoughtful frown.

"Any particular reason I *should* recognize some wadded-up piece of cloth?" she asked.

Fred took the wad in both hands and shook it out so that it hung down to its full length and shape, revealing a bright yellow, long-sleeved shirt with rust-colored stains all over it. "This make any difference?"

Maudie couldn't hide a bit of a smirk as she said, "Okay, I'll bite. Any particular reason I should recognize a wadded-up old shirt? I will say, though, that the bright color really . . . Wait a minute. Now that I study on it, maybe I *do* know that shirt." Her expression turned serious. "I think it used to belong to Merlin Sweeney. You remember, that big colored fella who played accordion in here for a while."

"Uh-huh. That's what we were thinking," said Hines.

"He liked to wear bright colors when he played. I don't think he had a lot of clothes so he always wore a yellow shirt like that, or a red one." Maudie suddenly looked concerned. "Where did you find that? Something hasn't happened to him, has it?"

"We're not sure," said Fred. "As far as we know, the only thing that's happened to him is he left town to go prospecting. We found this shirt stuffed in a gunnysack in the storeroom at the Shirley House where he slept as part of his payment for swamping out the place."

"The same deal and the same room John Larkin had . . . before he got into trouble," Hines said. "You see, it was John who told me where to find the shirt. As he was riding off, he hollered over his shoulder, 'Check the bloody shirt in the storeroom. Show it to the marshal. I think it might be something important' . . . In all the excitement that came next, the murder and all, I forgot about it for a while. But then I remembered and had Fred go with me to see if we could find what he meant."

"*Are* those bloodstains?" Maudie asked.

"I think so. I'm pretty sure." Fred scowled. "What I'm not sure about is what they mean or why Larkin thought they might be important. Hell, we don't even know for sure if the shirt *did* belong to that Merlin fella."

"It's about the right size. He was a pretty large man," Maudie said. "And it sure looks like the one he used to . . . Wait a minute, I think I might know a way to tell for sure. Let me see those sleeves, the cuffs."

She reached and lifted the sleeves one at a time, examining the cuffs.

"What are the cuffs gonna tell you?" Hines wanted to know.

"They're going to tell me if this was Merlin's shirt or not . . . And yes! It was. See right here?"

Maudie held up one of the sleeves with the cuff partially rolled back. Fred and Hines leaned in closer to look. It took a minute to spot it, but when they did, they could see where the symbol of a cross had been stitched with thin white thread on the underside of the cuff right next to the buttonhole.

Lifting his face, Hines said, "How did you know that was there?"

"Merlin explained it to me one time," Maudie answered. "It was a slow night, we were sitting around talking, and I happened to notice, from the way he sat with one of his legs propped up on a chair, that there was the symbol of a cross stitched on the cuff of his trousers. I asked him about it, thinking it was kind of nice, that he must be a very religious man."

"Was he?"

Maudie shook her head. "No, not really. Oh, he was a believer certainly, but not in a preachy, Bible-thumping kind of way. The business with the crosses stitched into his clothing, though, was a habit carried over from his childhood days when he was born and raised on a slave plantation. The owner of the plantation, it seems, refused to let his slaves practice any kind of religion. He claimed it led to them feeling uppity and developing an independent streak. So he wouldn't allow any kind of church services or prayers or anything—and for sure no crosses or other religious symbols.

"So Merlin's parents and some of the other slaves, they found a way to fool their owner. They took to sewing tiny signs of the cross into their clothing. It kept them connected to the Lord, Merlin's mama told him, even if they couldn't pray or sing His praises out loud. It let Him know that they still wanted Him in their lives so He would bless them and look over them. Merlin's mama instilled that in him very deeply, from an early age. To always keep the sign of the Lord about him so that He would be able to look on and know." Maudie paused and gave a little shrug. "So that's what Merlin did, even as a grown man and no longer a slave who had to hide his beliefs. It was a habit that he'd developed and never saw fit to break."

"I'll be damned," said Hines. And then, considering what had just been discussed, he suddenly blushed and stammered a little. "I mean, not really . . . That's not what anybody would want, I just meant . . . Wow. That's quite a story."

"Yeah, it is. Now," said Fred, with an oddly eager look on his face, "I got one more question that might make it even more meaningful . . ."

Half an hour later, Fred was conferring with Peter and Vern Macy in the office area of the jail building. He'd just finished telling them about the discovery of Merlin Sweeney's bloodstained shirt and Maudie's account of how Sweeney had a habit of marking his apparel with signs of the cross.

The brothers had listened attentively and now Fred was anxious for their response. "Well?" he prompted.

Peter and Vern exchanged looks. Then Vern said, "It all seems to fit, Fred. There's no denying that. The footprint in the alley with the cross pattern in its heel we've been wondering about for the past couple days . . . And now the bloody shirt with more cross symbols sewed in, combined with what Maudie was able to tell you . . . It all seems to point to this Merlin

Sweeney as the one who beat the snot out of Saul Norton the other night."

"In addition to the crosses sewn in his clothing," spoke up Peter, "Maudie was sure Sweeney also had that pattern on the heel of his shoe?"

Fred gave a firm nod of his head. "Yup. He showed it to her that night when they first got to talking about it. He even made a kind of a joke about how he was representing his faith in the Lord from head to foot."

"But then why would he, especially being a religious man and all, beat the hell out of Norton like that?" asked Peter. "Did they have some kind of argument or something?"

"Not that anybody seems to know about," said Fred. "Not as far as Maudie knew, and neither did Mike Bullock when we asked him. Nor did Norton himself mention anything when the marshal and me questioned him right after the beating about who might have had it in for him."

Vern pulled a long, thoughtful face. "So if we're right, if it *was* this Merlin who attacked Norton—and every sign indicates so—then it looks like he's the only one who can explain why."

"I've got another 'why,'" said Peter. "Why did Larkin call attention to the shirt? What made him think it was so important?"

"I'd say simply because he found it there in the storeroom after he moved in and recognized the stains on it as blood," said Fred. "That's something he can answer when the marshal brings him in. But that don't mean he'll have any idea as to what Merlin's motive was."

"Takes us right back to Merlin as the only one who can tell us that," said Vern.

The three of them went quiet for a minute.

Until Fred spoke again. "Okay, I'll say what we're all thinking. One of us needs to go after Merlin so we can get some answers out of him."

"The only thing wrong with that," Vern said, "is that I don't think the marshal would like it very much if he comes back and finds one of us gone off on the search. He stressed pretty hard about us sticking together while he was away, on account of the trouble brewing with those Rocking W gunnies and all."

"It might take days for that range war trouble to boil to a head. And it might take days for Marshal Hatfield to get back with Larkin," Fred pointed out. "In the meantime, the answer to what caused Merlin to go after Norton goes begging. For all we know, maybe that accordion player didn't head up into the gold fields after all. He might be hanging around somewhere, planning something else. We figured at one time that Norton's beating and the potshot taken at Jackson Emory out by the butte were possibly tied together, remember . . . ? Everything considered, I don't think we should wait to act."

CHAPTER 43

Around the forkful of bacon and eggs he'd just shoved into his mouth, Charley Drake said, "You mean this local law dog is actually a wanted outlaw down in Texas?"

Rance Brannigan nodded, a cup of steaming coffee raised partway to his wryly-grinning mouth. "That's exactly what I mean. Not only wanted, but wanted bad enough to have a big, juicy reward waitin' for whoever brings him in—dead or alive."

"That's the doggonedest thing I ever heard," marveled Wilbur Nixon. "A law dog with a price on his head."

"Him and his kind *all* ought to have a bounty on their otherwise worthless hides," snarled Drake venomously. "They pin on a badge and think it gives 'em the almighty right to stick their noses in other folks' business. It's about damn time one of 'em had somebody pokin' back into his."

"And that's exactly what we're gonna do when it comes to this so-called Hatfield," said Brannigan, his wry grin turning wolfish. "But we got to play it smart and go about it just right. We do this job for Wardell here and collect a nice fat fee for that, then we haul the marshal's sorry ass back to Texas for the even sweeter payoff that'll be waitin' there. All told, boys, it'll set us up in money and whores and easy livin' for a long time."

This conversation was taking place in the grub shack at the Rocking W ranch headquarters. The other wranglers and ranch hands had finished eating a bit earlier, then drifted on out to commence their morning chores. The three hardcases had the place to themselves except for a wiry old cook who'd loaded their plates and now was cussing to himself as he clanged pots and pans back in the kitchen area. Still, due to long-established habits of mistrust and caution, the trio was holding their voices to low, conspiratorial tones.

After mentally gnawing on it through much of the night, at first light Brannigan had finally revealed to his two cohorts the situation regarding the marshal of Rattlesnake Wells. Even at that, however, he only doled out the bare minimum of what they needed to know. Enough to hook their interest and make sure they were drawn into it with him, but not tipping his hand on every detail.

"After hashin' things out with Wardell last night," he continued now, "I think I got the picture of what he wants done here and I've even got a plan roughed out for how we can go about it. Hell, it shouldn't take more than a couple, three days. The key will be to pick out a handful of the right *hombres* from the crew of wranglers already on hand. If I got him spied right, Smoky Barnett, the ramrod, is the type we want right off. We get him, he'll be valuable for sortin' out the others. Once we've put together what we want, they'll not only play a part in takin' care of Wardell's cattle-rustlin' beaner neighbor, but they'll also back us when I call out that phony, two-faced marshal."

"You make it sound like we're stagin' some kind of military maneuver," said Drake.

Brannigan looked smug. "Why not? I always wanted to be a general. Remember that little uprising down in Mexico we hired into that time? I damn near got to be a general down there—would've been, too, if that ragtag so-called army we hooked up with hadn't all lost their balls when the goin' got tough."

"Yeah, I remember that Mexican foul-up," Drake said sourly. "We damn near ended up in front of a firing squad. We barely got away with the skin still on our asses, and we never got paid but a fraction of what we signed on for."

"Ah, but it wasn't all bad. Not in the beginning," said Nixon, the corners of his mouth lifting in a vaguely dreamy smile. "Remember all those plump, brown-skinned *señoritas* who welcomed us with such willing open arms when we first showed up to fight on their side?"

"You got a mighty soft way of looking back on things, Wilbur," said Drake. Then, his sourness turning bitter, he added, "If you recall, about five seconds after the *Federales* sent us fleein' for our lives, those same *señoritas* were willingly opening their arms, thighs, and everything else to the very scum they supposedly hated so much in the beginning."

"That may be true, *compadre*," allowed Nixon, his

smile remaining in place. "But it still don't take away the memory of how fine they treated us before that. And hell, far as what they did after, all they were doin' was findin' a way to survive. You can't hardly blame 'em for that."

"The hell I can't," muttered Drake.

"Never mind that kind of negative talk," said Brannigan testily. "That business is over and done. The thing to concentrate on now is what's before us here. The kind of money I'm talkin' about makin' off this, combined, will have more gals for you to dally with than you can shake a stick at, Wilbur. And the kind you like, too, Drake—the kind who'll let you rough 'em up and not raise a fuss about it. All that and plenty more can be ours . . . long as we do like I say and concentrate on gettin' these jobs done and done smart."

"Well, a-course, Rance," said Wilbur. "You take the lead, like always, and me and Drake will fall in line."

"When and how do we start?" Drake wanted to know.

Brannigan took a pull of his coffee, lowered it. "Soon as we're done eatin', we'll be takin' a ride out with Barnett. I want to see the lay of the land, especially where Wardell's property borders on that of this Mexican neighbor Wardell hates so much. I'll want a peek on the Mexican's side, too, and I'll want to see who's got cattle scattered anywhere close to the line."

Wilbur cocked an eyebrow. "Do I smell the drift of some beefsteaks still hoofin' around on four legs maybe mysteriously showin' up where they ain't supposed to belong?"

"Could be."

"Aw, shit. I had a hunch we'd end up herdin' cattle before we got out of here," grumbled Drake. "I suppose it'll be in the middle of the damn night, too, won't it?"

"Could be," Brannigan said again.

"A little cowboyin' I can handle okay," said Wilbur indifferently. Then, frowning deeply, he added, "But there's something else I been worryin' around in my head that's a site more bothersome."

"What's that?" Brannigan asked.

"This outlaw marshal we're gonna be takin' back to Texas for the big reward . . . Well, it's a mighty long stretch from here to Texas. Tryin' to take him all that way alive would present a whole lot of chances for him to be a problem. On the other hand, haulin' his dead body all that way would mean time for him to turn powerful ripe." Wilbur's face scrunched up unpleasantly at the mere thought. "I don't know if my tricky stomach could handle that so good."

Brannigan stared at him for a long moment, then wagged his head as if in amazement. "Wilbur, you think of the damnedest things, you know that?"

"I can't help it. I'm just sayin' . . ."

"Hell, there's a simple answer," said Drake. "If we take him back dead—which I agree would be a lot easier—we'll just lop off his head and take that. That oughtta be good enough for proof of identification, right, Rance? A head would be easier to lug along and, if we wrapped it up good and snug in a rain slicker or some such, it wouldn't hardly stink at all after the first couple days."

"Now you're just tryin' to get my goat," Wilbur said edgily. His expression nevertheless seemed to turn a little greenish. He cut his eyes over to Brannigan. "You wouldn't go along with doin' it like that, would you, Rance?"

"I dunno. It's an interestin' thought," replied Brannigan. "I've heard tell of bounty hunters who do it that way."

Wilbur looked on aghast, his gaze sweeping back and forth between his two comrades. Finally, Brannigan and Drake couldn't keep straight faces any longer and they broke into a round of teasing laughter at Wilbur's discomfort.

"Go ahead and laugh," Wilbur groused as he pushed away his half-eaten plate of food. "I hope you two jokers are happy—you've ruined the best breakfast I *almost* had in days."

"Don't worry, you've got plenty of great breakfasts ahead. I promise you that," Brannigan said when his laughter tapered off.

"Speakin' of what lies ahead, now something occurs to *me* about this outlaw marshal business," said Drake, a serious look replacing his own laughter. "You've told us who he is and that he's wanted for some mighty serious stuff down Texas way . . . but you ain't said exactly what he did or where it was he did it."

"That's true," Brannigan agreed. "But *I* know the answers to those things. Ain't that enough?"

"Well, yeah. As far as it goes." Drake scowled. "But

what if something happens to you? I mean, there's a risk to these things we're enterin' into, right? There always is. But what if we get to the point where we're ready to take that marshal back for the big money and . . . well, like I said, if anything should happen to you with me and Wilbur not knowing no more details than we do now . . . that'd sort of leave us high and dry. See what I mean?"

Brannigan didn't respond right away, instead took his time draining the rest of his coffee. His mind drifted to the old wanted poster in a pocket of his saddlebags, one of the ones issued on the Devil's River Kid more than half a dozen years ago. Until he'd run into the marshal of Rattlesnake Wells, Brannigan had almost forgot it was there. He'd carried it all this time for no particular reason other than he'd never bothered to dig it out and throw it away. But now, like Fate, there it still was when he'd gone looking for it—his *bona fides*, so to speak, for when the time was right to again go after the individual the poster was meant for. There was a description, an illustration (still a close resemblance, too), and a listing of the fugitive's crimes. Everything, in other words, anybody would need to claim the reward offered on the man now calling himself Bob Hatfield for his past deeds as Bob Hammond, alias the Devil's River Kid. But in spite of all he'd been through with Drake and Wilbur, Brannigan still felt better—safer, maybe, was the best way of putting it—keeping the existence of the wanted poster and its details as a sort of ace up his sleeve.

When he lowered his emptied cup, Brannigan's

face had lost all trace of the amusement only recently displayed. In a flat, uncompromising tone, he said, "Uh-huh. I do see what you mean, Drake. So I'd say what else that means is you and Wilbur, for the best chance at *all* of us seeing that big reward, had better make damn sure nothing happens to me . . ."

CHAPTER 44

Bob rose before sunup. Since he'd pitched a cold camp the night before, there was no coffee or bacon to look forward to. After rolling his bedroll back up and stowing the rest of his gear, he breakfasted on some beef jerky and cold biscuits dug out of his war bag. He washed it down with swigs of water from his canteen. The spring morning was crisp enough up here in the low range of the Shirleys to make him wish for even a cup of the dreadful coffee they brewed at the jail. Second choice, if he'd been more of a drinking man, would have been a belt of whiskey to warm his innards. Actually, there was a flask of whiskey in his saddlebags, but he didn't go digging for it.

By the time it was light enough to pick up Larkin's trail again, Bob had his horse saddled and ready. He'd staked the animal where it had sufficient graze for the night as well as access to a narrow stream trickling down from the higher rocks. Before climbing into the saddle, he took time to also treat the beast to a couple handfuls of belly-warming grain.

Bob felt agitated by the fact he hadn't slept well during the night. He'd been sore and exhausted from having spent the better part of the day in the saddle, he was cold, the ground was hard and uncomfortable, and he missed the warm curves of Consuela snuggled next to him. Adding to his agitation was the realization that these things affected him as much as they did because he'd allowed himself to get somewhat soft in the performance of his duties as marshal. Sitting behind a desk or leisurely strolling the streets of the town—even with the sporadic outbursts of trouble—weren't the same as being out on the trail, enduring the elements. He vowed inwardly that, in the future, he'd make it a point to ride out on some kind of regular basis in order to keep himself in better trail shape.

The only good thing about being so exhausted the night before was the fact it eventually led to him falling into a deep sleep. During the time he'd lain awake, however, his mind had churned busily. Coming as no surprise, there were two main things that his thoughts kept grinding on: John Larkin and the question of if he'd murdered Myron Poppe the way every sign pointed to; and Rance Brannigan and the questions of whether or not he'd recognized Bob (no matter how many times he came back around to it, Bob couldn't convince himself that Brannigan *hadn't*) and then how and when would the gunman act on it?

No answers were arrived at during the nighttime pondering and none were forthcoming in the light of the new day. In addition, now that it was evident running down Larkin wasn't going to be as easy or quick as Bob had hoped, there was the increasingly nagging question of whether or not he was doing the right thing by spending time pursuing Larkin at all, what with the matter of the pending range war and whatever Brannigan's role in it would be building pressure while he was away.

For the time being, he decided as he heeled his horse higher up into the Shirleys, following Larkin's steadily more broken trail, he would adhere to an old saying of his mother's: *In for a penny, in for a pound.* He'd set out and come this far, damn it, he wasn't ready to turn back yet.

By shortly past noon, Bob reckoned he had cut Larkin's roughly two-hour lead by half; maybe slightly more. This gave him encouragement to keep pushing on. Something else that gave him encouragement on a whole different subject was the inadvertent discovery he'd made a few hours back. In a shallow, grass-bottomed canyon that reached a ways into the Shirley foothills, he'd come within sight of dozens of cattle. Although he couldn't afford to take time to examine them closely, he was willing to bet that at least some of them carried the Rocking W brand. There was possibly some V-Slash beef among them, too. And it was altogether likely there were other such pockets of strays who had wandered this far to escape the harsh winter—the answer to Ed Wardell's missing cattle he was so hell-bent on believing had been rustled by Carlos Vandez. When Bob got back, he was counting on this discovery to go a long way toward soothing the range war friction he'd left behind.

But in the meantime, he was still intent on running down John Larkin. A task that was taking all his focus because his quarry's trail was getting harder and more erratic to follow. The cause for this was Larkin's tactic of choosing rocky passages that wouldn't take a hoofprint, even if it meant tougher going for himself, and veering at odd angles to the general northeastern direction he seemed to be heading. More than once Bob had lost several minutes switching back and forth over such hardpan breaks before he finally found an outlet point or a hoof scuff or some other obscure indicator that gave him a sign to keep following.

The higher peaks and sheer cliffs of the Shirleys, although not considered particularly large or imposing, not compared to the Rockies to the south or some of the various other ranges scattered through west central Wyoming, were nevertheless plenty rugged and steadily closing in. Combined with thickening pine growth and short, twisty canyons that led nowhere, suitable routes to continue north were becoming trickier. It was apparent that Larkin didn't know these mountains worth a damn and was simply blundering ahead in an effort to make his way through. Recognizing this, Bob's expectations had broadened from a plan of simply overtaking the fugitive to one that included the possibility of Larkin plunging into a blind canyon where he'd find himself cornered. The marshal cared little *how* the chase ended, he just wanted it over with so they could get headed back to Rattlesnake Wells.

With the sun in a cloudless sky beginning its slide downward toward the western horizon, Bob had picked Larkin's trail back up once again after an especially frustrating period of having lost it. The skunk had entered into a fast-running stream that cut deep through a long stretch of ground made up of nothing but flat, rocky slabs. Finding where Larkin emerged out of the water onto such a hardened surface that refused to take any kind of mark or hold a drop of wetness had required painstaking effort. When Bob finally found the trace he was looking for, he discovered the crafty bastard had traveled only a few hundred yards upstream before leaving the water and continuing on.

Cursing all the time he'd lost over such a short-ranged diversion, Bob heeled his own mount out of the water and locked on the trail again. When he did, the echoing crack of his horse's hooves on the slabbed surface sounded as angry and determined as his mood . . .

CHAPTER 45

"And this is well into V-Slash property—you're certain of that?"

Smoky Barnett scowled at the question put to him by Rance Brannigan. "Yeah, I'm certain. We're close to a mile over the line. I'm also certain that I don't like being here. Not one damn bit. I got an itch between my shoulder blades like some V-Slash brush popper is drawin' a bead on me and ready to trigger a round any second."

Brannigan emitted a dry chuckle. "Hell, son, that's a feeling I live with practically every day of my life. You get used to it, even learn to appreciate it. It's what keeps a man on his toes."

"I'll take your word for it," Barnett said dryly. "But I don't think I'm in any hurry to try and get used to it."

The two men, along with Charley Drake and Wilbur Nixon, sat their horses just back from the crest of a long grassy hump, what some would refer to as a hogback. The afternoon sun beat down on them, casting their shadows across the breeze-rippled grass. Over the crest, the land sloped gradually down into a fair-sized natural bowl with a few outcroppings of rock and some stands of trees around its edges.

Leaning forward on his saddle horn and gazing down into the bowl, studying it, Brannigan said to Barnett, "You might need to do some rethinkin' on that, on the gettin' used to it part. Because I got a hunch this ain't the last time we're gonna be visiting this spot."

"Why would that be?" Barnett wanted to know.

Brannigan jerked his chin. "Just look at the layout. If I was a dirty lowdown rustler in the habit of long-loopin' my neighbor's cattle in the middle of the night, this strikes me as exactly the kind of spot I'd bring 'em to. A sorta hidden little place where I could take my time re-markin' the critters' brands or maybe just holdin' 'em for a spell until I had some kind of sell-off worked out."

"And the fact we saw a nice little bunch of Rockin' W cattle not too far back on the other side of the property line," interjected Wilbur, "makes this spot all the more suitable. Wouldn't be but a short ride in the moonlight to nudge a few head of beeves from one location to the other."

"What are you talking about? Do you have some kind of tip that Vandez is plannin' a rustlin' raid soon and will be bringin' Wardell cattle here?" asked Barnett, an unmistakable touch of excitement edging into his voice.

"What if he did?" said Brannigan. "It wouldn't be the first time, would it? Maybe not for bringin' the stole cattle right to this spot, but takin' 'em somewhere all the same. Ain't that the way it's been going?"

"That's the way Wardell has been figurin', yeah."

"But the reason he's never been able to get the law or nobody to see it the same way, and the reason he's never taken any hard action on it—leastways not until he called in my pards and me—is because Wardell's never been able to *prove* what's goin' on. Ain't that right?" Brannigan pressed.

"Yeah, that's pretty much the size of it," Barnett allowed.

"Then that makes bringin' us in," said Drake with a sly, knowing grin, "all the smarter on Wardell's part. You see, we happen to not only be pretty damn good at findin' proof of this kind of dirty doings, but then, once we do, we are downright experts at sweepin' away the dirt."

"But no matter how good we are," Brannigan was quick to add, "we sometimes still need help gettin' things lined up in order to make it a clean sweep. That's where you could come in, Smoky. I've had my eye on you right from the start. Yeah, you're already the ramrod of this outfit, but I see a fella with the grit and savvy to be a lot more. And unless I'm wrong, something that would help you take that next step would be the chance at some real money—a helluva lot bigger payday than you're ever gonna get workin' for wages. Am I right, or am I right?"

"Well, yeah. Hell yeah. I like money as much as the next fella. But I gotta tell you, I ain't so sure I'm ready for—"

"We ain't talkin' nothing illegal. Not exactly," Brannigan cut him off. "But where has stickin' tight with the law got Wardell or you when it comes to this stinkin' greaser who's been robbin' you blind?

Sometimes you gotta bend the law a little, poke your elbows out past the edges some, in order to make it work to your advantage. That's all I'm sayin'. And I'm talkin' more than just this rustlin' business, too. When we get that taken care of, there's something even bigger practically right under your nose. That's where the real money is gonna be. You throw in with us now, you'll have your chance to get included in on that as well."

Barnett licked his lips. "You're throwin' an awful lot at me. But you've damn sure got my interest, I'll tell you that."

"Good. Then go with your gut," Brannigan urged him. "Hear us the rest of the way out, you won't be sorry. And another thing. Once you're in, we'll need you to find us four or five more men from your wranglin' crew who are also cut out for what needs to be done . . ."

Owen Dutton held a copy of the *Wells Gazette* at arm's length and gazed on it admiringly. It was a special edition—the first one he'd put out since starting the paper—and he felt as proud as a beaming papa holding up a brand-new son. Not only was his chest swelling because it was a special edition, but it also happened to contain, in Dutton's not-so-humble opinion, some of the finest, hardest-hitting journalism he'd ever run.

Given the rich subject matter of events from the past few days, how could it have been otherwise? The mysterious, still-unsolved sniper attempt on one of the community's most highly regarded citizens; a gunsmoke-shrouded shoot-out in the middle of the street; the murder of a beloved citizen by a vengeful former convict who'd betrayed all the chances he'd been given to prove himself reformed; the heroism of a fellow citizen who—in spite of still recuperating from a beating suffered in a craven, also still-unsolved prior assault—had tried valiantly to stop the murder victim from going to his doom; the ultimate tragedy of a widow now left heartbroken and alone. All of this capped off by a bold, insightful editorial that questioned the judgment of a marshal who didn't seem to hesitate when it came to gunning down a young, drunken rowdy yet failed time and again to restrain the actions of an obviously embittered individual who ended up taking the most innocent of lives.

Standing in horizontal slashes of late afternoon sunlight pouring through the blinds of his office, yet another tingle of excitement passed through Dutton as he scanned the layout of articles he'd single-handedly written and typeset. After working feverishly long into the night and then every minute of the day up to this point, he should have been exhausted. But he wasn't. He felt vibrant, energized. And for the first time in a long time he felt like he was truly representing the power of the press the way it was meant to be wielded.

Yes, he'd been well aware of how many people scoffed at the notion of a newspaper in Rattlesnake Wells. Especially when they saw that it was nothing more than a one-man operation cranking out copy from an ancient, rickety press on the cheapest paper to be had. Plenty still scoffed even after he began putting out regular editions and a loyal readership began to build. And yes, Dutton was well aware that he had a propensity toward sensationalism and the use of descriptive passages straight out of dime-novel prose. Everybody from his journalism teachers to Marshal Hatfield seemed to go out of their way to point this out to him.

But truth and accuracy were still what counted, damn it, even if presented in a less than polished style. And with the just-published editorial calling him to task for the way he'd handled the whole Larkin matter, if Marshal Hatfield was smart he'd be a lot more concerned about the perception of how he did his own job rather than how Dutton wrote his articles.

CHAPTER 46

Long, thick shadows thrown at crazy angles by the higher mountain peaks were hurrying the onset of dusk. Bob Hatfield was still locked on Larkin's trail and he sensed he'd shortened the time gap between them to possibly as slim as half an hour. Nevertheless, it didn't look like he was going to be able to close completely on his quarry before nightfall. Which meant another night's cold camp and then continuing his track-down into another day. Bob swore under his breath at the prospect.

But at least, he tried to console himself, he was confident he could catch up sometime tomorrow morning. The thing to consider at that point would be what was it going to take to secure Larkin's apprehension. In the back of his mind, Bob had been figuring all along that it somehow wouldn't come to a shoot-out. Although he couldn't say exactly why, he was counting on Larkin to give himself up if chased down. But maybe that was wishful thinking on Bob's part—he didn't want to kill Larkin to stop his flight, he was sure of that much; yet he would if he had to.

Conversely, he didn't believe Larkin was desperate enough to kill him, a lawman, even if to avoid capture. But all indications were that he'd already killed once and he sure hadn't hesitated to damn near knock Bob's block off for the sake of making good his escape in the first place . . . so nothing was certain.

What it boiled down to was that Bob needed to be extra cautious for his final close-in, making it all the more important not to push too far into the rapidly descending darkness.

Abruptly, with these thoughts running through his mind, the marshal came to a small, teardrop-shaped clearing. He'd been moving through a stretch of scraggly pine growth, following bent, broken twigs that marked Larkin's passage ahead of him more clearly than at any time all day. He reined his horse at the edge of the clearing before venturing out into the open. On the far side, he could see where the pine growth picked up again, although at that point starting to be interrupted by frequent outcroppings of jagged rock.

And then he spotted something else. Surprisingly, almost astonishingly, he could see the yellow-gold flicker of a campfire just within the pines on the other side.

Bob gripped his reins tighter. Man and horse froze into a single motionless shape. Only the rider's eyes moved—sweeping alertly from side to side, measuring, studying.

From the deep shadows within a thicket immediately to Bob's right, not more than a dozen feet away, a voice said low and clear, "Stay frozen just like that . . . And be especially careful not to move your hand anywhere near the Colt on your hip or the Winchester in the saddle scabbard."

Bob recognized the voice immediately. It belonged to John Larkin.

He wasn't aware of holding his breath until, after several tense clock ticks, he felt it hiss out through his teeth. "Well? Are you gonna shoot me or not?"

Larkin didn't answer right away. Then, after easing into view with a Winchester rifle leveled on Bob, he said, "I'm thinkin' on it . . . But no, I reckon I won't. If it was anybody else . . . maybe. But I should've known you'd be the one to come after me."

"You made it kinda personal by wrappin' that bucket around my head."

"And I could say you made it kinda personal by makin' me reach into that slop."

"By killing a man, you'd already reached pretty low all on your own."

Larkin's tone took on a sudden edge. "Apparently you don't listen so good, do you? Like I tried to tell you back in town, I had nothing to do with killing that little man! I opened the door and found him that way."

"That might sound a little more convincing if you hadn't immediately made a run for it and now are trying to plead your innocence from behind the barrel of a gun," Bob told him.

"I should've stuck around and done my pleading in front of a judge and jury—that what you're trying to sell?" Larkin sneered.

"It is."

"Well, in case you need remindin', I tried that once and it didn't work out so hot for me."

"You really think running and leaving everybody convinced you *are* a killer is any better?"

"At least I ain't behind bars."

"Not yet maybe. But as long as you're on the run and being hunted you're not really free, either. You'll never know when the next man you lock eyes with—wherever you go, after no matter how long—might not be somebody who'll recognize you and call you to account for what you thought you'd gotten away from." As he heard the words spilling out, Bob suddenly realized he was talking to himself as much as to Larkin.

Whatever Larkin heard on his end, it was enough to make him go silent for another long minute. Heaving a heavy sigh, he said, "Why do you think I built the fire over there and then scrambled back here to wait for you like this?"

Bob frowned. "To catch me off guard, I reckon. To puzzle me, make me hesitate for a second so's you could get the drop on me. Much as it galls me to admit, appears it worked."

"Uh-huh. And if I wanted, we're in agreement I could blow you clean out of that saddle right now and have a whale of a head start on anybody else who might come along next. Right?"

Bob just glared at him, said nothing.

"Okay. I want you to keep that in mind . . . And then I want you to be sure and remember this." So saying, Larkin lowered his Winchester and took a slow step forward. "I'm letting you take me in. It sank in a couple hours back that this runnin' shit ain't no good. I got a raw deal before but this time, with you behind the badge, I figure I've got a better chance. That's why I had to make sure it was you on my tail and then set this up so you'd see I was turning myself in of my own free will before you had me cornered to where I had no choice."

Bob gave a crisp nod. "So noted." Swinging down from his saddle, he reached out and relieved Larkin of his Winchester. "You understand," he said, "I'm gonna have to put you in cuffs."

"I understand," Larkin said woodenly. "I just hope you had the chance to wipe 'em off some."

"Understand, too, that I won't hesitate to shoot if you try any tricks to break away again."

Larkin furrowed his brow. "Now why in hell would I hand myself over, then try to make another run for it?"

"Just so we're clear." Bob took the irons from his belt and shook them out. "Hold out your hands . . . in front will do."

Larkin did as instructed. As the bracelets were being clamped around his wrists, he said, "I got me another hope or two."

"No promises. But what?"

"I furnished the fire . . . I hope you've got some coffee and grub to cook over it. On account of how sudden-like I lit out, I ended up a mite shy on provisions. Liked to froze my ass off last night, and I'm so hungry right about now my belly thinks my throat's been cut. You being an upstanding officer of the law and all, you got an obligation to provide proper care for your prisoner, don't you?"

Twisting his mouth wryly, Bob said, "I'll see what I can do . . . Would've been a sight easier on both of us if you'd made your decision to quit running a whole lot sooner. I didn't exactly have a warm, comfy time of it last night myself, so don't expect me to feel too sorry for you." Taking his horse's reins in one hand and wielding the confiscated rifle with the other, the marshal added, "Go on, walk ahead of me. Get started across the clearing while we've still got some light. That fire will feel mighty good in a few minutes. When we lose the sun this high up, the temperature's gonna drop like a stone."

CHAPTER 47

Twenty-seven hours later, Marshal Hatfield and his prisoner arrived back in Rattlesnake Wells. After camping for the night on the far edge of the teardrop-shaped clearing, they'd started their return from the Shirley Mountains at the first hint of grayness in the eastern sky. By pushing hard and steady, now without being slowed by the mechanics of one man trying to hide his trail while the other strained to follow it, they nearly halved the time initially taken to cover the distance involved.

Although it was full dark and the streets of Old Town were virtually empty, Bob nevertheless took extra pains to enter town in a way aimed at lessening any chance of them being noticed. This meant looping around the bottom end of Front Street and coming in from the west. This brought them to the rear of the jail where there was a hitch rail, a watering tub, and sufficient grass for the horses to be left overnight. There was also a rear door that gave entry to a storeroom adjacent to the cellblock.

"Home sweet home," Larkin muttered, eyeing the

back side of the sturdy, darkened building as Bob dismounted and snapped a match to light the lantern attached to the outer wall beside the door. "Never thought I'd be looking forward to stretching out on one of those hard-assed cell cots I've had the displeasure of getting acquainted with in the past. But after three days of being either in this saddle or on the cold ground, I gotta admit it don't seem like such a bad trade."

"Plumb warms my heart, hearing how eager you are to enjoy our accommodations," Bob replied dryly.

After lighting the lantern and unlocking the back door, Bob stepped inside long enough to light another lantern in the storeroom before returning to where Larkin remained on his horse. He reached up, inserting and twisting a small key to undo the second set of handcuffs that held the prisoner's chained wrists fastened to his saddle horn. Removing these, he motioned Larkin down, still with his first set of cuffs in place.

Minutes later they were inside, passing through the storeroom and emerging into the cellblock where a small candle burned on a wooden stool in one corner, casting the area in murky light. The fact this candle was lit informed Bob immediately that one or more prisoners were already in the lockup.

Even as this thought passed through his mind, the door separating the cellblock from the front office suddenly jerked open and a tousle-haired Fred Ordway was standing there with a gun in his hand.

"Marshal!" the big deputy blurted. "I heard noise back here and didn't—"

"Take it easy, Fred. It's just me," Bob told him, the corners of his mouth lifting slightly.

"Boy, am I glad to see you!"

"Same here, pal. I'm glad to see you and I'm glad to be back home."

Fred opened the door a bit wider so more light from the office spilled around him and better illuminated who was with the marshal. "Is that Larkin? Did you get him?"

"Yeah, to both questions."

"You glad to see me, too, Deputy Fred?" asked Larkin with a lopsided grin.

Fred showed no sign of returning his grin. "Not particularly. And you might have a lot less reason to grin than you think, buster."

"What's going on? Who've you got locked up?" said Bob, peering to penetrate the deep shadows of the far cell but unable to make out who was back there.

"Long story on our other prisoner," said Fred. His expression turned even more somber. "And there's been plenty going on since you been gone. Let's get the new addition put away and then I'll fill you in on all of it."

"Uh-oh. Sounds serious, Marshal. Reckon I let you catch me just in time for you to get back here and clamp a lid on things," remarked Larkin.

With Larkin behind bars and the rear of the building locked back up, Bob and Fred removed themselves to the office area where the marshal wasted no time plopping wearily into the chair behind his desk.

"Want me to make some coffee?" Fred offered.

Bob gestured at the pot already on the stove. "None left in there?"

"Yeah, but it's several hours old. Likely to be stout enough by now to—"

"No matter. It'll do. Throw an extra spoonful of sugar in it."

Fred poured a cup of the mud, doctored it with some sugar as requested, handed it to Bob. Uncharacteristically, the marshal doctored it a bit more by adding a generous splash of whiskey from a bottle pulled out of a desk drawer.

While he was doing that, Fred said, "So what's the story on Larkin? Did he confess to killing Mr. Poppe?"

"Not hardly. He still claims he didn't do it. Says when he opened that back door, Poppe was already laying there with a knife in his back . . . this one right here, as a matter of fact." As he said this, Bob picked up a knife that was laying on his desk on top of some papers. It was a folding lock-blade with a wood grain handle. The blade, about five inches in length, was currently locked open. A string had been tied around the handle with a paper tag on one end. On the tag someone had written *"Murder Weapon—Myron Poppe."*

"Doc Tibbs turned that in after he gave little Poppe's body over to the undertaker," Fred explained. "Poor little fella. Doc said if he'd been a heavier or more muscular man, a blade like that, in the back, might not have been enough to kill him. Anyway, I put that tag on it so we could keep track of it . . . you know, for evidence in the trial."

Bob nodded. "Good idea."

"Speaking of the trial, you don't believe Larkin's claim he didn't do the killing, do you?"

"Not much reason to. After a while, when trouble after trouble keeps showing up on a fella's doorstep, you can't help but wonder if he ain't inviting it in. All we can do is stand Larkin and his story before a judge and jury and let them sort it out."

"I guess. Although he'd probably be the first to say that didn't work out too swell for him the last time."

"Ain't no probably about it. That's exactly what he said." Bob put the knife back down and took a couple sips from his scalding, reinforced brew before leaning farther back in his chair. "But enough about him for now. Let's get to that other stuff you hinted at. Fill me in. Start with whoever it is we've got back there in the other cell."

"Okay," Fred said, hitching up a chair in front of the desk. "You know him. It's Merlin Sweeney, the fella who played accordion for a while at Bullock's . . ."

Fred went on to relate the sequence of events that had led from the pile of bloody clothes left in the back room of the Shirley House bar, telling how the cross symbols sewn into them had been connected to Sweeney via Maudie Sartain, who'd also been able to confirm that the same pattern existed in the heel of one of the man's shoes.

"Putting all that together," Fred went on, "made it seem pretty doggone likely that Sweeney was the one who'd assaulted Saul Norton in that alley beside

Bullock's. Naturally, that still left the big question of why. Plus, you'll remember, there was also the hanging question of whether or not Norton's beating was in any way connected to the potshot taken at Jackson Emory. So I made the decision that one of us deputies—Vern, as it turned out—needed to go find Sweeney in order to try and get some of those answers."

Bob drank some more of his coffee, waited for Fred to continue.

"Well, Vern found him easy enough. Turned out he'd staked a claim and started doing some digging not too far from where Vern and Peter's uncle has been working his own claim. And once Vern started asking his questions, Sweeney opened up like a bag of candy. Seems he's been tormented by guilt and hardly able to live with himself ever since the deed. He *wanted* to tell somebody about it, get it off his chest."

"If he felt that bad about it, what made him do it in the first place?" Bob asked.

"Get ready. The answer to that is bound to rattle your spurs." Fred paused to squeeze out some dramatic effect, then said, "Saul Norton *hired* him to do it."

Bob happened not to be wearing any spurs, but Fred's words nevertheless had an impact. "What? What the hell sense does that make?"

"You tell me and we'll both know. Hell, Sweeney don't even know." Fred wagged his head in puzzlement. "All he can say is that he was playing his accordion in Bullock's that night and Norton came up to him with the offer to make a very generous amount of money in a quick hurry. Naturally, Sweeney was interested in the chance to make some big money. He was scraping by on tips for his music and meager pay for swamping at the Shirley House.

"So the two of them went out back, out into the alley, and Norton held out a wad of money. 'All you got to do to earn it is beat the living tar out of me,' he told Sweeney. And then, to make sure he got his money's worth, he started taunting Merlin—calling him a nigger, questioning his manhood, saying every vile thing he could lay his tongue to. Sweeney exploded. Gave Norton everything he wanted and maybe a little extra. Next day, after he'd stuck around long enough to make sure he hadn't killed the man, he used the money he'd been paid to buy some prospecting gear and lit a shuck for the Prophecy gold fields."

"Has anybody asked Norton about this?"

Fred shook his head. "Vern only got back with Sweeney late this afternoon. To tell you the truth, we weren't exactly sure on *how* we were gonna proceed. We figured we'd make some kind of decision tomorrow . . . unless you showed up in the meantime to do it for us."

"What about the potshot at Jackson Emory and me? Sweeney have anything to say about that?" Bob asked.

"Nothing. He claims no part of it, barely even heard about the incident."

Bob pinned Fred with a very direct look. "You believe him?"

"Yeah, I do. On both matters," Fred said without

hesitation. "As a matter of fact, the only reason we put him in a cell was to give him a place to sleep tonight. Based on his story, Vern didn't really see anything to charge him with and wouldn't have brought him back if he hadn't insisted. Sweeney says he did wrong and he deserves to be punished, and, like the rest of us, he wants to know why Norton—or anybody else—would pay somebody to beat hell out of them."

"Yeah, that don't exactly fall under the heading of normal behavior," Bob allowed.

Fred scowled. "That and a lot more. There's no shortage of abnormal behavior going on around here these days, boss. And you bringing Larkin back is only gonna add fuel to the fire."

"I was afraid of that," said Bob, heaving a sigh. He held out his drained cup. "Pour me another one, will you? And then fill me in on the rest."

CHAPTER 48

"A big part of it is due to that damned newspaper-man Dutton. With the help of, coincidentally, Saul Norton." Fred had handed Bob another cup of coffee, but now, instead of sitting back down himself, he was pacing back and forth. "Dutton put out a special edition of his paper the day after you left. He had articles covering everything from that shot taken at you and Emory to your gunning of the drunken V-Slash cowboy to, of course, the murder of Myron Poppe. A heck of a lot of it was slanted toward making you look bad, boss. We had a copy of the dirty rag around here for a while, but I got disgusted with it and threw it in the stove."

"What did Dutton have to say about me?" Bob asked in a flat tone.

Fred made a face like he had a bad taste in his mouth. "The little weasel didn't really state anything direct. But it was like he put a negative twist, where you were concerned, on everything he reported. As if you had a choice in plugging that young fool drunk. And why, he asked, didn't you have any suspects for whoever shot at Emory or beat up Norton so bad? And when he wrote about the killing of Poppe, he painted Norton as some kind of hero who, barely getting around on a cane because of the beating he'd suffered, rushed to you as fast as he could to try and get you to prevent the confrontation between Poppe and Larkin. And then, in an editorial, he really let you have it—questioning why you hadn't been watching Larkin more carefully, knowing he was back in town for revenge, or why you didn't have him locked up after all the incidents he'd been involved in since returning. It was all . . . what's the word for it . . . 'innuendo.' But the little shit laid it on so thick that a lot of folks in town—folks I thought had more sense than to swallow that kind of garbage—are falling in line to either agree with him or at least to spout some of his same questions."

Bob raised his coffee cup, blew a cooling breath across its contents. "And how does Norton fit in as an accomplice to him?"

"After Dutton painted him as the brave, battered hero who tried valiantly to keep Poppe from harm," Fred explained, "he's been limping around town on that damn cane of his with a ready-made audience waiting wherever he stops to spout off. His target is Larkin. He's got a surprising number of folks stirred up about what a no-good, proven criminal Larkin is and how there's no more room for compassion or any hope of redemption where he's concerned. He gave the eulogy at Myron Poppe's funeral and darn near turned it into a lynch mob—or what would have been one if Larkin had been anywhere within reach."

"And now I've brought him back right into the thick of it," Bob muttered.

Fred's brow furrowed. "Yeah, that's what I'm afraid of. In a couple days, a lot of the folks Norton had so riled up at the funeral will likely cool down. But if those same people wake up tomorrow morning and find out we've got him right here in the jail . . . I'm afraid it could turn ugly."

"There's only one answer for that," Bob replied through clenched teeth. "No matter what it takes, no lynch mob is getting a prisoner of ours."

"No, of course not," Fred readily agreed. "But no matter how foolish and wrongheaded they might be, I hate the thought of fighting our own townsfolk, that's all—especially when we've got plenty of more dangerous troublemakers waiting on the fringe of everything."

Bob arched a brow. "By that, I take it you mean the range war situation with the Rocking W and Wardell's hired guns?"

"You got it."

"What are they up to?"

"I don't know, exactly. But I know it's building up to no good. Smoky Barnett, Wardell's ramrod, came galloping into town with a couple other Rocking W riders this afternoon, not too long before Vern got back with Sweeney. They went directly to see Dutton."

"Him again."

"Uh-huh. And when they left, he was riding with 'em. Me and Peter happened to be out on the street when they rode out, and that smart-mouthed Dutton couldn't resist throwing another dig our way. I don't recall word for word what he hollered, but it was something to the effect that once again he was going to open everybody's eyes to more illegal activity that the local law was ignoring."

"A week or so ago," Bob said, frowning thoughtfully, "he got talked into riding out so he could witness and report on some rustling activity that Wardell convinced him was bound to take place. Nothing happened, though. It was all wasted time on everybody's part. I'm surprised that even Dutton, no matter how eager he is for something sensational to report on, would get suckered into something like that all over again."

"He's on a roll now," Fred pointed out. "With all the crap he's stirred up, more people than ever will be paying attention to what shows up next in his paper. Maybe Dutton figures he can't afford to ignore anything that might turn out to be a story big enough to allow him to keep topping himself."

"That would fit his ego all right," said Bob, continuing to look thoughtful. "And you've also got to wonder about the timing of those Rocking W men dragging him out again with the promise of some real 'eye-opening' illegal activity. If it's rustling, like we expect, wouldn't you say it's awful accommodating of the rustlers to make a raid that Dutton can observe and report on . . . not to mention doing it so soon after those Texas hardcases have arrived on the scene?"

Fred looked puzzled for a long moment. It was clear the marshal was driving at something, but he didn't quite see . . . But then all of a sudden he did. His eyebrows lifted. "Say . . . you mean you think those polecats might be *staging* a rustling raid with

Dutton on hand to witness it so he'll then be able to swear to it as fact?"

Bob had set aside his coffee cup and now his hands were balled into fists on top of the desk. "I think there's a damn good chance of it, yeah. Don't you see? If the cattle end up on V-Slash property and that's how Dutton sees it and reports it, then anything that happens next—Rocking W men, led by those Texas gunnies, blasting the hell out of anybody riding for Vandez's brand—will be seen by most people as totally justified. There can be a wholesale bloodbath out there on the range, and Wardell will come out of it looking smug and righteous."

Fred licked his lips. "But we can't let that happen, can we? Jurisdictional limits or not, we got to go out there and try to do something. Don't we?"

Bob didn't say anything for several clock ticks. He stared at the front door as if seeing something beyond it. His fists remained balled on the desktop, knuckles standing out stark white against the taut flesh on the backs of his hands. Then, in a low voice, he said, "Yeah, I reckon we do . . ."

CHAPTER 49

Saul Norton had spent a miserable, nearly sleepless night. A worse one than even the pain-filled hours immediately following his beating. Only this time it wasn't physical misery that troubled him—it was mental anguish. Just when everything was going his way; everything from being lauded a hero to having the populace worked into an anti-Larkin frenzy to Victoria Emory looking at him in a more adoring way than ever before.

But now something unexpected had turned up that had the potential for causing it all to collapse.

Damn and double damn.

Norton had worried about leaving Merlin Sweeney as a loose end right from the get-go. But the idea and the opportunity to use him had presented themselves so fast—upon seeing Earl Hines walk into Bullock's that night minus the company of Larkin, meaning the damnable ex-con was left behind without an alibi—there'd been no time to formulate a more elaborate plan. He'd figured all along he would probably have to kill Sweeney at some point afterward, too, just to make sure. Yet since the potshot Norton had taken at old man Emory and Marshal Hatfield failed to achieve its intended results due to Hines being able to account for Larkin at the time of the shooting, this unexpected new chance to heap brutal blame on Larkin—with an alibi so clearly lacking—had to be acted on without hesitation. Dealing with Sweeney as part of the aftermath could be taken care of in due time.

Ultimately, of course, that bitch Brenda—Norton's future sister-in-law—had turned up as Larkin's alibi and Norton found himself the victim of a savage beating for no benefit to his cause.

Further, before Norton was even released from the doctor's care, Sweeney had fled to pursue his dreams of trying his hand at prospecting up in the Prophecies. So okay. At least for the short term, that was almost as good as having him dead.

It removed Sweeney from town so he couldn't inadvertently let something slip about the arranged beating. Plus, niggers being generally mistrusted (according to the way Norton believed), other prospectors up in the mountains would steer clear of him so he wouldn't have anybody up there to let something slip to, either. What was more, the black bastard had done such a good job with the beating he'd delivered to earn his money, Norton was left barely able to get around, let alone do anything to eliminate him as a loose end right away. But that didn't mean he didn't still intend to take care of the matter at the earliest opportunity he could find. After all, tragic accidents to lonely prospectors up in the mountains were as common as fleas on a dog.

In the meantime, the more or less impromptu murder of Myron Poppe and subsequent flight of Larkin had finally gotten the kind of reaction Norton had been trying for with his other schemes. And the laudatory way newspaperman Dutton had subsequently portrayed him was only icing on the cake. It all made the concern he had over Sweeney being a loose end something he'd been able to shove to the back of his mind—until the man suddenly showed up again, riding back into town, big as you please, alongside one of the town's deputies.

What the hell?

It had been late in the afternoon when Norton inadvertently spotted the pair from the porch of the Emory manse where he was still staying. Too late in the day to pursue trying to find out what was going on, what had brought about such a thing. All Norton had been able to do was wait out the evening, sitting through supper and parlor time with the Emorys, trying to act relaxed and normal while every second dreading a pounding at the front door that might announce the arrival of the authorities with questions concerning the outrageous claims made by Sweeney. But no such thing happened, and, somehow, that was almost worse. Nor had turning in early helped any; it only led to the endless hours of tossing and turning and wondering what it was that brought Sweeney back under escort by a deputy.

Norton rose in the morning determined to find out. But the news he heard at the breakfast table, from the household cook who had gone out early to buy fresh eggs from a neighbor who raised chickens, shook the hell out of everything all over again.

Merlin Sweeney wasn't the only one who was back in town.

So was John Larkin!

Bob Hatfield woke with the sun, as usual. What wasn't usual for him, however, was the fact he remained in bed after doing so. The warm, shapely curves of Consuela nestled against him weren't something any red-blooded male in his right mind would be in a hurry to separate from.

Before long it became apparent Consuela was awake also. She rolled over to face him and kissed him lightly on his cheek.

"Are we going to lie here like this all day?" she said.

"Don't sound like a bad idea to me."

"I don't disagree. But how long could we get away with it before Deputy Fred or somebody showed up with business that required your attention?"

"I could fire a couple warning shots. Give 'em to understand we weren't in the mood to be interrupted. How would that be?"

"It might work. But it would still be disruptive to our . . . uhmm . . . rest and relaxation, would it not? And then there's Bucky, remember? He'll need to be rousted up and sent off to school."

"Ain't that boy graduated yet? He ought to be out making his way in the world by now."

Consuela giggled. "He's only eleven, for heaven's sake!"

Bob sighed. "Okay. I guess we have to give him a few more weeks then."

Consuela snuggled a little closer. "Still, even though we may not be able to lie here *all* day, that doesn't mean we can't stay for at least a little while longer."

"You make the call," Bob told her. "I'm in no hurry to go face what's waiting out there for me today."

Neither of them said anything for a minute or so. Consuela's expression turned sober as her forefinger traced a random pattern through Bob's chest hairs. At length, she said, "You think if you ride out to try and deal with the situation between the Rocking W and the V-Slash today, it will end up in a confrontation with Brannigan, don't you?"

"Don't see how it can be otherwise," Bob said. "No matter what else happens, he'll have me dead to rights, smack in front of everybody. Won't be no better time for him to pitch his case, make his claim for having the grounds to take me back to Texas as a wanted outlaw."

"But you're not a hundred percent sure he even recognized you."

Although it had been nearly midnight when Bob came in last night, Consuela had gotten up to welcome him home and spend some time with him. It was the first chance he'd had to talk to her about coming face-to-face with Brannigan that day at the jail—only minutes before the discovery of Myron Poppe's body and all else that had transpired so rapidly after that.

"Brannigan recognized me all right," Bob said now. "In the days when he hunted me as the Devil's River Kid, he hated me too deeply and chased me too hard for him to ever forget. If nothing else, the fact he never caught me would be enough to sear it in his memory for good."

"You don't *have* to go out there today, you know. You've explained to me before that it's not technically within your jurisdiction."

"But if I don't go, there's almost certain to be some serious bloodshed. Lots of wranglers riding for one brand or other getting hurt or killed, all based on a phony setup. It may come to that anyway, even if I do go out. And not going won't prevent the confrontation with Brannigan. It would just come at some other time."

"What if, in all the violence and bloodshed you anticipate, Brannigan takes a bullet? Wouldn't that solve the whole matter where he's concerned?"

Bob emitted a short chuff. "Men like Brannigan have a way of surviving carnage, even while others are dying around them. Besides, hoping for something like that to happen after it's once again come this close between him and me . . . well, that wouldn't do."

"Why not? You make it sound like some ridiculous point of honor—that only you need to be the one to face him."

"It's not ridiculous."

Consuela lifted her face and regarded him. "No . . . for you, it's not, is it? I'm sorry I said it that way."

"It's okay."

Consuela laid her head back. "Men are so very strange . . . And even though you are one of the finest men I've ever known, I guess even you—or maybe especially a man like you—cannot help it."

CHAPTER 50

After all the years he'd lived in Rattlesnake Wells, it still never ceased to amaze Bob how fast word of even the most minor happening could spread through the town. Although he'd taken time for a bite of breakfast and spent a little while with Bucky before leaving home, it was still fairly early when he arrived at the jail. Yet already there was a crowd of more than a dozen men gathered out front, and the words the marshal overheard as he approached them made it clear they'd gotten the news of John Larkin being back in custody. Just as clear was what was on their minds as a result.

"Now that you've caught him, how long before you're gonna introduce him to a noose, Marshal?"

"You ain't gonna turn around and let the no-good skunk out again are you?"

"Go ahead, let him out. We'll throw a party for him—a necktie party like the dirty murderer deserves!"

Bob knew most of the faces and names of these men, but he didn't give them the satisfaction of responding in any way. Barely making eye contact, he strode straight through the mass and entered the jail.

Inside, all three of his deputies were already present.

"Did you enjoy a friendly welcome back from our loyal citizens?" Peter greeted sarcastically.

"Not hardly," Bob replied. "That how it's been since I been gone?"

"Like I told you," said Fred, "only after they got revved up by Saul Norton and that special edition of Dutton's damn newspaper."

"Only now, with Larkin returned," added Vern, "it's likely to get worse. They've never mobbed up out front like that before. I'd say it's a safe bet the crowd size will grow bigger as the day wears on. Leastways until they hear what you got planned for Larkin."

"Well, it sure as hell ain't what *they* got planned for him," Bob said. "Circuit Judge Stark is due in about ten days. I'll let him decide on what he wants to do about a trial and arranging legal representation. He might want to hold the trial here, he might want to hold it in Cheyenne and have a U.S. Marshal haul Larkin down there for it. But until he makes a ruling, we'll be keeping Larkin behind bars on charges of suspected murder."

"That's not gonna be too popular with our admirers outside," advised Peter. "They're looking for a verdict a lot sooner than that, and there's only one verdict that's gonna satisfy 'em."

"Well they're just gonna have to live with a little disappointment in their lives then, ain't they?" said Bob. "Speaking of that bunch, I didn't see any sign of their fearless leaders, Dutton or Norton either one. I'd be surprised if somebody hasn't rushed to tell them by now that I brought Larkin in."

"I don't think Dutton's back from riding out with the Rocking W boys yet. Far as that loudmouthed Norton, I expect he'll be showing up soon enough," Peter said.

Bob nodded. "Good. Maybe then, right in front of his eager audience, would be a good time to have him explain about hiring our other guest—Sweeney—to beat the hell out of him."

Fred raised his eyebrows. "You really think that's the best way to play it?"

"Maybe. Maybe not . . . Hell if I know. How *do* you play something as cockeyed as that?"

"That's a good question," agreed Vern. "It sure tops anything I ever heard tell of."

"Well, we need to decide *something* about Sweeney," Fred said. "We've got him behind bars, true enough, but I don't know if we actually have the right to call him a prisoner or not. You see, Vern didn't actually arrest him. And I don't know that there's anything in the statutes to use for a charge. What law did he break by successfully performing the job he was hired to do?"

"Never mind that for right now. If he's behind bars in our cellblock, then he's a prisoner until I say otherwise. At the moment, we've got bigger fish to fry." Bob poured himself some coffee, turned back to face his men. "I'm guessing," he said, "Fred has brought you up to speed on our other problem— leastways how him and me see it—regarding the two cattle outfits, the Rocking W and the V-Slash.

Like I've been preaching and as you well know, they're technically out of our jurisdiction. And it's largely speculation on my part about how the trouble between 'em is being stoked so that it's on the brink of reaching the boiling point mighty soon . . . But I don't think I'm wrong."

"Neither do we," said Peter and Vern in a demonstration of the eerie habit they had of often speaking the same words in nearly perfect unison.

"Good to hear your vote of confidence," Bob said. "But now we've got a situation right here under our own roof with the lid about ready to blow off, too. Any ideas on how to cover both at once?"

"The only way is to split up," said Vern. "Two stay here, two ride out to try and steady down those cattlemen."

Fred shook his head. "No good. Splitting up, in my opinion, is the last thing we should do. If we're gonna do any good at all out on the range, especially with those hardcases added to the Rocking W crew, I think we need to go in with a show of force. Two of us, maybe even all four of us, may not be enough. The opposing sides could catch us in a crossfire that would put us in bad shape plenty quick."

"Fred makes a good point," Bob said.

"Wait a minute, then," said Peter angrily. "If there's a chance we'll take fire from both brands, then why do we give a damn about either one of 'em? Let 'em go ahead and blast one anothers' brains out."

"The trouble with that," Fred pointed out, "is the number of innocent, hardworking cowboys who'll get caught in a lead storm totally not of their making."

"And if our speculating is right," added Bob, "ninety

percent of it will hinge on a falsehood, a piece of trickery pulled out from under the hats of those Texas hardcases. That's the part I dislike the most, having them horn in to make matters worse. Plus, with the Texans jerking the strings, the V-Slash crew will be caught off guard and are bound to suffer the heaviest if gunplay breaks out."

"That still leaves us stuck between a rock and a hard place unless we split up," insisted Vern. "We can't try to quell the trouble outside of town and keep a lid on things here, not both at the same time."

"Since you weren't around to know any better, I'll cut you some slack," said Bob. "But for your information, before I hired on you and your brother a couple years back, me and Fred managed to do a fair to middlin' job of dealing with problems around here when it was just the two of us. And the way we did it was with a helping hand now and then from some men in town we knew we could count on."

"You mean like that bunch out there?" said Peter, jabbing a thumb toward the front door.

Bob scowled. "Did it sound like I was describing anybody from that bunch?"

"No, of course not," Peter said, mollified.

"The way I see it is this," Bob went on. "The situation here in town is less volatile than what's brewing out on the rangelands. Out there, things are primed to explode and soon. While that pack of blowhards on the other side of the door might be talking loud and tough in order to try and impress one another, they're a long way from being truly ready to bust somebody out of jail and string 'em up, not even with half a dozen Nortons and Duttons egging them on.

Most of 'em are just regular fellas caught up in the excitement of the moment."

"So you're saying our first priority is outside of town, that what I'm hearing?" said Fred.

"For the four of us, yeah," confirmed Bob. "We'll gather some of the townsmen we know we can trust and leave them in charge here, while we ride out."

"I can go with that," said Vern.

Bob nodded. "Good. Because that's exactly what you're gonna do—go. You've got the fastest horse and you're the best rider, I want you to take off immediately. Hightail it out to the V-Slash and tell Carlos Vandez what's going on. Tell him I believe Wardell is planning to sucker him into a confrontation over some trumped-up rustling. Make sure he understands it's a setup designed to go very badly for him. Tell him to hold off, to sit tight at his ranch until the rest of us can get there."

"What if he won't listen to me?"

"Make him listen! Now get going."

"Want me to stay there and wait for you?"

"No, turn around and come back. Hopefully we'll meet you on the way. I want our group back together full strength as soon as possible."

Fifteen seconds later the front door was closing behind Vern.

Bob turned next to Fred. "Go tell Mike Bullock I want to see him. Tell him it's an emergency. Then find out if Angus McTeague is in town. If he is, tell him the same thing. If he's out at one of his mines, get a couple other men from the miners' council— Feeney, Nimitz, somebody like that. Get 'em back here as soon as you can, okay?"

As Fred was heading out, Peter said, "What about me? What do you need me to do?"

"Until we ride out, we've still got prisoners to think about," said Bob. "How about going up the street to the Bluebird Café and getting 'em some breakfast?"

"Breakfast?" Peter echoed.

"We can't let 'em starve, can we?" Then, smiling slyly, Bob added, "Besides, think how pissed off it will make those jaspers outside seeing a nice, hot meal fetched for Larkin."

Peter blinked a couple times, considering. Then his mouth spread in a lopsided grin, too. "Yeah. It sure as hell will, won't it?"

CHAPTER 51

The jail office had become very crowded.

In addition to Bob, Fred, and Peter, five other men were present. Mike Bullock, at no surprise to Bob, had shown up first. He was followed in short order by Fred accompanying Angus McTeague and three of his men. McTeague was head of the New Town miners' council and also a member of Rattlesnake Wells' overall town council. As owner of the three most successful mines up in the Prophecies, he was, hands down, the wealthiest man in the area. Despite that, he put on few airs (as prominently demonstrated by continuing to smoke the same cheap, dreadful-smelling cigars he'd puffed back in the days when he'd first arrived in the area as nothing more than a flat-broke prospector) and remained a big, ruggedly handsome character who charmed most everyone he met, right down to having a strong, loyal following from those who toiled for him in his mines.

It was three such employees, in fact—the three he'd brought along with him, none being strangers to Bob's jail—currently under discussion. The trio happened to be Ray Monte, Jimmy Russert, and Sam Kingston, the same men who'd tangled with John Larkin over a game of pool on his first night back in town.

"When Fred explained the predicament you were in," McTeague was saying, "I could see right quick the situation might be requirin' a bit more than just me and Mike. Not that the two of us *couldn't* handle a riot or three strictly on our own, mind you, but there comes a point in a man's life when he starts to see the charity in sharing such fun opportunities. Ain't that right, Mike?"

"You're doing the talking," Bullock said agreeably.

"Plus," McTeague went on, "it seemed particularly fitting that these three rascals I brought with me— good men all, says I—happened to be on hand for that very consideration."

"And there wasn't even a whisker of arm-twistin' to it," Ray Monte was quick to add. "When we heard what was up, we was more than willin' to pitch in and help. We'd consider it an honor, Marshal."

"I don't know about that. But having some extra men on hand for this situation sure ain't a bad idea," said Bob. "You fellas took your medicine for that scrap at the Grand a few nights back, so things are square between us. And a nod of approval from Angus McTeague ought to be good enough for anybody. So welcome aboard.

"Now just to make sure you know what you're up against—and that goes for all of you—I reckon you got a dose of the mood of that pack of jackasses outside as you came in. You wouldn't've had to hear much to figure out that I don't rate very high in their opinion and our prisoner Larkin even less so. Mike and Angus, like me, you probably know most of those men so you know they really ain't bad sorts given to making any kind of serious trouble. Way I figure, most of what they got stuck in their craws is just hot air. But they're stirred up. And stirred-up men, even decent ones, can get out of hand. So that's what I want you to keep in mind. I don't believe that bunch has got any serious troublemaking in 'em, but at the same time you've got to stay ready for that possibility."

"We'll be ready okay," said Bullock. "Speakin' for myself, ever since that kind of talk got started—putting you in a bad light and making noise about lynching Johnny Larkin—I've been practically *aching* to knock some stupid heads together. If this gives me the chance to do that, you damn betcha I'll be ready."

"Same goes all the way around for the rest of us," stated McTeague.

"All you need to do is hold the line," Bob reminded the two old bulls. "If all they do is gather out there and grumble and make noise, leave 'em to it. That's their right. But if they make any attempt to actually get at Larkin, then of course it's a different story . . . Now me and my deputies ought to be back by nightfall. We're either gonna have some luck taming down the situation between the two brands, or we're not. But we've got to try, otherwise I'm afraid there's gonna be a lot of blood spilled."

"Just make sure you don't get caught in the middle so some of that blood ends up being yours," cautioned Bullock. "If those stubborn damn cattlemen insist on blazing away at each other, there's only so much you can do."

"I know that," allowed Bob. "I also know that our first priority is this town. Those who've been finding so much fault with me of late will probably seize on us going out there as something more to bitch about. Maybe they're right. But like I said, we feel obligated to try. That makes us mighty grateful to you men for helping out here, so we're able to."

"Never mind all that. It's understood," said McTeague. "Now go ahead and get going. We've got the handle on things here."

Bob, Fred, and Peter had barely ridden beyond the city limits before they were brought to a halt by the sight of three horsemen on their way into town, pushing their mounts hard. Riding in the center of the incoming trio was Vern Macy.

Vern and the men with him reined up sharply and the two groups milled together as a delayed cloud of dust rolled over them.

"Sounds like we're running a mite late, at least for the initial clash between the two brands," Vern reported, slightly out of breath. "I ran into these two fellas on their way in to see you, Marshal. They're Rocking W hands . . . Leastways they were until this morning. I'll let them tell you what they know about what's going on."

As the dust thinned out, Bob recognized the two wranglers—Temple and Reese; the young cowpokes he'd singled out to give him a hand the day he'd broken up the attempted lynching of the two drifters,

Hicks and Streeter. While Ed Wardell, Smoky Barnett, and the rest of the Rocking W riders who'd been present that day looked all too eager to be participating in what was under way, Bob had recognized a measure of reluctance on the faces of Temple and Reese, which was why he'd ordered them out of the rest of the pack to gather up weapons and assist him in getting the two near-victims a safe distance away. On their faces now, he once again saw disturbed, unnerved expressions.

"We ain't rightfully positive about all the shenanigans that have gone on back at the ranch lately, Marshal," Reese reported. "But we've seen and heard enough—too much—to stick around and risk gettin' caught any deeper in it."

"As soon as those three Texas gunnies showed up," added Temple, "everything took a turn toward harder and meaner. Mostly on account of their leader, a fella who calls hisself Rance Brannigan. He is one cold-eyed polecat, yet Smoky Barnett and some of the other Rockin' W riders—even Mr. Wardell to a certain extent, it seemed like—started hoppin' to the way he called the tune."

"So what happened that caused you to be on your way in to see me?" Bob wanted to know.

After getting a nod from Temple indicating he should be the one to go ahead and tell it, Reese said, "Last night, Temple and me was scheduled to ride out on nighthawk duty over this small herd of cattle we'd only recently moved to a new pasture. But then, at the last minute, Smoky came to the bunkhouse and told us to sit tight, there'd been a change of plans and we could sleep in. Well, hell, that was pretty good news to our ears so we didn't think too much more about it. Not at first. But then, a little while later, we saw Smoky and those three Texans, along with three or four other hands, go ridin' out. That seemed kinda odd, takin' so many men if they was just on their way to cover nighthawkin'.' "

"Extra odd," added Temple, "that they was involvin' those Texans. From the time they showed up, they never before done a lick as far as ranch work."

"Anyway," Reese continued, "off they rode and we didn't think a whole lot more about it. We was just glad for the extra sack time, I guess. By the time mornin' rolled around, none of those who'd rode out late had showed back up for breakfast. Just about the time the rest of us hands was finishin' up eatin', though, here comes Smoky Barnett tearin' in like his tail was on fire and his ass was about to catch. He went straight to Mr. Wardell's house, and, not more'n a minute later, Wardell and that newspaperman he had with him came hurryin' back out with Smoky."

"What was the newspaperman doing there?" Fred asked.

"Wardell sent for him to come out the evening before," said Temple. "He wanted him—Dutton his name is—to do a story on the rustlin' Wardell is so bound and determined is goin' on. Dutton came around and talked to some of us hands, scribblin' down our thoughts about the trouble. 'Background,' he called it, for the articles he'd be puttin' in his paper."

Reese picked it up again from there, saying, "When it got late, Wardell had him to supper at the big house and then had him stay overnight. That's how he happened to be around in the mornin' when Smoky came a-thunderin' in with his big announcement."

"What announcement was that?" Bob asked, already having a pretty good hunch what the answer was going to be.

"New rustlin' activity that had took place durin' the night. Smoky and the boys ridin' with him had found sign of it and tracked the long-loopers onto V-Slash land. The rest of the men had stayed with the cattle, to hold 'em in place, while Smoky had come to fetch Mr. Wardell so's he could see for himself."

"Wardell *and* the newspaperman, right?" said Bob.

"Uh-huh. Dutton went with 'em."

Bob cocked one eyebrow dubiously. "Mighty convenient for the newspaperman to be so close by when the rustling took place, wouldn't you say?"

Temple and Reese exchanged uneasy glances. "That's, uh, what we got to thinkin', too," said Reese. "Not so much about Dutton, necessarily, but more to the point of Smoky and those Texans bein' out prowlin' on a night when the rustlers hit. In the first place, how could the rustlin' take place under the nose of all of 'em out there supposedly night-hawkin'? Not only that but, for the first time ever, then bein' able to track 'em over onto Vandez land."

"That's why we decided to take a look for ourselves," Temple said. "Sure enough, when we got to that herd we would've been nighthawkin' over if Smoky hadn't changed our schedule, you could quick enough tell there was a mess of 'em missin'. Four, five dozen at least. We didn't have no trouble seein' the way they got driven off, neither, and there wasn't much doubt it was in the direction of the V-Slash property line. So, our curiosity already pricked, we followed it for a ways.

"And before long was when we heard all the shootin'," Temple finished.

CHAPTER 52

Saul Norton finally decided that, since his voice had been such a big part of stirring up the very emotions they were displaying, he needed to make an appearance and join the crowd gathered outside the jail. He'd had reservations about going after hearing that Sweeney was also being kept in the lockup, though nobody seemed to be sure why.

Norton's concern was that his appearance on the scene might lead to the exposure of his past dealings with Sweeney. In the end, he'd decided that if the matter came up he would simply deny knowing anything about it. After all, lacking any kind of proof on Sweeney's part, who would believe a penniless black man over him?

When Norton arrived at the jail and found out the marshal and his deputies had ridden off to attend to some other trouble out of town, he was emboldened and suddenly very glad he came. By this point the crowd had swelled to nearly thirty in number and their mood was increasingly restless and rowdy.

When he stood before them and they shouted his name, Norton felt a rush of power and influence like he'd seldom ever known before.

"If anybody needed any further proof of our marshal's total breakdown of priorities and his repeated disregard for the importance of having a killer like John Larkin in his custody," he addressed the crowd, his voice raised high and quavering with outrage, "you have it presented before you in a stark display! Marshal Hatfield rides off—with *all* of his deputies, mind you—and leaves the confinement of a dangerous murderer in the hands of a handful of rank amateurs. Does that strike you as either prudent or competent? Are those the actions of someone who is committed to the safety and best interests of our community?"

Responding shouts came out of the crowd:

"Hell no! He ain't fit for the job!"

"We need to take responsibility for our own safety—we need to give Larkin what he deserves before he gets loose and kills again!"

"And then we need to get rid of that worthless damn Hatfield!"

Norton had stepped up on a porch-like strip of boardwalk that ran in front of the jail building, elevating himself slightly for addressing the crowd. When the front door of the jail opened behind him, the crowd suddenly quieted and Norton stepped aside with a bit of a start.

Mike Bullock came out onto the boardwalk. In the doorway behind him loomed Angus McTeague with a scattergun held on prominent display.

"It's getting awful stinking noisy out here," Bullock growled. "I not only don't like the noise, I double-damn don't like the words contained in it. Running down Bob Hatfield behind his back? That makes the whole lot of you not only gutless, it makes you about as wrong as wrong can be."

"It's a free country," argued Norton. "We have the right to assemble and the right to speak our piece."

"And I have the right not to like it and not to like you," Bullock told him.

"That may be, but it still doesn't change the situation."

"And what is the situation?" Bullock demanded. "When I hear 'give Larkin what he deserves' and 'get rid of that worthless damn Hatfield'—is that it? I'd call that more than talk, mister, I'd say those sound mighty damn close to threats."

"And if that's the case," said McTeague, crowding farther into the doorway, "then any of you loud-mouths wanting to try and make good on 'em by marching through us handful of 'rank amateurs'— well, you're welcome to try."

No one in the crowd appeared eager to take him up on the offer.

Sensing he was losing control over the group, Norton was quick to say, "Bullying honest citizens in-stead of protecting them against the likes of a John Larkin—yeah, it's plain to see Marshal Hatfield was the one who trained you for your acting deputy roles."

"You think anything we've said or done so far is bullying?" said Bullock, his face reddening. "Then maybe it's time to give you a demonstration of the real thing."

Before anything more was said, attention was shifted and heads were abruptly turned by a stirring in the group of onlookers that started toward the back and seemed to ripple quickly through to the front.

Brenda Emory emerged from the pack and stepped boldly up onto the boardwalk between Bullock and Norton. She was clad in a long maroon skirt, cinched at the waist by a wide leather belt, and a crisp white blouse. Her long reddish hair, looking molten in the morning sunlight, was pulled back and tied in a loose ponytail that flounced lightly when she moved her head.

"Enjoyable as seeing you give a demonstration of bullying to Mr. Norton might be," she said to Bullock, "I hardly think that's the kind of thing Marshal Hatfield left you in charge to do, is it, sir?"

Bullock scowled at her but didn't say anything right away.

Not waiting, Brenda turned her head and aimed a scowl of her own at Norton, saying, "And you, Saul—rabble-rousing when you belong at home still convalescing. Is this the wisest way for you to be spending your time?"

Norton showed no hesitation when it came to responding. "How I spend my time is my business. More to the point is what the hell are you doing here, Brenda?"

"I came to see John Larkin," she answered, thrusting out her chin defiantly. Then, narrowing her sparkling brown eyes and turning to rake them over the gathering, she simultaneously raised her voice so that everyone could hear, adding, "Unlike some, I happen to believe in one of the basic rules of our land that teaches a man is presumed innocent until *proven* guilty."

"Your behavior in coming here is scandalous," Norton hissed. "Do you know how hard it is on your father every time you—"

Brenda cut him off with, "Leave my father out of this! Where I go and how I choose to behave is my business." Turning back to Bullock, she said, "How about it, Mr. Bullock? Will you allow me a brief visit with the prisoner?"

Bullock looked momentarily uncomfortable, uncertain. But glancing past Brenda and seeing how displeased the notion clearly made Norton helped him make up his mind. "Probably not something the marshal would like for me to allow. But what the hell," he muttered. "Come ahead on in, Miss Emory."

CHAPTER 53

With Temple and Reese leading the way toward where they'd heard the sound of heavy gunfire, Bob and his deputies rode hard over low, rolling hills and in and out of brushy draws. The sun climbed higher in the sky overhead and the air was totally still. For a time the whole world seemed to be one of only thundering hooves, boiling dust, and a sensation of rushing toward danger they hoped they would be in time to help quell.

At last, as they approached a long, flat-topped hogback rising up a short ways off to the east, Reese raised one hand and they slowed to a walk and then a halt. Reese stood up in his stirrups and cocked one ear, listening sharply. When Bob moved up beside him, he said, "Somewhere about here is where we judged all the shootin' was comin' from. We was a ways back to the west. But by this point I'm pretty sure we've crossed onto V-Slash land, wouldn't you say, Temp?"

"For certain," Temple agreed.

Everyone sat their horses, remaining very still. The only sounds were the animals blowing, the occasional creak of leather, and the gentle whisper of settling dust.

After a minute, Bob said, "Let's move up onto that hogback and see if we can't make out something from there."

When they crested the hogback a handful of minutes later, they were indeed able to make out something. Something they'd been hoping to be able to prevent.

The back side of the hogback sloped down into a shallow natural bowl ringed by stands of scraggly timber and scattered, jagged rock outcroppings. Across the floor of the bowl, several head of cattle stood in two or three loose clumps. Interspersed among them were half a dozen carcasses sprawled flat and still, riddled with bullet holes. Two or three horses lay in the same condition . . . And then there were the bodies of the men. Five in all, three of them dropped flat, two others fallen in twisted, grotesque positions. All splashed with bright red smears of blood pumped by their dying heartbeats.

The six men looking down on this slaughter each uttered either a curse or a bitter lament to the Almighty under his breath.

Nudging his horse forward and down, Bob said in a low, husky voice, "Spread out. Look for any signs of life."

It didn't take long for them to work their way across the floor of the bowl. Other than the milling cattle, there was no living thing requiring closer examination or aid.

And then, partway up the slope on the far side of the bowl, something moved. Six Colts—none faster than Bob's—were swept from their holsters and leveled on the spot where the movement had taken place. The sound of hammers being thumbed back melded together like the exclamation point to an unspoken warning.

From behind one of the rock outcroppings, a disheveled-looking man emerged with jerky, unsteady steps. Minus his bowler hat and with his hair sticking up wildly and his face smeared with dirt, it took a moment for the man to be recognizable as Owen Dutton.

"Don't shoot," he said dully, holding out one hand. "For the love of God, no more shooting."

Bob and the others pouched their guns and converged quickly on the newspaperman, who looked ready to collapse.

"Take it easy, Dutton. Get hold of yourself," said Bob as he swung down from the saddle and reached back to grab his canteen. When Peter Macy stepped up to help steady Dutton, Bob unscrewed the cap off the canteen and held it up to pour some water down the newspaperman's gullet. When more started bubbling back out of the man's gaping mouth than going down, the marshal lowered the canteen. By then, the others were also gathered around close.

"What took place here? Tell us what happened to cause this," Bob said.

Dutton passed the back of one hand across his mouth. "Early this morning, back at the Rocking W, I was having breakfast with Ed Wardell when his foreman, Smoky—"

"We know that part," Bob interrupted. "You rode out on the report of some rustled cattle that had been tracked onto V-Slash property. What happened after you got here?"

As he answered, Dutton's eyes swept slowly over the carnage of the scene. "Not too long after we got here, some other riders showed up . . . V-Slash men. Carlos Vandez was with them . . . They had gotten reports of Rocking W men trespassing onto V-Slash land . . . Wardell and Vandez had a heated exchange. Wardell called him a thief, among other things, and pointed to the cattle as finally having the proof he'd always been lacking before. At first, Vandez simply denied knowing anything about how the cattle got here. But then, when Wardell refused to believe that, Vandez accused him of purposely *planting* the cattle in this spot for the sake of provoking a confrontation."

Dutton paused to catch his breath. The expression on his dirt-streaked face was one of anguish. It only deepened as he continued. "'And a bloody goddamned confrontation is what we're gonna have!' is how Wardell answered the accusation. And, God help us, was he ever telling the truth. The Texas gunmen Wardell had hired went for their weapons first and the rest of the Rocking W men didn't hesitate to follow suit. The V-Slash men were caught totally by surprise and badly outnumbered. Bullets started flying everywhere. Cattle, horses, and men were cut down. It was an unimaginable horror."

"The V-Slash boys must have made some kind of fight of it," observed Temple. "A couple of these fallen men are Rocking W riders."

Dutton nodded. "Oh, yes. They fought . . . bravely, desperately."

"And Vandez managed to get away?" Bob asked.

"Yes. I saw him get hit, though. It looked pretty serious but somehow he managed to stay in his saddle. Then he and the remainder of his men, some of them wounded, too, rode off."

"Wardell and his bunch didn't follow?" Bob asked.

"Not right away," Dutton said. "But Wardell swore this wasn't going to be the end of it. He said he meant to finish that thieving Vandez once and for all and today was going to be the day. But, to do so, he wanted more men. So he sent a couple riders back to the ranch for the rest of the crew. 'Tell 'em they'd better show up ready to ride and fight for the brand or not be anywhere in my sight when this is over' was the order he gave."

"That sounds like Wardell," Temple said sourly.

"At any rate, it was a message that got results," said Dutton. "In no time at all, a couple dozen more riders responded, all armed to the teeth. With Wardell in the lead, they took off hell-for-leather toward the V-Slash ranch headquarters."

"Why didn't you go with 'em?" said Fred.

"I started out. I didn't figure I had any choice," Dutton answered, looking like he was none too happy with the lack of an option. "But just over the rim of the slope"—he jerked a thumb, indicating the inclining ground behind him—"my horse stepped wrong and threw me. It's a wonder I didn't get trampled by the rest of the riders passing by. They either didn't notice I'd taken a spill or simply didn't give a damn. The good news was that I *didn't* get trampled; the bad news was that my horse broke its leg. So I had no means to follow or to go anywhere. I found some shade behind a rock and sat down to wait, hoping somebody would eventually come along."

"Did you put your horse out of its misery?" Vern wanted to know.

Dutton made a face. "I don't carry a gun—I could have gotten one off one of the dead men out there, I know—but the poor beast doesn't really seem to be suffering and I-I just didn't have the heart . . . not to do still more killing."

Vern made a face, too. One of disgust. "You don't put down a suffering animal for the sake of killing—and it *is* suffering, no matter what you think—you do it for mercy, you spineless fool."

"Go take care of it, will you, Vern?" Bob said.

The young deputy went quickly up the slope.

To Dutton, Bob said, "How many men total do you figure Wardell rode away from here with?"

"Thirty, I'd say, give or take."

"That sounds about right, if they cleared out most of the crew," said Reese.

"How long ago?"

"Less than half an hour. Maybe only twenty minutes," Dutton said.

Bob regarded Temple and Reese. "The odds are plain enough. You helped by guiding us this far, even after cutting yourselves clear of this mess once before. Nobody'd blame you if you wanted to finish riding clear now."

The two men exchanged looks. Then Temple said, "Odds ain't the whole of it, Marshal. Ridin' on the right side of a thing counts for something, too. Reckon that's what we'll be doin' if we continue to stick with you."

"Obliged," Bob said with a curt nod. Turning back to Dutton, he said, "We can't take you along. We can't be slowed by somebody riding double," he said.

"I understand," Dutton replied.

The flat crack of a rifle shot sounded from up over the rim of the slope.

"Let's get mounted. Somebody grab Vern's horse," Bob ordered. Once up in his own saddle, he looked down at Dutton again and said, "You can find water in the canteens of those dead horses . . . Maybe a horse from one of the fallen men will wander back through here now that the shooting has ended. That happens, you'll have a fresh mount. If not, we'll send somebody for you as soon as we can."

"I understand," Dutton said again. Then he added, "Good luck, Marshal."

CHAPTER 54

In addition to already knowing the way to the V-Slash ranch headquarters, Bob and those riding with him could easily see the tracks of Rocking W men who'd only recently gone before them. The way took them on a southwesterly slant from where they'd left Dutton and the "rustled" Wardell cattle, the terrain a continuation of the rolling, grassy hills and brushy draws that made up most of the rangeland north of Rattlesnake Wells.

This time Bob held them to a steady but more moderate pace, wanting to risk neither unexpectedly overtaking the Rocking W outfit nor warning them with the approach of a too-noticeable dust cloud. As they drew nearer to the ranch, he slowed them even more. Shortly after that they began to hear the reports of gunfire, both pistol and rifle.

Bob signaled a halt. "Sounds like once again the party has started without us," he said.

"Not unexpected, really," Fred responded. "Wardell and his bunch likely didn't wait too long to kick off the festivities. Fired up as they were after routing the V-Slash boys in that first skirmish, I expect they went tearing in on a full-out follow-up charge, hoping to hit with as much surprise as possible."

"Reckon that's how I'd've done it," agreed Bob. He settled back in his saddle some, not saying anything more for a minute. His eyes scanned the landscape ahead as he pictured in his mind the layout of the V-Slash headquarters from his recent visit there. Then: "Way I recollect, the main house would be about due west if we go in straight from where we are now. That puts the outbuildings, bunkhouse, corrals, and such on the near side to us. Figuring the Rocking W crew rode straight in, that would mean—after their initial charge—they could scatter, dismount, and take to cover in among those buildings and whatnot while they poured lead at the main house and wherever the V-Slash fellas tried to find cover of their own. With superior numbers on their side, the Wardell outfit could then steadily close in as they continued to blast away."

"That'd turn Vandez's front yard into a battlefield," said Vern.

"Judging by the sound of all that shooting," added Peter, "that's exactly what it's become."

"Whatever you call it," said Fred, "we go sashaying into the middle of it we'll risk drawing fire from both sides because each will suspect we might be there to help the other."

"There might be a way around that," said Bob. "But first, before we get too far ahead of ourselves, I want a better look at what the situation we'll be riding into actually is. To the north, there's some higher ground that sorta looks down on the ranch buildings. Let's work our way around to there and have ourselves that better look-see before we do anything rash."

Bob again led the way, swinging his mount north and heeling it to a gallop. He was less concerned about raising a dust cloud now, figuring that men engaged in a gun battle would be far more focused on keeping to cover and trading lead than noticing a few wisps of dust on the horizon.

Going by the sounds of the guns, Bob's group rode due north until they judged they were a distance above the battle. Only then did they cut to the west, ascending the swell of higher ground. At length, again going by the sound of the battle now somewhere below them, Bob signaled a halt. After dismounting and telling the others to stay put, the marshal proceeded on foot to the crest of a rounded ridge.

Crouching low in a fringe of knee-high grass, Bob gazed cautiously down on the ranch headquarters about five hundred yards below. He quickly saw that the way things appeared to be playing out down there was pretty close to what he'd expected. To the east, on Bob's left, the Rocking W bunch was fanned out, no longer mounted, and had taken up positions behind buildings, wagons, and fences. From this cover, they were pouring lead at the main house and a handful of sheds and structures close to it. To Bob's right, from the windows of the house and from behind the closer cover, V-Slash men were returning fire. Here and there were bodies—not necessarily discernible as to which side they belonged—sprawled motionless on the ground.

Scrambling back down to where he'd left the others, Bob said somewhat breathlessly, "It's about like we figured, except there might be a few less Rocking W men than we thought. They've still got the edge in numbers, though, and they're really pouring it on. A number of cowboys have already bit the dust. It ain't pretty, not by a damn sight."

"So what are we gonna do to try and tame 'em down—without taking a final taste of dust ourselves?" Fred asked.

"Mr. Temple," Bob said, gesturing toward the former Rocking W hand. "I see you're wearing a white undershirt beneath your outer shirt. Wonder if I might borrow it for little while?"

Temple looked abruptly and completely befuddled. "I, uh . . . The thing is, it ain't just a shirt, it's a whole set of long johns."

"I don't care exactly what piece of apparel it is, I want the color," Bob told him. "Didn't you ever hear of a white flag of truce?"

"Hey, I got a pair of white socks if that'd be any help. They'd be a lot easier to get off," Vern offered.

Before Bob could say anything, Peter spoke. "They wouldn't be big enough to make a decent flag. Besides—meaning no offense, little brother—but I've seen your so-called white socks after you've worn them a few times and I ain't so sure they'd even rightly pass for white."

Vern scowled indignantly and started to reply but Temple cut him off.

"Just give me a minute. I never said I *wouldn't* hand over my long handles. I need time to get to it, that's all." Temple was down out of his saddle by this point, starting to unbutton his shirt. Moving quickly, with the gun-thunder from the ranch battle growing more intense by the minute, he kicked off his boots, shucked down to his skivvies and then more as he hopped about on stocking feet. Tossing the long handles to Bob, he began pulling his clothes back on even quicker than he'd peeled them off.

Temple was dressed again by the time Bob had the commandeered undergarment tied to the barrel of his rifle. It flowed out nicely, making a unique yet hopefully still effective white flag.

"Hard to believe what a difference a thin layer of cloth like that makes when it comes to sittin' a saddle," remarked Temple sourly as he climbed back into his. "My business is floppin' awful loose in these britches, I gotta tell you. I hope I get my long handles back and not shot full of bullet holes, Marshal."

Bob gave him a look. "If this flag gets shot full of holes, that'll probably mean I will be, too. Comes to that, I hope you understand if my concern for your skivvies might be a little lacking."

Temple looked somber. "Well. I hope neither of you get shot full of holes, then."

CHAPTER 55

Down the northern slope they descended in single file. Bob was in the lead, prominently displaying the impromptu flag of truce. He was followed, respectively, by Fred, Vern, Peter, Reese, and Temple. Their standing orders were simple: In the event any of the gunfire was turned on them, they were to scatter and take cover. But in any event, they were to hold their own fire for as long as possible.

Bob was nearly at the bottom of the slope before any of the shooters appeared to take notice. Heads began turning at the unexpected sight he made, and gradually the tempo of the shooting slowed, became sporadic, and finally stopped. This, however, did not prevent several of the guns on both sides from being aimed at him.

Emboldened by the cease-fire, not to mention the fact he hadn't been shot yet, Bob held his horse to a slow walk and proceeded out into the flat, open area between the ranch's main house and the out-buildings and fences behind which the Rocking W men were hunkered down. No-man's-land. Behind him, his men fanned out on the edge of the open area and braced to cover him in case the quieted guns started up again.

Bob drew back on the reins and stopped his horse. For a minute he just sat there, looking ahead at nothing, saying nothing. Then, slowly, he turned his head to look in the direction of the main house; after several clock ticks he turned his head and looked the other way, seeking out the deeply frowning face of Ed Wardell peeking out from behind a corral gate.

Finally, Wardell couldn't hold it in any longer. "What the hell are you doing here, Hatfield? What are you trying to pull?"

"I'm not trying to 'pull' anything. What I'm trying to do is stop any more of this senseless killing and maiming over a completely wrongheaded notion," Bob answered.

"There's nothing wrongheaded about a man fighting to keep what's rightfully his from being stolen away from him," insisted Wardell. "Besides, you had your chance to get involved in this and you wanted nothing to do with it. I practically begged you. But your answer was always that it was out of your jurisdiction."

"It still is. That part hasn't changed," Bob told him. "But—"

"Then get your interferin' ass out of here! Ain't no 'buts' about it," hollered out Smoky Barnett. "That badge of yours don't mean nothing out here but a shiny target to aim at, and I, for one, am itchin' to do just that."

Bob made it a point not to look at Barnett, instead keeping his eyes locked on Wardell as he said, "I thought you ran the show at the Rocking W, Ed. Since when have you started letting this yappin' mutt do your talking for you?"

"Go ahead and run your mouth, law dog," Barnett said. "That just makes it all the more—"

"Be quiet, Smoky," Wardell cut him short. "I'm handling this. You keep your place."

"Now that I know who I'm dealing with," said Bob, "let me finish my point about the wrongheadedness of what's going on here. You see, the missing beef that started all this—the ones you're so hell-bent on blaming Vandez for—ain't really missing at all. Leastways, not a good chunk of 'em."

"What the hell are you talking about, not missing?" hissed Wardell. "I know when I'm short cattle and when I'm not."

Bob wagged his head. "I'm not saying you're not short cattle on your spread, on the range where you expect them to be. What I'm saying is that they can be found where you just haven't looked yet."

"You're not making any sense!"

Bob made a placating gesture with his free hand. "Just hold on, I'll explain. But before I do"—the marshal turned away momentarily and called toward the main house—"Carlos Vandez! Are you listening to this also?"

After a sight pause, Vandez called back, "*Sí*, Marshal Hatfield. If I was not listening, the bullets would still be flying."

"Well, just keep listening and keep holding off on those bullets," Bob told him. Then, turning back to Wardell, he said, "Two days ago, I had occasion to chase a fugitive up into the Shirley Mountains. I was able to stay on his trail, but he sure didn't make it easy for me. In the course of following all the zigs and zags he pulled to try and throw me off, I came upon an interesting sight in the lower reaches of the Shirley foothills . . . Several pockets of cattle—each one numbering three or four dozen, maybe more, I didn't take time for a tight count—nestled in a series of shallow, grass-bottomed canyons. Your cattle, Wardell . . . and some of yours, too, Vandez . . . scattered off their regular range by the hard winter and finding places to hunker in and survive, even thrive."

Wardell slowly straightened up and eased partway out from behind the gate. The corners of his mouth were turned down and his eyes were boring into Bob. "That's a helluva yarn you're spinning, Hatfield."

"Maybe so. But tell me it's not possible," Bob insisted. "You know how mean last winter was. Wasn't plenty of the cattle you *did* manage to gather up this spring scattered far and wide over your spread?"

"That's true, boss," said one of the Rocking W men crouched behind a wagon near where Wardell now stood. "We chased cows from hell to breakfast and back again; yet some of us fellas had a hunch there still might be others—"

"Shut up, Evans!" barked Barnett, treating somebody else to getting his words cut off. "Mr. Wardell is handling this. He wants anything out of you, he'll ask for it."

There was movement from the front of the main house, causing all eyes to snap in that direction. The front door slowly opened and Carlos Vandez emerged. His left shoulder was heavily bandaged, the arm suspended in a sling. Splotches of blood had seeped through the bandaging, and as the cattleman came forward it was obvious he was in a good deal of pain. Two V-Slash wranglers walked on either side of him, each fisting a drawn gun but holding it down alongside his hip.

Watching Vandez approach, Wardell stepped the rest of the way clear of his concealment and edged forward, too. For the first time, Bob saw that he also was wounded. His left arm hung limp, punctured by a bullet hole just below the elbow. Blood was dripping from the cuff of his shirtsleeve.

"I, too, found myself short of cattle this spring, and many of those we rounded up were widely scattered," said Vandez as he drew closer to where Bob still sat his horse with his flag held out at a sagging angle. "It seems I was not missing as many as my neighbor, however, so neither did I think to send my *vaqueros* searching as far as the Shirley foothills."

"I'm not saying *all* the missing cattle are to be found there," Bob tried to make clear. "The winter no doubt claimed many. But some good-sized bunches of 'em survived. I saw 'em with my own eyes."

"If that turns out to be true," said Wardell somewhat woodenly, "then all of this . . ." He let his words trail off as his gaze swept over the grounds of the ranch headquarters. Wispy layers of gunsmoke remained hanging in the still air. It became clear that the sight of the fallen and the wounded and the thought of what had been transpiring here only moments earlier were suddenly weighing heavy on the embittered cattleman.

"Now hold on a minute," said Barnett, also stepping out from behind a wagon wheel. "You'll have to excuse me, boss, but I need to speak on this. You can believe the marshal's fairy tale about those far-wandered beeves if you want, but what about the stolen cattle we found in that hollow where we skirmished only a little while ago? That was smack on V-Slash range, and those cows didn't get there by wanderin' off in no winter storm."

"That's a real interesting question, Barnett," Bob said through clenched teeth. "What *about* those cattle back in the hollow? Maybe you can explain to your boss and the rest of us how—after you pulled the nighthawk crew originally slotted to watch over that herd and then rode out yourself at the head of a re-placement bunch including three Texas gunnies who never worked cattle before—you all managed to let a rustling supposedly take place right under your noses. And then, miraculously, you were Johnny-on-the-spot when it came to tracking 'em straight onto Vandez property so's you could raise the big alarm that set this whole thing in motion."

Wardell glared at Barnett, his expression clearly saying he expected a response.

Bob nudged it along, saying, "Come on, Wardell. You don't have to ponder those facts for very long to see that they stink to high heaven. Those cattle ending up where they did was a setup job aimed at fi-nally blowing the lid off the powder keg you've been packing full of your hate for Vandez ever since he bought land bordering yours."

Wardell's glare melted into an expression of an-guish. "Is it true, Smoky? Is that how and why those cattle got moved to where you showed me?"

Barnett looked half-confused, half-angry. "I thought it's what you wanted. All this time you been lookin' for proof . . . Brannigan said it was up to us to make some for you."

As Wardell's eyes cut in his direction, Brannigan came out around the opposite end of the same wagon Barnett had been behind. The Texan's mouth was spread in a wide sneer. "Spare me the violins and the mournful looks, Wardell. For Christ's sake. I told you right from the get-go that me and my boys weren't here for the long haul. I told you we'd do things our way to get the end results you wanted. What the hell did you expect?"

"*What did I expect?*" Wardell's voice was strident, quavering. "I wanted an end to the rustling I was convinced was taking place. I was willing to fight and even kill to protect what was rightfully mine. But I never wanted . . . *this.*" He swept his good arm, indicating the battlefield the V-Slash ranch headquarters had been turned into. "Certainly not over some trumped-up piece of trickery."

"Well, it's what you got," Brannigan said coldly. "You made your statement, you whittled down your enemy, and, if the high and mighty marshal is to be believed, your rustlin' problem is solved. What more do you want?"

"What I want right at this minute," Wardell said in a strained voice, "is you gone from my sight. Gone from these parts. Damn my soul for ever bringing you here! And if you think for one second I'm going to pay you the balance of what we agreed—"

"You damn well will pay the rest of what you owe me," Brannigan snarled. "If you think otherwise, then this little bit of lead tradin' that seems to have turned your spine to jelly will look like a game of patty-cake compared to what I'll rain down on you, you crawfishin' bastard."

"I might have a little something to say about that," drawled Bob.

CHAPTER 56

Brannigan's snarl turned into a condescending smile. "Well, well. Mr. High and Mighty Marshal. I was about ready to get around to you anyway. So let's cut to it. You and me have got some long-unfinished business. What say we go ahead and get it settled?"

"You need to be settled with. No argument there," Bob allowed.

"Señors," spoke up Carlos Vandez, "perhaps you should take time to look to the south. I think something more is about to happen."

All eyes followed Vandez's words. What they saw was a group of riders approaching at a hard gallop. Riding at the head of these new arrivals was a wide-shouldered figure immediately recognizable to some. The U.S. Marshal's badge glinting on the front of his shirt was recognizable to everyone.

Moments later, one-eyed Marshal Buford Morrison reined up just short of where Bob still calmly sat his horse. Behind Morrison, a half dozen other riders also reined to a halt, fanning out slightly. All of these were Rattlesnake Wells townsmen familiar to Bob. Among them was Ray Monte, one of the "deputies" he'd left behind to guard the jail with Bullock and McTeague.

"Well now," said Morrison in his booming voice. "Bein' the sharp-eyed lawman and trained investigator that I am, I can quickly see you fellas have had yourselves a real eventful morning. So the only question that leaves is: What in hellfire thunderation is this all about?"

"It started out as a matter of rustling," Bob began to explain.

"Wait a minute," Morrison interrupted him. "First, I've got an even bigger question. Why in blazes are you sitting there holding out a pair of your long johns?"

"It's a flag of truce," Bob said, feeling his ears burn a little. He lowered the Winchester and pulled off its "flag," adding, "And just for the record, they're not my long johns."

Morrison looked skeptical. "You folks around here sure have some mighty strange practices when it comes to fighting a range war, that's all I got to say."

"Be that as it may," said Bob, "I think this particular range war has about run its course. Is that a statement you can agree with . . . Vandez? Wardell?"

"*Sí.* My *vaqueros* and I want no more of shooting and killing . . . Though we remain ready to fight if attacked," replied Vandez.

"You got no more worries about being bothered by me or mine, Vandez," Wardell told him. "I may have been misled but, like the marshal pointed out right from the get-go, I came into this with a chip on my shoulder and a whole wrongheaded notion . . .

I'll carry the blame and the guilt of what happened because of that all the rest of my days."

"There's blame to go around," Bob stated. "But what's more important to worry about, right at the moment, is getting some of these injured men tended to. We need to send a rider back to town to fetch the doc as soon as possible."

"Way ahead of you, son," said Morrison. "I was afraid we wasn't gonna make it out here in time to stop the trouble, so I asked the doc to come along before we left. He's trailing a ways behind in his buggy, but he should be here before long."

"That'll be good." Bob squinted. "And not that it ain't good to see you, too—but how come you to show up here?"

Morrison smiled. "That pretty wife of yours sent me a telegram. Said you were in trouble but too proud to ask for help, so she was asking for you. After that inquiry you sent a couple days prior to hers, I decided there must be something serious enough going on to warrant paying a visit. I got into town on the train just minutes after you and your men lit out. The fellas at the jail told me what was up and where you was headed, then these gents"—he jabbed a thumb toward Monte and the others—"offered to show me the way. So here we are."

Bob's eyebrows lifted during the telling. "Seems like I got more friends than I thought I needed. Reckon you ain't got a patent on being wrongheaded, Wardell."

Brannigan edged forward some more. His sneer was back, wider than ever. "You keep believing that, Hat-field. But before you tally your number of friends too high, let's find out how chummy the federal man wants to be with a wanted outlaw who used to go by the name of Devil's River Kid."

"Who the hell are you? And what are you talking about?" Morrison wanted to know.

"My name's Brannigan," the Texan said. "I'm going to reach into my vest pocket for a piece of paper that will explain everything. So don't nobody get too proddy with none of those damn guns."

Slowly, Brannigan did what he'd announced. Unfolding the wanted poster, he walked to where Morrison still sat his horse and handed it up to him, saying, "That says it quicker and plainer than I can with words."

Morrison scowled down at the paper, studying it long and hard. When he lifted his face again, his single eye darted back and forth several times between Bob and Brannigan. Then it settled on Brannigan and he said, "Seems like your idea of what's supposed to be so plain must differ quite a bit from mine. What am I supposed to be looking at here? What is this supposed to be telling me?"

Brannigan's eyes bugged and his mouth sagged open in astonishment before he was able to find his voice. "Are you kidding me? Are you blind? The man described and depicted on that wanted dodger is who everybody around here calls Bob Hatfield! He's really a wanted outlaw and killer from down in Texas. He's been on the run for seven years, but now I've caught up with him!"

"You'd better haul back on the reins a little, bub, before you blow a gasket," advised Morrison. "In the first place, I may only have one eye but I am a long way from being blind. I can see just fine, thank you, and what I can see in this instance is that there ain't a damn thing on this wanted dodger to make anybody think it pertains to Bob Hatfield. I say you're making a big mistake and you owe a big apology to the good marshal and everybody here for wasting their time."

"Like hell! I chased that bastard and came within inches of nabbing him all those years ago." The cords on Brannigan's unshaven neck bulged like they were going to burst from his neck. "You think I'd ever forget that face? It's the same damn one that's right there on that paper!"

"You calling me a liar?" Morrison challenged.

"For God's sake . . . Will you please at least show it to somebody else? Get another opinion?"

Morrison considered this, his expression stony. At length, he gave a single nod of his head. "All right. One more pass at humoring you, then that had better be the end of it . . . Deputy Fred, will you and those two other young fellas come over here and have a look at this, please?"

From over on the edge of the open space, Fred, Peter, and Vern nudged their horses into motion and moved toward Morrison.

"Now wait a damn minute!" Brannigan protested. "That ain't fair. Those are his own men. They won't call it straight!"

"Straight?" Morrison echoed. "You strike me as the type who never gave one single damn about the straight of anything in your whole miserable life, mister, so stop your caterwauling. Three honorable officers of the law are going to look at this paper—at your request, I might add—and give their judgment on your claims. In the meantime, you'd be advised to keep a civil tongue in your head."

The three deputies took the paper from Morrison and quickly passed it among themselves. When Fred handed it back, Morrison said, "Well?"

"No likeness I can recognize, sir," said Fred.

"Never saw that face before in my life," said Vern.

"Nobody I remember ever seeing, and it's a mug too damn homely to forget," said Peter.

"This is outrageous!" wailed Brannigan. He spread his arms and turned in a circle, imploring all the cowboys looking on. "Are you going to allow this kind of injustice from those who are supposed to be upholding the law around here? You deserve better than that. *I* deserve better than that—me and my pards are here to remove a dangerous fugitive from the midst of decent, hardworkin' folks like all of you, and this is how we get treated?"

Something abruptly clicked inside Bob. This business with Brannigan had dragged on for too long. It was time to end it. And he saw now, before anybody else got dragged into it or hurt, there was only one way.

"You're right, Brannigan," he said as he swung down from his saddle.

"Huh?" said the Texan, his face snapping around.

Bob stepped clear of his horse and planted his feet wide. "You heard me. I said you're right . . . You got deserves coming."

Brannigan shifted to face Bob squarely. "What is that supposed to mean?"

"You figure it out. You said a minute ago you deserve different than what you're getting. I agree, though I imagine what each of us thinks you deserve is something mighty far apart. So have those two noble, civic-minded pards of yours step up there beside you and let's settle it. We'll let the winner *earn* what he deserves."

"Oh, yeah, that's rich," scoffed Brannigan. "Us three against you and all your lyin', badge-wearin' pals, eh? Five on three. Real fair odds for *earnin'* the right outcome, ain't it?"

Bob said, "You're right about the odds being a little lopsided. But your numbers are off . . . I'm calling it three to one, and I want everybody to understand that's the way I *demand* for it to be."

"Now wait a minute, Bob," protested Morrison. "You can't—"

"Yes, I can! You and the fellas did what you could, Buford, and for that I'm grateful," said Bob. "But now it goes to this. I'll be damned if I walk away and leave these three peckerwoods alive to hound me— and possibly my family, because that's the kind of lowlife scum they are—at another time. No, it needs to end now. Once and for all. If these bastards can take me . . . they can have me. I'm giving my word on that."

Morrison's mouth pulled into a tight, grim line. Then he said, "Okay. If that's the way you want it, then go ahead . . . Sundown Bob."

Brannigan frowned. "What's this 'Sundown Bob' shit? How many names you got, Hat-field?"

"No need to concern yourself over it," Bob told him. "Ain't like you're gonna be around long enough to have to worry about remembering all of 'em."

By now Drake and Wilbur had moved up on either

side of Brannigan. They didn't look quite so eager to be participating in this, but neither were they backing out.

Brannigan showed his teeth in a wolf's smile. "I been waitin' seven years for this. I can't tell you how much I'm lookin' forward to sendin' the Devil's River Kid to finally meet the Devil . . ."

Nearly fifty men stood looking on when the gunplay suddenly erupted between the four men. Not one of the onlookers could ever claim afterward to have been able to follow the speed of Bob's draw. It came quicker than an eye blink. One instant he was standing poised and ready, the next his Colt was in his fist, spitting flame and thunder and hot lead.

Bob took out Brannigan first. Two rapid-fire slugs, punching less than an inch apart, straight into the bounty hunter's black heart. Then a quick adjust to the left to plant a pill in Drake's throat, blowing his Adam's apple out the back of his neck. Wilbur was targeted last but no less effectively, taking two hits, one to the center of his chest, then another to the outside edge of his heart as he twisted away from the first impact.

Brannigan and Wilbur toppled together in a heap. Drake was slammed backward three or four feet and hit the ground that far separated from his pards.

With his remaining bullet under the .44's cocked hammer, Bob swung the gun one more time in a flat arc and brought it to bear on Smoky Barnett. "How about you?" he grated. "You wanting any of this?"

Barnett lifted his hands, jerking them away from his body like they were on springs. "N-No, not me. I'm no part of it," he stammered.

Bob continued to glare at him for a long count, then broke open the Colt and methodically reloaded before returning it to its holster.

For their part, the Texans got off a total of three shots. None came anywhere close to Bob. Brannigan's gun never cleared leather, so he didn't fire at all. Drake triggered one round into the dirt as his throat was exploding. Wilbur fired skyward twice as he was twisting and falling away.

It all happened so fast that one of the Rocking W wranglers would later lament how he turned his head to stifle a sneeze and missed the whole thing in the brief time his face was averted.

CHAPTER 57

Unfortunately too late to do any good for the men who were killed or injured, the range war between the Rocking W and the V-Slash was over.

And so was the threat posed by Rance Brannigan to Bob Hatfield's present and future—based on his past. Even though everyone present that day heard Brannigan's accusations, thanks to the loyalty of Buford Morrison and Bob's three deputies no one else ever saw the wanted poster offered as proof of his claims. As a result, there was no choice but to take the word of the four lawmen that the poster bore no resemblance to Bob and therefore had no validity. In the months and years that followed, the accusations by Brannigan were rarely, if ever, even mentioned around Rattlesnake Wells. In a private ceremony held in the jail office before the U.S. Marshal left town (and also never spoken of again), Morrison passed out cigars and lighted them with the poster, rolled tight and set aflame.

Thanks additionally to Brannigan's greed and innate distrust in anyone and everyone—as evidenced by his insistence on first finishing and getting paid for the Wardell job while never sending advance word down to Texas that he'd discovered a still-alive Bob Hammond/Devil's River Kid—Marshal Hatfield's secret became once again secure as soon as Brannigan, Drake, and Wilbur bit the dust.

Bob reflected deeply on these things during the ride back to Rattlesnake Wells. He naturally felt relieved but, at the same time, there was still the matter of a murder suspect waiting in his jail and the lynch mob mentality of the many townsmen he had every reason to expect would also still be there, wanting to get their hands on the prisoner. That not only wasn't something to look forward to but needing to deal with it stood directly in the way of something he *was* looking forward to—spending time with Consuela and Bucky.

The lengthening shadows of early evening were reaching inward from the buildings on the west side of Front Street as Bob, his deputies, and Marshal Morrison came plodding back into town. An uncharacteristically muted Owen Dutton was also with them, riding double with Vern after they'd swung back by the site of the first skirmish to pick him up as promised.

Drawing abreast of the newspaper office, Dutton wordlessly peeled off from the group. Citizens on the boardwalks lining the street and faces in the shop windows gawked as the riders proceeded on toward the jail.

Nearing the sturdy building, Bob was surprised to see there was no crowd gathered out front. As he and the others swung down from their saddles and tied up at the hitch rail, the front door opened and Bullock and McTeague stepped out to greet them.

"It's good to see you not only back, but all of you back in one piece," said Bullock.

"Too bad the same can't be said for everybody who got caught up in the trouble out there," Bob responded wearily. "The doc is still with them, taking care of the ones he can do any good. But at least it's over. And if you think it's good to *see* us back, let me tell you how good it feels to *be* back."

"Amen to that," said Fred, joined by agreeable muttering from the others.

"But what happened here?" Bob asked, looking this way and that in an exaggerated manner. "We left you with all sorts of chattering citizens to keep you company while we were away, only now it appears they all abandoned you."

"That they did," said McTeague. "The thanks for that goes to your friend Marshal Morrison there. He showed up, did considerable barking and cussing at 'em, all the while flashing his federal credentials, and danged if those fellas who'd been milling around all morning didn't all of a sudden remember other places they needed to be and things they had to do. Ain't seen a whisker of any of 'em since."

"The girl had a little something to do with it, too, after she took the wind out of Norton's sails right in front of everybody," added Bullock. "But, yeah, it was the appearance by Marshal Morrison that mostly broke 'em up."

"What girl?" Bob wanted to know.

"This girl right here—me," said a voice from behind McTeague.

A moment later the mine owner was edged aside, and filling part of the doorway beside him was Brenda Emory. Before Bob could say anything, she spoke again. "Don't get angry with either Mr. Bullock or Mr. McTeague for allowing me to be here, Marshal. They tried their best to be gruff and stern in their refusals to let me stay, but I can be a pest when I don't get my way and they are, after all, two gentlemen and just a couple of puppies when it comes right down to it."

Bob arched a brow and said dryly, "Yeah, I've often heard them described just that way."

"Besides," Brenda went on, her eyes shiny with eager excitement, "I convinced them you not only wouldn't mind me being here when you got back, but, once you heard what I had to say, you'd actually be very pleased . . . After all, I'm ready to reveal to you who really killed Myron Poppe. And it wasn't Johnny Larkin!"

It was full dark by the time they arrived at the Emory house. Inside, suppertime was over and, as was the custom for the family, all present had repaired to the parlor for wine and conversation. Jackson Emory was seated in his comfortable easy chair while Victoria and Saul Norton shared the chesterfield.

"Miss Brenda has returned, sir . . . with guests." That was the announcement Graedon barely had time to get out before Brenda marched into the room leading those who accompanied her. The latter included Marshal Hatfield, Marshal Morrison, Deputy Fred . . . and John Larkin, brought along at the insistence of Brenda, though not without the restraint of handcuffs.

The instant their eyes fell on Larkin, both Victoria and Norton shot to their feet. "What is the meaning of this outrage!?" Victoria exclaimed.

Smiling wickedly, Brenda said, "Calm down, sis. You'll have plenty to be outraged over before the evening is done. But this is just the start."

"Marshal Hatfield," said Emory, glaring at Bob, "I've come to expect certain escapades such as this from my daughter. But from you, I would have expected more professionalism, not to mention courtesy. There's been talk of late about you and the performance of your duties. Talk that I chose to disregard. But right at the moment, I find myself questioning my judgment on that."

"I'll admit our barging in like this is a bit unusual and inconvenient, sir," said Bob. "But by the time we're done, I think you'll better understand."

"Understand what?"

"Our purpose here," spoke up Morrison, "is to arrest a killer and a thief."

"You already have such a person in your custody," declared Norton, an alarmed expression gripping his face. "He's right there—John Larkin!"

"You're awful sure about that, ain't you?" said Bob.

"He's proven himself time and again to be someone of low character—and he's an ex-convict to boot! What more do you need?" demanded Norton.

"I'd like to give you what you need," Larkin said.

"Did you hear that? He threatened me! Are you going to let him get away with that?"

"By the time we're finished here, I don't figure on anybody getting away with anything," Bob replied.

He held out his hand and Fred gave him the large, lumpy cloth sack he'd carried in with him. After pushing aside some wineglasses, Bob placed the sack on a low, polished table positioned in front of the chesterfield where Norton and Victoria had been sitting. Reaching in, he withdrew an object and held it up for everyone to see. It was a lock-blade knife, blade exposed and locked in the open position. It was, in fact, the evidence knife that had been resting on the desk in his office until only a short time ago. The tag reading *Murder Weapon—Myron Poppe* had been removed.

"Does anyone recognize this?" Bob asked, extending the weapon so everybody could have a closer look.

Brenda moved over to stand by her sister. "Doesn't it look familiar to you, Victoria?"

Victoria made a distasteful face. "Why should an ugly old knife look familiar to me?"

"Maybe," said Brenda, "because you gave one just like it as a birthday gift to Saul about three years ago. Remember? It came with a fine leather case with a belt loop that you had Saul's initials engraved on."

"So what?" Norton interjected. "Sure the knife looks like the one Victoria gave me and sure it looks familiar—because there are dozens of knives just like that being carried by men all over town and up in the mining camps. What's so special about that?"

"What's so special about this particular one," said

Bob, "is that it's the murder weapon that killed poor little Myron Poppe."

"You might wonder why the killer would leave a nice knife like that behind, wouldn't you?" said Fred. "Why not do the deed and then take the knife for use another day and to keep from leaving behind any evidence? Well, according to our undertaker when I asked him those very questions, it seems that, in this particular instance, the blade got shoved so deep into Myron Poppe's spinal column that it lodged in the vertebrae and was difficult to pull back out. So the killer, being in a hurry to get away after he'd done the stabbing, didn't want to take the time to twist and yank the blade free out of all that blood and gristle."

"For God's sake!" Victoria wailed. "Must you go into such gory detail?"

"By the way," drawled Bob, "where is that birthday knife of yours, Norton?"

Norton bristled. "In my apartment, along with various other personal items."

Brenda shook her head. "No, it's not. I went and looked . . . You see, when I was at the jail earlier to visit Johnny, I spotted that knife on the marshal's desk with an evidence tag on it. I recognized it right away. It's not really that common, Saul, not with those features or that finish on the handle. Victoria paid top dollar and went to a lot of trouble to pick out that knife for you. And when I searched your apartment, looking for it, all I found was the empty case."

"You had no business being in my apartment. That's a crime—burglary or breaking and entering or something!"

Victoria looked aghast. "Surely you're not suggesting that Saul was the one who used that knife to stab poor Mr. Poppe."

"Can you explain what happened to your knife, Norton?" asked Bob.

"And while you're at it," said Morrison, "maybe you can explain why you would pay good money to a man and hire him to beat the living hell out of you like you did a few nights back."

"What kind of nonsense is that? Who in their right mind would do such a thing?" demanded Emory.

"That's what I'm trying to find out from Norton."

"It's a preposterous allegation, one I know nothing about," huffed Norton. "Are you going to take the word of a dirty nigger over me?"

"Who said anything about the man who beat you up being black?" asked Fred. "How could you know that specific detail?"

"And while you're explaining that, along with the rest," said Bob, continuing the bombardment, "maybe you can explain this, which was also found hidden in your apartment . . ." So saying, he pulled a moderate-sized carpetbag from out of the burlap sack. Yanking it open and turning it over, he allowed some of its contents to spill out onto the table. There were fat rolls of paper money tied with string and two or three small cloth sacks stamped with the logo for Emory Mining.

"Good God!" exclaimed Emory. "That looks like . . ."

"It is," Larkin told him. "Those smaller sacks are nuggets and dust from your mine. *Stolen* from your mine, Mr. Emory. The very thing Norton framed me for all those years back so he could get rid of me because I was starting to be suspicious of him. The rolls of money—tens of thousands of dollars by a quick count—represent what he's managed to siphon off and convert to cash over the years while he's been your only foreman."

"Enough!" shouted Norton. This came with the appearance of a large-bore, two-shot derringer that he drew from inside his jacket. Before anyone could react, he reached out, grabbed Brenda by her long ponytail, and jerked her viciously to him. Jamming the muzzle of the derringer against the side of her head, he snarled, "Nobody make a move on me or I'll blow this sneaky, troublemaking bitch's brains out!"

"Saul, you don't really mean . . ." Victoria whimpered.

"Shut up! I meant every word I said! And that goes for you, too, Graedon, you and your military and police background. Get in here and stand by the old man so I can keep an eye on you as well."

"You'll never get away with it, man," Bob tried to tell him. "I've got two more deputies outside. Even if you get past them, I'll hunt you down. You harm that girl, I'll hunt you and kill you."

"As long as I got this girl you won't do shit— except what I tell you to do!"

"But why, Saul?" said Emory, his voice choked with emotion. "Why the need for the stealing and all the rest? You were on your way to having a piece of it, at least half, regardless. You were going to marry Victoria; everybody knows I'm not going to be around much longer . . . it was all lined up for you."

"Maybe. But it wasn't always that way, was it?" sneered Norton. "In the beginning all of that was in the cards for Larkin. So okay, after I got rid of him it started to turn around. But you been dying in pieces for years, old man, yet you never seem to get there. Still, I might have been able to wait you out. I was trying, I really was . . . And then that damned Larkin came back in the picture again. Him and his stinkin' early parole. I should have just killed the bastard and been done with it. But no, I tried to be clever and set him up to get hauled away like before . . . and look where it got me."

"What you're trying to do is just digging yourself in deeper," Bob told him. "Give it up, man. Now, before anybody else gets hurt or killed . . . You don't have a chance."

"I think otherwise. Long as I got this gun and this bitch for a hostage, I say I got a *good* chance."

"At least trade her out for another hostage. Let the girl go, take me," Bob said.

"No good, hero. I'm stickin' with the cards I've dealt myself and playing them all the way. What you're gonna do is holler out and have a couple horses saddled and ready for us real quick-like. Including grub, guns, and ammo . . . Oh, yeah. And also my little bag of goodies from there on the table.

"As soon as all that's ready, me and Missy Brenda are gonna ride away from this shithole of a town. Once we're a couple days in the clear and providing you behave yourself and don't follow close after us, I'll let her go. We will have parted ways with fond memories and sad hearts and that will be the end of that."

"You harm one hair of my daughter's head, I swear I'll live for however long it takes to see you hanged," said Emory in a harsh whisper.

"Sure you will, old man," chuckled Norton. Then, sobering, he added, "But by the way, I'll guarantee one person who won't be around for that momentous occasion . . . and that's *you*, you bastard Larkin!"

With no further warning, Norton lifted the derringer from Brenda's temple just long enough to aim it at Larkin and trigger a round to the center of his chest. Larkin threw up his hands reflexively but there was no stopping the bullet. It slammed into him and knocked him flat. Victoria screamed as the room shook with the sound of the gun blast. And then the smoking muzzle was jammed once more against the side of Brenda's head.

"Damn! Did that ever feel good!" Norton exclaimed. "But no matter how much fun I'm having here, I still want somebody to holler out for those horses . . . and don't forget I still got one bullet left for Missy Brenda. As you just saw, that's plenty to get the job done. Yeah, you're all thinking how you'd be able to blast me to bits afterward, but who's kidding who? You know damn well you're not ready to pay the price of her life just to get me."

It was Fred who went to the window and hollered out for Vern and Peter to get the horses like Norton was demanding. Following that were several tense minutes that dragged by like hours.

At one point Victoria sobbed, "I can't believe I ever thought I loved you."

"Yeah, well it cuts both ways, sweetheart," Norton responded cruelly.

Finally, Peter called in to say the horses were ready.

"Okay," said Norton. "Gather up my money and gold from the table, Marshal. Put it in the bag and close it tight. Then hand the bag to the girl. We're getting near to the end now, so don't nobody do anything stupid that'll cause things to go very bad for Missy Brenda."

Once the bag was in Brenda's hand, Norton said, "Now we're in the home stretch. Me and Missy Brenda are gonna make our way, real close and slow, out the front door. All of you stay back. Keep doing that, keep being smart and staying clear, and in a couple days from now I'll turn her loose somewhere where she can be found. By then I will be long gone and you can all spend the rest of your days entertaining each other by talking nasty about me."

Norton and Brenda began edging toward the front door. Their way meant having to step over the feet of John Larkin's body. Brenda went first, hesitating slightly and emitting a ragged sob as she did so. Norton gave her hair a jerk and told her to knock it off. His eyes were darting back and forth between the front door and where Bob and the others were grouped around Jackson Emory's chair. As he raised his foot and began his step-over, he was paying no attention to what was beneath him.

That's when Larkin lunged into motion. First his left leg kicked upward, high and hard, slamming into Norton's crotch. At the same time he twisted his upper body from the way he'd fallen onto his right side and partly facedown, jackknifing upward as he swung his chained-together hands. In his right fist he was gripping the evidence knife—the same one that killed Myron Poppe—which had been knocked from the table when he fell and he'd been able to seize unnoticed as he lay supposedly dead. He sank the full length of the blade just below Norton's belt buckle and yanked savagely downward.

Norton screamed as his body spasmed in excruciating pain, first from the crotch blow and then from the knife ripping his abdomen. He lurched to one side and started to double over, involuntarily pulling the derringer away from Brenda's temple. When it roared again, the bullet it spat this time smashed harmlessly into a wall of the parlor. In the same instant, Brenda pulled free and threw herself to one side.

That was all the opening Bob needed. His Colt streaked from its holster and he triggered two rapid-fire shots. Both hit high on the side of Norton's neck, just below the hinge of his jaw. The impact sent him staggering partway out the parlor door where he finally dropped and skidded to a halt on the fine carpeting, soon to be taking on the stain of widening pools of blood.

EPILOGUE

What saved John Larkin's life was his handcuffs. When he threw up his hands as Norton shot him, the incoming slug hit the connecting chain between the two wrist clamps. This fragmented the bullet into three pieces, each of which struck with enough impact to knock him down and do fairly serious injury, but with the force lessened to a degree that was never truly life threatening.

Larkin still required a lengthy recovery period, however. At first it appeared there was going to be some conflict over which of the Emory sisters would help nurse him back to health—Victoria, whom he had returned thinking he still had feelings for; or Brenda, who had believed in him when no one else did and who'd been instrumental in proving his innocence for the murder of Myron Poppe. It didn't take long for the patient to realize and express that his heart had been won over by the brave loyalty of Brenda.

Nor did it take long for Jackson Emory to indicate his faith in Larkin had been restored and his old job as mining foreman would be waiting for him as soon as he was well enough . . . along, it seemed, with the hand of his youngest daughter.

Outside of town, the peace between the Rocking W and the V-Slash brands, though tenuous at times, continued to hold.

In town, the anti–Bob Hatfield feelings that had been stirred up quickly dissipated and faded from thought and tongue. The only lingering wisp of it may have resided in Owen Dutton—something that concerned Bob, particularly on the off chance the newspaperman might have heard a vague mention of Rance Brannigan's claims about Bob's outlaw past. To assuage his concerns, Bob finally decided to confront Dutton about it one day. Careful not to make any direct references or certainly not to use the phrase "Devil's River Kid," he poked and prodded in order to try and get a read off the man. In the end, he came away satisfied that Dutton's firsthand experience seeing gunplay and violence at the skirmish in the draw and then in the aftermath of the battle at V-Slash ranch headquarters had cured him of finding glory in that sort of thing and seeking to sensationalize more of the same. The only thing that came close was Dutton's parting words, suggesting that one of these days he'd like to sit down with the marshal and learn more about "Sundown Bob."

Bob's response was to smile wistfully and say, "Yeah . . . One of these days I'm gonna have to find out a little more about that fella myself."

But the truth of the matter, he knew, was that the only person he really wanted to be was Bob Hatfield, husband and father. And whenever he went home and found Consuela and Bucky waiting for him to fulfill that role, he realized he was genuinely blessed.

Keep reading for a special preview. . . .

A HIGH SIERRA CHRISTMAS
by WILLIAM W. JOHNSTONE
with J. A. Johnstone

*A Jensen family holiday takes a dark and dangerous
turn—on the infamous Donner Pass—in this thrilling
epic adventure from the bestselling Johnstones . . .*

It's beginning to look a lot like Christmas in the
High Sierras. But Smoke Jensen and his children,
Louis and Denise, won't let a little snow stop them
from heading to Reno for the holidays. There are
two ways for them to get there: the long way, going
around the Sierra Nevada Mountains, or the short
way, going right through them. Smoke decides
to take a gamble. They'll follow the trail that
decades earlier brought the legendary
Donner Party to a gruesome, tragic end . . .

And so the journey begins.

Coming soon, wherever Pinnacle books are sold.

CHAPTER 1

"Give me all your money and valuables, mister, and be quick about it!"

"No, I don't believe I will," Smoke Jensen said as he shook his head.

"I mean it!" the would-be robber said, jabbing the gun in his hand toward Smoke.

He had stepped out of an alley a moment earlier and threatened Smoke with the old, small-caliber revolver. Smoke was on his way to an appointment and had taken a shortcut along a smaller street, which at the moment was practically deserted.

A few people were walking along the cobblestones in the next block, but they were unaware of the drama playing out here . . . or ignoring it because they didn't want to get involved. It was hard to tell with big-city folks.

The thief wore a threadbare suit over a grimy, collarless shirt. Smoke couldn't see the soles of the man's shoes, but he would have bet they had holes in them. The man's dark hair was lank and tangled, his face gaunt, his eyes hollow.

"Opium?" Smoke asked.

"What?" The man looked and sounded confused as he responded to Smoke's question.

"That's why you've resorted to robbing people on the streets? So you can afford to go down to Chinatown and visit one of the opium dens?"

"That ain't none o' your business. Just gimme your damn money!"

"No." Smoke's voice was flat and hard now, with no compromise in it. "And you'd better not try to shoot that old relic. It'll likely blow up in your hand if you do."

The man turned the gun's barrel away from Smoke to stare at the weapon. When he did that, Smoke's left hand came up and closed around the cylinder. He shoved the barrel skyward, just in case the gun went off.

At the same time, Smoke's right fist crashed into the robber's face and sent him flying backward. Smoke was a medium-sized man, but his shoulders were broad as an ax handle and the muscles that coated his torso were thick enough to make his clothes bulge if the garments weren't made properly.

Smoke had pulled his punch a little. The robber looked to be on the frail side, and Smoke didn't want to hit him too hard and break his neck.

For many years he had been in the habit of killing or at least seriously injuring anybody who pointed a gun at him, but this time it seemed like enough just to disarm the varmint and knock him down. Smoke expected to see him scramble up and flee as quick as his legs would carry him away from here.

The man got up all right, but instead of running away, he charged at Smoke again with a wolfish snarl on his face. His hand darted under his coat and came out clutching a short-bladed but still dangerous knife.

That made things different. Smoke twisted aside as the man slashed at him with the blade. The knife was probably more of a threat than the popgun the man had been waving around.

Smoke tossed the revolver aside, grabbed the man's arm with both hands while the man was off balance, and shoved down on it while bringing his knee up.

The man's forearm snapped with a sharp crack. He screeched in pain and dropped the knife. When Smoke let go of him, he fell to his knees in the street and stayed there, whimpering as he cradled his broken arm against his body.

Smoke picked up the gun, took hold of the would-be robber's coat collar, hauled him to his feet, and marched him stumbling along the cobblestones until he found a police officer.

The blue-uniformed man glared at him and demanded, "Here now! What've you done to this poor fellow?"

"This poor fella, as you call him, tried to rob me," Smoke said. With his free hand, he held out the gun and the knife. "He pulled this gun on me and demanded all my money and valuables, and when I took it away from him he tried to cut me open with the knife. I'd had about enough of it by then." Smoke shoved the would-be robber toward the officer. "His arm's broken, so he'll need some medical attention before you lock him up."

"Wait just a blasted minute! I'm supposed to take your word for all this?"

"It's true, it's true!" the thief wailed. "Lock me up, do anything you want, just keep that crazy cowboy away from me!"

"Sounds like a confession to me," Smoke said. He started to turn away.

"Hold on," the officer said. "At least tell me your name and where to find you, so I can fill out a report."

"The name's Smoke Jensen, and my son and daughter and I are staying at the Palace Hotel."

The policeman's eyebrows rose. The Palace was the city's oldest, most luxurious, and most expensive hotel. The man standing in front of him wasn't dressed fancy—Smoke wore a simple brown tweed suit and a darker brown flat-crowned hat—but if he could afford to stay at the Palace, he had to have plenty of money.

Not only that, but the name was familiar. The officer recalled where he had seen it and blurted out, "I thought Smoke Jensen was just a character in the dime novels!"

"Not hardly," Smoke said. He was well aware of the lurid, yellow-backed yarns that portrayed him variously as an outlaw, a lawman, and the West's fastest and most-feared gunfighter. All of those things had been true at one time or another, but the fevered scribblings of the so-called authors who cranked out those dubious tomes barely scratched the surface.

These days he was a rancher. His Sugarloaf spread

back in Colorado was one of the most successful and lucrative west of the Mississippi, not to mention the wealth that had come from the gold claim he had found as a young man. He could well afford to stay at the Palace Hotel. More than likely, he could have booked an entire floor and not missed the money.

Instead he had a suite, with rooms for himself; his son, Louis Arthur; and his daughter, Denise Nicole. He was on his way to meet the twins now, and he didn't want to be delayed.

"Is it all right for me to go on to the hotel?" he asked the policeman.

"Why, sure it is, Mr. Jensen," the officer said. He took hold of the thief's uninjured arm. "I'll tend to this miscreant. I'm sorry you ran into trouble here in our fair city."

"Don't worry about it," Smoke said. "For some reason, I tend to run into trouble just about everywhere I go."

Connect with  U s

Visit us online at
KensingtonBooks.com
to read more from your favorite authors, see books
by series, view reading group guides, and more.

for sneak peeks, chances to win books and prize packs,
and to share your thoughts with other readers.

facebook.com/kensingtonpublishing
twitter.com/kensingtonbooks

Tell us what you think!

To share your thoughts, submit a review,
or sign up for our eNewsletters, please visit:
KensingtonBooks.com/TellUs.